PENGUIN BOOKS

# A LATE LARK SINGING

Sybil Marshall was born and grew up in East Anglia. A villager all her life, she witnessed the breakdown of the old way of life in a rural community following the sudden growth of mechanized farming and the post-war attitude to sexual morality. Having been a village schoolteacher, at the age of forty-seven she went to Cambridge University to read English. She became a Lecturer in Education at Sheffield University and subsequently Reader in Primary Education at the University of Sussex. In 1965 she devised Granada Television's popular programme *Picture Box*, and continued to act as adviser and to write the teacher's handbook until 1989.

As well as works on education, Sybil Marshall has written non-fiction books recording life in her native fens in their pre-war isolation, including *Fenland Chronicle*, *The Silver New Nothing* and *A Pride of Tigers*. She also won the Angel Prize for Literature for *Everyman's Book of English Folk Tales*. The Swithinford series, of which *A Late Lark Singing* is the most recent part, also includes her first novel, the bestselling *A Nest of Magpies*, written when she was eighty years old, *Sharp through the Hawthorn* and *Strip the Willow*. She has also written a collection of short stories, entitled *The Chequer-Board*. Most of her books are published in Penguin.

Dr Sybil Marshall lives in Ely, Cambridgeshire, with her husband, Ewart Oakeshott, FSA.

D0452410

# A
# LATE LARK
# SINGING

Sybil Marshall

PENGUIN BOOKS

PENGUIN BOOKS

Published by the Penguin Group
Penguin Books Ltd, 27 Wrights Lane, London W8 5TZ, England
Penguin Putnam Inc., 375 Hudson Street, New York, New York 10014, USA
Penguin Books Australia Ltd, Ringwood, Victoria, Australia
Penguin Books Canada Ltd, 10 Alcorn Avenue, Toronto, Ontario, Canada M4V 3B2
Penguin Books (NZ) Ltd, 182–190 Wairau Road, Auckland 10, New Zealand

Penguin Books Ltd, Registered Offices: Harmondsworth, Middlesex, England

First published by Michael Joseph 1997
Published in Penguin Books 1998
3 5 7 9 10 8 6 4

Printed in England by Clays Ltd, St Ives plc

For Love, Life, and Laughter,
and the memory of two fathers
who from their very different backgrounds
nevertheless endowed their children with
the love of words, from which arises the
education of the heart

Dad: William Henry (Will 'En) Edwards (1870–1950)
born and bred a 'fen-tiger'
and
Pa: Ronald Lewis (Tommy) Oakeshott (1881–1947)
Civil Servant, Novelist and Poet.

### THE SKEIN OF HOPE

Above the clamour of embattled foes
Rings out the lark's song from the empty sky,
Among the unmarked graves of those who die
Upthrusts the tendrils of a budding rose.
And even where the storm its refuse throws,
Where branches of the riven saplings lie,
Comes presently a shy hare creeping by,
Or baby rabbit with its wrinkled nose.
So mingle life and death; so intertwine
The good and ill in such a tangled skein
We can't unravel from it joy or pain
Or any strand but love.

R. L. OAKESHOTT

(By permission of my husband, Ewart Oakeshott)

It was going to be another sweltering day.

All East Anglia lay baked in the sunshine that had begun in June, just in time for the 'wedding of the year', a great occasion for everybody in Old Swithinford because it was 'as it should be'. Charlie Bellamy was a farmer's daughter, marrying Charles Bridgefoot, who was a farmer's son. Rural England was not dead yet.

The wonderful weather had gone on all through harvest, right up to the end of August. By that time drought was threatening, the fields already ploughed lying baked in the glaring sun, the landscape chequered by other fields where stubble had turned to brittle, shining white, some of them textured by bales of straw casting dark shadows. Trees in the garden of Benedict's House had begun to look dry, dusty and sad. Ned, the gardener at Benedict's, meeting the postman under them one morning, had complained that he had had quite enough of 'that bloody blue sky' to last him a lifetime.

The two at Benedict's had returned from a holiday in Wales in time for the wedding, bringing with them the parson who had come specially to perform that ceremony. What they had not expected was to arrive home a respectably married couple themselves, instead of openly 'living in sin' as they had been. It was only *en route* home that they had made up their minds to keep quiet about it, so as not to steal all the limelight from young Charles and Charlie, and persuade their friend the Rev. Nigel Delaprime to aid and abet them. So they had said nothing, and the longer the time went on, the more difficult it became to spring the surprise on their friends. It was now three months, and still no word had been said.

When September came in and the only difference to the weather was that the dry heat had changed to day after day of cloying, sticky humidity, even Sophie complained.

Arriving for work at Benedict's on the first Thursday of

September, she found Fran and William still sitting at the kitchen table, lingering languidly over breakfast as if Time had for the present suspended all meaning for them. Nothing so common-place as a spell of hot weather was likely to put Sophie out of her routine of keeping Benedict's swept and garnished, but even she was a little put about by the heat that morning.

She accepted the offer of a cup of tea before she began work without her customary half-hearted protest, albeit with one eye on the clock. Thursday was her day for doing the bedrooms, and do them she would, including the four guest-rooms that didn't need even a duster. She had set her cup down and prepared for her onslaught on them by loading herself with a vacuum cleaner, brooms, mops, dusters and tins of polish when Ned tapped lightly on the back door and came in. She paused, curious to know what he wanted, and to exchange a few words with him about the weather.

'Hotter than ever, I reckon,' Ned said, wiping his forehead with a sunburnt forearm. At Fran's invitation he sat down with them and hung his cap, countryman fashion, over his knee. Fran noticed the red welt it had made across his forehead, and the deep, sweat-soaked ridge in his hair round the back of his head.

It was Sophie who answered. 'I don't complain in the hordinary way about whatever 'Im Above chooses to send us in the way o' weather, seeing as there's no 'elp for it, but I do think as 'E'd hev more sense than to keep it up as mulfering as this 'ere, day after day. There ain't a breath of air to be 'ad nowhere, hinside or hout.' She set down all her impedimenta on a handy chair, turned up her voluminous apron and delved into the pocket of her overall for a handkerchief with which to wipe her sweat-beaded face and neck.

William was watching Fran's face. It was registering her amuse-ment both at the layers of clothing Sophie was wearing despite the heat, and at what for Sophie was very nearly a 'blastpheemious' remark, showing as it did of her disapproval of what ''Im Above' 'choosed to do' with regard to the weather. He was afraid that for once Sophie might not take with her usual good-humoured aplomb Fran's delight in her use of the vernacular. He rushed into the breach himself, to give Fran time to compose herself.

2

'Mulfering?' he said. 'That's a new one on me. What does it mean?'

'Ain't I just told you? Though seeing as you were brought up 'ere same as I was, I should ha' thought as you'd ha' knowed anyway. "Mulfering" means weather like this 'ere, and I don't know no other word for it.'

'More don't I, come to think on it,' said Ned. 'I don't know as there is one. But it ain't no use you grumbling about it, Soph, 'cos you know as well as I do as it won't get no cooler till we've had a storm, and it's bound to be a real old souser when it comes. So don't leave no windows open a-nights, only just enough to get a breathe of air, 'cos after heat like this them storms come sudden, so as carpets and things get soaked afore you can shut 'em. And keep some candles handy in case the power gets cut off.'

Sophie sniffed and gave him a look of withering scorn. 'I keep candles ready all'us,' she said, 'winter and summer alike. Time was when we didn't hev nothing but candles, afore the 'lectric come this way. And as to winders, I all'us leave mine open in a storm, so as to let out the thunderbolt do one come down the chimney. We wasn't allowed to take no notice o' thunderstorms when we was children. Mam wouldn't let us. All we ever done was to fetch a towel and cover the looking-glass up with it, and put anything shiny like knives and forks and things into drawers, do they might draw the lightning. Not like some as I could mention, as used to start squealing at the first rumble o' thunder and run into the cupboard under the stairs and set there with a coat over their 'ead till you'd think they'd be stifled. But there, Mam all'us said you could tell them as 'ad a guilty conscience, come a thunderstorm.'

They all understood that the reference was to William's sister, Jess. Sophie's 'Mam', Kezia, had been housekeeper at Benedict's for their grandfather, and had looked after them as children during long holidays spent there. She had had little sympathy with Jess's sense of the dramatic. Sophie still had reservations about Jess, though about Fran and William she had none. She loved them, and if they hadn't returned her love for its own sake, which they did, they would have been obliged to reciprocate her loyalty to them, and the care she lavished on them and their beautiful old house. She was an integral part of their household, and one of the many blessings Fran's decision to return to Old Swithinford and restore her grandfather's old house had showered on them. The greatest blessing of all, of course, had been finding each other again.

William was accustomed to Fran's endearing way of finding small things irresistibly and overpoweringly funny, even at the most inopportune moments, such as now. He tried to turn the conversation by asking Ned what he wanted.

'Nothing as I know on,' Ned answered with a twinkle, quite aware of the situation. 'Only it were so mulfering hot out there in the garden that when I see Soph come I thought there might be a cup o' tea on the go, and I were right – so I'm had what it was I come for and I'd better be a'going again to do what I can out there. Not that I can do much, till that rain.'

He got up and went, putting on his cap from sheer habit. Sophie loaded herself again with all her paraphernalia. 'Ah,' she said, 'and I'd better be gooing and getting on wi' them bedrooms as well as I can, seeing as 'ow my clo'es is all sticking to me as soaking wet as if I'd put 'em on straight out o' the washtub.'

The door closed behind her. 'Now you can laugh,' William said, getting up and standing behind Fran's chair. She leaned back against him and let the repressed laughter bubble out of her.

'I don't wonder she's mulfered,' said Fran. 'She's still wearing an overall and an apron over her frock, and black wool stockings. I'd like to bet she's got a "vestie" on as well as her corsets, and a petticoat. I hope she doesn't die of a heatstroke upstairs. She won't shed anything while she's at work, "bending about and such" with you and Ned around. Just think what might be revealed if she did!'

'I daren't think,' he said, running his hands down over her, 'because you, you hussy, feel as if you have nothing on under that sunfrock but a bra and a pair of pants.'

'Ssh!' she said. 'Sophie would have a heatstroke if she heard you mentioning such things – married man though you may be now.' She leaned back against him, and took her head away again. 'Your shirt's sticking to you as much as Sophie's, er, underlinen are sticking to her! Just look at the wet patch I've made on your chest.'

4

'That's nothing to be wondered at,' he answered, pulling her head back against him and leaning over to kiss her. 'What with the heat and the feel of you through that flimsy frock – and the knowledge that you are my *wife*. My wife – here in this hot kitchen in the morning as much as you are in bed at night. I still can't believe it.'

'Perhaps that's just as well, at present,' she said. 'Put the kettle on again. I'd love another cup of tea – china tea with lemon in it, to cool you down. But aren't you a bit out of date? I thought that marriage nowadays was regarded as the ultimate passion-killer.'

'Like Sophie's fleecy lined bloomers?' he said. 'Well, maybe there is a connection. Familiarity breeds contempt. She's worn them all her life, so she doesn't think about how hot they make her. She's had fifty years to get used to them. But it's only about ten weeks yet that you have been my lawful wedded wife – absolutely and irrevocably mine. Give a fellow a chance! Sometimes I think I've just dreamed it. Maybe we ought to have waited till we could tie the knot here, "in the sight of Sophie's god and the congregation" of our friends. I have a feeling that Sophie disapproves of us more for our "hole and corner wedding" than she ever did for living together in sin.'

'She understood the reason for that,' Fran replied. 'She can't see any logical reason for us getting married in secret and then not telling anybody. She probably suspects that there is some dark and deadly secret in your life.'

'And if that's what she makes of it, what on earth will other people invent? Sophie's the only person we've actually told yet – but I get the impression that it's got out, somehow. Unfortunately, the usual reason for hasty and unadvertised weddings is not applicable in our case, so even our nearest and dearest friends wonder.'

'It wouldn't make any difference now, in any case,' she said. 'As far as the scandalmongers are concerned, we should only be shutting the stable door after the horse had bolted. We shall go down in the annals of the village as a couple of shameless, unrepentant adulterers. None of them will ever believe that we are married, unless we have our "wedding lines" framed and hang them up in the post office for all to see.'

She saw the hurt pass over his face like the shadow of a cloud over a sunny cornfield and wished she hadn't made a joke of it.

'You can't keep a secret in a village,' he said, 'and we were silly to try. I'd have liked to come home and shout the news from the housetops – but we couldn't do that to Charles and Charlie. It made no difference to anybody but us, did it? I thought all we had to do was to wait till the excitement of that wedding had died down, and then gather our friends together for a grand announcement and a little celebration. How did it get out?'

'Ask me another,' she said. 'In a village walls have ears. Does it really matter?'

'Yes. It matters to us that we don't lose our friends by letting them think we didn't want them to know. I think I must have been a bit punch-drunk. I'd been through a pretty tortuous couple of weeks – and I couldn't see how anybody here could know. If by a millionth chance one of them had read in *The Times* the reported death of an American politician and his lady-friend in Spain, why should they connect it with me? It only got into our papers because of the bizarre details. I did consider carefully before telling you that I knew Janice was dead, and I was free at last of my promise to her. Oh, sweetheart, do you mind very much? It was terribly selfish of me – but I had waited so long, and those last two weeks had been hell. Did it spoil everything for you?'

'Don't be silly,' she said. 'It was all very romantic, and our reason for keeping it quiet was anything but selfish. They'll all appreciate it when they know. I'm quite sure I'm right about that.'

He turned his head and smiled at her. 'You usually are. So how do you propose we go about letting them know now? The longer we leave it, the more difficult it will be to do it naturally.'

Yes, she understood that. She, too, had noticed that their friends had been rather pointedly keeping aloof from them in the last week or two. She had put it down to the heat and the need for a bit of a let-up after all the excitement of the Bridgefoot–Bellamy wedding. She was suddenly aware that he was truly troubled about it.

He had turned back to the kettle, made the tea, and was standing looking out into the garden. His stillness and silence meant that he was worrying. The levity of their breakfast-table talk had given way to something more serious. She had always known that it had meant much more to him than it had to her that they had not previously been able to legalize their marriage. She'd been too happy to care, but he'd never been able to accept their situation as serenely as she had. She'd put that down to the fact that the obstacle was on his side, the silly promise that he couldn't bring himself to break; but she loved him, and didn't want him to be other than he was, especially as she knew he wouldn't have been happy with an extra load of conscience towards Janice to carry. She had got glimpses of the suffering that pea under the mattress of their happiness had caused him now and then when he confessed how insecure he felt being only her 'lodger', or, to use the current ugly phrase, her 'live-in lover'.

And there were his sudden flashes of irrational jealousy when any eligible unattached man swam into their orbit. That made her angry, though she tried to hide from him how much it hurt her too. If her love for him didn't give him security, nothing else would – except, it seemed, to be able to marry her legally. Well, that he had now done, and was, apparently, still finding new things to 'whittle' about.

She had been a little bothered that their secret had got out and that none of their friends had made any reference to it. They either didn't believe it, or were too well-bred to poke their noses into what was not their business. But surely it was nothing for William to get himself upset about?

He turned to face her again, still looking anxious. 'Let's go somewhere cooler to drink this. Shall we go into my study? And darling – if you can bear it, I need to talk to you seriously.'

So there was something else on his mind. She got up, and he followed her into his study, carrying the tea tray.

What was now William's study had been Fran's sitting-room, converted from the huge kitchen when she had first done up and then occupied what had been the servants' quarters while the rest of the house was being restored. It had been left furnished as it was then, and William's office equipment had been added. It was certainly cooler and more private than the kitchen.

Two large armchairs flanked the fireplace, and into one of them Fran sank gratefully while William set the teapot on his desk, poured out a cup of tea, and took it to her. She had expected him to take his own to the other chair, but to her surprise he sat down in his swivel chair by his desk. What it was he had to say must be more serious than she had expected.

He didn't seem to know where to begin, and fidgeted with an ivory paper-knife, with his back towards her. When the silence grew too long, she broke it, saying lightly, 'I'm not at all sure this is a good idea. It's too hot to think. What's wrong, darling? What is it making you so downhearted all of a sudden?'

'This,' he said, laying his hand on a thick pile of typescript on his desk. She knew it must be the research project he had been working on. She hadn't known he had got it nearly so far towards completion. 'It's only the first draft. When I went into college last week I took it with me to ask Morag to make me a fair copy, in her own time, as she has done before. After a whole year off, I shall have to concentrate on my job again. I've had enough of this, and the sooner I get rid of it to the publisher, the better.'

'Are you really so fed up with it?' she said. 'And why did Morag refuse? There must be a good reason! She adores you – it's a marvel to me that you ever found any other woman to satisfy your every want after all these years of having a slavish secretary's undivided devotion and attention.'

Her teasing raised only the ghost of a smile before he resumed his uncharacteristically anxious expression. 'She didn't refuse. She wasn't there,' he said. 'It seems that Canistor – our visiting professor and my stand-in – didn't get on with her. So without so much as a word to or with me, he colluded with my erstwhile colleagues to get himself a secretary more to his liking. Chance helped. Apparently the Master's secretary had to leave at short notice, and as he is in his last year it was sensible for him to be given a secretary who already knew all the ropes. So they chose Morag and moved her – but they might at least have told me!

'I'd written to let Canistor know that I should be going in that day, and asked him to have lunch with me. I thought it a bit strange that he didn't even acknowledge my letter, but of course he could have been away, and I thought I might find him there

8

waiting for me. But when he didn't turn up, I can't honestly say I was surprised. The surprise came when I opened Morag's office door and found a strange female sitting in her chair. A glamorous young dolly-bird, who looked highly offended at my intrusion and asked me haughtily who I was and what I wanted. Canistor couldn't even have told her of my letter.'

He paused, and added wryly, 'Not exactly an auspicious welcome back!'

He put down the paper-knife and fingered his typescript, as if that symbolized all he was feeling.

'Maybe the dolly-bird will prove every bit as good a secretary as Morag when you get used to her,' Fran said, soothingly. 'She'll probably be glad to earn a bit extra in her spare time.'

'You haven't seen her,' he replied. 'My guess is that her boss has kept her spare time pretty occupied with duties other than official ones in his spare time. I didn't bother to ask her anything, except where I could find Morag.

'Morag was upset that nobody had had the courtesy to inform me of the change. She had to be circumspect, of course, but I gather that my absence has been made the most of to effect a lot of the changes I managed to hold in check in the past. Morag said they had got plans for next year pretty well sewn up, on the presumption that any alterations I might want to make could only be cosmetic at this late stage, anyway. Nobody else was there to consult with me.'

The smile he turned towards Fran was sardonic. 'I suppose we all overvalue our own importance. I got the message. They have taken the opportunity of my absence to demonstrate how well they can get on without me.'

He got up and went to relieve her of her cup. She was struggling to find words of comfort, and her face her distress. He sat down on the arm of her chair.

'I haven't told you before because I've had to look at the entire situation in a new perspective, and assess the consequences. I have tenure, of course, so they can't get rid of me; but once a new Master is installed, every effort will be made to put me on the shelf. When you get to the top as young as I did, it seems to the others that you've been there for ever – blocking the way up the ladder. Quite irrespective of your actual age or ability, you are written off as an old-fashioned fuddy-duddy *they* have to carry. Sometimes it's true – you can see such pathetic has-beens wandering about most universities, stuck in the past and only ticking off the years to retirement. They put me into that category the moment I gave them the chance.'

'But my darling – they know better! You're neither old nor doddery! I think you're just being morbid because they hadn't put out the red carpet for you.'

'No, sweetheart, honestly. I'm simply being realistic. University life isn't what it used to be – I've told you that often enough before. And a lot more changes are on the way. I can't really blame the young whizz-kids who have to fight for themselves. They regard me as an anachronism – which to some extent I am, like the Master. That's why he's going before his time.'

'So what is it you are trying to tell me?'

'That I know now what to expect. To put it bluntly, they don't want me back any more than I want to go back. I'm utterly disenchanted with all of them – and my future there amongst them.'

She sat up, and looked into his face. He stroked her hair and looked down at her.

It was she who found words first. 'William! Is that true – that you don't want to go back? You've hinted it before, but I've never believed you. Are you sure?'

'Quite sure. I hate the very thought of it – though that doesn't signify. I have to, whether I want to or not.'

Her expression changed, and her back straightened. 'Why?' Her tone, as well as the question, was blunt. She knew what his answer would be. They had been over this before.

He reached for her hand again, because he could feel the resistance in her, and he needed her support, not her opposition.

'Because I have to be fair to my old colleagues, for one thing. If I gave up suddenly and at short notice, the chances are that his being *in situ* would give Canistor an unfair advantage to stay there. He's just the sort the younger intake would support in preference to one of the older brigade. Of course the Chair would have to be advertised – but in university politics there are always wheels within wheels. You see what it means. When I go back next month, there will be a solid phalanx of youngsters in organized opposition to me. I shall have to fight them on every tiny issue. With a new Master, and even the change of Vice Chancellor in the offing, I can't rely on much loyalty or support. I don't find it a very pleasant prospect.'

'So? If you can't help yourself, you won't be able to do much for your old colleagues who are being overlooked. That excuse won't wash. Why must you go on?'

'Do I have to spell it out to you yet again? Finance, my darling. The result of all my mis-spent years. With inflation running as high as it is, and still likely to rise, my pension at this point would be approximately worth half what it will be if I serve my time out. No – you have to listen to me.'

He held her against him. 'We must consider this, seriously. We are safe and comfortable financially as we are now, but we can't take it for granted that it will always be so. We have heavy commitments, for example to Sophie and Ned. Besides, if they were to give up, their replacements – which we couldn't do without – would cost us twice as much for half the service. And – please don't be cross with me for saying this – but there's no guarantee that you can go on for ever being as successful as you are now. Popularity of your kind is notoriously fickle. We can't go on expecting your earned income to go on being our cushion – even if I were prepared to let you be the main breadwinner. Which, quite frankly, as your husband, I am not. I wasn't prepared for the miracle that has happened to me. All that I can offer you is the security of as big and regular a pension as I can make it by seeing my time out.'

'You've always expected to have to go on providing for Janice. At least you don't have to fork out maintenance for her, now.'

'No – but you won't be able to rely on the very adequate war-widow's pension that you had to give up when you married me, either. They more or less balance each other out.'

It was always the same, when they discussed ways and means. She knew it hurt his old-fashioned pride that they lived in 'her' house, and that she contributed to their very comfortable life-style at all. That was part of the pre-war ethic they had been born into,

11

in his case reinforced by his natural courtesy and his chivalric code of 'honour'. As much part of him as his head of white hair. Part of the man she loved and didn't want altered. But she couldn't let him make an issue of it at this point. She'd had no option but to look after herself until he'd turned up again; she valued her independence, and wasn't prepared to give it up and let her own talents rust just to save his over-sensitive *amour-propre*. She had no intention of being anything but an equal partner in this marriage. Her reply had a tinge of asperity.

'You know perfectly well that I haven't relied on my pension since you objected to "another man keeping me", as you put it. I went on drawing it, of course – it was my right – but I didn't use it. As I told you, I had it paid into a separate account in my bank – to be used for the grandchildren if we never needed it. So there it is, and has been accumulating compound interest. A nice little nest-egg that will keep us from starving if we are ever on the breadline. But I'm not nearly so prepared to write myself off yet as you seem to be – any more than I am prepared to write you off. If, to satisfy that tender conscience of yours, you must earn something to supplement whatever pension you would be entitled to, there are dozens of avenues open to you. Finished – at your age? Don't be such a push-over! When or if the time does come, we'll cut our coat according to our cloth. To provide for the future is, as you say, plain common sense. To mortgage the present for it is nonsense. Anybody who has lived through a war ought to remember that! Are you truly being realistic – or just "maunch-gutting", as Sophie would say? You'll be fifty-four this month. That means you have eleven more years at least to go to your full pension age – thirteen if you choose. Are you honestly gearing yourself up to face that because you are scared we shan't have enough to get along on if you don't? I never heard anything so idiotic!'

She stopped, aware of him grinning down at her – the first 'William-ish' reaction she had seen since they had begun this discussion. She was afraid she might have hurt him by being so forthright, but that mischievous smile reassured her.

'Gosh!' he said. 'You aren't half handsome when you're fired up like that. I'm glad I had enough sense to ask my landlady to marry me. At least she'll keep me warm at night when we run out of fuel. All that fire inside her, as well as being soft and cuddly into the bargain.'

She boxed his ears. 'I'm surprised you had enough sense,' she said. 'She was glad enough to accept you. Opportunities like that don't often come to middle-aged women of her shape and size. She didn't stop to consider whether or not you might be able to keep her without her soiling her lily-white hands with anything called work. As long as she'd got a man to call her own, she didn't care much about his bank balance – especially as the man was you.' She was holding up her face to be kissed.

'Then may we go on talking a little longer?' he responded. 'You've just put it all into a nutshell. I'm not the same man now that gate-crashed into your life. I'd considered myself reasonably lucky insofar that if I didn't have a wife, at least I had a mistress I thought I could never tire of: history. But when at my age you fall for somebody new, old mistresses lose their charm.'

'I see. The mid-life crisis. Middle-aged men leave their wives for younger and more exciting ones, and find they've got to keep up the old grind to finance both. Are you really telling me you have lost interest in history? Darling, that worries me. What's wrong?'

He got up and went to stand looking out of the window. Then he turned to face her again.

'My whole view of history has changed, and the way we teach it. I shall always love history. But I don't any longer want to be an academic historian, teaching the same old stuff year after year. You know the old joke about the definition of "education" – the process by which knowledge passes from the notebook of the tutor to the notebook of the student without passing through the minds of either? That's what's turned people like me into old fuddy-duddies, but it at least had the advantage of being structured. Now it's all changing too fast, and leaving such as me behind. We've lost cohesion. It's every man for himself, tutor or student, scrambling up the ladder somehow, and the devil take the hindmost.

'In this last year, I've been feeling that I'm a part of living history – actually helping to make it. That's what's always happened. I don't see it now from the merely academic viewpoint of historical "periods". I see it now as Will Durrant defined it: "*the parade of egos across the landscape of Time*". I don't want to be stuck to one period. I want to roam about in the landscape of Time, and see whom and what I meet.

'But that, my sweetheart, is where we came in. What I'd like to do and what I must if I remain a professor of medieval history are two very different things. I'd like to explore things that crop up – like that fascinating old manuscript Bob found in the church up at Castle Hill. Probably seventeenth century, and therefore not my "period". Even thinking of it is selfish and impractical, as well as being financially impossible, besides amounting to me committing academic suicide. So of course I shan't.'

Fran stood up suddenly and faced him, looking very determined.

'Oh yes you will!' she said. 'I've listened to you, so now you listen to me. When Archie Marriner attacked you personally on the question of our adultery, you defended yourself by saying that though you were a historian and he a priest in Holy Orders, *you were both men first*. That still applies. You're a man who, to quote yourself "is making history".

'Are you really going to contemplate wasting the next eleven years of what is left of your tiny span of life doing what you don't want to do – just to be a "good husband" to me? Being a good husband depends on a lot more than simply keeping the wolf from the door! It depends on you making your wife happy – and you can't do that unless you're happy yourself.

'Where do you think I shall stand in the list of your priorities if you spend the next decade just pumping up the size of your pension? You'd hate me for being the cause of you ending up one of those useless old dodderers you mentioned. I don't want that to happen, and I won't let it. So if you want to please me, you'll go back next month and tell them you'll be leaving at Christmas. Oh, my darling, please! Please do. Promise me!'

'I'll do everything I can to please you,' he said, 'except promise. I've learned from experience what a mistake it can be to make unredeemable promises.'

'That's all in the past,' she said. 'Haven't we done with all that

14

– especially Janice, for ever? It's the future that matters. Can't you take a gamble on love, and me?'

He was too moved to speak, but he wrapped his long arms round her and held her. When they came apart, both mopped damp faces with their handkerchiefs. It seemed hotter than ever.

He was still struggling to find adequate words when the telephone rang.

As an interrupter, the telephone has no equal. Its strident, authoritative voice brooks no defiance. They both knew that they had not done with the subject altogether, and would have to return to it. It was far too important a decision for William to have to make on the spur of emotion only. But for the present, somebody had to silence that insistent bell.

William picked up the receiver, listened, and handed it to Fran. 'It's Jeremy,' he said. 'There seems to be some sort of emergency.'

There was. Kate, Fran's married daughter, had been coming downstairs with a load of dirty washing in her arms, had tripped over a trailing sheet and fallen the rest of the way. She had badly sprained an ankle so that she could put no weight on it, and wrenched a shoulder so badly that she couldn't even lift a cup of tea. It was still in holiday time from her little daughter Helen's playschool, and Andy, still a toddler, was 'into everything'. The trouble was that this had happened just when Jeremy was about to leave for a week's business conference that was very important to him, but there was no way he could leave Kate to cope by herself. Even the daily help was taking her annual holiday in Blackpool.

'It's always the way, in any sort of crisis,' Jeremy said, 'and I hate to ask you, but could you possibly stand in for a few days?'

'I'd hardly call it a crisis,' Fran said. 'Nothing more than a temporary emergency. Of course I shall come. What are mothers for?'

The relief in Jeremy's voice was evident, but he still sounded a bit hesitant. 'I'm afraid it's an urgent one,' he went on. 'I have to leave tonight. Can you make it today?'

William had been picking up most of the conversation. He

took the receiver. 'Yes,' he said. 'As long as we don't waste time now.'

He turned to Fran and said, 'Ask Sophie to get lunch early. We can be there by tea-time. I'll take you, and stay with you if you want me to. Two children and an invalid to look after in this heat will be more than a handful.'

'I don't know how I ever coped without you,' she said. 'But haven't you got a lot of plans made? And we must consult the troops! There's Cat, for one thing.'

'You go and talk to Sophie,' he said. 'I'll go and find Ned. He doesn't usually mind coming to stay here to keep an eye on the house, and Cat-sit.'

Sophie was not quite her instantly obliging self. ''Ow long do you expect to be away, then?' she asked, with an air of embarrassed reluctance.

'I don't know. Till Jerry gets home and Kate can be left, I suppose. Why?'

'There's things to be seen to,' replied Sophie darkly. 'Let's see what Ned says.'

Ned had come in from the garden with William. Fran did not miss the swift though silent communication between him and Sophie.

Ned appeared to be as unwilling to oblige as Sophie. He addressed himself to William. 'I don't reckon both of you ought to be away together till we've got this storm over,' he said. 'It ain't that I wouldn't help if I could – but I can't be in two places at once. Come that storm in the middle o' the night, my place is as likely to be struck as this – and this as likely as mine.'

'Do you mean we're likely to get it tonight? Because in that case, we'll get off now, and I'll come straight back.'

Sophie intervened with her usual common sense. 'There's no call for you to rush off and travel through the 'eat o' the afternoon,' she said. 'Leave it till the cool o' the evening. That'll give us all a bit more time to see to things.' Again, there was that conspiratorial glance between her and Ned. Sophie saw him out, standing at the back door to converse with him. Fran was getting irritated by their joint lack of cooperation. She and William didn't often take advantage of their devotion.

'Whatever's got into them?' she asked William.

He raised his eyebrows, as nonplussed as she was herself. 'Something unusual's in the wind. People like them don't get upset at the prospect of a storm. But if I'm going to get you there tonight and come back, I'd better go and get the car filled up and whatnot, while Sophie prepares lunch. Then we shall be ready to start when they'll let us.' He went, and Sophie returned.

In the ordinary way, Fran would have let Sophie take her usual verbal route 'round by Will's mother's' to discover the cause for the reluctance and the slight air of embarrassment that accompanied it. But there was no time for finesse. Fran guessed that Ned had told Sophie of some wild bit of rumour going round with regard to their hasty and hidden marriage, to which another sudden and unannounced trip would add a lot of salacious details. Under the circumstances, there was no time to play Sophie's game. She would ask outright what was the matter.

'Is there any real reason why we shouldn't go to Kate's help?' she asked, with a little more asperity in her tone than was usual.

Sophie flushed a deep beetroot red, and had difficulty in finding her tongue.

Fran thought that Sophie must, by nature, be the world's worst conspirator. She spoke the truth – but it had to be the whole truth, and nothing but the truth. If she couldn't give chapter and verse, she said nothing. If she did repeat anything, her tale went like a children's game, up highways and down bye-ways, through bushes and briars, and 'in and out of the windows'.

'It's as Ned said,' Sophie answered at last. 'You 'adn't both ought to be away come a storm. Don't you remember when Miss –'

Fran cut her short. 'I haven't lost my wits because Kate's fallen downstairs,' she said. 'I know as well as you do that it isn't the likelihood of a storm that's worrying you.'

Sophie took refuge in prevarication. 'It were Ned as made all the hormpolodge about a storm,' she said. 'Not me! I never mentioned no storm!'

'Then don't waste your breath and my time now. Tell me the truth.'

It was as near as she had ever been to giving Sophie an order, and for a moment Fran thought Sophie was going to burst into tears. Sophie, seeing there was no help for it, sat down and 'bluthered it all out'.

'It's all to do with you and 'im getting married like that in foreign parts so's none o' your friends knowed nothing about it – only me, and I'm wished a good many times as I didn't. What call 'ad you to goo and do it in secret be'ind all our backs? You might ha' knowed as it'd get out some'ow! Everybody's talking about it, and asking me. I'm sure I'm 'ad to come as near to telling lies about it as anything in my whull life! There's some say as it ain't the truth, and he's heving to pretend 'e's married you, 'cos don't, 'e'll lose 'is job. There's others as'll vouch for the fact as you'd been living together for years afore you come 'ere, and it was 'cos of you as 'is wife ever left 'im – anybody could see as 'e were Roland and Kate's father, only it stood to sense as you wouldn't say so, seeing as when your own 'usband got killed, you could goo on drawing a pension for 'em till they was growed up. You never did 'ear such tales! I'm been so put-about by it as I were downright glad when George Bridgefoot come up 'ere one day when you wasn't 'ere and asked me outright if I knowed the truth of it. And I told 'im I did, and 'e knows as I wouldn't tell 'im no lies even for you. So then 'e said, could we tell Ned an 'all, 'cos there was something to be done as they would want our 'elp with. And that's 'ow Ned comes to know, as well as me.'

Fran went through several phases of reaction while listening to Sophie's recital. Indignation, softened by a yearning wish that saying so could make it true that William was the father of her children, followed by amusement that it had not been loose or lying tongues, but silence the golden that had caused this farrago of nonsense in the first place.

'So George knows?'

'As much as I do. All you told me when you come back was as you 'ad been married and I wasn't to tell nobody till you was ready to tell 'em yourselves. Why, I couldn't tell 'im, 'cos you never told me for why. And 'e said as all your friends guessed it must ha' been a register-office wedding after William's divorce 'ad come through, and I said I 'adn't 'eard nothing about no divorce. But 'e seemed satisfied, and told me why 'e'd wanted to know. Seems as all your friends is made up their mind to jine together to give you a present, and want to give it to you at a little do somewheer on the Sat'day afore 'is birthday on the last Sunday o' the month. But there was some reason why they couldn't set the date, so we don't know yet. But they can't have no do if you ain't 'ere, so me an' Ned tried to stop you going afore one of us 'ad 'ad time to nip down and tell George about you heving to be away. Tha's all. We was trying to do our best.'

The warm glow that had started to spread from Fran's diaphragm was threatening to overwhelm her. She reached her hand across the table to Sophie, who took it and returned the squeeze.

'I don't know what we can have done to deserve such friends as we have,' she said. 'And of course we'll fall in with any plans they have. But we must tell you what did happen. William found out that his wife had died – and wanted us to be married as soon as we could. The Reverend Delaprime married us – in a little Welsh church. But ours wasn't the wedding everybody here was looking forward to, and Charles and Charlie's was. We just didn't want to spoil anything for them. We didn't tell anybody but you –' She stopped because Sophie was allowing herself the luxury of a few tears.

Then while Fran went to pack, Sophie set with a will to preparing a hasty lunch.

William came back, and was given the facts as far as Fran knew them.

'I imagine they're waiting for Effendi to come back,' William said. 'They wouldn't want to do anything like that without him. I don't think it would be fair on them for both of us to be away long, so if you are sure you can manage without me, I'll only stay at Kate's tonight, and come back tomorrow morning. That should reassure them. So if you are asked again, Sophie, you can tell any of them that they'll find me here until I go to fetch Fran home again.'

They set off in the late afternoon, in a much happier mood. What Sophie had told them rid them of the niggling worry that they might have unintentionally hurt or even offended their friends by such unwonted secrecy.

In the enclosed seclusion of the car, they returned to the subject of William's future. He wasn't prepared to consider it settled; so he was glad that he need only be away from home for one night, because whatever his final decision, he had no intention of giving anybody the chance to accuse him of dereliction of duty while he still held his post. He'd made up his mind to be seen about in college as often as he could in the next three weeks, ostentatiously preparing to take up the reins of office again, and teaching that precocious little so-and-so sitting in Morag's chair what her official duties as secretary to the head of a department were likely to be from then on.

He also wanted to test the temperature again – not, as before, in a mood of outrage, but calmly and objectively. He told Fran that though he hated to be separated from her, the decision that had soon to be made absolute might be easier that way.

'I must be sure I didn't make it up!' he said. 'It's all too easy to find reasons for not doing what you don't want to. I honestly hate the very thought of going on, but I must consider all the consequences of acting out of pique, and on a selfish whim.'

She sighed. 'I thought we had been over all that this morning,' she said. 'I suppose you mean the financial consequences? I do wish you wouldn't. I think the heat must be getting at you. Can't we forget it for now? Let's stop and have a meal at the next good hotel while we can still afford it. I don't suppose there'll be much to eat at Kate's.'

He laughed, took her at her word, and pulled into the car-park of The Old Mill about three miles further on. It was getting a little cooler, and they were more at ease, physically and in general, than they had been for a week or more. By mutual consent they talked of everything else but his dilemma till they reached their destination.

He left early next morning, having arranged that he should ring her every night around eight o'clock, after she had made supper and put the children to bed.

Alone on the way home, his nagging problem returned. There were things to be put into the balance on the other side, besides the question of finance. Silly things, some of them, but real. He had dreamed of being able to lay in Fran's lap the perks of being his wife, that so far she had never enjoyed. To show her off, in so very different a way from that of Janice. To be able with her at his side to enjoy as never before the social life of Cambridge as the respected academic he now was.

But – to do what he wanted to do, when he wanted to do it . . . ? Fran was right that there would be plenty of avenues open to him. No one could rob him of the reputation or prestige he had already earned. So why was he still shilly-shallying?

Because a man did not live on his wife's money. He hadn't had much of an opinion of Greg, who had been forced to let Jess work. He'd remembered telling Fran about 'Jess and that hopeless husband of hers'. Greg had made good the moment he'd had a chance. He hadn't deliberately given up what he did have in order to do it. That made a lot of difference. His friends would understand how he felt, but apart from Elyot, they all still *worked*. If he had something to go to that they – and he – could regard as a 'job', he'd feel a lot better about giving up the job he had.

A man did *not* rely on his wife's earnings. It was part of the moral code in which they had been brought up. Much akin to the one they had already been through, holding off from consummating their love for each other for so long. In the ethos of those prewar days, men didn't give up a good job just because they were fed up with it; they stuck it out – just as both sexes resisted sex outside the marriage bond on the grounds of a 'morality' unknown to those born after the conflict. He was torn both ways now, as he had been then, wanting Fran so desperately but unwilling to break through the hedge of thorns that guarded her reputation. It had been she who had been able to set convention aside. She was made of sterner stuff than he was. Without her always at hand, he would be able to see and judge his position more objectively. How would he feel when it came to the crunch and he was only an idle country gentleman, while Canistor sat in his 'Chair' and showed all the adoring youngsters what a 'real' academic could do?

He came to a halt in a tailback at some roadworks, and the sun was high enough by then to be beating without mercy on the metal box on wheels he sat in. He opened the windows, but there was no air. The cool of his own study at home had never seemed more alluring. If he took the gamble Fran seemed to want him to, he could spend the rest of his working life there! But that was the rub. He gazed out into the heat-haze all round him, coloured as it was with exhaust smoke and diesel fumes, till the smell of it began to overpower him, and he decided he would rather be hot than be sick. He began to find the hold-up unbearable, mainly because he was stuck in it through no fault of his own, and there was no way out – very much like the position he had got himself into *vis-à-vis* his job.

He tried to make himself think of something other than the heat and fumes and his predicament, but found thinking difficult. His brain was as muzzy as the surrounding atmosphere. What was there he could offer as a good reason for getting out of the university traffic jam? A project of some sort he had to have, or his guilt at his own idleness would defeat his purpose in getting free to choose what he did. If there were something to occupy him that he could genuinely call 'work', even though he did it with a pen instead of a shovel, he would feel much more justified in taking the plunge.

The traffic began to move again, and so did his mind. In the heat of his discussion with Fran yesterday, he had mentioned that what he wanted to do was to explore Bob's book. He began to explore its possibilities now, as home and Benedict's, even without Fran in it, beckoned him on.

William's friendship with Bob Bellamy was an unusual one, probably because Bob was such an unusual man. While most of the other farmers in and around the old village farmed land that had been in the possession of their families for generations, Bob had come to try out 'highland' farming as a tenant, while still working his own land in his native fens. It was one of the changes the postwar period had brought with it that as the value of fenland for agricultural purposes had dropped, that of 'highland' had gone up. Once huge new mechanical implements became readily available, farming on hard clay land became as easy and as profitable as working the extremely fertile but sometimes too soft and friable fenland. Bob was a fen-tiger to his very core, but astute enough to see that his university-educated son's reasoning was right when he had advocated getting a foot in on a highland farm while the going was good. It was therefore for his son's sake that he had uprooted himself and taken on a rather neglected highland farm on the outskirts of Old Swithinford. It hadn't worked out, and Bob had been at a very low ebb when William and Fran had met him, and found what a loveable character and extraordinary acquaintance they had made. Like many fenmen, Bob was 'fey', though much more so than most. It was when he had discovered that neither William nor Fran scorned him for being 'only a tenant farmer', nor scoffed at his extraordinarily well-developed sixth sense that he began to trust them, and from that time on the friendship had ripened fast.

In Fran, he had found a woman who was everything his hard, grasping, selfish wife had never been. He gave to her the same sort of devotion his pagan ancestors might have given to a tribal goddess, and though as a man he envied William, he saw their love for each other as something beautiful in its own right – as he saw the first primrose of every new spring.

In the darkest period of Bob's life he had, against all William's advice, gone up into the cracked and unsafe tower of the little church so close to his isolated house, and come down with a 'find', a book-shaped package carefully sewn, nautical-fashion, into several layers of what William later judged to be fairweather hempen sailcloth. The fascinated historian guessed that it had never been unwrapped since whoever had hidden it put it where Bob had found it. It hadn't got there of its own accord – so who had hidden it, and why? There had to be a story attached to it, and both men were avid to discover what the story was.

Keeping records and/or diaries in times of war or pestilence was no new thing – many such had been found and studied. The mystery here was why, if such it was, it should have been so carefully preserved and so well hidden. Records were left in order to be read by survivors: diaries, if they contained personal secrets, were not left in public buildings to be found by just anybody, or abandoned lightly. Who had taken all that trouble with it? A dying man couldn't, a man in a hurry to save himself from infection wouldn't, and if all it contained was a record of a bad outbreak of plague, there was no reason why anybody should. Plague and small-pox and such devastating epidemics were far too prevalent for anybody to go to such trouble about.

Bob had agreed, not relying on knowledge he didn't possess, but on feelings that he did. Why didn't they rip it open and find out exactly what it was there and then?

William was in a scholar's dilemma. This, he told Bob, was the sort of 'find' that historians dream about as gamblers dream of winning the jackpot and adolescents dream of waking up to find a prince or princess in their bed. The fact that Bob had found it didn't make it theirs. William's academic integrity was at stake if he didn't report it – *exactly as it had been found*. He told Bob he could not be party to undoing the package, but would, if Bob agreed, be responsible for handing it on to the rector, the Rev. Archibald Marriner.

Bob demurred. As he saw it, if he hadn't found it when he did, it would probably have never been saved at all, because it was evident that before long the church would either fall down or be reduced to rubble by a developer's bulldozers to make foundations for another estate of horrid little houses. It was no secret that such 'finds' that might hold up progress were hushed up and hurriedly disposed of by road-making contractors and their like, before local historians or archaeologists got wind of them. Money was at stake. But he, Bob, had found this and rescued it. He wanted his friend William, and only William, to be the one to open it and discover what it was. If he wouldn't, Bob saw nothing wrong in hanging on to it, just as it was, until William changed his mind.

William, looking up at Bob's amused but determined face under the old pork-pie hat the farmer had pushed to the very back of his head, had got the message. If it was going to be a contest between William's knowledge and Bob's intuition, there was no doubt which had the most chance of being right. William compromised, and agreed that Bob should take care of it at least till William had had time to make discreet inquiries and finish the bit of research he was already engaged upon.

And that is how it had been left until one evening just before William and Fran had set out for Wales, when Bob had taken the package out of the ancient Bible box in which he kept it, tossed it into William's lap, and left him alone with it. The historian's curiosity conquered the academic's touchy conscience, and William had unpicked the black thread stitches to find a thick, leather-covered book filled with manuscript.

Circumstances alter cases. There was now no rector, nor likely to be. Bob, returning, took the situation in, re-wrapped the book, handed it to William, and bade him take it home with him.

Temptation had been too great and he had succumbed. But he had known himself well enough to judge that if once he began to study it, his official research would never be finished – and he still had remnants of guilt about it. So he had added a plastic wrapper to the oilskin Bob had placed round it, put it into the bottom drawer of his study desk, locked the drawer and put the key away in his little private safe.

He had done his best to forget it – until now. What had happened in college last week had demonstrated to him all too clearly that other people's integrity now bore very little relation even to the ragged ends of his own. The knowledge that the manuscript was there had begun to torment him.

He always hated going into the house when Fran was not there. Sophie and Ned had gone home. While he waited for the leaden finger of time to reach eight o'clock so he could ring Fran, he could think of nothing but that old book. He told her all about it, adding that every time he sat down at his desk he could feel his nose quivering and his mouth watering, like a dog following a man with aniseed in his trouser turn-ups. She laughed aloud, and at the sound his heart and spirits rose like a helium-filled balloon.

'Darling Fido!' she said. 'Still following the scent of honour! But honestly, sweetheart, aren't you overdoing it a bit? How do you know what it is until you've looked more closely into it? It may still turn out to be only a miserly old churchwarden's accounts, or the confessions of a randy old parson about his interest in the local bawdy house. He might even have kept the madame's accounts in return for services rendered. I think you really ought to find out. At least it would keep you out of other mischief till

I get home again. Go to it, my love! Dare to be a Daniel, as Kezia used to sing. Oh dear – Kate's calling and I think I hear Andy crying. Sorry, my darling, but I must go. Duty calls. Only till eight o'clock tomorrow, but I've got to say goodnight, sweetheart.'

She cut him off.

William replaced the hand-set in its cradle, satisfied and soothed. The physical distance between him and Fran tonight seemed to have concentrated rather than detracted from their rapport. Knowing they had only minutes to talk instead of as long as they liked, and that at any moment they might be interrupted, they had somehow distilled a lot of meaning into a few words and summed up all the long discussions of the past few days.

She had made it quite clear that she was not simply 'going along with him' in advising him to give up. If he didn't want to go on, then she didn't want him to. She genuinely wanted whatever it was that he wanted, and was prepared to take any consequences. That was Love, with a capital L. For the first time, he believed her wholly, and to Luck, Fate, God – whatever it was that had brought them back together again – he offered gratitude unlimited.

She was right. She had tried to make him see that once before. He had too much life still ahead of him to waste it plodding along simply for the sake of safety and financial security.

'You don't *have* to become a lotus eater just because you give up whatever is beginning to pall on you,' Fran had said. 'Think of old Odysseus, finding Ithaca so boring and still wanting to go forward to "seek a newer world".

> "How dull it is to pause, to make an end
> To rust unburnished, not to shine in use!
> As though to breathe were life."'

He smiled at the remembrance. She wouldn't be his Fran if she hadn't got an apt quotation on the end of her tongue! She hadn't been able to persuade him. He had been all too conscious that he had to go on plodding, mainly because of his obligations to Janice. He guessed Fran remembered, too, and would know the real reason for his hesitation now, though he had never voiced it. It was still that question of his 'duty', and the outdated concept of honour that lay behind it. He owed duty to his college, to the university, to scholarship in general, still; but more than all these, he now owed duty to Fran. He was her husband.

He had discharged to the letter all his obligations to Janice, though aware that it meant Fran taking a lot of moral flak, because having given his word, his obligations to Janice were fixed and immovable. There had never been a chance for Fran to rely on him financially, because even on his good salary he couldn't have done enough for both. That Fran hadn't needed nor had ever asked for that sort of help had only served to make him feel his inadequacy towards her even more. The obligations he felt towards her now were far greater than he had ever felt towards Janice – from whom, God be praised, he had been freed for ever. He sat down and heaved a huge sigh of relief and content. She had hung over his happiness with Fran like the sword of Damocles suspended by one of her brittle coppery hairs. He closed his eyes and yearned for Fran's soft, dark head against his cheek. It was Fran who was his wife now. Until tonight, he had never been able to make himself believe there could be a woman living who could forget and forgive all that he had put Fran through in the last three years, and still without a trace of resentment be willing to let him renounce all that she had a moral right to – financial security, academic prestige, and all the social cachet of the Oxbridge culture to which his position entitled him. But then, Fran wasn't just any woman. Nor was she content for either of them to live out their lives just breathing. Every day with her would be 'a newer world'.

He concluded that she had been well aware of the way his mind had been working all along. She had seen through him and all the specious arguments he had put forward as to why he could not retire yet – had known they were camouflage or weak substitutes for the real reasons for his ambivalence. That was what had made her so forthright tonight. She was afraid lest, in this period of enforced separation, he might convince himself that his honour and duty to her lay in self-sacrifice, and take a unilateral decision on a principle she did not share, that the harder way must neces- sarily be the right one. Shades of medieval chivalry as interpreted by the Victorians! He gave the sitting-room ceiling a huge amused grin – to think that it was him seeing through her motives instead of her always seeing through his! She was truly afraid that, without her in sight, he would do something irrevocably silly. That's why she had dangled the temptation of Bob's book before him. Not that it was a bad idea at all. She had hit on a crucial point when she had said that until somebody read it, nobody would know whether it was worth a lot of trouble or not.

And it was in his possession, and besides Fran and Bob, nobody knew of its existence. The thought of it giving up its secrets to anyone but himself filled him with the same sort of unreasoning jealousy that in the past he had felt towards any other unattached man who had looked with appreciation upon Fran. Possession may be nine points of the law – but the thought of Fran – or that book – in any other hands but his own was almost more than he could bear. He tried again to consider it dispassionately. He had to confess that he had missed the rarefied atmosphere of university life very little, if at all. Or the academic view of history that he had allowed to form like a patina over his more general interest in it. History was not the preserve of university departments only. He hadn't been deprived of history in the last twelve months, even without the research he had lost interest in. He had been living through history, and in his infinitesimal way, helping to make it. He had watched the village he had known from early childhood, once a unified community, being ripped apart and split into two. He had become involved in the struggle enough to take sides, something a trained historian surely should never do? He couldn't have told anybody why he had felt obliged to throw his lot in with the old and traditional against the new and progressive. Now education was at a crossroads, and he didn't care much for the way it looked like going. That was why he was giving up.

Giving up? Was he? He was quite startled to find that he had more or less made up his mind. He turned his mind back to the book. They had agreed that it was probably seventeenth-century. How many people there must have been then, as he was now, vacillating before choosing sides. Weighing the pros and cons of the case – yet always watching the balance of reason being tipped one way or the other by personal involvement or love for someone on the other side. All war was ghastly, as he knew only too well; but of all wars, civil war was the worst. He went to find a book to do a bit of background reading. But Cat appeared from somewhere, climbed on to his chest, pushed the book aside with her little black nose, put one of her seal-dark paws each side of his neck, and tucked her head under his chin. He couldn't repulse her any more than he could have pushed Fran's head from its place on his shoulder. He stroked her and caressed her and listened to her purring love song, till both of them contentedly slept . . .

He was late to bed, and late getting up, oppressed by the heat and depressed by the thought of a whole weekend alone without Fran. It was as hot and sticky as ever, though the morning mist still hovered.

He had taken a fairly firm decision overnight, but by the light of day he began to have a few doubts again. Cat obligingly came and sat in Fran's chair, so he talked aloud to her, and her throaty replies, in a wide range of Siamese, were reasonably satisfactory.

He would have to begin on the procedures of getting himself released – giving his official resignation to the Registrar, and his personal reasons for it to the Master, to whom full courtesy was due. He foresaw that they might request him to continue for the whole of the next academic year. It would have some advantages.

It would bring him round to his fifty-fifth birthday, which for some totally inexplicable reason presented itself as a far less foolish age at which to retire than fifty-four, though God only knew why! There would be more time for him to get used to the idea, and to placate that still rather sore place in his conscience about the financial aspect. It would mean one more year's service to be taken into account in the calculation of his pension and the accompanying lump sum. It was all very well to rely on the Lord to provide, but as Sophie's mother would have said, 'God helps them as help theirselves.'

Besides, he had remembered little Tanner/Jasper/Jonce. He had given his dead friend a solemn promise that whatever happened to the rest of the children, he would keep his eye on the

29

one who was John's own son, and when the time came had a proper education. The child was settled for the moment – they all hoped permanently – with Jess and Greg. But even if they did get official permission to keep him, without financial help they might not be able to cope on Greg's precarious income as an artist. It had just struck William that Jonce was very much of an age with Fran's grandchildren, and that Kate and Jeremy might also need help then, too. It was the question as to where his moral duty lay raising its head again.

However, the last obstacle still lay in his own mind. He had to be absolutely sure that he was not running away from his job in a fit of middle-aged pique. Only a fool or a coward would condemn himself to years of purposeless decline by any pretence that there was waiting for him a task worthy of his talent and ability. Bob's book might very well still turn out to be no more than a chimera created by his need to provide himself with an excuse.

He didn't consider himself a fool, but he did sometimes wonder if he was a moral coward. The way to find the truth about that manuscript was to go after breakfast and open it. Nobody had ever forbidden him to: certainly not Fran, certainly not Bob. He knew the reason to be that *he had been scared of being disappointed*. That it might yet turn out to be nothing, and not his reprieve from becoming 'an old dodderer', despite his doctorate and his reputation. He had to prove to himself that though he might be a fool, he was not a cringing coward – and there was no time like the present.

Five minutes later, the big, brown, leather-covered book lay open before him on his desk. After the first glance down at it, he lifted his head and took a deep breath. Outside the window, the sun had lifted itself above the tops of the trees and driven off the cool morning mist, beating down from a sky as broad and blue as he had ever seen. The garden swam in a haze before his eyes. Then he sat down and began to read.

The firm, elegant Roman hand was quite legible, though the ink was somewhat faded. The Latin was that of a scholar: grammatical, clear and concise. William's first reaction was one of elation. A couple of lines was enough to convince him that unless it changed drastically as the writer went on, he would have no more trouble with it than if it had been modern French. Finding it so invitingly possible almost overwhelmed him.

The sunlight on the scorched garden outside was too bright. His heart was thumping in a most uncomfortable way, and when he stood up to draw the curtains, his head swam. It must be the brightness of the light. He went to sit with his back to it, till his head should clear. There was no hurry. It was still barely nine o'clock and, being Saturday, he'd be alone all day.

Though he longed for Fran to be there to share his elation, there was a perverse satisfaction in being forced to play a husband's part and take a final decision himself. He was, he supposed, the same man as the lonely academic who, on the spur of the moment, had decided to write that stiff little note of congratulation to his cousin after their long years of separation, and that tiny, unpremeditated action had changed his life. Today's anything-but-unpremeditated action could change it even more.

If he hadn't sent it, he would now be going downhill towards nothingness, like an old long-case clock with its weight slowly descending till at last the pendulum stopped swinging and it ceased to tick. Meeting Fran had rewound his clock. She had restored life to the bit of him that was becoming moribund. He'd always be a scholar, but she had restored his essential manhood. Life was different now in every way. Coping with internal politics within a university, and petty quarrels with incompatible colleagues was one thing; facing up to matters of life and death among friends and neighbours with the woman you'd always loved at your side was quite another. He knew now which of the two communities he really belonged to. That book lying behind him on his desk could be another gift to him from the gods, as Fran had been. He had posted that note to Fran with no advice but his own. There was no one but himself to rely on today.

It was already getting hotter. There was no air to breathe. He was damp and clammy, sweating profusely, he guessed because of his excitement and a violent reaction to having made the decision after such hesitation. He slumped back into his armchair.

He had been far more worried than he would ever admit to anyone but himself. The bright days – actually and metaphorically

– since he had brought Fran home to Benedict's as his wife had been clouded by the knowledge that every one of them had brought his return to the university job inexorably closer. And he had been dreading it, long before the visit that had brought his feelings to a head. With his conscience shaming him for his disloyalty to his chosen and till now so beloved profession, he had used Bob's book as an excuse, pinning his hopes of release on it. How stupid could one get! Why did he need any excuse? There were opportunities galore for a man with his reputation. As long as Fran was willing to go along with him, there really had been no need to worry. What a silly state he had got himself into! Especially about that old book . . . In these last few days, it had become a sigil, an occult prediction guiding his future actions. Exactly as people of Kezia's generation still as a last resort slipped a knife into a Bible, taking as a sign whatever text met their eyes. He hadn't expected it to work quite the magic that it seemed to have done, and the reaction had been too strong.

He was reluctant to move while his head still swam, but he could think. The book was not a diary or a journal, because that presupposed daily entries. This was a continuous narrative in a style that was easy, gracious and personal. In the little of it he had read, he had felt himself warming to its author, who seemed to be writing because he had the means, the time, and a good story to tell. The best of all reasons for putting quill to paper! He wanted to go back to it, but he could not summon the energy.

The study door opened and Sophie came in, bearing his morning coffee, exactly as on a weekday. He jumped to his feet.

'Sophie! I didn't expect you – it is Saturday, isn't it?'

She looked hot, disgruntled, put out. 'I should ha' been 'ere sooner only for heving to goo to Thirz's and calling at the butcher's for some neck o' lamb to casserole for your dinner. And I'm got you a lovely bit o' fillet steak for tomorrow, seeing as it's Sunday and I shan't be 'ere to see to your meals. Do you don't want it, see as you put it in the freezer. It's no weather for anything to be kept long. I ain't been told what your plans are.'

'I haven't got any. I'll eat it when I fancy it. Thanks for thinking about me.'

'That's just it. You ain't been yourself at all since you come

32

'ome from being away in Wales. Ned's noticed it, and all – as if you 'ad something on your mind. I don't wonder as there is them as think you're only pretending to be married – but what sense there is in such a fool's tale I can't make out, seeing as everybody knows as you're been living together as man and wife for all this while a'ready. But as I said to Thirz' this morning, "'E's got plenty on 'is mind without us bothering 'im." But there, she is as she is.'

He pulled himself together to consider what she had said. 'Thirzah? Is she ill again?' he asked, realizing that he was being requested to stand in for Fran as Sophie's confidante with regard to some altercation between Sophie and her strong-willed, didactic elder sister.

'No, not she!' said Sophie, her face red with suppressed irritation. 'There never was much wrong with 'er, if you ask me. She made 'erself bad 'cos she couldn't hev 'er own way. When that Welshman stood up to 'er, praying as loud as she did, 'er temper just got the better of 'er. Soon as 'e'd gone away, she was right as rain again, so long as the rest of us would give in and let 'er 'ev 'er own way about everything.'

She mopped a glum face. He knew of old that it was no good trying to hurry her.

'Fetch yourself a drink and sit down and tell me what she wants that you don't want to bother me with,' he said. 'I have got something on my mind – but it's nothing to do with us being married. You'll be the first to know what it is, when I can tell anybody. There, does that satisfy you? Now you tell me what it is that has upset you this morning.'

The relief on Sophie's face as she faced him from the other armchair, sitting primly on its edge, was reward enough to him for making an effort for her.

'If only it wasn't so 'ot!' she said. 'I can't abear heving to go anywhere in weather like this, but Thirz' says as we shall hev to goo.'

He took his cue. 'Where to, and why?' he asked.

'Thirz' 'ad a letter come this morning, from Cousin Tilda's 'usband.'

William kept his face straight only with an effort. Mention of

33

Cousin Tilda was almost too much of a sudden let-up for him. They had first heard of Cousin Tilda and her tendency to headaches (which Sophie had called the megrims) while in a particularly hilarious mood, since when 'the megrims' had become a euphemism for an attack of love on his part that nothing but taking Fran to bed would cure. Sophie's face warned him it was no time for him to show the least sign of frivolity now.

'Seems as Cousin Tilda's been heving them megrims so bad she 'ad to 'eve the doctor. She went to the 'ospital to be tested last week, and it turns out as it ain't megrims at all as she's got.'

She dropped her voice to a tone suitable for bad news. 'It's a tumour on 'er brain. 'Er 'usband says in 'is letter as she ain't like to last long – days rather than weeks. Poor Tilda! She never did hev no luck. 'E's never been no good to 'er for one thing, from what we're 'eard. But Thirz' says give even the devil 'us due, he done right to let us know, and we shall hev to go and pay our last respects. Tilda is our kin, when all's said and done, though as far as I remember we ain't seen 'er since we buried Mam. She would ha' wanted us to go for Aunt Sar'anne's sake, even if it is all the way to the other side o' Norwich. 'Ow we shall ever get all that way in this 'ere 'eat, we dread to think.'

'But she isn't dead yet! It may be snowing before you have to go. How old is she?'

'Same age, near enough, as our Het. She were Aunt Sar'anne's youngest o' six.'

'So she's your first cousin?'

'No. Aunt Sar'anne's Mam's cousin. Tilda's out of 'ospital till the end, and Aunt Sar'anne's looking after 'er.'

William was lost in a maze of genealogy 'Sorry – I don't understand,' he said. 'Aunt Sar'anne's your mother's first cousin? Are you sure? Your mother would have been in her late eighties by now – any of her cousins must be too old to look after anybody else.'

Sophie pursed her lips, a sign of disapproval. She mopped her face again, setting her coffee cup down with a thump. The heat was making her as short-tempered as everybody else. He mustn't lose his patience with her.

'Tha's all you know!' she said. 'Aunt Sar'anne'll be ninety-two

34

come 'er birthday, but you don't know Aunt Sar'anne. 'Er and Mam never got on together.'

Well, that explained a lot. Kezia had been tough for anybody to get on with, as he knew. She, like Thirzah, had had an iron will, especially about getting her own way.

'So by that Thirz' says as we're all got to hev our arrangements made for this coming Friday.'

In spite of his resolution not to interrupt her, he was startled into replying to this instance of 'Thirzary'. 'It's a lot of trouble to take, to go all the way to a funeral of somebody you haven't seen for twenty years and didn't like anyway. What good can it possibly do?'

He could see he had taken the wrong line. It implied a criticism of what 'Mam' would have thought right. The pursed lips became tighter.

'That's as maybe. We goo by th'old wayses. What's worrying us is 'ow we're gooing to get there. This week and with Fran away and all.'

This *non sequitur* gave him a clue at last. Sophie had been sent by Thirzah to ask a favour of him; and she had been 'going round the sun to meet the moon' to find a way of getting to it without asking outright. It was against her principles to take advantage of friendship. He spoke gently, which Sophie was quick to notice.

'Oh, I understand now. You want to go while she's still alive?'

Sophie showed her surprise at his stupidity. 'Ain't I just said as we're going to pay our last respects?'

'But – you can't make arrangements to go to the funeral of somebody who isn't dead!'

'So you may think, seeing as nobody's got no respect for the dead no more. All they want now is to get 'em out o' the 'ouse, and leave everything else to the hundertaker. But in times gone by folks '*ad* to get things planned afore'and. Thirz' reckons it's like to be Friday, do Tilda's gone a'ready. They couldn't keep 'er longer than three days.'

This macabre conversation was getting William out of his depth, but it was no good wishing for Fran to come to his aid. She wasn't there. He had to deal with it himself.

'Dear Sophie,' he said, 'I think the news has upset you all more than you know. Undertakers keep bodies now in refrigerated rooms till it's convenient to bury them.'

'That wouldn't do for Aunt Sar'anne. She won't let nobody put Tilda in 'is fridge. She's a-dying at 'ome, and they'll keep 'er there. Even if they hev to screw 'er down afore time 'cos o' this weather. Like when my Dad died. You see, we hadn't got only them two tiny little bedrooms upstairs, with doors only about four foot 'igh as you 'ad to bend double to get through, and the stairs no better than a twisted old ladder. There wasn't no way as a coffin would go up or down. So soon as Dad were dead, they 'ad to get 'im down while they still could. Rolled 'im up in a sheet and got 'im down, and then laid 'im out on the house-place table till 'is coffin come and they could put 'im in it for all the neighbours to come and view.

'And our Mam just set there aside of it, day and night. We was too little to understand, but the neighbours and Miss was very good to us. It weren't no worse for us than it were for other folks. Our next door neighbour set with Mam every night till the last one afore the funeral, 'cos they'd 'ad to screw 'im down by then. They couldn't bury 'im no sooner 'cos the shop at Swithinford couldn't get our new blacks ready no quicker. Mam wouldn't have nobody to set with 'er, that last night. She said she wanted 'im all to 'erself just that once more. All I remember is us three little'uns walking in our new black up that long old path, with Mam follering the coffin all by 'erself, and us trailing after 'er.' Sophie was wiping tears, as well as sweat, from her face now.

'Don't upset yourself remembering, Sophie – unless talking helps. I've never heard you speak of it before. I suppose we weren't here when it happened, though your mother worked here before then, didn't she?'

'You wasn't old enough to remember any more than we was, but if you 'ad been they wouldn't 'ave told you. I'm only telling you now so's you can see why some still stick to their old wayses. Things was different for the likes of us to what it would ha' been for the likes o' you. Poor folks 'ad to 'elp each other out. There was a hundertaker 'ere as made coffins and arranged carriers if enough neighbours didn't volunteer.

'My Dad were a big, 'eavy man, and they 'ad to 'ev six to carry 'im. 'E went to church in Mr Thack'ray's best new wagon, with the bearers a-sitting three aside o' the coffin. All of 'em neighbours, as 'e'd worked with, like, or for. Tom Fairey's father were one, and George Bridgefoot another. They were young and strong then. Like Dad 'ad been. 'E'd carried a good many to the grave 'isself. It was expected of such as 'im.'

'When was it?' he asked.

'October of 1918, just afore the war were over.'

(So little time ago? Yet it seemed to belong to another era. That was the sort of detail even social historians mentioned only in passing. He was no stranger to death, God knew – and young Robert Fairey's funeral had been halfway back towards what Sophie had been describing; but the poignancy of hearing the difficulties of such a bereavement first hand from one it affected personally showed it up in all its stark reality.)

'How long had your mother worked here?'

'Since your grandfather had been left a widowman. It were another funeral as got 'er the job 'ere.'

'Grandmother's? Grandfather's wife's?'

'Lawks, no. Some old man's as they'd found drownded in the river. The parish 'ad to bury 'im. I don't know as they ever found out who 'e were. It were wartime and they didn't take no more trouble than they 'ad to. Besides, 'e'd been in the river a day or two afore they found 'im. But the Rector would give 'im a proper Christian burial, and asked for volunteers to carry 'im to the grave. There weren't many young and strong enough left 'ere to do it then, 'cos most of 'em 'ad 'ad to go to war, so it fell to my Dad to 'elp. But that were only a pauper's coffin, and that leaked – in the very corner what Dad had got on 'is shoulder – all the way down the path and back out to the corner o' the churchyard where they'd pushed the old stranger in under the 'edge. Mam tried to wash Dad's jacket, and left it out on the line for a week, but that smell just wouldn't come out. Dad couldn't never wear it no more, and 'e 'adn't got no other. They was too poor to buy one, and too proud to let folks know. But then one o' your grandfather's men as 'ad went to the war and got wounded bad come 'ome and died. Your grandfather wanted 'im to 'ev an 'ero's burial, with a Union Jack over 'is coffin and suchlike, and said 'e'd pay for it all. Of course 'e expected Dad to be willing to carry, but Dad 'ad to say no, 'cos 'e'd got nothing fit to wear at a fun'ral.'

She paused, looking back with a sad smile. 'The soldier 'ad been one of 'is own friends, and Mam knowed 'ow bad Dad felt about it, 'specially when she 'eard as the squire 'ad took it all the wrong way and thought my Dad were just being awk'ard for some reason, it never crossing 'is mind as what the real reason could be. But 'im taking it like that hupset Dad even more, till Mam couldn't stand it no longer. She never said a word to our Dad, but she come up 'ere and asked to speak to your grandfather and she told 'im the truth. She's told us many's the time about it.

'She said 'e just stood straight up in front of 'er as tall as 'e could make 'isself, and said, "Would you say as your 'usband's about my size?", and then, afore she could answer, 'e'd gone and fetched 'er two of 'is own old suits, one for ordinary Sunday wear and one for funerals. And they both fitted Dad a treat. Mam said she were so pleased that she just set there and cried – and Squire Wagstaffe was so kind to 'er as you'd never believe.

'And afore she come away, 'e told 'er as 'e 'ad made up 'is mind to 'ave a 'ousekeeper, and if she wanted it she could hev the job. So by that, when you used to come she looked after you, and we was let to come to play. Thanks be to 'Im Above. What would 'ave 'appened to us if she 'adn't 'ad that job when Dad died, I don't know. But it were all through that poor old chap a-getting drownded as Mam worked 'ere, and 'ow I come to be setting 'ere now.

'But there,' Sophie said, 'you can't live in the past. That's all 'istory, now.' Which was just what William had been thinking. She had dried her face, though William still had a lump in his throat that prevented him from speaking. Sophie looked up at the clock.

'You 'adn't ought to ha' let me run on so,' she said severely. 'It's too late now for me to get that casserole done for your dinner. If I get it ready, and put it in the real slow oven, it'd be done beautiful for your meal tonight. Will that do?'

'It would suit me better,' William said. 'It's too hot to eat much in the middle of the day. But you haven't told me what it is Thirzah wants.'

'To be took to Tilda's fun'ral all the way by car. All five of us, Thirz' and Dan, Het and Joe, and me and Wend's little old boy if she can't get nobody else to look after 'im.'

'I don't know if I can promise to get away,' he said. 'Tell Joe he can borrow my car to take you. I can use Fran's if I have to.'

Sophie's eyes glistened. She stood up, and faced him. 'You're like what the Bible says,' she said. *"A very present 'elp in time o' trouble."* Just like your grandfather was to us. O' course, I know as well as you do as 'e weren't your real grandfather, but that don't make no difference. You're just like 'im.'

William couldn't answer. He got up and put his arms round her, and kissed her.

She was bereft of words, till at last they exploded from her, straight from her heart.

'Well!' she said. 'Tha's something as I shan't never forget! Nor tell Thirzah about! Though to think what Mam would have said! She'd ha' been *so* proud. Thenks.'

When Sophie had gone, William sat down again in the armchair, and was very glad she had not had time to prepare any lunch, which he would have felt bound to eat. The sort of details she had been relating were not those he would have chosen to think about while he was feeling as queasy as he did, though he was no stranger to death in its guise of war. It was almost noon, and the heat was increasing. He felt inertia like a heavy weight holding him to his chair.

He had been touched and made to think by all that Sophie had told him. The past – meaning the prewar years – was truly a different country from the one they now lived in. The days she had been describing in such vivid detail had already been sifted and riddled till all that remained were the nuggets of 'fact' that appeared between the covers of history textbooks, which the young were constrained to read, remember and regurgitate for exams. The sort of detail Sophie had been recounting about the lives and deaths of ordinary people during that period had already been reduced to the 'facts' about 'The Great Depression', 'The General Strike' and 'The Rise of the Weimar Republic'.

Having spent his life dealing with such nuggets of history, he felt after listening to Sophie that the dust which had gone through the sieve might have been more worth his study. The knights whose exploits had been recorded had been made into heroes; but those who had fallen in the mêlée had been forgotten. It was all such a matter of chance. It seemed wrong to him, somehow, that such details as Sophie had been recounting should be lost for ever when such voices as hers were silenced by time. In half an hour she had made him *feel* more than four years of research into the end of the Hundred Years War had done – although there were a lot of such stories he could have put in if he had dared. It was not regarded as being within the academic's province to dwell on human anecdotes. Those who did were written off as 'popular historians', a term used pejoratively to denote second-rate scholars. Academics should deal only with proven, documented fact, not human lives. People should be made to *feel*.

Well, he had more or less decided to cut the knot that bound him to academia. He looked sadly at the pile of typescript, thinking how much more interesting he could have made it if he had been less of a scholar and more of a writer.

He himself had been involved in the last war. Who could tell the young now studying it for their next exam what it was really like to be a Spitfire pilot if such as he didn't? They hadn't then thought of themselves as making history; they were too concerned with the matter of living or dying to think about such things. It had been left to novelists and playwrights and the makers of films to make their actions seem real, even to themselves. History dealt with the facts; it was left to the other arts to add the feeling.

Yet all such as he had memories, more often than not kept hidden. The Battle of Britain to him had receded into a sort of film fantasy – except for the eternity of time during which he had watched his best friend plummet to the earth dangling on the end of an unopened parachute. That still caused him to have nightmares. He felt that in some way it made him worthy to stand and listen to Sophie. He knew that Elyot Franks's searing memory of being torpedoed and his long ordeal adrift in an open boat with a burned-alive boy's tortured eyes on him would make him feel the same. History? They didn't tell how a man like Elyot had stood it till he could stand it no longer, and with his own hands had administered the overdose of morphia that had put the boy out of his suffering. Nobody could ever record, in any medium, all such tales. It was useful, though, to be reminded now and again that a beach is made up of individual grains of sand, and the sea of drops of moisture. Fiction probably came nearer to real history than any reportage of fact.

He really shouldn't have thought about Mac. He dropped off into a heat-induced doze and immediately dreamed that Mac and John Petrie had both been on the end of the 'Roman candle' and had landed and sunk the boat containing Elyot and Petrie's 'family' of eight waifs. He was very glad to wake up from it, and betook himself to the bathroom for a cold shower which made him feel much better, though not at all well.

He had been asleep longer than he had thought. The sun was already westering, and he had begun to feel hungry. He must have his supper before eight o'clock, when he could ring Fran and tell her that the die was now cast. He would be writing his resignation first thing tomorrow morning.

The lamb casserole Sophie had prepared for him, together with some good wine, put new heart into him. He told Cat so as he shared the meal with her, cutting off the most succulent little gobbets of lamb from his plate and transferring them to her dish. Fran would have approved, but not Sophie. In Kezia's time, cats were obliged to earn their keep. It was held that if you didn't keep them hungry, they wouldn't hunt. Yet all through history animals had been of great importance. It had been Cromwell's cavalry that had made the difference in the Civil War. What a lot there was he didn't know about the seventeenth century! He'd better get down to a bit of general reading before he opened that book again. He had to be able to think in a different time-frame, just as people like Sophie were having to adjust to the new decimal currency and the 24-hour clock at present.

'Pees?' Sophie had said scornfully. 'Them's things as you eat – if you can get any worth eating. Dried peas I cannot abide, though them as are been frez and kept for donkey's years in a freezer ain't a lot better. Dan'el swears 'e'll never goo shopping no more, 'cos 'e can't deal with these 'ere new 'pees'. But 'e were laughing about what Beryl Bean said. She was telling somebody in 'is 'earing

41

that the government should ha' left it till all the old'uns 'ad died off. But then, she never 'as been more than 'levenpence-'apenny in the shilling.'

He looked at the clock. It still wanted twenty minutes to eight o'clock – no, he corrected himself – till 20.00 hours. His new digital watch told him it was now 19.40. 'Just time to wash up, Cat,' he said, 'before I ring our mistress. Mistress? I shall have to be careful. Fran could have been "mistress" of the household, but not of the man in it. Well, not without causing a lot more talk than pounds and pees do now.'

He went to the telephone chuckling. His senses had all been engaged while listening to Sophie. To get it right, he had to be able to see and hear, smell and taste, think and feel as they did three hundred years ago. It wasn't going to be easy. But the die was now cast . . .

When he rang Fran, it was the turn of her heart to take flight.

'What's happened?' she said. 'I know by your voice that something has. Tell me!'

He told her; she crowed relief and pleasure. She quite understood what a huge step it was he was taking, and had been a little afraid of influencing him too much. She said so. He answered her in the same serious tone.

'I think you have been right all along,' he said. 'Things have changed so much in so many ways. At my age, even ten years ago, one would have been more than middle-aged. Far too old to take risks, or change direction. But life is what you make it, and the old saw of "*Nothing venture, nothing gain*" is as true as ever. If I'm a coward now, it's mainly because of you. I used not to be such a weak-minded, dithering fool, once.'

She interrupted. 'You, a coward? Afraid to take chances?'

'Darling – I know I used not to be, but I hadn't you to live for, or to take care of. It makes a lot of difference. I'm afraid to take chances now because I've got so much to live for, and I'm afraid I shan't be able to give you what you want. Does that make sense?'

'All I shall ever want is for you to be happy. The best way you can be sure of looking after me is to look after yourself first. Now don't go back on it, will you? Whatever happens, we're in it together. Isn't that enough?'

'Yes. I won't change my mind again. Let's talk about something else, if it's only the weather.'

'The forecast is predicting heavy thunderstorms. Let's hope they'll hold off till Wednesday, because I've got good news for you. Jerry's conference is a flop because of the heat, so they've decided to cut it short and close it after the weekend. He'll be home tomorrow night, and I can leave on Tuesday.'

Their mood changed like magic to the levity that was like yeast in their lives.

'I'll come for you on Tuesday –' he began, his voice airborne. But she chipped in, her voice filled with life and love and laughter. 'Like the highwayman?' she said.

> 'I'll come to thee by moonlight,
> Though hell should bar the way.'

'No – he only had a horse! I shall come for you by midday, and pray that fallen trees don't bar the way! Only two more days!'

'And then after Christmas we shall be free to do whatever we like when we like. *Free* – from now to eternity. At least till we're both eighty.'

'Make it ninety.'

'OK, if you say so, but we shall need a new doctor. We can't rely on Old Henderson for that long.'

'I'll see about getting a replacement for him at once. Till tomorrow, then. I'm going to do a lot of background reading. Including literature – especially the Cavalier love poets.'

'Is love the prerogative of any period?' she teased.

'No – but Charles the First fell in love with his own wife. Maybe we've never given the Stuarts their due, at least about knowing how to love properly. Perhaps it was a Stuart characteristic.'

'Careful. What about Old Rowley, and his goings on?'

'We don't know everything. All those other women could have been balm for a broken heart after Lucy Walters – Monmouth's mother. I'll try to find out.'

'Do you mean to tell me there is anything you can still learn about history? Or love, if it comes to that? Tell that to the Marines! Goodnight, Galahad.'

Sunday. Not quite like other Sundays, because of the empty space by his side. After Christmas, Sundays wouldn't necessarily be so special. William turned over, and lay on his back luxuriating in the thought. No more turning out on foggy mornings, no more anxiety about what time he got home because of Fran worrying about black ice on the roads. No more sitting restless through those long-winded, get-nowhere-in-the-end committee meetings. No more having to subdue every other activity to the entries in his diary. He would be *free*. Free as he had not been for years and years and years. Free, above all else, of Janice, and the perpetual threat that she could and if it suited her would wreck his happiness.

He'd be glad now when his letter of resignation was a *fait accompli*, written and posted. There were cords still binding him, from which he had to free himself.

He got up and went straight to his study to compose the letter, and a personal one to the Master. He stood both letters in full view on the mantelpiece, and went to make himself breakfast. He felt like a balloon, floating free after escaping from its tether to a child's little fist.

It wasn't altogether as pleasant a sensation as he had expected. Till he engaged himself with something else, he would feel a sense of guilt at being aimlessly restless – or restlessly aimless; but there was no point in starting to prevaricate again this morning. He had given Fran his word, last evening, and he would never go back on that.

Under the circumstances, until things were finalized, he didn't particularly want to meet his close friends, especially without Fran at his side. It was only forty-eight hours before he could set off to fetch her home.

Meanwhile, he faced this whole day alone. He had put Bob's

book away again, for one thing because he needed a lot more background knowledge before tackling it seriously, and for another, when he did begin on it, he would need to be able to give it his whole attention. He had to disengage himself gently from all his university obligations first.

There were the long hours of today to fill. Heaven knew their library was full enough of information about the seventeenth century, what with his history books and Fran's literary ones. There was no hurry, but he had made up his mind to start today.

He was surprised to get a phone call from his sister, Jess. They had been very much out of touch with everybody of late – mostly because of the enervating heat.

'I hear Fran's deserted you,' Jess said. 'Are you OK?'

'Quite, thanks. Why shouldn't I be?'

'Just sisterly concern. What are you doing about lunch?'

'Nothing. It's too hot to eat in the middle of the day.'

'You wouldn't care for me and Jonce to come round and get it for you?'

'No, thanks. I have work to do.'

'No need to bite my head off. So has Greg. That's why I need to get out of his way. His paint won't dry and he's acting like a bear with a sore behind. Sounds as if you are, too – like everybody else. But I expect in your case it's because you don't like being a grass widower so soon after becoming a real husband at last.'

She rang off, and he felt a twinge of remorse. He needn't have been quite so inhospitable – but at least she had acknowledged that she knew of their marriage, and that there was no ill feeling.

He fetched a pile of books and began to read. He found it all so fascinating that when lunchtime came he stopped only to get himself a drink, and went on reading until the heat of the afternoon conquered him. It was worse than ever. He went to the open window, aware of his need for fresh air – but the whole world was still caught in airless torpor. Not a leaf moved, not a shadow stirred. The sky seemed as relentlessly blue as ever – though a more intense shade, if anything . . . as if somebody up there had dipped a brush by mistake in crimson and given his cerulean wash a hint of purple.

*

He fell into a deep, heavy snooze, and woke hungry. He ate the fillet steak, read until it was time to ring Fran, then propped his book up in front of him again and read on. He was very late to bed again, reflecting that in spite of Fran's absence, he had enjoyed his day.

He didn't sleep well, and had a nightmare in which he was lying in a ditch with cavalry thundering over him. Sweating, he woke up, and realized what had wakened him. The storm had come. A blinding flash and an even louder crash of thunder roused him further, and sent Cat scuttering to take shelter under the bed. Rain was lashing the windows and the branches of trees buffeting the walls. He had difficulty separating himself from his dream, but at last reality returned. That's what came of reading too late into the night!

But he shouldn't be lying there in bed. He had stayed at home especially to deal with any consequences of the 'souser' Ned had predicted. The last stroke of lightning had been very close, and rain was coming down in bucketfuls if not from a genuine cloud-burst. He put out his hand to switch on the bedside lamp, but nothing happened. Power had been cut off.

He stumbled out of bed and fumbled his way down the staircase, through Stygian darkness lit by intermittent flashes of sheet light-ning from the now receding storm, but in the hall the sheet lightning did not penetrate.

Somewhere in the house there were candles – Sophie had said so. She didn't trust new-fangled things like electric light. Why should she? She'd been brought up by candlelight, as everybody from king to pauper must have been in the period of his too-vivid dream. She would have left candles close at hand, but even Sophie, the ever-prepared, would have to trust to a match to light her candle with. He could hardly credit that she had a flint and tinder-box secreted somewhere – as he should have had a torch. Or at least a box of matches. He'd seen one somewhere very recently but couldn't remember where.

When his eyes had accustomed themselves a bit to the blackness, he found that he could see the slightly luminous glow of the hands on the long-case clock, and on a table beside it there was something vaguely circular. Of course – the old Queen Anne candlestick that

Sophie took such delight in polishing. It always had a new candle in it, and a box of matches in the saucer. He felt for them, and lit the candle. It was 4.20 a.m., and electricity or no electricity, the Aga would still be hot enough to boil the kettle.

The storm was passing, and his tour of inspection of the house revealed no obvious damage. It was too late to go back to bed. He fetched his book, and by the light of his candle went on reading.

Ned arrived almost before it was light. 'I told you we should get it,' he said. 'That were right overhead, and I reckon something pretty close must have got struck. Have you been round the house?'

'Yes, inside. As far as I could see the roof's all right. But the power's cut.'

'It's gone all over the village,' Ned said. 'Perhaps the transformer got struck. Now as it's light, I'll go and look round outside.'

He was back in less than ten minutes. 'It was us as got struck,' he said. 'Though we was lucky. It got that biggest old macrocarpa tree down in the spinney, and cut it slap into two.'

William went to view the damage, astounded afresh by nature's elemental power. He needed to find out at once if Fran and Kate's household were safe, but the lines were damaged and there was no chance of him getting through.

Dejected, he went into his study to await whatever was in store. Either the effect of his nightmare, or the thunder itself, was making him feel queer. It did, he knew, have that effect on some people, though he had never been troubled by it before. He dozed uneasily until he heard Sophie's voice and went to greet her.

She was full of the storm. Yes, she assured him sturdily, her place was all right. Such low, stud-and-mud cottages as hers were safe enough in a storm, only if a thunderbolt should come down the wide old chimney, but she'd never known one to, though Mam had always made them prepare against such thing. Such little places, she had assured him, bent to the weather, as you might say. They never took no harm.

But hadn't him and Ned heard the news? Right in the middle of the storm, old Dr Henderson had stood out of bed, and fell down dead! Whatever would they do without him?

47

William felt the shock run through him. How long was it since he had been joking with Fran that he would have to be on the lookout for a replacement for their dear old doctor?

'Ah!' Sophie said. 'That'll mean a lot more change as we could 'ave done without. Storms all'us bring about changes in the weather, come good or bad, and there's other sorts o' storms besides such as we 'ad last night.'

The morning so far seemed good. The air was fresh, the sky was clear though coolly, limpidly blue after the hot burning blue of the last many weeks, and everywhere the thirsty earth was soaking up puddles, and parched grass lifting up faded blades to catch the dust-filled tears dripping from rain-washed trees. But it wasn't doing much to cheer William. He went back to his study, wanting to be alone, just waiting and hoping to hear Fran's voice soon.

Sophie came in with the post. 'The lights is on again,' she announced, laying down a pile of mail. Hopeful, he lifted the telephone receiver yet again, and listened. The dialling tone was like music against his ear.

'Storm?' said Fran. 'We heard thunder in the distance, but that was all.'

Assured that she was well, he didn't hold the line, even to tell her about the death of their old doctor. She had said she was busy, and he still felt rather queer.

Consoled by contact of any sort with her, however, he picked up his mail. There was the usual pile of bills and bumpf, and one long legal envelope. From his solicitor? He wasn't expecting anything else from that quarter, so he supposed it could only be Robin Drake's bill. William had given him a watching brief on what happened to little Jonce, his hippy friend John Petrie's own son, whose mother and therefore the little boy's legal guardian didn't want him, while Jess and Greg certainly did. Nothing had as yet been finally resolved about any of the children who had been abandoned after Petrie's death, and other friends who had stepped in so nobly to help William and Fran at the time of crisis by giving homes to the children were by this time rather taking it for granted that as long as the drug-addict mother made no claims, the local authorities would turn a blind eye on the case and let well alone. It would break a lot of hearts if there were to be partings after all.

William felt a shudder of apprehension as he prepared to open the letter. That utterly amoral mother would have no scruples at all about trying blackmail on the couples who had relieved her of her offspring and grown too fond of them to want to lose them now. He slit the envelope, and began to read.

It was indeed from his solicitor, but not about Jonce, or any other of the children. It was a bolt from the blue as unexpected as a fireball down the chimney in the storm could have been. He read it again and again, barely able to take any of it in once he had caught sight of the word 'Janice'. His new-found freedom was shattered like the bursting of a rainbow-tinted soap-bubble.

Dear William,

I enclose herewith information received from Blackdell and Curtis, NY concerning the death of your late wife, Mrs Janice Aurelia Burbage, and the winding up of her estate.

When you have had time to peruse the relevant documents, I shall be pleased to receive your further instructions.

Yours sincerely,
Robin.

There were several bulky documents. William read on with increasing anxiety and a sense of dread. Janice, she from whom he had thought himself at last to be wholly free, was reaching from her grave to keep her hold on him. He had so feared her grip on his happiness in the past that even her name still touched the sore spot her manacles on him had left. Fran averred that as far as she was concerned, Janice had not existed for a long time past, but he had had difficulty in believing her. He hadn't been, and still wasn't nearly so magnanimous about Fran's former husband. He was afraid that any mention of Janice was still a threat to their happiness, and that she could put poison into their relationship even now.

Though it was so much cooler, he broke out in clammy sweat all over as he forced himself to tackle the letter from the American

49

law-firm. Well, at least the fact of her death was not being disputed! When his eye had at first fallen on her name, he had endured a moment of heart-stopping panic; but it appeared that this correspondence was concerned only with her 'estate'.

He braced himself to read on. Since she had left him, he had always been afraid that one day he would find himself responsible for her accumulated debts. He had borne in his mind recently, while so often mentally balancing his budget, that if she had died in debt, he would be morally if not legally bound to settle them. He knew only too well from experience the sort of woman with regard to money she had always been.

It would depend now on the figure he had to find whether or not he could post his letter of resignation. Fran would be bitterly disappointed if he couldn't, but he could and did trust her word that whatever happened, they were 'in it together'. She hadn't envisaged anything of this nature though. He had told her last night that he was no longer a coward or weakling. He had to prove it to himself, now, by squaring his shoulders to finish reading that letter.

Janice had died intestate, and consequently, as her legal spouse, he was her next of kin and residual legatee. Legatee! Fran wouldn't want her clothes or her bits of jewellery.

He would find herewith an audited statement of their outstanding charges to the time of her death, which they had deducted (thereby reminding him, as if he didn't know, that for the past twenty years and more he had been paying two lots of legal fees for the handling of any communication between himself and his wife, including his monthly maintenance cheques). The letter went on to say that their firm had also been responsible for acting as Mrs Burbage's financial advisers, and overseeing her investments, which he would note had proved both secure and profitable.

Investments? He could read no further. Anger and resentment almost choked him, and for the second time in three days his eyes blurred and his head swam, this time much worse than before.

Investments! He didn't understand, except to see clearly that she had used his maintenance of her as a means of keeping tabs on him. A rein by which she could at any moment that suited her drive him into redeeming his promise to take her back if she

50

wanted to come; and, of course, by taking it from him, make sure that he had a much-reduced income to offer any other woman. He had known by the time she left him how hard-headed and mercenary she was, but this . . . ? She had always been astute where self-interest was concerned, and she had always wanted money at her immediate disposal when she wanted to indulge herself in any way. He hadn't been able always to supply it, and that had been her major complaint about him. His salary as a junior academic had not been large enough to cope with the sudden demands she made on it, and in the end she had taken off with a man whose means were in another league altogether.

He had felt guilty for failing her in that respect, and had tried to compensate her by making her as secure as he could if other men failed her. She had used him and his promise callously as an insurance policy against the possibility of the supply of rich men running out! What an unmitigated fool he had been. No wonder she hadn't wished to let him free. Even if he had died first, she would have had a claim on his estate on the grounds that he had continued to 'support' her.

It had probably never occurred to her as a real possibility that, to use the legal jargon, she might 'predecease him', which was also very possibly the reason for her never having made a will. His mouth twisted into a sardonic smile. She had probably been unable to make herself believe that she would ever die.

Then, suddenly, the penny of understanding dropped. He'd been reading it all wrong. The letter was telling him that he was her *residual legatee* – which must mean that she must have left *money*. Real money. She hadn't needed, so she hadn't spent all that he had been sending her, and she had stashed it away, even re-investing the interest.

His first reaction was purely one of physical revulsion. A wave of nausea swept over him as he remembered that that scheming woman had been his wife, and then conjured up Fran's warm, soft body, as sweet-scented as an English rose-garden, lying close to him with her head on his shoulder and her loving face and eyes openly expressing the languorous content they shared. Would he ever feel clean enough to make love to her again?

He stood up too suddenly, but the room began to swim round

and he collapsed back into his chair again. He began to think he must be ill, but after closing his eyes briefly, his head cleared and he went on reading the letter. It referred him to the separate statement attached. They would be pleased to receive his instructions, if he wished, as formerly via his own solicitors Drake, Blundell and Roberts. Till they heard to the contrary, they had thought it advisable, as the late Mrs Burbage's solicitors, to hold a watching brief on the case referred to in the second separate document. They advised him to consult with them soonest if he wished to contest the claim.

It was all complete gibberish to him. His head was too muzzy at the moment to understand a word of it properly. He went on turning the pages. Then he glanced with breath-taking incredulity at the astounding figure his accumulated payments, plus profits, had amounted to, and had by no means absorbed the shock of it when he heard Sophie at his study door. He laid the sheaf of paper down on his desk, and turned, gasping for breath, to face her. His face was the colour of old parchment, and his knuckles gleamed white as he tried to keep himself from falling by clinging to the wooden arms of his chair.

Sophie took one look at him, plonked down the coffee she was carrying, together with a large white envelope, ran to the back door and screeched at the top of her voice for Ned.

By the time Ned arrived, Sophie had pushed William back into his chair and opened his shirt collar. Ned took charge, but the shock was receding and William, though still feeling very sick, took from Sophie's hand the sopping wet cloth she was about to deluge his face with.

'Thanks, Sophie, I'll do it. I'm all right, really. Ned – do you think you could fix me a gin and tonic? I'm afraid to move, in case I throw up.'

'You're got an 'eat-stroke,' Sophie said, in a tone that defied contradiction. 'I'm seen men at 'arvest work in 'ot weather took just like that. Set still. Do you want to goo for the doctor?'

'A doctor as is dead won't do him a lot o' good,' said Ned, coming back with the drink. 'This'll do more good. There ain't nothing like a drop o' gin for the dry heaves. How d'you feel now?'

William was feeling well enough to want to laugh. It wasn't often Sophie lost her cool enough to have forgotten that their beloved old doctor was dead, or Ned to show so plainly how perturbed he was. God bless them both – how he must have scared them! And himself, if he acknowledged the truth. He pulled himself together and began to sip the drink, conscious of four anxious eyes upon him. He wanted desperately for them both to go and leave him alone.

'Don't fuss, Sophie,' he said. 'I was very late to bed, and had a dreadful nightmare. I guess you're right, and it's only the heat affecting me a bit.'

Ned took the hint, and left, though reluctantly. Sophie still hovered over William. She picked up the large white envelope she had brought in with his coffee. 'That Mr Choppen was 'ere just afore you was took, and asked me when Fran would be back. I said as you were fetching 'er 'ome tomorrow and asked 'im to come in and speak to you, but 'e said as 'e was in a 'urry and 'e'd leave this 'ere, and you could please yourself whether you opened it straight away or waited till she was 'ere to open it with you, like, 'cos it's meant for both of you.'

'Put it on the mantelpiece for now,' William said, and she did as he requested before leaving him. 'Shut the door after yourself,' William said, afraid to offend her but well aware that she wouldn't take her eye off him till she had to. But he must finish reading that letter.

Pages of legal jargon. He had to read every sentence twice to make sure he was taking it in. It began by telling him what he already knew, that for the last few years Janice had been conducting what they termed 'a very close liaison' with one Humphrey K. Joseph (born Humboldt Fredreich Josephstein), Chairman and largest stockholder in a huge chain of hotels and restaurants.

The said gentleman had died following an accident while in Spain accompanied by Mrs Burbage. In his will, he had settled upon the lady, Mrs Janice Aurelia Burbage (alias Denton) the sum of $250,000 if he should predecease her 'while the liaison was still active'. His family was disputing this bequest on the grounds that there was serious doubt about the actual facts.

At the inquest it had been stated that the deceased had slipped

53

while descending the steps at the deep end of the private swimming pool of the villa he had rented for the summer, sustaining injuries that prevented him from helping himself. Mrs Denton, who had been present, had dived in to help him, and eventually had succeeded in lifting him out before summoning other help. He had been admitted at once to hospital where it had been established that he was suffering from osteoporosis, and had sustained several fractures from the effects of which he had died two days later.

However, in those two days, Mrs Denton had also had to be admitted to another hospital, where she, too, had died. Medical evidence given was that her heart had already been weak and had been considerably overstrained by her efforts to lift Mr Joseph. She had been found dead in her hospital bed by the nurse on duty in the early hours of the morning of the same night that Mr Joseph had died, aged seventy-one.

His family were disputing which had died first, and whether, at that period, the liaison was still 'active'. Staff at the villa deposed that though they had had separate rooms, it had been accepted that they were 'man and wife'. Such wealthy couples often had separate rooms prepared for them. Who could tell? It was not their business.

The time of the lady's death was difficult to establish. It had been a very hot night. The nurse in evidence said she had looked in on Mrs Burbage before midnight and had found her very peacefully asleep. The next time she had found her dead. A doctor hastily summoned could only guess an approximate time of death.

William was sure he must be fantasizing; this was the stuff of television drama – it didn't happen in real life. The whole affair was mad and the last thing he wanted to be mixed up in; but there it was, in black and white, and however he felt, he must pull himself together and get in touch with his solicitor. He was still enough in command of himself to see the implications. If it were proved that Janice was still the old man's mistress, and had outlived him, even by a few minutes, she had inherited a great deal of money – in the region of £100,000. No wonder his family were disputing it! But – if they lost, as part of Janice's residuary estate it would fall to him. It was utterly preposterous. It made him feel terribly sick again. He didn't want a penny of her filthy money!

This was what he got for his ridiculous notion of being 'honourable' to a woman who hadn't known the meaning of the word when the romantic boy he had then been had married her. It served him right that it should turn on him now, considering what he had since done to Fran, whom he had loved long before his one desire had been to live long enough to get Janice into bed. This was Nemesis.

He had to see his solicitor now, at once, today, to find out where he stood before he had to face Fran again tomorrow. Not all the money in the Middle East would be worth one word of dissension between them now.

The solicitor greeted him with outstretched hand, a smile, and congratulations. William accepted the salutation with pleasure, thinking it referred to his marriage. He was soon disillusioned. The congratulations were upon his inheritance.

Robin Drake was an old friend. They had been undergraduates together, and had been professionally, if not socially, in touch ever since. He knew what William had come to see him about, and was quite disturbed by his friend's strange attitude towards it.

Of course he would deal with it, he said, as he had in the past dealt with all legal matters concerning William's first marriage. He had been expecting to be asked to see a divorce through, but everything appeared to have resolved itself, so what was William so upset about? Why be so apprehensive about such marvellous news?

Wearily, William tried to explain. Part of his reluctance to go into details was that, for him, it was all too deeply personal. He was not a fool. He had as much respect for what money could do as the next man – but in the present instance he could not rid himself of dread that the source from which it came was poisonous, and that the whole sequence of events smacked of the devil. That instead of heading for a new green valley flowing with the milk and honey of peace and content, his steps were being redirected willy-nilly by some *force majeure* into a dry desert.

William could see perfectly well how stupid his attitude must appear. No man in his right senses would be looking the gift horse in the mouth as he was, and questioning such a windfall. He could almost see the solicitor's thoughts.

*Poor Old William. Got left behind the times, immured in that ivory tower of his. Probably a nervous breakdown pending. Better handle him with care.*

'There are no legal difficulties about your late wife's will,' Robin said soothingly. 'If I were you, I would leave the investment as it is for the time being. I'll deal with it for you. I agree that the other matter is much more difficult, and we shall just have to wait and see. The judgement may well go your way. If two people die in the same accident, without proof of time of death, it is usually assumed that the elder died first. The case will take a long time, and if you get the best of it, there won't be much for us to do. Just accept the fortune and thank your lucky stars. All you have to do is decide whether or not you want to be represented in the dispute.'

'No!' said William, almost violently. 'I don't want to have anything to do with it! Mixing it with American lawyers? Not bloody likely. I'll stay clear, thanks.'

'Not even a watching brief? Are you being fair to your new wife? There's a great deal of money involved, you know.'

'Fran won't want it. She'll say we have no right to it, or think of it as blood-money. She's old-fashioned about such things. So, if it comes to that, am I.'

'Need you tell her anything about it?'

'I think so.' William's voice was curt. What was the good of trying to explain? He rose to go. 'Do as you think fit,' he said.

Drake put out his hand again with an expression of genuine concern on his face. 'Are you all right, William? Not hiding anything? You came to me as your legal adviser, but I'm inclined to think you need a doctor more than a lawyer . . .'

The inference was clear. For the first time since he had opened the letter, William's face broke into a genuinely amused smile.

'Do you mean a psychiatrist, or a marriage-guidance counsellor?' he asked. 'You're barking up the wrong tree, Robin. I haven't made the same mistake twice. I've got all those rolled into one – my wife. Come and meet her. Then you'll be able to reassure yourself about my sanity, which it's obvious you're doubting now.

There are still a few things more important than money, you know. Keep a watching brief for me if you feel you must, and I'll see you again when I've had time to come to terms with it all.' What he meant, of course, was when he had heard what Fran's reaction to it was. It was the thought of telling her that he was most afraid of. *Afraid?* So he was a moral coward, after all.

He ate the lunch Sophie had made for him so as to please her, and then went back into his study. He'd quite forgotten that card Eric had left. It was still standing where he had put it. He reached for it, and fingered it. Was it of any significance? No harm in finding out. It would make more sense, in his present uneasy state, he thought, than putting a knife into a Bible!

He opened the beautiful envelope very carefully, so as to be able to seal it again if he wanted to. The card inside was gilt-edged, and lettered and illuminated like a medieval manuscript.

*THE FRIENDS OF BENEDICT'S*
*request the pleasure of your company*
*at a wedding ceremony between*
*Frances, née Wagstaffe*
*and*
*William Burbage,*
*to be conducted by*
*the Reverend Nigel Delaprime*
*at*
*3 p.m. on Saturday, 30th September,*
*in*
*St Swithin's Church, Old Swithinford,*
*and afterwards for a presentation of their respects to the*
*bride and bridegroom at*
*Benedict's House,*
*to be followed by a Wedding Breakfast*
*at The Swithinford Hall Hotel.*

*Formal Dress, please.*                    *RSVP as soon as possible to*
                                            *Eric Choppen,*
                                *Monastery Farm, Old Swithinford.*

William goggled at it, not sure he could believe the evidence of his own eyes. It couldn't be a hoax. No one, least of all a hard-headed man like Eric, would carry out a joke in such doubtful taste. He began to feel quite disorientated, and sat down to clear his head. He began to be concerned on his own behalf, in case Robin Drake might be right and he was imagining things.

Blessings in church following civil weddings were becoming fashionable, he knew – but it must be a unique occasion for a couple to be asked to attend their own. On the other hand, if their special group of friends really believed the rumours Sophie had disclosed about his secret divorce and remarriage, they were just the sort to do something unusual. He examined the card again. It had been most carefully worded, and Nigel must have lent his name to it as a *bona fide*.

But – formal dress? All the trimmings, in fact. Why?

Guilt flooded over him. He knew perfectly well why! Because they guessed what Fran would have wanted, if he had had enough sense to leave it to her. He didn't know, because he hadn't wanted to know, what sort of a wedding she had had first time round. How could he have been so senselessly selfish as to rush her as he had done? What difference would it have made if they had waited? For all he knew, Fran may have been terribly disappointed. Somebody – probably the women – cared enough about her feelings to try to make up to her all he, who was supposed to love her, had deprived her of. '*The Friends of Benedict's*.' His eyes misted over.

If only Janice had kept out of it! Nothing was more likely to take the gilt off this bit of gingerbread than Janice and her damned money. He and Fran, in spite of being so happy, had always had the threat of Janice hanging over them. These last few weeks, thinking they had done with her for ever, had been like paradise. For her to intrude again, now, just at this juncture, might be the very last straw for Fran. A constant reminder of what both of them wanted to forget.

There was a queer feeling of pressure in his chest. Waves of nausea swept over him. He closed his eyes against another attack of vertigo, because if the room spun round him again as it had done before, this time he would have to vomit.

He was ill. He had better tell Sophie before she left. He got up, and began to stagger into the hall, where he saw her at the sitting-room door with two blurred figures behind her. Friends, thank God, capable of dealing with any emergency! He recognized Eric Choppen, whose business activities included the hotel where his own sister Jess was Eric's PA, and the equally reliable war-veteran padre of ex-commando Eric's unit. One of them caught him as he fell, and the other reached for the hall telephone. Then he lost consciousness altogether.

'Jess? This is Eric. Get me that doctor who booked in about an hour ago, and send him to Benedict's, pronto. Yes – Dr Terence Hardy. Yes – William. Red alert. No, you stop where you are. I can cope.'

William came round to find himself prone on the sitting-room floor. Eric knelt behind him, holding his head, while a strange man knelt at his side, just folding up a stethoscope. Standing against his feet, seeming to William as tall and leaning as peculiarly as the Tower of Pisa, was Nigel, clutching a bowl. 'What the hell?' began William, trying to focus his eyes on Nigel, and struggling to sit up, only to be pushed flat again by the doctor.

'A doctor and a parson? Whatever for?' William asked, and started to giggle, only to find he couldn't stop. Then he began violently to vomit.

They were prepared for that, and dealt expertly with it. By the time they had led him to the bathroom and cleaned him up as much as possible, he felt a great deal better.

'You'll be OK now, I think,' said the doctor. 'My guess is that you are simply in shock – and under a good deal of stress. Have a cup of hot, strong, sweet tea, and sit quiet for a bit. If you take my advice, you'll take it easy for a week or two. You've been overdoing it somehow.'

Sophie, who had been hovering where she could see and desperately anxious to do something to help, said, 'I'm got a pot o' tea all ready to mash. You set down there with 'im, and I'll bring it in.'

The doctor was packing his bag. 'Don't go, Dr Hardy,' Eric said. 'It looks as if you've got your first patient. Stop long enough to make sure you'll recognize him again.' While the doctor hesitated, Eric turned to William. 'It must be your lucky day, William,' he said. 'We had a doctor on the spot because I happened to be there when he booked in, and talked to him. He came to see old Henderson, with a view to buying his practice. We did have a stroke of luck!'

The tea had restored William. He thanked the doctor, who then left, saying he would see him again before the day was out, if that would be suitable to him.

'Don't fuss, Sophie,' William said. 'You get off as well, while I still have company. You can see that I shall be well looked after.' Unwillingly, she allowed herself to be persuaded.

As the door closed behind her, Eric said, 'Now, William, what's this all about? Our prospective GP diagnosed shock and stress. I hope that card you were clutching wasn't the cause of it – though that's what we came about, and why we were on the spot when needed.'

After a minute's reflection, William decided to tell them everything.

'He said I had been under stress. That's an understatement, if ever there was one! I've been under stress for the last twenty-five years. I'd got used to it when Fran reappeared, and made things worse. The more you've got to lose, the more you fear burglars. Then there was all the trauma of John Petrie and the children last year, and we went to Wales while we had a chance, to recuperate. Eric doesn't know what happened while we were there – though Nigel does. Thanks, Nigel.'

He went on to tell them everything. The awful ten days in Wales when he couldn't confide even in Fran; his hustling Fran into marriage; last week's academic politicking, and his near despair at the thought of having to return to his job; the decision they had taken, and the relief. Until this morning. He poured the whole story out to them – including his awful fear.

'I know you must think me the most goddamned moral coward,' he said, bitterly. 'But the university business had got me down already, without the bombshell of this money business. I just can't take it!' He leaned forward suddenly, and hid his face in shaking hands. He had meant to imply only that he couldn't take any further stress or shock. Both his friends thought he was referring to the legacy. They eyed him with distress, till Eric lifted his eyebrows in interrogation at Nigel, and received in return a reluctant nod. Then Eric got up, and strode over to stand in front of William.

'Sit up, shut up, and listen to me,' he ordered – and there was no mistake that it was an order.

William looked up, startled. The Eric standing before him was not one he had seen before. It was the Commando officer, with 'war veteran' written all over him. His voice matched – loud, cold, crisp and clear, and he didn't mince his words.

'Pull yourself together! You're a man, not a bloody plaster saint, though to me it looks more like lack of guts than saintliness, playing silly buggers at the sight of a legal envelope. Not take the money? Don't be such a sodding fool! It isn't blood money.

'I think you're lashing yourself into this frenzy because you feel guilty for being glad that that blasted wife of yours is dead and you've taken advantage of it to marry the one you've been sleeping with. No, shut up. It isn't your turn, yet.

'She wants a man, not a saint. By God, you give me ideas. If you hadn't stolen a march on me, I'd have got in first and seen that she got one – especially in bed!'

William had leapt to his feet, his face contorted with fury. He found to his disgust that he was still unsteady, and Eric looked him disparagingly over before turning an insolent back on him to wink broadly at Nigel.

'Be ready to catch his halo, Nigel,' he said. 'I do believe I've managed to kick him where it hurts!'

'I thought you drew it pretty mild, actually,' said Nigel with a twinkle that William caught, looking from one to the other. 'It was clear we had to do something – but all he needed was a bit of a kick on the backside. He hasn't really got cold feet, you know. They're just a bit numb with shock.'

He turned to William. 'Take it easy, William. Let's have a drink and take a bit of a recce. Eric was only demonstrating the sergeant-major act he used to keep up his sleeve to put on for wilting privates before a dangerous mission.'

Eric had sat down and taken his pipe from his pocket, filling it placidly while Nigel poured the drinks. 'You know none of it was meant personally, but we did feel we had to do something to bring you to your senses. I fear I'm out of practice – and I was a bit inhibited by being in your house –'

'Yes, I gathered that,' William said, his still rather wan face creasing into a smile, and speaking with a deliberately over-plummy Oxford accent. 'I wondered what had happened to that ubiquitous copulatory adjective which is necessary as every alternate word in any serviceman's vocabulary.'

They took the glasses Nigel handed to them.

Complete amity having been restored, Eric puffed thoughtfully on his pipe. and took up the serious theme again. 'About this legacy. You seemed to be suggesting that it was on Fran's behalf you wanted to refuse it. If you've got even half the sense I give you credit for, you'll accept it for Fran's sake, not in spite of her. My guess is that she'll take a more practical view of it than you do. Why on earth should either of you mind taking the money?'

'Because we have no moral right to it. We've been discussing ways and means a lot just lately, in view of my thinking of giving up my job. We're both perfectly prepared to tighten our belts if we have to. I want to be free to do as I like, because I don't care to be involved in other people's politics, nor what may happen to higher education because of them. I expect to have to pay for that privilege – I happen to believe that what you pay for is in the end of more worth to you than what you come by for nothing. I don't really expect a businessman like you, Eric, to go along with me, but the fact remains that I'm squeamish about taking money I haven't worked for. I've done nothing to earn this windfall. Why don't I welcome it, or expect Fran to? Because of where it comes from, and because it isn't ours. We should be happier without it.'

'I think it's time for me to act as referee,' Nigel interrupted. 'There are usually two sides to any question.' He rose, and paced up and down in a very clerical manner, hands clasped behind him. 'As I see it, this legacy falls distinctly into two categories. William says he can't accept it because he hasn't earned it. I can appreciate that. But if William didn't earn what he contributed towards the first Mrs Burbage's maintenance, who did? That he did contribute is to his credit. But looked at with plain common sense, it has been his money all the time. If she hasn't spent it, all that has happened is that he will be getting his own back. I'd like to bet that Fran will find that funny! And believe me, William, accepting it will do nothing whatsoever to tarnish your halo.

'But the other quarter of a million dollars is a very different matter. If you had given your solicitor instructions to make every effort to get it, I should have been disappointed in you. And if to get it you would have had to endure an American-style lawsuit, you would probably have ruined yourself financially, and all you would have got out of it would have been a real pair of wings and a halo – and Fran would have been a widow for the second time. Open to such as Eric's advances. That lot of money isn't worth losing any sleep about. If, in the course of time, the law decides it is legally yours, then accept it without fuss and look round for somebody who does need it.'

Eric was now puffing happily, pleased that his broadside had done nothing but what he had intended, which was to soften William up enough to accept sensible advice. 'There is danger in living in an ivory tower, you know,' he said. 'It makes people like you forget that, whether you like it or not, you must move with the times. You can't fight today's battles, even the moral ones, with yesterday's weapons. Remember the Poles in 1939, trying to stop Hitler's tanks with cavalry – courageous, even heroic, but damn-all good.'

William hadn't told them about his dream; he thought Eric's choice of example was completely fortuitous, and was also very apt. 'OK,' he said, 'you win.'

'This is all very well, Nigel,' Eric said suddenly, 'but we haven't done what we came for. To talk to you about that invitation. We felt we owed you an explanation.'

'Can it wait while I go and have a bath and change my suit?'

'No hurry. Freshen yourself up, and then, if you feel like it, we'll all go down to the hotel for a meal.'

William was back twenty minutes later, looking almost himself again. They set off together for the hotel.

'When's Fran coming back?' asked Eric.

'Tomorrow. I'm fetching her just after lunch. Thanks to you two, I can now face her again. I was dreading it.'

Eric eyed him dubiously. Then turning to Nigel, he said, 'Padre, do you think you could knock a bit more sense into our saintly idiot? He wouldn't be safe to drive a child's tricycle! You can come, William, but I shall be driving. We're taking no risks till this wedding party is over.'

William gave in as meekly as any angel. While Eric was present, the confession and apologies to Fran would have to be put off. Better to do it at home than in the car.

Eric left them with a tray of drinks, and excused himself. William found Nigel calming. They chatted about everything except William's breakdown that afternoon.

When Eric came back he was accompanied by Dr Hardy. 'I went to find him and asked him to join us for dinner,' Eric explained. 'We are all interested in his plans.'

He invited Hardy to explain. He was the senior partner of a multiple practice in a suburban town. They had been keeping an eye open for another practice with growth potential, if possible in a pleasanter, semi-rural location, and had been negotiating with Dr Henderson for his. Though Henderson had wanted to retire from work, his wife didn't want to leave the village or the house, so the problem of finding some other premises was what had held things up so far. He had set up another consultation with Dr Henderson – but of course the sudden death of the doctor had changed everything, and made swift decisions imperative.

'As I already had reservations here for three days, I decided to come to be on the spot. A practice like this won't hang about long, and I wanted to be here, in case – though I shall have to wait till the funeral's over, of course. But things have changed. I drove straight to the Hendersons' to offer my condolences to Mrs Henderson, and was told that she now intends to move to be closer to her daughter – so the house will be sold with the practice after all. That's a considerable snag, because that house is no good to us, but I don't want to let the practice slip through my fingers. I was wondering what to do when I had the luck to meet Mr

Choppen. Just the sort of person to tell me what I needed to know. He was both interested and helpful.'

'Which is where you came in, right on cue, William. I had to get a doctor quick, and I knew exactly where there was one. His problem is that he doesn't want the house. Mine is that I do. It's a gem, as you know – and properly restored, as we've restored others, it would rival any in the village. So I'm in a cleft stick, too. I daren't let Bailey get his hands on it, or on the site – with that big garden and a five-acre paddock at the back, he'd have six modern bungalows on it before we could say Jack Robinson! Right in the centre of the village – it doesn't bear thinking about from any point of view, my commercial interests included.

'The long and the short of it is that I've put a proposition to Dr Hardy. If he'll buy the house in with the practice, he can use it as it is as long as he needs to; then I'll give him a profit on it, and restore it. Another doctor buying it at once would spike Bailey's guns – especially as Hardy was already involved before old Henderson died.'

William was appalled by the prospect of Bailey getting hold of it. An estate of new 'luxury' bungalows right in the middle of the village? If Bailey got in first, there'd be no difficulty about planning permission. If by any chance Bailey's cheque-book failed there were other kinds of what Sophie called 'jiggery-pokery' not to be overlooked.

'It sounds to me like lifebelts at the ready before the ship is holed,' he said. 'What can we do or say to persuade you to take Eric's offer? We need you – you've had proof of that. We have been spoiled in the past by our dear old-fashioned GP. How soon can you make up your mind? Mr Bailey's ruthless methods of development worry us all.'

Eric smiled. 'It's already made up. So why don't we celebrate? Here's the menu. You choose while I order up some champagne. Let's hope we're not being too optimistic. I think we should warn Hardy that Bailey is no gentleman. He'll be there with his cheque-book at the ready, funeral or no funeral.'

'I imagine,' said Nigel wisely, 'that we can put our trust in Mrs Henderson. It takes two to make a bargain. I don't know her personally, but I know her kind. Nothing would be more likely to put her back up than that sort of social gaffe from an "outsider" like Bailey. Play your game according to the rules that apply in a place like this,' he said to the doctor. 'Your rival has yet to learn them. And keep your own counsel till everything's settled. Bailey has spies, and it seems as if news is blown on the wind, here.'

As they ate, William had a chance to sum up the newcomer. A slim, handsome man in his early forties, with a pleasant, easy manner and rather more than his fair share of social charm. More suited to Harley Street than a country practice like Old Swithinford and its surrounding new estates? They asked no personal questions, but as the meal progressed they learned more about him without asking. They gathered that he was unmarried, while two out of the three of his junior partners had small children, which was one reason for them wanting to move to the country if they had to move at all.

'I hope you all understand what important people doctors are in this sort of community,' William said. 'There's a kind of hierarchy, you know, left over from the past. Parsons and doctors still carry a kind of mystique which puts them only just a little below the angels. Especially with the old-fashioned sort of genuine villagers – like me and Fran, or our Sophie and her sister Thirzah.'

'Oh, Sophie won't cause any trouble,' said Eric. 'He's probably won her heart already by his prompt attention to her favourite man. Forgive me for interfering, William, but you scared us with your little exhibition this afternoon. I took the opportunity just now of talking about you to Dr Hardy. As he's going to be here, will you agree to see him again? Apart from our concern about you, we can't have all our deeply laid plans for this spoilt by you being ill and unable to attend.'

He produced from his pocket the invitation card he had whipped from the mantelshelf at Benedict's just as they left, and laid it on the table for all to see. William was just in the act of glancing at his watch.

'Good God! Is that really the time? I must ring Fran! May I use your office phone, Eric? Oh, of course, Dr Hardy, if you really think it's necessary. Tomorrow, early evening? I see no reason why not – we shall be back by then. That will suit me fine.'

He made for Eric's office, carefully closing the door behind himself.

'I don't suppose you know any cure for love?' Eric asked the doctor with an amused smile. 'That's really all that's the matter with him! And don't bother to quote the usual answer, that the only cure for love is marriage. He's tried it twice, once disastrously during the war and again in May this year, splendidly, as we thought. But that's what's worrying us now. It only seems to have made him worse.'

'No – I'm afraid I can't claim to be any sort of expert with regard to affairs of the heart,' replied the doctor, a little wryly, Nigel thought. 'Except that experience has taught me what stress they can cause. And though I'm not a psychologist, I can claim to know a fair amount about the effects of stress. I'll do my best – especially if he'll open up and tell me what it is that's got him into this state.'

'If he doesn't, we will,' Eric assured him. 'But it's his business.'

Hardy waited till William came back, and then excused himself, leaving the three friends together.


When Eric's pipe was drawing to his satisfaction, he picked up the invitation card again and said, 'Now let's talk about this.'

'Start right at the beginning,' William said.

'Right. When it leaked out – God knows how – that you and Fran had stolen a march on us, and we were left to draw our own conclusions, we all took the same line. That it really was none of our business – though I have to say we were puzzled. It was so unlike either of you. But as Jane Bellamy kept telling us, she'd had her reasons for doing the same thing, and no doubt you had yours. It was already August when Nigel let slip that he knew you'd been married in May, and the tales here were getting riper and riper. Some of your friends, especially the two old Bridgefoots, were making themselves miserable in case it meant that you really were in trouble. I recalled that it was you who brought Nigel here to marry Charles and Charlie, and in the end I rang him, to ask if he had been given any clues to work on. He told me the truth. Of all the idiots I've ever met, I think you two take the biscuit!'

William attempted an excuse. 'It seemed the right thing to do at the time,' he said. 'We'd intended only to keep quiet till the other wedding was over, but such a wedding didn't get over, and the longer we left it, the more difficult it became. When my return to the University began to loom near, it occupied so much of my time that we let it drift.

'We didn't suspect anybody had got wind of it until Fran had to go suddenly to Kate, and Sophie showed such distress that Fran forced the truth out of her about the rumours. It must be one of the world's greatest mysteries how such tales get about. She gave the game away that you had something up your sleeve. So what had happened?'

'Well – the more it got round that none of us knew anything, the blacker villains you became. We felt we had to put a stop to it. So a few of us met here, and became "The Friends of Benedict's". Again and again we came back to the same thing. If only we knew *why* you had kept it dark so long. I rang Nigel again, and came back to report.'

Eric smiled the amused smile that none but those close to him saw very often. He had created an image of himself as a poker-faced businessman, which suited his purpose well enough, but belied him absolutely. 'We had been expecting an atom bomb, and it turned out to be a rather beautiful firework. I wish you could have been a fly on the wall for the next few minutes, when I told the others. They were all stunned. Incredulous.

'Charlie recovered first. "They did it for *us*?" she said – and we old-stagers had to look the other way while Charles comforted her. They're such a lovely young couple, they make even crusty old codgers like me feel it's still good to be alive.

'By then the others had had time to take it in. "It's just like Fran and William," Beth said. "But it isn't fair. It was those two who made our wedding possible."

' "They saved our marriage," Greg said bluntly.

' "And ours," Brian Bridgefoot added, "because of New Year's Eve. I daren't think what would have happened to me and Rosy if I hadn't been stopped in my tracks then."

'Then old George Bridgefoot put his finger on the spot. You know what he sounds like when he's really moved by anything –

slow and thoughtful and dignified. It's almost like listening to the voice of God.

'"I met 'em first at my Lucy's wedding," he said, "when all we knew about 'em was that they were Old Squire Wagstaffe's grandchildren. Folks said they were living in sin – but when I saw them together that day, I didn't care. They *were* our people come back to us. Since then, I've hoped and prayed that if the day ever did come when they could marry each other, I'd still be alive to see it, in church here, where all my family's been married. I've come to think of Fran as one of 'em, you see. But if William's got a divorce after all, and it had to be a registry-office wedding, couldn't they still be blessed in our church? And couldn't we give 'em a proper wedding party?"

'"If we had a rector," Beth said, "it would be a wonderful idea."

'"There's Nigel," I said – and that was that. I was sent to phone him again, to see what he thought. He said he'd already married you once, in church, and explained how it had come about. But he saw no reason why he couldn't bless you, or, if it came to that, marry you all over again.

'Then the balloon really did go up. The idea just took off, and I must say it has been fun for us all. If you agree – and that's all we're waiting for now – you are going to be married as you should have been in the first place. All that remains is for us to tell you the details, and get your permission to get on with it.

'It has been like casting a play – everybody wanted to be in it. Who was going to give the bride away? Fran's son Roland? "Nonsense," said Monica. She knew who Fran would want – nobody but George. I thought the old man was going to burst into tears, but we knew she was right. So did he. He just sat there silent, consulting Somebody, like he so often does, and then nodded. "Only I can't make speeches and such," he said.

'"No more than I could ha' done at Charlie's wedding," Bob said. "But Jane's father didn't want to be left out, anyway, and he's used enough to making speeches. He'd love to be asked."

'Greg wanted to be at the organ, and nobody challenged his right to that. That left the question of the best man. We had too many candidates. The one thing we all knew we mustn't do was to leave it to William to choose among them. Jane settled it by saying that royal weddings like this one didn't have a best man – the bridegroom had two "supporters". They would have to be Elyot and Bob, because William had been best man at both their weddings. That left me, and a few others. I should have to cope with the organization, so I put myself down as toast-master and a sort of major-domo. All the rest – Roland, Jeremy, Charles and Brian – would act as ushers. There's only one real snag – there hasn't been time to clear the barn. But everybody said that you had to be able to dance at your own wedding, so we have compromised. The celebration will be in the ballroom here.'

William had difficulty in finding his voice.

'What about bells?' asked Nigel, to give him time to recover. The look Eric gave him would have silenced the Speaker of the House of Commons. Nigel subsided.

William asked Eric not to say anything to Fran about him being ill and having to have a doctor. Or about the wedding plans, till he had told her all the rest as well. He would rather do it at home, in private, he said, and there would be time before Hardy arrived for the consultation. The reply Eric gave him was rather evasive, and put William on his guard. Surely she didn't know?

Eric asked him if he had genuinely lost his grip to such an extent. Did he think they wouldn't let Fran know, and give her the chance to get home at once, if it should be necessary? It hadn't been, and he had persuaded her to stick to the pre-arranged plan, especially as Eric assured her that he would be at the wheel. As far as he knew, she didn't know about 'the wedding'.

But once at Kate's house next day they found that she did. In conversation, Kate had let enough slip to put Fran on the trail, and she had soon been in possession of more facts than even William had been told. Kate, covered in confusion and self-reproach, had begged her mother not to say anything to anybody, but to pretend she knew nothing. It was unfair to all the others, especially William, for her to be briefed before he was, and in any case, it was not Kate's secret to let out. For Kate's sake, Fran had promised, but she had been genuinely pleased to know details. There were only two weeks left, and even if William was well enough to go through with it, what about things like apparel?

'I've never been a real bride before, you know – but I shall draw the line at a white wedding dress and a veil. William won't have any problem – I shall never forget my first sight of him in his own gorgeous grey tails.'

'We've got it all in hand, Mum – or at least, Monica has. Just relax and enjoy it.'

It was well after tea-time when Eric deposited them back at Benedict's, so William was let off the hook of telling Fran about Janice yet again. There wasn't time to start on it before Hardy was due to arrive. William assured Fran that the doctor's visit was Eric's idea. He had gone along with it because he hadn't wanted to do anything to spoil the new doctor's goodwill towards them.

'But it really isn't necessary,' he said. 'Honestly. I'm sure it was only the heat. Let's talk about this wedding instead. Is there any limit to the number of times a couple can go on marrying each other? I think we must be in line for a record – if marrying each other means giving pledges. First on Hunstanton pier; then at Lucy Bridgefoot's wedding, when we both answered the responses meant only for her and Alex; then again when we woke up for the first time in the same bed, and exchanged rings; and still again when I put the ring on your finger just as Elyot said "With this ring, I thee wed" to Beth.'

Fran joined in. 'Then we really were married at Rhulen, but the next week we still felt that Charles and Charlie were only standing in for us. Maybe that means we still didn't feel properly married.'

'This time will make seven – our lucky number. Do you want a new wedding ring?'

'No! Never!' She pulled off her engagement ring, and the eternity ring, and left the little plain gold band only on the hand she held out to him. He took it, and bowed his head over it, leaving a kiss planted on the ring as he closed her fingers over it.

If only she already knew what he had to tell her – soon. He sighed, and she was quick to notice it, and put her own interpretation on it. The doctor was not coming for nothing!

By the time he arrived they had both got themselves thoroughly worked up again. Hardy was introduced to Fran, who then excused herself while the men went together into William's study, where

71

the doctor carried out a thorough routine examination, and told William to get dressed and sit down.

'Now, Dr Burbage,' he said, 'you are just about as healthy a physical specimen for your age as I've met in a long time. But your pulse is racing, your skin is clammy and you look like a burglar who has just felt the cop's hand on his shoulder. Physically, you're fine – but psychologically I'm not nearly so sure. Why are you so het-up now? What's got you into this state? It isn't my visit – you welcomed it last night and knew it was only your friends making doubly sure you wouldn't fall flat on your face in church. So what's wrong now – this evening?'

'I haven't told my wife about that bloody legacy yet! Don't pretend you don't know – Eric wouldn't have got you here on any false pretences. And about our friends' plans to marry us all over again. Fran knew about that – and we'd been apart for too long for me to blurt it out as soon as we were alone together – but what it amounts to is that I can't go through with that silly ceremony unless she knows. I've got to face telling her – now, at once. I must.'

The doctor's face twisted wryly into a smile of sympathy and understanding. William might just as well have added what he was thinking – 'before bedtime'.

'If you work yourself up any more, we shall have a repeat performance of yesterday afternoon. So – why not tell her while I'm still here? Within call, as a doctor, or to act as a referee? I think that might be wise – but of course it's up to you, Professor Burbage.'

'Oh, for heaven's sake!' said William, relief flooding all over him. 'Stay with us while I tell her, and help me out! Be the friend you were obviously meant to be, and for God's sake don't be so formal. I shan't be a professor after Christmas, and what right have I to be called a "doctor" compared with you? My name's William.'

'And mine's Terry. Eric Choppen did outline the case to me, and I'm at your service. Call Mrs Burbage in.'

'You mean Fran,' said William, as he went to the door, and called. Then he put his back against the mantelpiece, his face like chalk and his hands shoved deep into his trouser pockets to keep them from shaking. Fran came in, took one look at William, caught her breath in fear and, completely ignoring the stranger's presence, rushed into her husband's arms.

Hardy watched, again with that wry smile. He should have had more sense than to have suggested himself as a third party. Breaking the very first rule in the doctor's book, never to get involved with your patients. But this was different. He had too often been the third party when the news to be broken was the worst that could be.

Fran pulled herself away from William and looked up into his face. 'Tell me,' she commanded, 'whatever it is. We're in this together as well as everything else. That's part of the bargain.' Her face had lost its colour, and the light that Hardy had noticed had gone out of her eyes.

William led her to a chair, sat on the arm of it, and told her all. He watched her face, and the doctor watched them both. Fran, very silent, wiped her eyes with the tightly screwed up ball of a handkerchief she held clenched in her hand. She didn't speak.

William was afraid. 'Fran?' he said urgently, 'Fran! Are you all right?'

She leapt to her feet and the sudden change in her startled both men. Colour flooded her face, and her eyes loosed arrows of indignation at both of them. 'Of course I'm all right, you flaming idiots! Frightening me to death about nothing! *Janice!*'

She spat the word out with such disgust that it became almost visible in the tense atmosphere. 'All that fuss about a woman like that – and a dead one too, thank God. I don't know what you've been putting yourself through, but you deserve every pang you've had – unless, of course, you're grieving for her. In which case our bargain is void from this moment on. *Janice!*'

William had no idea how to deal with this raging virago, but by instinct he did the right thing and went to her. She turned to him, and clung. Then she remembered the doctor, and tried to take herself away, but William wouldn't let go. So she remained within the circle of his arms, but turned towards Hardy.

'I'm sorry, Dr Hardy. Please forgive that exhibition – but I was bracing myself to hear you tell me he'd got cancer! And it turns out only to be something about his former wife – who's dead, anyway! Really, sweetheart, are you sure you aren't losing your marbles? She's been dead as far as I'm concerned for years. Dear old Mary Budd put me wise and I knew she was right. Do you know what Mary said? It was when I'd got myself into such a tizzy when you'd gone to the USA and Jess said she guessed that this time Janice might really have claimed you and held you to your word. I asked Mary what I should do if it turned out to be true. She only laughed, and said *"Janice claim William? She doesn't want him! If only he'd be man enough to stop shelling out the shekels, she wouldn't care if the cat ate him."*

'Since then, the only threat she's ever been to me was in what she was doing – to you. You don't give me much credit if you thought I was jealous of her enough to care what she's done with her *money*, do you? She didn't even intend to leave it to you, anyway. She'd reckoned without the gods. You can't fool them. Once I knew that all she loved was money, and that you loved me, I wouldn't have cared if the cat had eaten her! And you've been making yourself ill about it. Oh, my darling.'

She had forgotten the doctor in her vehemence, and turned herself back to face William, whose arms tightened round her as he hid his face in her hair to hide his tears.

Hardy sat still, trying not to remind them that he was there. If he moved, he would break the spell the pair of them had cast on him. They belonged wholly to each other, and to the house and its setting. It overflowed with a warmth he hadn't felt for a long time. It was a bad start with his first two new patients to have to realize that he envied both of them.

Fran finally pushed William away, and when she turned back to Hardy, her eyes were shining with some other emotion. She said, 'It's so ironic. I do wish Mary could know that it was Janice herself, after all, who had to shell out the shekels.'

'Don't go away, Mrs Burbage. I don't think William will recover quite so quickly as you seem to have done. May I explain what I believe to be the reason for his little breakdown yesterday?

'Stress is a bit like money,' he said. 'It builds up at compound interest for as many years as William has suffered it. He hasn't understood how much of it there's been, and to forget the cause of it has got into the habit of shouldering everybody else's troubles as well as his own. I heard a lot from Eric and Nigel last night.

When such a load gets too heavy, the strength to carry it gives out. The patient gets low in spirits, and less able to go on – which then loads him afresh with guilt. The worst burden of all.

'Then if the pressure is released too suddenly, that's the last straw. Like divers with the bends, the patient is in great distress, and can't help himself. That's all William's suffering from. Too much relief and happiness after all those years of doubt and guilt – first towards his first wife, most of all towards you. This money business simply brought it all out into the open.

'Be patient with him. Help him to start again. I think if I were in William's shoes, I should hope to put all the past behind me, and grab the future with both hands.'

Fran took his hands and held them tight. 'How lucky we are to have got you', she said, giving him a smile that William knew meant that if she dared, she'd kiss him. He tied a knot in his mental handkerchief to take a bet with her that she'd be kissing Terence Hardy before the year was out.

They saw him to the door. As he shook hands with William, he said, 'You may need my medical attention again, but you won't get any sympathy. I'm more likely to need yours.' With which cryptic remark, he drove away.

'Now what do you think he meant by that?' Fran asked.

'I don't know and I don't much care!' William answered.

'It's dark,' Fran said, surprised. 'Well past supper-time. Are you hungry?'

'Hungry?' he said, slamming the big front door and turning the key. 'I'm starving – but not for food. Just for you again.'

So much to be said, so much to be done. The whole incident of William's sudden collapse had given both of them, though particularly Fran, a severe jolt. She felt how near they had been to the edge of an abyss, and if there had been time, she would have smothered him with care like an old hen with one chick. Luckily for him, there wasn't time for her to coddle him.

Buoyed up by her return home and her sturdy acceptance of everything, William's reaction swung the other way. He was ashamed of the fuss he had made, and tried to make too little of it. After two days of skating dangerously round each other's feelings, it was Sunday morning again, and they went back to it, both revealing feelings that had been kept hidden for fear of upsetting the other. In close, warm intimacy, they notched up yet another high-water mark of their oneness. Fran relaxed and went back to being more or less her normal self, except that she had been badly scared, and reminded herself constantly to count her blessings and give William the time it would take him wholly to recover. There were too many changes to be swallowed whole at one gulp, as he was inclined to want to do.

Feeling completely secure, for the first time since he had left his undergraduate days behind him, he made swift and sensible judgements. He went to see the Master before posting his letter of resignation. The interview soothed him; both were giving up before they need have done, much for the same reasons. They understood each other. The letter was posted the next day.

It was only a short time before the reply came, to the effect that his resignation was reluctantly accepted and would take effect, as he had requested, from the end of the Michaelmas term. However, as he had been absent from his department for a whole academic year, it would be to everybody's advantage if he would agree to the status quo remaining until he left. In effect, it meant that he was released as from now – though they hoped he would agree to give a course of lectures on the subject of his latest research. The bon-bon was reserved to the last paragraph: he would retain his title of Professor, to which the Master and his former colleagues wished to add their formal acknowledgement of his previous excellent work by granting him the addition of 'Emeritus'.

So he was free. All he had to do to finalize it was to clear his college rooms. Then when the wedding-blessing party was over, he could take out Bob's book and begin on it in earnest.

Fran, reviewing their new situation with delight, found her usual apt quotation:

'And in the afternoon they came unto a land
In which it seemed always afternoon.'

'Hold on,' William said. 'It was you who said that I needn't become a lotus-eater just because I didn't have a regular job. I don't propose to, anyway.'

'I didn't expect you to – though I must say I feel as if we've reached a sort of peaceful afternoon in our lives.'

He eyed her with the mischievous twinkle she hadn't seen for what seemed a very long time. 'I seem to recall an occasion, just after you had decided to let me through your hedge of thorns, when you suggested we might enlighten the young that being fifty didn't spell the end of love in any of its aspects.

'You are, as usual, quite right. I can hear the wheels buzzing in your mind already, and I'm looking forward to attacking Bob's book. There's no point in beginning on it now till after my birthday.' They agreed they would be happy just to drift towards the end of September. It would take time to get over their little earthquake.

A few days later, Sophie arrived with the news that Cousin Tilda's megrims were over for ever. She had been sent to remind William of his promise to lend Joe his car for them all to go and pay their last respects.

'No problem,' William had assured her. 'Tell Joe to pick it up whenever it suits him.'

In consequence, Joe appeared the next Monday morning, suitably mournful and mournfully suited, accompanied by an equally funereal Sophie. Fran, surprised to see Sophie, thought it must mean that as she had been the one actually to ask for the loan of the car she regarded it as her responsibility, and did not intend to take her eye off it again till it was safely back in the garage. For once she was wrong. Joe drove gingerly out of the front gate alone, telling Sophie he would call back for her when he had got all the others loaded up.

'I wanted a word with you,' she said, 'to tell you not to get worried if we're late back. For one thing, Thirz'll want to make the most of a houting like this 'ere, and she'll want to goo back the 'ouse even if it's no more than a cup o' tea and a biscuit. But I know Thirz'. She'll want all the tale o' Tilda's death-bed and such, and be 'inting as we shall all want keepsakes of 'er.

'Thirz' never lets nothing goo by 'er. It ain't as she needs nothing, 'cos she don't – and she never were on good enough terms wi' Tilda to want no keepsakes of 'er. But folks is all the same when there's a death in the fam'ly. It's as if something comes over 'em, so's they can't abear nobody else to hev nothing. There's usually a row about something, even if it's only a old cracked pot won at a fair and broke so it won't 'old water.

'Thirz' 'as been going on about what'll 'appen to all the bits and pieces as come down to Tilda through Aunt Sar'anne from our great-grandmother. She says we are got more right to 'em than Tilda's 'usband. She's give Het instructions to ask about this, and me to ask about that, till last night I told her straight as I didn't want nothing, and she could do 'er own asking. Do, that'll very like turn out real nasty. So I thought if I could get a word with you this morning, pr'aps when Joe picks me up you might 'int as you'll need the car tonight.'

William promised. Fran was thinking how accurate Sophie's view of people was, especially among those who still clung to their roots. The young of today didn't. They had no use for family treasures unless they had intrinsic value. Nothing counted with them but money. She was glad, though, when a few minutes later, Joe drove the car up to the front door as sedately as if it had been a hearse, and she watched Sophie squash herself into the back seat between her sister Hetty and Thirzah's husband Daniel, all with faces put on to match their suits of woe. Fran had much ado to maintain her own dignity as Joe turned the car and came back with Thirzah sitting in full view beside him. Her broad behind more than filled the passenger seat, and she sat upright, very sedate, almost regal. As the car passed the door, Thirzah bowed her black-hatted head graciously towards Fran, her solemn face set like plaster of Paris as she lifted a black-kid-gloved hand in royal salutation.

Fran held her breath as Joe changed up the gears and cautiously cleared the gateposts with at least two feet to spare on either side – and then let her laughter loose. 'I wouldn't have missed that for all the tea in China,' she said. As she told William, up to her eyes as she was with preparations for the 'wedding', she couldn't wait to hear Sophie's account of the funeral next morning.

It was clear that she had been, and still was, very perturbed. They had gone back to the house, and all had been just as Sophie had feared. Thirzah had had 'eyes everywhere' and had embarrassed them all, even Het. Tilda's husband had 'just set there', Sophie said, letting Thirz' run on till he asked her if she was done, 'cos if she was, he had something to say.

(Sophie had dropped into her deepest vernacular speech, which warned them that there was something seriously amiss. They gave her their full attention.) As far as he could make out, Tilda's husband said, they'd only come to poke and pry and claim as everything in sight by rights belonged to them. Well, he said, if they wanted all them things, they could have another as he didn't want and welcome – Aunt Sar'anne. Now he'd got rid o' Tilda, he had plans for hisself. He'd give notice, as he was getting out of the house come Michaelmas. So they'd better take Aunt Sar'anne, 'cos he wasn't going to. She wasn't his responsibility.

Sophie wiped away a tear, but whether it was of sorrow or indignation, Fran couldn't be sure. 'I'm sure I can't tell you what it was like,' she said. 'We was all so took back, we didn't know what to say. But Thirz's face was as red as beetroot, and I could see as she'd bust if she couldn't soon find 'er tongue. But she did! She reared up like fried bread and told 'im just what she thought of 'im. Dan'el tried to stop 'er, but every time 'e opened 'is mouth, she 'eld 'er 'and up in front of 'is face like this 'ere, and 'e couldn't get a word in till she'd 'ad 'er say.

'Then we all just set dumb, like, till Het 'ad a fit o' sterricks, squealing as she 'ad a job and two little child'en to look after, and couldn't and wouldn't do no more. Thirz' said we all knowed as *she* was like to be next after Tilda, and the doctor 'ad said she 'adn't ought to do 'alf as she did do a'ready. She couldn't take no more on, no more than Het could – but there wasn't no reason why I shouldn't, seeing as 'ow I 'adn't no man to look after, and 'ad plenty o' money as Jelly left me.

'I'm sure I felt sorry for poor old Aunt Sar'anne – but I 'ad to say as I only 'ad one bedroom, 'cos I'd 'ad both them rooms made into one when I bought my little 'ome that time. And I did hev a job, and a big 'ouse to look after, so I couldn't do no more than anybody else, though willing to do my bit as long as they done their'n. And there poor old Aunt Sar'anne set for all the world like a mouse in a cats' 'ome, till we'd all 'ad our say. She never shed a tear, nor nothing but when we'd all finished she said as 'ow, so far as she knowed, she'd never been no burden to nobody, and she wouldn't be now.

'"Not to my Perce I weren't," she said, "even when we 'ad six child'en, and 'e was out after other women. And I'm all'us 'elped my poor child'en, as 'ad plenty o' troubles o' their own – specially poor Tilda. I'm 'ad to stop 'ere to look after 'er, 'cos 'e wouldn't do a 'and's turn for 'er. I'm knowed all the way along about '*is* fancy woman, same as I did about my Perce's, but I kep' it from Tilda. You can see what's upsetting 'im – 'e 'oped I should go afore Tilda did, but 'e didn't have that luck no more than my Perce did. But if I hev to live on the roadside under a humbrella I shan't stop wheer 'e is. I all'us did 'ope as I shouldn't hev to be put in the Union, but if it comes to that it wouldn't be for long, that's one thing."

'Then Dan upped and told 'er that afore it come to that, 'e'd see to it that she was welcome in their 'ouse, whatever Thirz' said. I thought Thirz' would hev a stroke then and there, that I did. But she just set 'er jaw square, and looked at Dan'el like a snake at a rabbit, as if she'd swaller 'im whull when she'd got 'im 'ome.

'But Aunt Sar'anne, she stood up, and said, "You'd all better be getting off 'ome. I shall be all right, you'll see. God don't pay 'is debts wi' money."

'So by that, we come away. I could see as Dan'el felt as bad about it as I did. 'E still thinks as 'im and Thriz' ought to take 'er in, 'cos they are got plenty o' room for 'er, them never heving no children, and a big spare bedroom as is never used. But if 'e put 'is foot down and made Thirz' agree, it wouldn't last five minutes. She's too much like Mam for 'er and Aunt Sar'anne to get on. I don't know what'll become of Aunt Sar'anne, nor what to do for the best. We shall hev to leave it to 'Im Above, and trust 'Im as never lets even a sparrer fall to the ground. It's all in 'Is 'ands, now.'

She got up sadly, and went to get on with her work.

'And in ours, I imagine,' said William after her retreating back. 'She's probably thinking that if with our help the Lord saved seven out of eight of John Petrie's little sparrers, there's hope for one more.'

'One day at a time, my darling,' said Fran, mentally squaring her shoulders. 'Let's just hope she doesn't turn out to be another like Rosy Bridgefoot's aunt.'

'I don't like it, though,' he said. 'It's another sign of the times, and it's soon going to become a serious social problem. Sophie's been telling us for years that "people ought to look after their own", but when it comes to it, even such as she can't or won't. The Welfare State has no plans for the number of Aunt Sar'annes there will be in another twenty years. And it's as clear as a pikestaff that "their own" will be the last to give them house-room. Houses like Thirzah's were built to expand – like a goldcrest wren's nest. By the time ten children had been reared there and flown the coop, there was room left for Granny or Grandad. That isn't the case with Bailey's brick boxes, even if all the women didn't have jobs. Not a very pleasant prospect for our plans to live to be ninety.'

'When I'm ninety, you'll be ninety-two, and, as the song says, "As long as we're together, it wouldn't matter at all." We've got enough on our plates just at present.'

He gave her his lopsided-eyebrow smile, and her heart turned over. God was still in His heaven, and all was right with her world.

Fran stood before her own image in the long mirror of the best bedroom at The Old Glebe, with Monica crawling round her feet and Kate imploring her not to spoil her make-up by starting to cry.

Fran gulped. How on earth could they expect her not to cry?

81

This was her real wedding day. The sort every adolescent girl dreams about, and which she'd had to wait for till she was over fifty. It was right that there should be this bit of ritual to seal her marriage to William. It might be unconventional, but it was *right*.

Ritual was atavistic. It was the way men had found to put themselves in touch with whatever supreme power they called God. She couldn't differentiate between Bob Bellamy's worship of Nature and Nigel and Beth's devotion to Christianity. She knew where she stood. Her supreme power was called Love. 'Where Love is, God is. Where God is, Love is.' That was enough.

Not that a lot of ritual connected with weddings wasn't nearer to superstition than religion. Bits of tradition such as

> Something old, something new,
> Something borrowed, and something blue.

Kate had supplied her with a borrowed blue handkerchief, and she was wearing the gorgeous old tortoiseshell comb Roland had given her in her hair; William had this very morning supplied a new rose-quartz necklace and ear-rings, and sprays of white heather to mix in her bouquet. But it had been Sophie, of all people, who had been absolutely adamant that she and William must not catch sight of each other today until they met in church. It meant one or the other of them spending the night somewhere other than Benedict's. Wasn't that really carrying pretence a bit too far?

Not at all, said George and Molly Bridgefoot. It was only right and proper. If George was going to stand in for Fran's long-dead father, then they claimed the privilege of having their 'daughter' in their house the night before her wedding. She had given in reluctantly, forbearing to remind them that it was not exactly a wedding. *Only* a blessing? It was much more. Which of course was why she was at present standing before the mirror in The Old Glebe, trying not to cry, while William was dressing at Monastery Farm, where a stag-party luncheon had been laid on by Eric, who had made it clear that William was to go straight to the church from there.

Fran had feared that all the glory of it could be spoilt if Beryl Bean – the queen of scandal-mongers – got her nasty tongue round it. '*Lot of silly nonsense, if you ask me! Seeing as we all know very well as they are been living together in sin as man and wife all this while.*' She had said so to William, who confessed to having his doubts, too. But they could not and would not do anything to disappoint their friends.

She had soothed her own misgivings by talking to Nigel. He had been a bit surprised that Fran should care what anybody said or thought. 'Those who don't understand what it's all about don't deserve to be part of it,' he had said. 'To those who do, it's a sign of spring when Old Swithinford was heading for the depths of winter. The two of you stopped the rot, and then set a pattern for others like Beth and Elyot to follow. Nobody's forcing anybody who doesn't want to take part. But I think a lot will be there in church. They'll pretend to go, as they do to most weddings, to "see the peep-show". They're only fooling themselves, you know. And as for your other misgivings – don't people know love when they see it? And what's new about your situation? How many young couples nowadays haven't anticipated their marriage? The number of pregnant brides I've married since the war saddens me, not because of their "sin", but because I fear that, but for the baby, there would have been no wedding. In which case, the marriage hasn't much chance of being a happy one. That's the only scruple I have about marrying them. If they've found by living together that they're ready to make a genuine commitment to each other, I rejoice with them. But when I look into their faces as they stand before me on their wedding day and fail to find there anything to hold them together once the pageant's over, I worry. As Martin Luther King said, "Divorce is an endless tragedy." That's the road too many of them go down.

'But you and William?' He took her hand, and she clung to his. 'Frances, some marriages are truly made in heaven. I am honoured to have been chosen to make such a marriage public here on earth.'

(How had he known that what had been needed to set her mind at rest was the touch of a warm human hand? She had argued no more.)

She drew a deep breath, and looked at herself again in the mirror. Monica had excelled herself. It was part of her flair as a designer that she always strove to make the most of her client's best features. In Fran's case this was her flawless skin, especially on her throat and chest, where plump women have an advantage over their skinnier sisters. The dress of gorgeous creamy-pink silk and lace Monica had concocted for her was cut low, tight to the waist and then billowing out with lace panniers, almost mid-eighteenth-century style. Fran lost touch with reality, unable to believe the image she saw was her own.

Kate and Monica were now adding the final touches. Monica's own hairdresser had set Fran's hair up into a pompadour style in keeping with the dress. Monica had added the comb, attached to which was a single pink rose on a circle of frothy lace.

'Now just the spray,' Monica said, taking it from the bed just as a loud bang on the door made them all turn in apprehension.

It was only Jeremy, with a huge grin on his face. 'William's in a dreadful panic because Elyot's just asked him for the ring, and he's remembered you're still wearing it,' he said.

Fran pulled it from her finger, and passed it out to her son-in-law. Her hand looked terribly bare without it – but it wouldn't be long now before William could put all her rings back. She simply mustn't let herself think of him now, or the tears would spring in spite of her. Kate was trying to hand her another package Jeremy had left. He had said that Effendi had defied all instructions about not giving presents, and begged Fran to accept his little offering – an exquisite, carved ivory fan. Fran floated away again, searching her memory as to where, somewhere, she had seen one before just like it.

'You must carry it instead of the spray,' Monica said, ripping the spray to pieces and expertly fixing a couple of pink roses and the white heather to the closed fan. 'It's absolutely right with the dress. Effendi must have spent all day yesterday searching for it, once he knew what you would be wearing. There, now you're ready, and it's time we went down.' They both kissed her, and went ahead of her to the stairs. They needed five minutes to get to the church themselves before Fran set out.

At the top of the staircase, Fran paused to look down. There stood George, top hat in hand, looking up at her with all he was feeling showing in his grand old face. He might have been her grandfather come again – a yeoman farmer who had climbed up the social ladder and yet remained wholly himself. By the other newel-post was her second 'stand-in father' for the day – Effendi, the polished cosmopolitan diplomat who had made the same journey in the opposite direction. Among them in their rural simplicity he had found balm for old wounds that still hurt, and had learned that love was kind, and truly suffered long.

They both watched her down, admiration and affection in both pairs of moist eyes. She went straight into George's arms, and he no longer tried to hold tears back. She turned from him to Effendi, more skilled in hiding the emotion she knew was there.

In the church porch George held her and kissed her again, just as she had seen him do at his own youngest daughter's wedding. The first notes of the Bridal March reached her, and she heard the congregation rise. At the foot of the chancel steps stood the magnificent figure of Nigel, every inch the Brigade of Guards Officer he had once been, every inch the man of God he was now, every tall inch of him now a friend.

Then she saw William's grey-suited back, upright between Elyot and Bob. *Waiting for her.* From that moment the church's six hundred years of accumulated atmosphere took over and she gave herself up entirely to living this dream come true.

She had gone into her 'overdrive gear' at the first note of the organ, that state of extra perceptiveness that sharpened all her senses and enabled her to think and feel on several planes at the same time. Though she did not miss a single moment of its personal intensity, she was still able to feel the symbolism of it all. The church itself – the repository of emotions of all kinds for six centuries past; the marvellous, rolling phrases of the prayer-book, enhanced by Nigel's wonderful, cultured, feeling-filled voice; the music, into which Greg was putting his heart and soul; then back again to the wonderful memory shared with William as he slipped on to her finger again the ring he had first put there at the end of Hunstanton pier – and looking up at him she knew that he was remembering, too.

Then Greg was thundering out the Wedding March, and she and William were stepping out to it down the aisle together in unison, as to the measure of a stately dance. Fran took in the

85

rows of grey-suited men and gorgeously apparelled women still standing in the pews as they passed, while at the back of the church the people of the village were hurrying to the door, as they always did, so as to be lining the churchyard path ready to greet the couple in their own way, with the solid earth underfoot and the limitless sky overhead.

Many more of them than Fran had thought there would be. She and William must play their part. It was, said her sensitized antennae, not just for them themselves that they were being thus honoured; they were symbols of all that in the past their family had stood for in this still close-knit community. So she brought William to a standstill, to greet and be greeted. She also became aware that at this moment convention was being broken. The formally dressed ranks were slipping out of the church behind their backs, and were being ushered discreetly by Eric down to their waiting cars. Out of the corner of her eye she also caught sight of Sophie and all her family heading down the back path to where William's car, with Joe at the wheel, awaited them. Of course – they had to get away first to be at Benedict's with the champagne opened for the next little bit of the programme, which, as Eric had warned them, was a secret restricted to the Friends of Benedict's. All very mysterious.

When only that special group was left, she guessed that they were now just waiting for Greg. As the sound of the organ ceased, the clamour of bells above them took over in a peal as riotously joyful as Fran had ever heard. Nothing had been left out. And still she and William stood, letting all the best of Old Swithinford look their fill.

When Greg had taken his place beside Jess, Eric signalled to his formed-up procession to precede them down the path. It must all have been rehearsed, Fran decided, and William briefed at lunch-time today what to expect. Eric came quietly to his shoulder, and whispered, 'Now, as soon as Nicholas and I are at the wheels of our cars, you two can run the gauntlet.'

They had no time to wonder any further as they hurried through the shower of confetti, rice and flowers to the lych-gate where Effendi's new Mercedes awaited them, with ushers holding open the doors. Eric issued his last order to their Effendi, Jane Bellamy's diplomat father. 'Don't let them out, whatever you do,' he said, 'till all the rest of us are inside the house. You can drive away now, and we'll all follow.'

William, holding her hand, raised his eyebrows in interrogation. She shook her head. Both were by this time beyond speech. As the bridal car started to move, the others all fell into line behind, and Fran saw that every one was decorated with a bunch of ribbons on the bonnet. Fran had overheard Sophie remarking to Ned about 'that there cavalrycade as they are planning' being more like a funeral than a wedding. She had forgotten, but it was now clear what Sophie had meant. Those gay bunches of ribbons made quite sure that there was no chance of any misunderstanding. She had given up trying to fathom out the reason for this trip to Benedict's before going to the hotel, except that the invitation had informed them that the friends of Benedict's wanted to give them in private the only wedding present they were prepared to accept. The joyous noise of the bells was still being flung out in wild abandon across the golden September East Anglian landscape.

The car drew up at the front door of Benedict's, where they alighted to stand at the door to greet their special guests. Everyone passed inside to take glasses from trays held by Sophie and Joe – Ned being still in church ringing his bell. Eric made sure everybody was there, directing them, Sophie and all, into the sitting-room. They were left alone.

William bent to kiss Fran. 'Welcome home, my darling,' he said. 'The most beautiful bride that ever a bridegroom carried across a doorstep,' and taking her completely by surprise, swung her off her feet and set her down again in the hall. Only Eric saw.

He gave William a huge, congratulatory grin, and a minute to get his breath back, before leading them to their sitting-room door, where he, on purpose, blocked their view. He called to the assembled company, 'Has everybody got a drink? Ah, there you are, Ned. You're just in time.' Then he moved aside, and let them see.

The scene was set for yet another ceremony. On the right side of the hearthrug, in front of the marble fire surround, stood Greg. On the left, facing him, was Charlie Bridgefoot, still a new bride herself, looking her loveliest, and between them stood Effendi. Leaving them standing just inside the door, Eric announced, 'Ladies and Gentlemen, I invite you to raise your glasses to *The Burbages at Home.*'

Every glass was raised, but no one drank. A silence fell, broken by Effendi.

'William and Frances, to me has fallen the honour of asking you to accept from us here assembled, The Friends of Benedict's, this token of our love and esteem.'

Then he stood by Charlie's side while she pulled on the end of the silken cord she had been holding, and the velvet curtains above the mantelpiece opened to reveal a large framed picture. The glasses were raised and salutations called, through which Fran detected a muffled sob. Greg's face was not the only one streaming with tears.

They gazed as if mesmerized. There it was – almost but not quite a replica of the picture that they both remembered from early childhood. It was the same size, designed, as the original had been, to fill the space. The heavy swept gilt frame was an exact replica. So was the composition of the picture. There was the house as it had once been, in the background, fronted by a grassy lawn in which stood a graceful beech tree in early leaf. Beneath the tree stood a woman holding a fan, and by her side knelt a man in a full coat, embroidered waistcoat, and knee-breeches. His hair was black and inclined to curl, and by his side was a dog.

Just like the other had been – except that this was William looking up at Fran and Fran looking down on William, with that ineffable look of love in her eyes that had haunted Bob in his recurring dream of the room and the picture long before he had ever been inside the house.

The new picture was incredibly beautiful in its own right, and quite overpowering in its emotional effect. William and Fran turned to each other. The Burbages were at home. When at last William let Fran go, he turned to Greg – Greg now triumphant, though with tears still coursing down his cheeks from eyes lit as with some hidden fire.

Fran, still unbelieving, remembered that muffled sob. She crossed to where Bob was hiding his tears on Jane's shoulder in the far corner. Jane moved away to let Fran get at him, and she was folded into his arms.

'It was your idea, Bob, wasn't it?' she said.

He nodded, shyly, but said, 'I didn't do much, only sketched it for Greg as near as I could remember it from my dream – and lent him my old Bonzo, 'cos you hadn't got a dog. But I never thought he could bring it off like that!' There was awe in his voice, and the appreciation of an apprentice for a master. 'I just can't get over it.'

'It's a masterpiece by any standards,' said William, who had come to fetch Fran to stand beneath it by his side while he made an impromptu speech of thanks, so warm and heartfelt that it was, Fran thought, another masterpiece to crown this part of the day.

At two-thirty next morning, tired but sated with happiness, they sat in front of the picture again. Fran's chair had been pulled round to face it, and William sat on the arm of it. It had been a day to remember for ever.

The wedding breakfast had gone off with all the panache Eric had intended it should. Never, Fran told herself, had she heard speeches of such elegance and wit. Under Eric's expert organization the whole occasion had slipped along with the gentle, colourful, fragrant glissade of a dewdrop sliding down a roseleaf.

There had then been an interval to break the formal breakfast away from the informal evening party. It gave them all a chance to change into more casual clothes, with which it was hoped the spirit of former wedding parties held in the barn would transfer itself to the hotel ballroom.

Fran and William changed in the hotel, and then foregathered with a few others in Eric's private quarters. Within that intimate little circle they had reviewed and relived the marvellous day again.

Handing Fran a drink, Eric said, 'Relax and rest while you can. You still have to be the belle of the ball this evening.'

'What and whom are we to expect?' William asked.

'All the usual – and possibly some strangers,' Eric answered. 'We took trouble to make sure people like your Sophie and Ned and their families and friends would be as welcome here as in the barn. We've laid on extra, temporary staff, because our normal routine has to go on as usual, and there are a lot of wedding guests staying here as well. Then there'll be all our local wedding guests, and – I do hope you don't mind this – but, well, after the first brash mistakes I made, I saw that it was up to me to try and help to preserve all that was best of village life. My only idea at first was to make it a viable commercial venture, but I have other concerns as well, now.

'A lot of the values that a place like Old Swithinford used to set such store by have something to be said for them. You never know when we may need them again. Nicholas here knows exactly what I mean, I think. You can't put your finger on exactly what they are, until you see the whole social mix letting their back-hair down together at a party, especially a wedding. The Marlands had no idea, until they met the Bridgefoots, for example. They'll be throwing themselves into the fun tonight as if they had been born to it. I thought about it a lot, because you two are such prime examples of what it takes. You understand village life from the inside out.

'So – I've briefed all the staff on duty tonight so that they know exactly what sort of thing is going on here. They have permission to explain to any interested casual guest, and to tell any one who is at all interested that if they care to look in, they will be welcome, too. I can't think anybody will, though you don't know till you try – but I'd like them to know that this is not wholly commercial, nor simply a convenient caravanserai, but an essential part of the community, the successor of the medieval hostelry and the village inn. Then there are one or two others who stand between the known and the unknown – Dr Hardy, for instance, who came to the wedding and the reception. Good for him – he's got off to a good start; but whether he'll feel able to show up tonight, we shall have to wait and see. And the two girls at Beth and Elyot's. It will be their first party of this sort ever. They're starry eyed about it – I do hope they'll have a good time. Which reminds me to ask you, William – if we need to introduce them to anybody, what is their surname?'

William didn't hesitate. 'Officially, Garnett – but Ammy refused point blank to be registered at school as anything but Petrie. They hate to be reminded of their mother, and love the memory of the man who wasn't their father. There's no law against you calling yourself whatever you like, as far as I know.'

'Ammy isn't going back to school next term,' Fran said. 'Beth told me.'

'Any more than I'm going back to the University,' said William, 'though I think all of you knew that, except perhaps Effendi. There's no secret about it, now.'

'It isn't the only change in the wind, either,' said Eric, looking towards Nigel and receiving a slight nod.

'What else then?' asked Fran eagerly.

'We've got a new doctor – and even a new rector. It seems Nigel doesn't want to leave us any more than we want him to. I believe he has sort of taken to the parish.'

'Oh! Oh! What wonderful news! Is it true, Nigel? Honestly?'

'Not for public knowledge, yet, or George would have given you the news as an extra wedding present. He's busting to tell you – but you can tell him you know, if you like. It really would make his day.'

'It's made ours, on top of everything else. Where will you live?'

'My dear Fran, where do you suppose? Down Spotted Cow Lane, of course. There must have been a pub of that name down there once. Do you know which house it was?'

'Where else but yours!' she answered.

'No! I can't believe it,' he said, his face lighting up like a naughty schoolboy's. 'Eric – did you hear that? If there's a blocked door, I shall have it opened, knowing it must lead to what was once the cellar. So here and now I give you an order to keep it filled with bottles of the same quality you supply to Elyot Franks.'

'Certainly, Padre,' said Eric, saluting smartly.

'The band is here,' said Jess, putting her head round the door. 'I can't get Greg away from the piano. He's having a wonderful time with the drummer. Don't bother to come, Eric. I'll make sure they know what they're doing.'

'I imagine Greg's prospects are about to alter drastically, too,' Eric said. 'I've already heard Rupert Marland giving him a commission to paint young Georgina. They'll come thick and fast, once they start.'

'What about Monica? He won't let her down.'

'She's already seen it coming, and made other arrangements for everything except the adverts. He'll still do those. Are you all OK while I pop home to fetch Marjorie and see that all is well? Monica's two Petrie girls are baby-sitting for everybody in my house tonight, so that the two oldest can come to the party. I promised Marjorie that I'd go and get her, or she wouldn't have come, and that would have spoilt George's evening.'

He was back within half an hour, by which time the ballroom was filling up. 'We'll go down,' he said, 'but you two stay where you are till you receive our summons.'

'Now what have they got up their sleeve?' William wondered.

'I've stopped wondering. I just hope I don't lose my slipper on the way home.'

'I shall be there to pick it up if you do,' he said. 'Poor Prince Charming had to organize a countrywide search.'

The summons came, and they went down together. At their entrance, the band played a long introductory chord, and then from the piano came the sound of two pairs of hands playing a duet in the slow, dreamy waltz from yesterday, appropriately named 'Destiny'. They knew what was expected of them. Fran moved into the dance in a daze of emotion, and then gave herself up wholly to the pleasure of the dance itself. She simply could not remember the last time she had been on a real ballroom floor, and not just making do with a carpeted room or a rough-boarded barn floor, or even magic flagstones under a winter moon. The two at the piano, Greg and Beth, had chosen right. It was their destiny to be always as they were at that moment, thinking, moving, feeling as one. They danced as naturally as they breathed.

At the end of 'Destiny', the pianists swung into a fresh, faster tempo, though still in waltz-time. The dancers took the change literally in their stride, recognizing 'You will Remember Vienna'. At the first note, William pushed Fran to arms' length, and their feet closed in, toe to toe, turning them into the spinning-top shape best suited for the swirlings and turnings of the Viennese waltz, until again without warning they went back to the romantic strains and tempo of 'Sweetheart, Sweetheart, Sweetheart'.

The spellbound spectators were silent, not wanting them to stop. They finished in the centre of the floor, with William still holding Fran tight before letting her go, looking down at her as she looked up at him for a long, lovely sliver of time stolen from eternity. Then applause broke loose.

'Bravo! Encore!' came from every direction. The band struck another chord for silence. Eric went to the quite unnecessary microphone, and said, 'Yes, Encore! Encore! But for everybody. Find your partners and on with the dance!'

Fran had little hope of being able to dance with William again – but for once she didn't care. She was prepared to share him, looking forward to the dancing for its own sake, whoever her partner. She had no idea whether or not dancing was one of Effendi's accomplishments, but guessed that, because of his age, it must have been part of his training. She was right. He was a graceful, correct sort of performer, though without William's superb balance and the perfect timing which marks the natural dancer. Nigel, she found, had more zest than skill, one reason being, he told her, that he was eons out of practice. Both were a little too sedate for Fran's top-gear mood.

The band had been well briefed to keep to ballroom dancing for the first half of the evening, and warned that during the second half they might be asked for anything except the rocking, jiving, twisting contortions the young put so much effort into these days. A gathering of this kind was more likely to look to the past than to the present or the future. The band-leader said all he needed to know was the rhythm and the tempo. They were good at improvising.

Fran watched Bob trying to persuade Jane on to the floor. Was she too shy – or afraid that her 'countrified' husband wouldn't be able to compete? Did she know what she was missing? When the band struck up a quick-step, Fran found Bob at her side. She was glad he had got there first – on a floor like this!

She felt the eyes of 'the London folk' on them, wondering perhaps, Fran thought, at Bob's daring. William, failing to persuade Jane to try her luck with him, turned to Charlie, who said she was willing to try anything once. 'Me next then,' Greg called, his eyes brimming with delight just to look at her. That girl had everything

– the *joie-de-vivre* that came with happiness, and beauty that was by no means all external. Young Charles had picked a winner, and no mistake. But Greg was soaked in beauty tonight, seeing it everywhere, especially in those pre-Raphaelite Petrie girls, no longer waif-like and ethereal, but glowing with youth and stunning in their first party frocks.

Other couples were out on the floor when a spotlight beam picked out Bob and Fran. The rest drew aside at once to watch. Bob was a big man, broad as well as tall, with muscles well developed by hard work, but his twinkling feet might have been those of Fred Astaire. William, pulling Charlie close to him, stood to watch with the rest.

'Dad rivals even you,' she said. 'Do you mind?'

He squeezed her. 'Not any more,' he said. 'We're like blood brothers and obey our pagan instincts, that's all. Dancing is in our blood. In everybody's, I think, but most people are afraid to show it. It just draws your dad and me closer now.'

Bob restored Fran to William, and went back to Jane. 'Now, my beauty,' Fran heard him say, 'will *you* try dancing with me if Fran dares?'

Greg said in Fran's ear, 'Can't you feel the temperature of happiness rising? It's infecting everybody.'

'Greg,' she said, 'it's almost too good. I always get afraid when I'm too happy. What have we done to deserve anything like today?'

He answered her, understanding how she felt. 'You get what you give,' he said. 'And you do deserve it.'

Time for the supper. Small tables set out all round the room, and a long, damask-covered table groaning under an extravagant finger buffet. Wine in the charge of a wine waiter, and tea and coffee in the charge of two less experienced 'extras'.

Fran and William went to join Sophie and her family.

'I never did see or taste nothing like this 'ere in all my life afore,' said Sophie.

'Nor me nothing better than this,' added Daniel, holding up a glass of wine.

'You're had too much a'ready,' said Thirzah forbiddingly.

'It's wine, gal, not strong drink. You know as it says in the Bible that wine's all right. The Lord turned water into wine at just

94

sich a do as this – and don't it say in the Bible, "Wine, that maketh glad the heart of man"?'

William wondered if Dan had any idea just how potent Eric Choppen's good wine was. Or Joe, either, if it came to that. They were there to enjoy themselves, though, and he hoped they would.

The band had gone outside for a breather, the ladies to the cloakrooms, some of the men to have a quick smoke. Waiters and waitresses were scurrying about to restore the floor for the second half of the dancing. The room was filling again as the band tried out some of the country-dance tunes they were likely to need.

There was a startling crash. One of the extra waitresses, who had piled high a huge tray with wine glasses, tumblers, cups and saucers, and plates still sticky with jam and cream and crumbs and dregs, had stepped on a wet patch and slipped. The loaded tray cascaded before her into a wide circle of broken glass, crockery, messy scraps of food and sticky little wet patches.

The nearest men rushed to help the girl to her feet, and escorted her, crying, to the head waiter. The sound made by their shoe-soles as they returned was a warning as to the state the dance-floor was in.

Eric went to the microphone. 'Accidents will happen,' he said calmly. 'Don't worry – Freda isn't hurt. The floor *will* be if any of you tread on the mess. We'll have it put right in no time.' He turned to the head waiter, who was afraid he would get the blame for allowing an untrained waitress to pile up a tray like that. 'Tackle the mess in the right way,' Eric commanded. 'It needs brooms, not vacuum cleaners. Fetch the brooms we use for sweeping the patio. And a dustbin bag.'

Sophie was horrified at the mess. 'Come you on and help me, Het,' she ordered, getting to her feet. 'They'll be till bulls' noon clearing that mess up. It's nothing new to the likes of us.' Daniel ordered her to stop where she was.

'You'll muck your new frock up,' he said, ignoring Thirzah's forbidding frown. 'Let me and Joe do it. We're been sweeping barn floors up all our lives.' He possessed himself of the two brooms – long-handled with brushes at least twice as long as the household sort, and handed one of them to Joe. Then the two of

95

them, one tall and big-boned, the other small and compact, showed how they should be used. When the floor was cleared to their satisfaction, they stood up, leaning on the brooms, facing each other.

As if on cue, the band tried out a country tune with a polka rhythm. Dan stood for a moment as if bewitched, the broom still in his hand. Then he slid his hand down the wooden handle of the broom till it was fairly balanced, and began to dance. His big, heavy-soled, best Sunday boots stamped out the polka rhythm, feet flat down to the floor, knees bent, but at each step brought up high.

'Good God,' said William. 'What will Thirzah say?'

'Ssh,' said an awed voice in his ear. 'For God's sake don't stop him. It's pure Breughel!' Greg was moved beyond words. Fran looked round the ring of faces, from Thirzah's, red and outraged, to others, somewhat embarrassed of the town-bred ladies who thought Dan was drunk and feared a scene, and on again to the few who understood just what it was they were being privileged to witness. History. Peasant dancing for the pure joy of living while there was a brief chance. Earth feet, heavy feet in clumsy boots, lifted in country mirth.

Goose-pimples rose on her skin. But Dan had finished his circle, and had come back to where Joe stood watching. Then he faced Joe, signalling to him to join in – and now the brooms were held in sweeping position in front of them as they faced each other. This time the polka was performed without the knees being bent or lifted, but with an elastic step that beat out the rhythm, accompanying a tapping made by the alternate ends of the broom heads being struck on the wooden floor. There was, the amazed spectators began to understand, a ritual pattern to the dance, as the dancers moved towards each other, drew away, met again, or parted to bend and twirl the broom heads round themselves close to the floor, then upright again and back to the dance. Helped by the band, whose musicianship told them what they were watching, the tempo increased a little, and the two figures drew closer to each other, continuing the dance till each had to watch the other's broom as it came round, and without breaking his step leap over it. With an extra-loud clap of wood on wood they came to the end, close together, shy and red of face, puffing a little, to a roar of astounded applause.

In the long silence that followed, it was George Bridgefoot who spoke. 'Well done, both of you. You couldn't have pleased me more.'

Voices begged him to explain. 'I didn't ask 'em to do it,' he said. 'I reckon it just come to Dan natural, like, to show how happy he was. Just like they used to in the old days when the harvest was in and they'd finish by sweeping the barns out after the threshing. I've seen Dan do it before, but I shouldn't ha' thought anybody as young as Joe knowed how. And now I'm going to ask the band if we can all dance "Haste to the Wedding".' He took Fran by the hand, and the dance formed up. Elyot and Beth took no persuading, and Jane at last gave in to Bob, Jess and Greg, and all the rest lined up in pairs. William was the odd man out, and went to try his charm on Emerald Petrie.

'I'm sorry, Dr William,' she said, prettily shy and using without thinking the name her little brother had bestowed on him, 'but I've never had the chance to dance before, and I don't know how to do it. Besides, I'd rather not leave Ammy all by herself.'

'Come and learn, then,' said William. 'Everybody should know how to dance! Didn't you see Mr Bates and Mr Noble? Dancing is good for you, body, mind and spirit. Isn't it, Dr Hardy?'

Startled, the doctor replied, 'How should I know? I don't dance, either.'

'Then you'll have to learn, too,' said William. 'Quick – take Ammy and come with Emmy and me. We shall be too late if you hesitate. There's nothing to learn in this dance. Just watch everybody else, and you'll see.' He got his way.

It was getting on for midnight, but there was no sign of anybody but Thirzah's group wanting to stop. Sets for an eightsome reel were being formed. 'We're one woman short,' Greg called. 'Come on, somebody. We'll push you through.'

While they waited, young Nick Hadley-Gordon appeared in the doorway, talking to a woman nobody recognized. They had both been standing outside, watching, and Nick was apparently urging her to go in and make up the set. Eric, in his capacity as

Master of Ceremonies, went to add his invitation. She was not dressed for dancing, but he didn't miss the detail of a silver thistle brooch at the throat of her high-necked blouse.

'I'd love to,' she said, 'but it's quite impossible. Thank you for asking me, all the same.' Then she turned on her heel and almost ran away.

'I'm the man without the partner,' Eric said, coming back into the ballroom. 'Come on, Emerald – I'm not the dancer Dr Burbage is, but here's your chance to teach me.' She stood up, shy, but in a surprising way self-assured, and obliged.

Fran had not missed young Nick's late appearance. He came straight to her when the reel was finished. 'And where have you been till now?' she asked lightly. She was not prepared for his reply.

'Poppy said she wouldn't come at all if I did,' he said, blushing. 'I was miserable, because I didn't want to offend you, so I've been watching from the door. Poppy caught sight of me, and left. She didn't come back. I was still standing there feeling miserable when that other lady joined me. I liked her a lot. But she's sad – I know, so am I.'

The clock struck midnight, and it was now Sunday, and William's birthday. As they had been briefed, the band and the company struck up 'Happy Birthday' and the last bottles of champagne flowed.

So William and Fran sat before their new painting, reliving the day and not wanting it to end.

'George told me his great news,' she said. 'He's giving up the management of Bridgefoot Farms Ltd at Michaelmas, but keeping all the Glebe land for himself and Daniel to tiffle about on. How wise of him. Brian will hold the reins of all the rest except for Charles's bit down Danesum Lane, which is his to do just as he likes with, though as a junior partner he'll be expected to help where he's wanted. Marjorie remains a shareholder. It all seems to make a great deal of sense to me. And it's turned out so much better than George thought it would. He's a happy old man, after all.'

'He didn't appear all that old, tonight. He'd forgotten his bad hip – 'specially when Stripping the Willow with you. But then you'd make a lamp post dance.'

'So, it seems, could you! How did you get the new doctor to try? He told me that he had two left feet.'

'I think Dan and Joe cured him. He's just begun to understand what lies below the surface here. I think tonight has taught him that if he is going to be in it, he has to be of it, as well. Nice man. I like him.'

Fran's eyes went back to the picture. 'That,' she said, 'accounts for us having to spend last night apart. They had to manoeuvre us out of the way while they hung it. Fancy them being able to wheedle Sophie into acting a lie!'

'She loved being part of the secret. Besides, she was doing it for us. Like she stayed at least fifteen minutes into "the Lord's day" so as to be able to wish me a happy birthday with all the rest. The happiest birthday I've ever had – with you as the best present. Even better than the picture.' They studied it afresh.

'We must mount that fan Effendi gave me,' Fran said, 'and put it up somewhere in a prominent place. He must have scoured Paris for it.'

'On Bob's instructions. Only Bob knew what the lady in the original picture was holding. Or what her dress was like. He made Greg a rough sketch with as many details as he could. Effendi and Greg both say the original must have been a Gainsborough. I'm glad Greg didn't make me look like that awful gun-toting Mr Andrews.'

'So am I,' she said. 'Gosh, I am tired! Let's go to bed.'

'Believe it or not, so am I. I'm absolutely dead beat – too tired for anything else. Which is not exactly what any bridegroom ought to confess to his bride on their wedding night. All I can do is to tell you again that I love you – more and more with every day that passes. And I always shall.'

'We start a new era from today,' Fran said. 'The Burbages are at home – and their guardian angels are in residence. Bless Bob. Bless Greg. Bless Eric. Oh, bless 'em all.'

He was more than half asleep when she roused him.

'William,' she said, sitting up, 'why on earth do you suppose Grandfather had to sell a *Gainsborough*? *And where is it now?*'

He pulled her head back on to his shoulder, and began to laugh.

'You really are what Ned calls "the master-bit",' he said. 'I confess to you that I'm too tired and too drained to make love to you on our wedding night, and what do you do? Wake me up to ask me a question as impossible to answer as that! I don't know. Ask Bob. Only not in bed.'

He was asleep again before she had time to answer him.

Sunday morning again, and what was left of William's birthday. Nothing special to get up for. Everything to stop in bed for, as long as they liked.

'I feel suspended,' Fran said, 'floating between heaven and earth like a little parachute from a dandelion clock. Just hovering. Not pinned down by anything, especially clocks or calendars. No past to tie me, no future laid out for me. How long do you think this unfettered feeling can last?'

'Not long, if I know you. This morning, it's probably just a normal reaction to yesterday. It's put a hiatus into our lives. It's wonderful to know we haven't any longer to count the days to the beginning of the Michaelmas term. But I know you. You'd hate it if it lasted long. So we'll take today off, and get back to normal tomorrow. I want to get everything cleared up, and start again. Maybe afresh. Having at last been made respectable in the sight of God and the congregation of Old Swithinford, we ought hence forward to get up early on Sundays and go to communion, taken by our new rector.'

She looked so horrified that he laughed aloud. 'Not every Sunday, but it might be a good idea to go occasionally. We – or at least, I – poked my nose into the church's affairs to "keep the old wayses" going, so we really ought to do what we can to support them, now. Besides – we ought to make the most of things while we can.'

'What do you mean?'

'I've warned you all along that we can't prevent change. We

can only slow it down a bit. Any tide running too fast can cause flood and havoc. There were straws in the wind last night – didn't you notice that only Church Enders were there? Lane Enders wouldn't have any interest in dancing as their grandfathers did, even if they knew how. The modern culture they want to belong to demands "individual expression", even in dance – and music so loud that it inhibits all but the briefest verbal exchanges. As different as can be from ours. I expect they regard us as pampered rich idlers with no idea of what they call "work". Work for them is something you go to. They work in order to be able to keep up with the Joneses. We work – in our own way – so that we don't have to try to keep up with anybody. But the future belongs to them and their culture. That's something we can't even slow up.'

'You mean they don't consider what we do to be "work" at all?'

'No – because we don't do it with a pick and shovel, or commute to an office – though they see your name on the screen. I'm the drone. There are things I must do, but after that I don't propose to "touch collar", as Sophie would say, till I start on Bob's book.'

'And I have to try to find ideas for a new series. I haven't got a clue at the moment. But all will be well. I know it.'

'How? Aren't you tempting a benevolent providence?'

'No! Acknowledging with gratitude our many blessings. And feeling safe with our guardian angels looking down on us. I believe they are as glad to be home as we are to have them.'

'You think they mean us to put our noses down on the grindstone?'

'I don't really know about you. Your nose will be down to the grindstone when other people's affairs let you. Like last year.'

'You're a fine one to talk, I must say. It depends on the new pattern. We may never have to get ourselves so deeply involved again.'

'Some hopes,' she said. 'Want to bet?'

'No, Mrs Burbage. I have too much sense to want to bet against you. What I do want is my breakfast.'

Over breakfast they picked up the same threads again. 'What is it you must do in the next day or two?' she asked.

'Clear the last few thing out of my college rooms. I left some things there. When Mother died, the family was split up by the war and Benedict's lost as the family base. I never had anything approaching a home again till I found you. So I lived – if that's what it could be called – in the flat, and kept a few things in my room: my gown, and my dress suits – for handy convenience – and a few other bits and pieces. I honestly can't remember what, except that there are cardboard boxes full of papers that Jess said she thought I ought to have. I didn't bother to go through them, and there they still are. I can either go through them there or bring them back to sort – but I rather dread poking into a painful past, wherever. I think I'll just go and throw everything into the car, and you can help me sort through them. I'd like you to be on hand.'

'We must keep your academic gear here,' she said. 'It shouldn't take long. I suppose we ought to make a round of "thank-you" visits, soon,' she added. He nodded. 'Especially up to Castle Hill. That picture originated with Bob.'

'Yes,' she agreed. 'Which reminds me to ask you – did you happen to notice when Poppy Gifford left? When Nick came so late, he was miserable, and it was something to do with Poppy. That's funny, isn't it?'

William didn't appear unduly disturbed. 'Lover's tiff, I expect,' he said. 'People in love quarrel just for the pleasure of making it up again. You ought to know that.'

'Yes, darling, but when? Effendi and Nick only arrived back just in time for yesterday, and Effendi came first, without Nick. Nick and Poppy can't have seen each other since just after Charlie's wedding, when he and Effendi went off so suddenly. I don't like it. Something's wrong that we haven't been told about.'

'There you go again! Running to meet trouble. I agree it looks a bit queer, but there's probably a very ordinary reason for it. Don't start digging anything up that might spoil yesterday. Besides, it's Sunday. What shall we do?'

'Need we do anything?'

'No. I hoped you'd say that. All I want to do today is just *be*. As long as you are here just being, too.'

Monday morning brought Sophie, full of talk about Saturday's great occasion. There was, she declared, nothing as anybody could find fault with – well, nobody except Thrizah. 'I do believe,' she said, 'if Thirz' ever gets as far as the Pearly Gates, she'll find fault with 'em 'cos they ain't opened wide enough for 'er to get through! I couldn't see no wrong in it myself – and I told 'er so. "It were no disgrace to me," I said, "and I don't know why it should be to you. They was just enj'ying theirselves."'

They were accustomed to her way of prolonging the pleasure of reaching the kernel of a story as long as possible, but they couldn't think what she meant. Fran asked.

'Dan'el and Joe a-dancing the broomstick dance,' she said. ''Specially Dan. "To think my own 'usband would let me down like that there," she kept saying yest'day. "Making such a hexibition of 'isself in front of all them posh folk from London. What's more, 'e was drunk! 'E'd never ha' done such a thing if 'e hadn't ha' been." She knows very well as 'e wasn't drunk. What upset 'er was that it reminded everybody as all 'er 'usband 'ad ever been was a labourer as 'ad swep' a barn hout. Sich wayses I can't abide.'

'Oh dear,' Fran soothed. 'It was wonderful – from every point of view.'

'Ev'ry point o' view only 'er'n,' Sophie said. 'Trouble is, she can't rile Dan'el. 'E's such a patient man, and don't let 'er upset 'im. But once or twice yest'day, I thought 'e were going to answer 'er back – and I was afraid as if 'e did she'd hev one of 'er turns. She's very near as bad now with them turns as Het used to be with 'er sterricks. As I told 'er yest'day – she'll goo too far with Dan one o' these days, and 'e'll let 'er know as when all is said and done, 'e's the man o' the 'ouse. Is there anything special to be done?'

'Not much,' Fran said. 'William's going to fetch the last of his things from college. Could you find him some room for them in the spare-room cupboards?'

'I'd better clear that big old me'ogany wardrobe in the one in the hend room,' Sophie replied. 'There's room to 'ang things and a lot o' big drawers as well as a little bit of a cupboard. They don't make furniture like that no more.' And with that, she went.

William went, too, after warning Fran not to expect him back till she saw him.

Now that the time had come, in spite of everything, he felt a twinge of nostalgia about breaking this very last link. There was such an extraordinary confusion of emotion and memory folded into those academic robes, not all of it sad, nor by any means all happy.

When he had taken all he wanted to save down to the car, William felt impelled to go back just once more to sit in silence in the room that for so many years had been his personal base. He didn't understand why he should be stirred by a sadness he hadn't expected. Feeling, perhaps, that he was leaving a lot of himself there? That was silly, because he wasn't. But this had been his home. He had told Fran so. College had been to him the home he had never had with Janice, or any home since the family at Benedict's had been broken up when he was only in his early twenties. He didn't remember any home before his mother had married Fran's uncle. He'd only been three, after all, and had thought of himself as a Wagstaffe – but of course he wasn't. With Benedict's deserted, and the Wagstaffes scattered by bereavement and war, he had been out on his own. It wasn't until he had first occupied these rooms that he had begun to feel attached permanently to anything, anywhere or indeed to anybody again. Now that he was attached again to Fran and Old Swithinford by bands that could not be easily broken, why on earth should he feel that leaving his connection with his college left a gap?

Because there was a gap. At Cambridge he had not been a Wagstaffe. He had been a Burbage. That was the bit that was all his own, and nobody else's. It gave him a desolate feeling of regret that he knew absolutely nothing about his Burbage roots; nothing more than his birth certificate told him, and the fact that his father had been killed on the Somme. He didn't blame anyone; his mother, like other young war widows, had had to put that part of her life behind her, and the Wagstaffes, having accepted him as one of their own, went out of their way not to dwell on his difference. He didn't remember his father, had never seen a photograph, and had been told nothing.

Well – it was too late, now. It was a consolation that they had let him keep his name, which he had now endowed Fran with. In apposition came the grief that there would be no more Burbages. He stood alone, without past or future, as far as his name was concerned. A name that meant more, here in this room, than it did anywhere else.

He took a last look round, smoothed the old wood of his desk with a caressing hand, tried not to look at his successor's gear rather obviously strewn everywhere around, and remembered the pert little secretary in the next room. He heard her voice, and it was time for him to slip away. No need even to lock the door and give her the key. He shut it behind him and walked resolutely away.

But the feeling of sadness wouldn't leave him – and the last thing he wanted was to let Fran suspect it. Passing the hotel, he yielded to a sudden impulse and turned in to the car-park. A drink with Eric was just what he needed.

The receptionist told him that Mr Choppen was in his office with another visitor, and she didn't know whether it was possible for William to see him. There was, she said, a bit of a crisis on, but she would ring up and ask.

'Go up,' she said. It was already past normal lunch-time, and William was not surprised to find Eric and Nigel sitting with a bottle between them, waiting for lunch to be sent up.

'Have a brandy, and I'll order another lunch,' Eric said. 'You're just in time – unless Fran's waiting for you.'

William was glad he had given himself leeway at home. 'Brandy?' he asked. 'Yes please. Exactly what I could do with.'

'Same here,' said Eric, pouring generously. 'Whisky's a depressant, and no good in any sort of crisis. Brandy's a stimulant.'

'What's wrong?' William asked. 'It isn't often I find you in such a state.'

'That blasted Anne Chessman's ratted on me. Just at the wrong time – with Christmas conferences and parties and all the rest in view. I don't suppose it's her fault, actually, and there would never have been a right time. But we'd settled into the changed routine she forced on me when she kicked up such a stink with Jess after she'd married the Chessman fellow. I had to rearrange everything to keep her and Jess apart, by giving her the top job here and letting Jess work from the central office down at Monastery Farm. It was a good move – but a fat lot of thanks I get from Anne. She's left our employ without warning. Just a note. That's enough to make me swear in it's own right, but there are all the other strings attached to it to worry about as well. I'm fond of Marjorie, and I hate to see any of my friends in distress. Damn Bailey and all his bloody works!'

He picked up his glass and tipped back the contents. William raised his eyebrows at Nigel.

'Don't get worried, Padre,' Eric said. 'I'm mad angry, but I'm not round the bend yet. That's the worst of a bloody village. One ant steps out of line, and the whole ant heap is affected. Let's get our grub here, and I'll explain.'

'So what's bitten Anne?' asked William.

'Did you know her new husband had been a Japanese POW for four years? Poor bugger – we've all got scars of some sort but I think his must be the worst. He's all right as long as things go smoothly, but he breaks when they don't. Working for Bailey can't be easy. I have no real idea what caused this, but all of a sudden he had an overpowering desire to get away from here – and they have upped sticks and gone to live in Newhaven. Just like that. There's nothing I can do about it but begin to look out for somebody else with a couple of languages at her tongue's end. Anne was a nasty bit of work in many ways, but she was an absolutely first-class asset here.

'It's having a knock-on effect on Marjorie, too. Our arrangement has worked so well – I couldn't have believed it could have been so good. Once we'd sorted out our personal relationship with each other, it's been all gas and gaiters. She's as practical a woman as I am a man – she's settled for independence, just as I have, and we understand each other. She loves to be busy, and to be needed. She likes looking after me, and I like being looked after.

106

It's just like having a twin sister in the other side of my house, and she has already made it plain that once Nigel moves into his cottage she proposes to take him under her wing as well. After all, she is a Bridgefoot!

'But she's not happy about either of her children. Poppy's been home since before Charles and Charlie's wedding – and, as Marjorie says, she isn't the girl she used to be. No life in her. Then there's Pansy – well, the contact between her and the rest of her family since she went to live with Darren Bailey has been minimal, to say the least. Of course, Poppy has to go back to college on Thursday, and I knew how Marjorie would miss her. I wasn't surprised to find they had both been crying, yesterday morning. I was surprised to be told that it was Pansy, not Poppy, who was the cause. She had just rung her mother to say that she and Darren Bailey had been married for a month or more, because she is pregnant, and that they're about to move away as well. Obviously a big shake-up in the Bailey camp. Naturally, Marjorie's upset. And there's nothing anybody can do to help.'

He filled the glasses, and it was William who asked, 'Where's Pansy going? Too far for her mother to be in on the baby's advent?'

'Apparently to a rented house in Deal, on the East Coast. Just too far. And I've heard a rumour this morning that "Casablanca" is on the market. That's one that I shall not be making a bid for!'

'Well, there'll be no tears at this end of the village if that rumour's truth,' William said. 'It looks as if Bailey has come unstuck somewhere, doesn't it? But he's got far too many irons in the fire round here to move far. I expect he's only going back into Swithinford – or even to Cambridge. I must go home. But I've just said goodbye to the first half of my life, and needed that brandy, Eric, before facing Fran again.'

As they were seeing him out, one of the girls from the office was about to knock on Eric's door. William was in his car and on his way home before he recalled who it was that had been with the office-girl. He wouldn't have recognized her face – but he knew where he had seen that high-necked blouse and the thistle brooch before.

He was glad of Sophie's offer to get Ned to help her to unload his car and put the things away in the wardrobe she had cleared. He told Fran that he had had his lunch with Eric and Nigel – anxious that she should not suspect the mood that had made him seek their company. He'd had a sudden urge to go in and thank Eric, he said, and, finding Nigel there and Eric in a stew, he had been inveigled into stopping. And what a budget of news he had gathered.

'What an extraordinary thing!' Fran said, as usual feeling her response to it rather than simply thinking. 'Poor Marjorie – as if she hasn't had enough to put up with already. But really, Pansy is the odd one out in the Bridgefoot family, isn't she? Her becoming Mrs Bailey Junior leaves Poppy the only Gifford among them. But why Newhaven? Why Deal? Sounds to me as if there's been a bust-up in the Bailey family, as well as in the workforce. I don't think there will be much mourning about Anne removing herself – especially on Jess's part. Or mine, if I tell the truth. What shall we do with what's left of the afternoon? I had thought we might walk up to Castle Hill, but it's too late now for us to invite ourselves to tea. Just laze?'

'Suits me,' said William. But it was not to be. He got up and answered the telephone to Charlie Bridgefoot.

'Yes, we should love to,' she heard him say.

His smile was wry as he told Fran, 'Not Castle Hill – Danesum. And I warn you that Charlie didn't sound too happy.'

It was the first time they had been to Danesum since the newly married young owners had gone there on the night of their wedding in June, postponing their honeymoon because Charlie declared that the house which Charles had striven with all his youthful strength and idealism to make ready for his bride 'wanted them'.

William left the car at the top of Danesum Lane, and they walked the rest of the way until the old house came into view, lit by the warm glow of the autumnal sun lowering itself towards the western horizon. It showed them the same house they had known when the hippy family of Petries had lived there, but even from a distance they were aware of a glow that now came from the inside, too. It was alive again. The rowan tree that stood in its front garden was a huge torch of red berries, and behind the house itself, between it and the newly thatched granary, old apple trees bent under the weight of fruit as they had not done before, having after many years at last had their roots cleared.

William found their approach to the house too full of memories for comfort. He had formed a close bond with the cultured vagabond whose heart had been made too big and whose courage was that of a lion. John Petrie ranked in William's list of friends second only to Mac; that the voices of both had been silenced for ever only made the memory of them dearer. Mac had left him nothing but memory, and the recurring nightmare of an unopened parachute plummeting to earth. John had left him a legacy of concern for eight children.

As the front door opened to admit them, William could hardly bear the sight of the other door on the right just inside the hall, a door that led to the room where he had sat with his condemned friend. He almost expected to hear the continuous racking cough, feeling down his spine a thrill that brought goose-pimples on the back of his neck. But it was not Emmy Petrie who was opening the door to them, as in the past, thinly clothed, barefoot and hung about with baby brothers. It was Charlie, looking so robustly healthy and so glowingly beautiful with happiness that she almost took his breath away. He had stood back for Fran to go in first, and Charlie had greeted her with warmth; but when she turned towards him, she simply put her arms round his neck and her face close to his, so that she could whisper into his ear.

'I feel his presence too,' she said. 'It just fills the house with love. That was his wedding present to us.' William returned her kiss with a good deal of feeling. She was outstanding in so many ways – in her beauty, in her intellect and her gift for languages, in her whole attitude to life. Most of all, perhaps, for those who knew her father well, in her resemblance to him at moments like this. She had inherited a great deal of his sixth sense. She had foreseen that William would be dreading this first visit to Danesum and had known how to comfort him as nobody else could, not even Fran. And it was into that very room where he had first seen John that they were ushered – but what a difference there was now!

Charles was escorting Fran, and proudly telling her what they had managed to do so far. They were only furnishing half the large house at present, till they were quite sure what it was they needed. Charlie had only done one year out of three towards her first degree. For two more years she'd be officially in residence at Cambridge in term-time.

'Which puts Grandad's hopes on the back-boiler till then, at the earliest,' Charles said with a grin. Charlie was prettily dispensing a substantial afternoon tea.

'So what are your long-term plans?' Fran asked, accepting the invitation his conspiratorial grin had offered.

'No young Bridgefoots till Charlie has that first degree in her pocket. The usual procedure for an aspiring vet is to work "out in the field" in a practice with a qualified vet. Two years ought to give us time to get this place round so that we can establish a practice here, and offer a qualified vet a partnership that will allow Charlie to work with him from here till she gets her own final qualifications. It will take a lot of hard work and money to bring it up to scratch for regulations, partly because, being so much off the beaten track, normal services have passed it by. Jack Bartrum got electricity down to his farmhouse, so the electricity mains were near enough for Mr Petrie to get connected. I had to start by having mains water laid on. How on earth the Petries managed without it – eight children, including two babies – I just can't think. But my greatest problem was sewerage. Everything was absolutely primitive. No chance of getting connected except at my own expense, which couldn't even be considered, though I had to get a system of some sort completed before I could bring Charlie here. It was going to cost the earth in any case, and if in time we were going to run a vet's practice from here, and it had to meet regulations, it would be cheaper in the long run to get it done first as last. But that's when I got scared that I had bitten off more than I could chew.'

He flushed, a bit embarrassed, but went gallantly on, 'I got so het up that I nearly wrecked everything. I'd spent most of what I had, and couldn't see any way round the sewerage problem without borrowing. I'd promised Grandad I wouldn't do that. Charlie's father told me he was sure it would all turn out right in the end – and it did – though not as anybody would have expected. I was short-tempered enough to kick up a dust about nothing all the time, and threw a fit about the plans for our wedding. I resented it being in the hands of Charlie's family, and not a Bridgefoot wedding at Bridgefoot expense. I went about muttering to myself that I never thought the time would come when Bridgefoots had to accept charity from anybody, and when Charlie's grandfather offered us a month's honeymoon on the continent for a wedding present, I worked it up into an insult. The honeymoon at any rate would be at Bridgefoot expense, I said, with my nose in the air. That was when Charlie actually threw her engagement ring back at me, and told me there wouldn't be any wedding.

'Charlie's father knew how I felt and explained it to Effendi. And what happened was that we had a short and cheap honeymoon at *my* Grandad's expense, while a very expensive sewerage system was installed at Effendi's. His wedding present in lieu of the honeymoon. It must be one of the queerest wedding presents ever – but it means we've got the very latest in septic tanks and all the rest. We'll show you round after tea.'

William listened with mixed feelings. Charles was no longer the Adonis-like youth he had been in the spring – touchy and proud and very vulnerable in his love-sickness. He was now a fully fledged Bridgefoot, with his feet on his own land and his own wife at his own table. William had delighted in the boy up to his ears in love – but it was only as it should be that marriage to a girl like Charlie should put the last bit of maturity to the man. He found himself wondering philosophically which of the two couples round the tea-table today was the luckier. If only he and Fran could have had this wonderful mating-time together – but on the other hand, they had had the unexpected experience of old love blazing up into life again at a time when dusk might otherwise have been falling too early. These youngsters, with luck, could have the best of both.

Looking at their bright faces, he came near to praying for them. Then he caught Charlie's eye, and saw that she knew what he was thinking. She was directing his gaze to where John's apology for a bed had stood, and where now she had put a comfortable divan.

She had deliberately preserved John's presence there. William didn't need to worry, her eyes said. Benedict's wasn't the only house with a resident guardian angel.

Fran was telling Charles that they would love to look round, but Charlie chipped in. 'Another time, darling, you shall show them the wonders of our sewerage system. But – please forgive us – we need to talk to you. We're worried about Poppy and Nick.'

She cleared away, but they went on sitting round the table. Sound judgement again, William thought. Fran was sending him silent messages that this was what they might have guessed. Surprisingly, Charlie left it to Charles.

'Have you heard about Pansy?' he asked. 'She couldn't have timed it worse! Aunt Marge is just about beside herself with worry – and all the rest of my family as well. They're so concerned about Pansy that they haven't noticed what's happening to Poppy. She'll be gone back to college by Thursday, and – well, we don't know what to do.'

'Dad and Jane and Effendi can't understand what's come over Nick,' said Charlie. 'And we've gone and put our feet in it right up to our elbows.'

'Start right at the beginning,' Fran said gently. 'We're a bit out of touch.'

'Sorry,' Charlie answered, 'I forgot. You were away. Nick had got his memory back before you went, hadn't he? And they'd decided he'd got to go back to his doctor in London? Well, we were up to our necks and missed what had happened between Poppy and Nick. Poppy threw herself about with Aunt Marge – but we only heard it at second hand, because I was doing exams and Charles was worrying about our cesspit – or something.' (William had the feeling that the smile she threw Charles would have made the Sphinx roll over and ask to have its tummy rubbed.)

'Whatever it was blew over – because everybody was hiding it so as not to upset anybody before our wedding. I knew something was worrying Dad, but things seemed to be all right when Nick came back to be best man. Well, you were there, so you saw. I don't need to tell you how perfect everything was, do I? I shall remember every moment of it till the day I die – but one moment more than all the rest. One that you didn't see, because you were all still in church.'

She paused – and had difficulty going on. Charles moved his chair closer to her and put his arm round her. 'Go on, my lambkin,' he said.

'Charles and I came down the aisle – married – with only Nick and Poppy following us – out of the door. It was eerie. None of us had said a word to any of the others, but – there we stood at the door, and a few feet away from us was Robert's grave. We all four turned towards it, and stood round it, looking down – thinking he ought to be there. Both Charles and Nick were crying, so we went into a huddle with our arms round each other so that the folks standing down the path shouldn't see, and Charles held me and Nick held Poppy. We felt that it was only a question of time before we'd be doing the same again with roles reversed, and Nick and Poppy in our shoes. Then the bells started and we skedaddled back to the porch for the photos and all the rest. Poppy put her bouquet on the grave – so all the folks who'd seen it thought it had all been planned.

'Then there was all the reception, and the do in the barn that night,' Charles said. 'And both Poppy and Nick looked as happy as we felt. If anything could have made us happier than we had expected to be that night, it was that Nick was himself again, and Poppy with him like she used to be before he was ill.'

There was a long pause before Charlie took up the tale again. 'But before the week was out, Nick was whipped off for a month on the continent with Effendi. Harvest hit Charles before we were ready for it because of the weather, and as soon as it was over, we went off on our honeymoon. As soon as we got back, the news about you being married leaked out, and we began planning a party for you as soon as Effendi and Nick were back. We didn't pick up that anything was wrong – that Nick and Poppy were no longer on speaking terms – until he didn't show up on Saturday.'

'And when he did, Poppy slipped away like greased lightning,' Charles interpolated. 'By Sunday the fat was in the fire about Pansy, and we felt awful. We couldn't just let it go like that – but we couldn't ask anybody on either side to help.

'In the end, we thought that perhaps it was just a lovers' tiff,

113

and that maybe if we got them together we could put things right ourselves. So I went and waylaid Nick, and brought him back here. And Charlie got Poppy here on false pretences without telling her Nick was going to be here as well.'

'It was awful. We should have minded our own business, and kept out of it,' said Charlie, trying not to cry.

'So tell us what happened,' Fran said. 'I expect it is only a lovers' tiff, and if it is, only the two of them can put it right. I seem to remember you and Charles in the same boat at least twice.'

'It's all so *silly*,' Charlie said, though still in deep distress.

'I agree,' Charles said. 'I'd like to knock their heads together to bring them both to their senses if I didn't think they were both as soft as rotten mangolds.'

'After the first shock of seeing each other here,' said Charlie, 'we might as well all have been in an ice house. Nick looked and acted as if he had been frozen and would never be warm again, and Poppy was limp and wilted, all weepy, wiping tears away that she didn't want Nick to see. He was all stuck-up and proud and haughty – he looked down his nose at Poppy like a Regency Buck with a quizzing glass. We'd made things a thousand times worse, silly idiots that we are. We're afraid it's really serious, and Charles said if we had to talk to somebody, it had to be you. We do hope you don't mind.'

'So what is the trouble?' asked William. 'We can't advise till we know.'

'You tell them,' Charles said, and left it to Charlie.

'It appears that when Nick fell off the straw-stack – the fall that restored his memory – he fell literally straight into Poppy's arms. And he didn't know he'd been ill at all, let alone for so long. He thought he was a schoolboy again, kissing Poppy in the straw while they waited for Robert and Pansy to come back. Poor Poppy had to tell him what had happened. She took him as far as the house, and then went home, leaving him with his family. She was in a dreadful state because she'd never stopped loving him. But she'd given up hope after his accident, expecting him to die, like we all did – and she'd faced up to life without him. Then, suddenly, there he was again – all just like it had been before, and as if there

114

had never been the awful gap of his amnesia. But *she* knew what had happened in that time, and knew that things weren't the same as they had been, and never would be again.

'When he'd been knocked out, he'd been the illegitimate son of the village charwoman who wasn't good enough for her father. Nick who'd fallen back into her arms was a pampered invalid and Effendi's spoilt, darling grandson. His mother was my Dad's wife. Everything was upside-down. It was her who wasn't good enough for him, now, poor Poppy.'

'She should have had more sense,' said Charles, ruffled because of the implied suggestion that anything could be better than to be born a Bridgefoot – as Poppy's mother had been.

'Don't be silly, Charles. Remember all the rest of the circumstances. The more she thought, the worse it seemed. Her father had been killed – with all the scandal attached to his death – and the whole village was talking about her mother's "goings-on" with Mr Choppen, though of course there wasn't even a hint of truth in that. She blamed her mother because she was so miserable – and took herself off back to college. But not before she had seen Nick again. That's what we didn't know. He wanted to go on where they'd left off, but she told him it was too late, and made him think she'd got somebody else. Poor old Nick was left flat. He was still trying to adjust to having his memory back, and having to put two very different sorts of lives together. Dad and Jane guessed Poppy had something to do with him being miserable.

'But our wedding was coming up, and when Nick came down from London for it and they met again, everything was marvellous. Poppy had just begun to hope again, when Nick disappeared to the continent with Effendi – after writing to her that nothing would ever come of it so they might as well stop seeing each other at once.'

'Why?' This was William, straight and to the point. He was having trouble in believing that of Nick.

'I don't think anybody, even Dad, could realize what Nick was enduring. With all the wedding and everything, they hadn't really given him enough thought – besides, it seemed so much like a miracle that he had got his memory back that they didn't stop to think what it must be like for him. None of us did. You see – he told us all this after Charles had taken Poppy home – he could remember what his childhood had been like, and he began to ask questions. Why had his mother been so poor? Where had his rich grandfather been, and why had he left them in such poverty? Why had he suddenly turned up out of the blue, like a rich Nabob? And above all, who was his father, and where was he now?

'So he went home one afternoon and demanded to be told. They wouldn't tell him – none of them. I don't know why, but they wouldn't then and they still won't – especially his mother. Until his accident, he had only had his mother, and she had only had him. He thinks she's lost all interest in him now that she's got her father and my Dad and, to top it all, "two of the little Petrie bastards". His words, William, not mine. He's terribly bitter about his mother's love for them. He tried asking people in the village, but all they could tell him was that he was a bastard as well, and that his mother had lived with some horrible old man – whom he just remembers. He couldn't take it, and still can't.

'You can see what a terrible mistake we made, thinking that just putting them together would be enough. They do belong to each other, I'm sure they do, and they always will, but Poppy can't forgive him for changing her resolution to do without him, and giving her hope again, and then squashing it like swatting a fly without telling her why. All he would say was that he was worse than a nobody, had no right to anything, least of all to a Bridgefoot, and that as soon as he could possibly escape he was going to, even if he had to beg for his living or starve. He's almost out of his mind. We haven't seen either of them since.'

'Why won't they tell him?' asked Fran.

'Why does it matter so much?' asked Charlie. 'He knows who his mother is, and what she did for him, and who his grandfather is, and what a wonderful man he is – he's in no worse a position than I am, is he? I'm a Bellamy and proud to be my Dad's daughter and Charles's wife. That's enough. I do know who and what my mother is – and wish I didn't. I think what I've got far outweighs what I haven't. I think he should count his blessings. It's Poppy I'm sorry for, not Nick.'

Fran was remembering Nick's mother as she had been before her transformation – carrying such a burden alone and without a

116

word of complaint. She wished she dared tell Nick – but of course, he must remember Jane like that too. That was why his mind was set now on finding out *why* it had been like that. There must be some very good reason why they wouldn't tell him. She was wondering if she dared ask Bob.

William was being unusually silent. He sat looking down at the table, rather abstractedly rolling under his finger a crumb that had escaped Charlie's clearing up. When the silence grew long, he looked up and reached over to take and hold Fran's hand with a look of apology to her in his eyes. 'I have to sympathize with Nick,' he said. 'I'm more or less in the same boat. If you know both your parents – however unsatisfactory they may be – you know who and what you are. If you don't, there's always a great question-mark in your mind. Charles stands on firm ground, there; so does Fran. They not only know who they are, they have memories to help them. Charlie knows – she has memories that she doesn't particularly like, but because she knows, she can rationalize. It's not knowing that's the worst. You see, nobody ever told me anything about my father except facts – and not many of those. I was only three when my mother married again, to Fran's uncle. They made me into a Wagstaffe – and no one could be more grateful than I am for what they did for me. But I wasn't born a Wagstaffe. My name is Burbage, and I know from seeing documents that my father was Frederick Ross Burbage who died at Beaumont Hamel on the Somme when he was twenty-six and I less than a year old. Naturally, when she'd married again, my mother didn't wish to talk – or her new husband to hear – about him. He was dead. He didn't live to know me, and I've no memories of him. Happy as I am now, I still want to know him. At least I know something. Apparently, Nick knows nothing. You two did your best – but in this case, there's nothing any of us can do. There are times when all any of us can do is to leave it to time and the gods – or as Charles's grandfather would say, "in the hands of God".'

He felt the pressure of Fran's hand on his own, and knew how moved she was at his confession. But she didn't dwell on it; she wanted to comfort all of them.

'I would say that it is all just that love has got its hair in a tangle,' she said. 'Getting the tangle out is bound to be painful – but if it is real love, and I think it is, it will be worth it in the end. William says leave it to time and the gods. I say leave it to love.'

'Same thing,' he said.

The new term began. Poppy left without encountering Nick again. William luxuriated in his freedom. He had lost all nostalgia for his job, and had accepted that there was no need to cut himself and Fran from all the rest that being part of Cambridge meant. All that was left of his last visit there was that his feelings about his identity had been strengthened by his empathy with Nick. They had talked a lot about Nick and Poppy since their visit to Danesum, but Fran had been careful not to rub the slightly sore place William had exposed. She knew that if he wanted to talk about it to her, he would choose his own time.

'What I can't understand,' Fran said, 'is why Bob isn't aware of the situation.'

'I'm sure he is,' William answered, 'and probably suffering because he must know there's a very good reason why Nick can't be told who or what his father is – or was. He'll know that the only thing he can do to help is nothing, and that must hurt. He'll protect Jane. She and Effendi are probably the only two who know the truth they can't tell Nick. Bob won't make it worse. Nobody can wipe out the past.

'And it's made much more complicated for them by Poppy being Charles's cousin – and a Bridgefoot. The Bridgefoots are as proud as Lucifer – and if they get the idea that Nick thinks Poppy isn't good enough for him, the fat will be in the fire.'

'But he isn't,' Fran retorted indignantly. 'He's saying he isn't good enough for her – because he's only a nameless bastard. And nobody will put him out of his misery.'

'And we can't, and mustn't, interfere.' William's voice was gentle, but firm. He knew Fran's penchant for soaking up other people's troubles. This was more than she could handle.

'I shan't promise anything,' she said stubbornly, her chin stuck out. 'We may have to. What if Beryl Bean gets hold of the tale?'

He had to agree that they couldn't just put their heads in the sand and hope it would go away. He pursued his own thoughts.

'There's more to the Pansy business than meets the eye, I think. How is it that Anne whatever-her-name-is-now has pulled out without warning, at such short notice? Why in such haste skedaddle to *Newhaven*? Her husband is – or was – Bailey's clerk. Apparently, he suffers from bouts of deep depression as a result of his four years as a guest of the Japanese – like so many others of the Cambridgeshires. But as an excuse for this unpredictable move it doesn't hold water. He's on home ground here, and common sense says that the last thing he'd do of his own accord is to dig up his roots and throw away his wife's plum job. It smacks to me of Bailey. And what connection is there between that and young Bailey whipping Pansy off to Deal? Has Bailey got some huge development plan in prospect for the south-east which needs two key men to cover? Could it mean that we might be going to get rid of Bailey and all his works?'

'Didn't you tell me there was also a rumour that Casablanca was on the market?' she asked.

'It does add up!' he exclaimed. 'I must go and glean some more news from Eric.'

'You'd probably do a lot better to find some excuse for going to the DIY shop. Beryl will know, because of her Ken being so thick with the Baileys.'

'Thanks – but I'd rather hear truth than fiction. One creative mind at a time is as much as I can deal with.'

'If you mean me, I haven't got a creative idea in my head,' she said. 'Too many other things, like worrying about Nick and Poppy, are getting in the way.'

He was sober in an instant. 'I'm not forgetting them,' he said. 'I happen to think Eric and Nigel are the best bets for a bit of advice. Don't let this upset you. Relax for a few more days, and then, when we both begin again, ideas will come out of your ears.'

'All right. Go and see what you can glean from Eric. Nigel's gone back to Wales to clear things up before coming here for good. That's one bright spot, anyway.'

William went to find Eric at the hotel, and tentatively offered his services as an emergency translator. Eric was both touched and amused. He answered gravely that if after Christmas, when his resignation had taken effect, William was *still* convinced that Fran was in danger of starving, he would consider giving William employment on a part-time basis – but at the moment he was coping better than he could ever have hoped. He had brought Jess back to prevent confusion becoming more confounded, and had already come by a temporary substitute for Anne – the woman who had popped up with young Nick at the end of last Saturday's festivities.

'She's staying here,' he said, 'and I make a point of talking to our guests – especially lookers like her! She's at a loose end – possibly as a result of a marriage break-up. It's the fashion, nowadays. Anyway, when she heard that I had need of a translator, she offered to help while she was here, part-time. She has no other commitments, so it may last until I can get another suitable office manager. Nigel's gone to clear up in Wales. He'll be back as soon as he can, partly because Kenneth Bean is making a fuss about him not being resident down Spotted Cow Lane. Once he's inducted, he and George together will be more than a match for Ken, who's only Bailey's cat's-paw, when all's said and done. Other bits of news are in the wind, though nothing's finalized, but I know I can trust your discretion. Things have moved fast – because Dr Hardy happened to be on the spot at the right time. Property changing hands is still geared to Michaelmas, here.

'Hardy's still here, and will cover the practice himself as *locum tenens* till he can clinch the deal with Mrs Henderson. But it's another stroke of luck for him – and in the long run for us – that the rumour about Bailey's grand new house being on the market is true. After his ambition to become the new lord of the manor here was thwarted, his wife wasn't satisfied. She wants to move back to "civilization" – to a Victorian mansion on the outskirts of Swithinford – as soon as they can sell their white elephant. Hardy's been to look at it, and though Bailey's asking the last penny for it, he's interested. It does have a lot in its favour as far as he's concerned. It's in the right position, between the old village and the new estate, and big enough to be split into two homes for his married partners, with plenty of out-houses to convert into modern consulting rooms. He can hardly believe his good luck, but I've warned him about Bailey. Who sups with the devil needs a long spoon.

'He's not badgering old Mrs Henderson to get out – but she's expected to take over her new house from Michaelmas. Bailey's sort don't bother about such things – old customs don't make a lot of sense these days to those with eyes on the biggest penny "soonest", as our American friends put it. "When it suits him" will be Bailey's motto. It would have been mine, once. As a business man, I'm not wholly sure where I stand. It's the obverse side of living in a community intermarried and interlinked for generations. You have to learn to fall in with ways everybody takes for granted. Only – when you come up against a character like Bailey, you can't be too careful. I wish I could rid myself of a suspicion that he's behind Anne's leaving me in the soup – though I can't see what good it would do him. It makes no sense, and that bothers me.'

'We've been following the same line of thought this morning,' William said. 'But we mustn't make Bailey an idiot. He wouldn't remove Anne just to annoy you.'

'No. That's why I'm suspicious. His mistake before was to underrate us. I don't underrate him. I don't know what he's up to, but I shan't take my eye off him. What made you interested?'

'Pansy Gifford's involvement with him and the fact that Charles and Charlie are worried about Poppy and Nick. There's trouble between them, so of course the Bellamys are involved. I came up here this morning hoping I might still find Nigel with you. I wanted to ask his advice.'

Eric had been listening quietly, following William's track. 'I must be blind,' he said. 'I took it for granted that Marjorie was resigned to Pansy's association with the Baileys, but I should have known she'd be upset by Pansy getting married without telling her, and all the rest. She's never mentioned it to me, and though Nigel did, we decided to keep out of it, especially as we were all up to our necks in plans for your party last Saturday. It was only

121

when Marjorie said she didn't want to come that I put my oar in. I went home and more or less made her show up, so as not to spoil the whole evening for all the rest of the Bridgefoots. I haven't seen much of her lately, and once or twice when I have, I could swear she'd been crying – but really, it was no business of mine to ask what about. Poppy's been home and hasn't been very happy either – but she's Pansy's twin and I guessed that accounted for it. It's clear to me now that Poppy's miserable on her own account, and Marjorie's miserable about both. I can't interfere. It would only make matters worse.'

'Us as well,' William said ungrammatically. 'But failing Nigel, I'll talk to Bob.' He was rising to go when a knock came at the door, and Jess put her head round it.

'Come in,' she said to someone behind her, 'and meet the man you told me you'd noticed dancing last Saturday evening. He happens to be my brother. William, this is our new temporary member of staff, Anthea Pelham.'

Jess and Eric both enjoyed watching the impression they made on each other, William at his most suavely polished and courteous, the lady at her most strikingly beautiful, socially cool best. There was a moment's silence before Eric said, 'Sorry, William, but we have work to do. Give my love to that wonderful wife of yours – and remember that if after last Saturday you ever cause her another moment's anxiety, I am pledged to come personally and break your neck.'

Jess said, rather dryly, 'I don't think either of you is in much danger on that score. I'm the one who has to keep my eye on my husband, not Fran.'

'I don't think you have much to worry about, either,' said Eric. 'Not now.'

It was a very strange exchange to have arisen from a bare introduction, William thought. Jess, too, was aware of it, and, turning, offered a jocular explanation to the stranger. 'There are too many handsome men in this village for peace of mind, Anthea,' she said. 'I warn you, beware.'

Ms Pelham, with a dazzling smile, replied lightly, 'How splendid. 'I do like men to be nice to look at – from a distance.'

*

122

William reported everything to Fran, including an account of his introduction to Anthea Pelham.

'Tell me all about her,' Fran said.

'Eric was right when he called her "a looker",' he said. 'She's very beautiful, though if you ask me in what way I can't answer. I'd say about thirty – dark, with hair cut short and inclined to curl round her face – rather like an older version of Poppy Gifford, with the same sort of face – clean-cut and delicate, but strong, somehow. I really can't tell you any more. Except perhaps that her smile was rather too bright and meant to dazzle – I think that is how she trapped us into that silly conversation. I wasn't thinking consciously then, but now you make me, I'd say the smile was genuine enough, but overlaid with professionalism. As if she smiled to order whether she felt like smiling or not. And I have no idea how I got that impression – unless something about it told me that she wore it like a mask and it didn't mean much.'

'She certainly made an impression on you,' Fran said, somewhat dryly.

He looked up, startled at her tone – and found her looking intently at him. They held each other's eyes for a second, William's inclined to twinkle as a long, slow smile spread over his face. He got up and went to stand over her, giving way to a chuckle that came straight from his heart, forced out of him by surprise and delight.

'I've been wondering if I'd ever hear that tone in your voice again,' he said, 'waiting and hoping that I would. I've really only ever heard it once before – walking home from Hen Street one Sunday when I was about to leave for the USA. It was the first time I ever believed you could love me enough to be jealous – matching my love for you. Now I know – I've caught you out. You even took all this last business about Janice without batting an eyelid – yet I startle you into showing jealousy because I'm able to describe a woman I met for five minutes! That was the truth, because you didn't have time to guard your tongue. Oh, my darling, as if you don't know by now that beauty lies in the eye of the beholder – and that in any case it's always more than skin deep. For me there's only one truly beautiful woman in the whole world, and she's mine, now and for ever.'

He leaned down to her, and then slid to his knees in front of her and took her hands, making her look back at him again. 'My precious, only love,' he said, opening her left hand to kiss the wedding ring before closing her fingers over it, and laying his face on them in her lap. Anthea Pelham and Poppy and Nick and everybody else dissolved into thin air and drifted out of the windows – shadows, not substantial things.

It was much later, after supper, that they returned to the more general content of his visit to Eric.

'So we're no farther forward,' she said.

'No. And we have to accept that. We, like Charlie and Charles, want everybody to be as happy as we are. But we can't make Poppy and Nick happy. We mustn't even try. We must do a much harder thing, and stand aside.

'As Eric made quite clear, without actually intending to, the time's wrong. Other things, by rule of custom, take precedence just at present. However anxious Bob and Effendi are, they have to attend to the business of Bob's farm. And Jane, who ought to have been able to rejoice, is being left at home while they see lawyers, wondering how to deal with her miserable, bad-tempered son who used to be such a paragon. Watching him taking his misery out on everybody, even little Jade and Aggie. She knows what's the matter with him, but can't – knows she mustn't – apply the cure. The Bridgefoots are in the same boat – breaking an age-old pattern and setting up a new one makes nobody but Brian wholly happy. They don't need family problems just now. It's like a row of dominoes, or playing Postman's Knock when the call is "general post" – the circle breaks up and has to be reformed. So we must try to keep out of it, and spend our time counting our blessings.'

She knew he was right. 'I couldn't count my blessings,' she said. 'It would be like trying to count the stars in the Milky Way.'

The long silence that followed her remark was very eloquent. She broke it by being deliberately flippant.

'I nearly said "My cup runneth over", but though I have quite a lot to say for clichés in the ordinary way, I'm not very happy with that one. Cups running over are anything but nice – slopping over, dripping stuff that's too hot or too cold in your lap, or making you all wet and sticky – and if you try to put them down they leave rings on your polished table or the carpet. Really, people shouldn't parrot things like that just because they come from the Bible, without thinking about what they mean.'

'Words don't mean as much to everybody as they do to you,' he replied. 'Most folk just like to show off by quoting. You don't. You dip into your treasure chest and always find something exactly right. Most people can't.'

'Then they shouldn't try,' she said. 'Poets make magic with words. When magic goes wrong, it's dangerous. Like the fashion for calling Kipling a racist because they can quote "*O, East is East and West is West and never the twain shall meet*", without knowing that it's only the first line of a stanza that means exactly the opposite to what they accuse him of. One should think about what one is saying, and how it may be interpreted. But Jess got it right about the men here being such a nice lot, didn't she? I don't know where else you could find such a gathering of winners – from any point of view. You and Greg and Eric and Bob and Elyot and Effendi – and Nigel and George and Charles and Nick –'

'And Joe and Daniel and Kid Bean and Arnold Bailey and Darren his son and –'

'Stop it!' she said. 'Now you're not thinking. Joe and Daniel, yes. Not the others.'

'You're simply proving my cliché about beauty being in the eye of the beholder. In his way, Arnold Bailey's quite a good-looker, big and handsome, and he knows how to dress. You can't compare Eric with Elyot for looks, now can you? Or George Bridgefoot with Effendi, though they're both older. *You* see what they are, not what they look like. And because you love us, you see us all through rose-coloured glasses.'

'I won't yield that George isn't every bit as handsome as Effendi,' she said. 'Or Nigel, if it comes to that – as a looker he takes a lot of beating. I love him but I don't know much about him. We know the others well, even Eric hiding his soft, broken heart under that businessman's carapace. Nigel's out on his own though, as his name says – "of the first rank". So why is a man like that without a wife or a family? He's the only one among us all without anybody of his own to love. I want to know why.'

125

William, who had joined in the game to please her, suddenly saw that it had taken a serious turn and that she wanted him to answer. 'I don't know any more than you do,' he said. 'We are all to some extent a mixture of our nature and nurture, and products of our own times. George Bridgefoot and Nicholas Hadley-Gordon and Nigel Delaprime are about the same age, so they have lived through the same times – but in different cultures. George has just followed the same pattern as his father and grandfather, back to the year dot. Effendi was the son of a famous politician, had private tutors at home till he went as a day-boy to his public school, and then up to Oxford still young.

'I don't know about Nigel, but I can guess. Like Kipling – bundled off to a boarding school when he was seven, and then on to a public school where unhappy little boys were turned into men. Boys who weren't allowed to cry, because men don't cry. Public-schoolboys were intended to be Empire builders, not husbands and fathers first. My guess would be that Nigel sublimated his need of women and children by becoming a priest, and has never really ceased to be a man's man first. That's why he was such a marvellous padre in wartime – besides not having anything to prevent him from giving all the best of himself to other men in fear or danger. Greg said *he* would have deserted and been shot rather than not get back to Jess if he had known how much she needed him in wartime. So would I have done – if it had been you carrying my child. I think Nigel is the great man he is because he can still give even the merest stranger of his very best. Those of us with the love of women in our hearts are men all right – but men of a different kind. Does that explanation satisfy you?'

She nodded, afraid to speak. 'He's the right one to talk to about Nick and Poppy,' she said at last, 'when he comes back. But – if you'll agree, I'd like to talk to Beth. Soon.'

126

Of all those they felt obliged to visit and thank for being among the Friends of Benedict's, only Commander Elyot Franks RN, (Rtd) and his wife Beth were unconnected with either Nick or Poppy by blood or marriage, and only they were not involved in some sort of change this Michaelmas. Fran really had no hope of doing anything more than spending a pleasant hour with Beth, keeping her ears open for any hint of truth or rumour. William declined to go with her, though he liked visiting the Old Rectory, being fond of the company of Elyot. He had his own reasons for not accompanying her, and took it upon himself to warn her not to tell them about the Nick–Poppy problem unless they already knew.

He was quite as anxious as Fran to help if there was any way he could – and it had occurred to him that village gossip could give a lead. Had Jane really been able to keep absolutely secret all facts concerning herself and her son for twenty years? And if she had, what tales had been invented to fill the vacuum? He thought that Nick's present despair could be due to a mixture of two things – the great fog of not knowing and not being allowed to know, and the cruel taunts of other children in the past that he couldn't forget. Just what had the village been saying about him and his mother recently, that he might possibly have heard, or even been maliciously told?

It was no use asking Sophie. If she couldn't vouch for the truth of it, she wouldn't be drawn into repeating any gossip. But she had a tendency to 'mother' William when Fran wasn't in evidence, and he proposed this morning to make use of it. If she found him sitting alone looking rather disconsolately idle, he might inveigle her into a chat.

They had now had two days of indolent inactivity, and both had begun to feel restless, though neither would have admitted it to the other. In fact, by now both were wanting to get on with something, especially as all their friends were more than busy. William suspected Fran's intended visit to the Old Rectory was more to fill time than to gather information, and smiled at the remembrance of her little tirade about her cup running over, which came as near as she would come to actually telling him she'd had enough of doing nothing. He, too, confessed to himself that having got all he thought he had wanted, a cup running over with idleness was almost too much of a good thing.

Sophie arrived, as usual, while they were still at the breakfast table, and spent five minutes telling them about Daniel's new arrangement with George Bridgefoot, who was, as she reminded them, 'the first Bridgefoot as ever retired to anything but his coffin'. Her tone was not exactly robust with approval.

Thirz', she disclosed, was having a lot to say about it, mainly because George's new plans involved Daniel. 'What she's a-putting 'erself out about,' said Sophie, 'is 'er rights.' Somebody had told her that if Daniel was still working for George when he turned sixty-five – several years ahead, yet – when he became eligible for his old-age pension, they would have to pay some of it back till Daniel was seventy. Even the fact that in future they wouldn't have to pay George the few shillings a week rent for their cottage 'would be took into account, so Thirz' is 'eard,' Sophie said, and Thirz' had declared 'as she *would* hev her rights, and she wouldn't hev no charity, from George Bridgefoot nor nobody else. Dan'el 'ad paid 'is stamp all them year so's they should get their pensions come 'e was sixty-five, and draw their pensions they would. Dan'el would hev to give up work, do George was still alive and still wanted him.'

'Wait a minute, Sophie,' William protested. 'If Daniel stopped work while he could still go on and George still wanted him to, he'd die of boredom in six months!'

Sophie snorted. 'Thirz'd hev 'er own way if it killed Dan'el and she 'ad to suffer like a 'erring on a gridiron 'erself.'

'What was it about them not having to pay George rent for the cottage any longer?'

'Same as I said,' Sophie retorted. 'George would ha' give 'em their 'ouse outright after all these year, do they 'ad 'ad child'en;

but seeing as they 'adn't, and nobody near to leave it to, he said they could hev it rent-free as long as any of 'em needed it. Thirz' thinks 'e might ha' give 'em it, child'en or no child'en. She says George is so well-britched 'e'd never ha' missed it, and she don't like to hev to be be'olden to 'im for the rest of 'er life. I don't know 'ow it is,' Sophie said grimly, 'but the holder Thirz' gets, the more ungrateful she is. Never satisfied with nothing. It all comes, she says, o' George giving up afore 'e ought, 'stead o' going on working 'is land, like 'is father and grandfather did, till 'e dropped.'

She had had her say, and was now going to work.

'I'm afraid Thirzah has a lot to learn,' William said to Fran. 'Old customs such as fathers handing down to sons are on their way out. Sons no longer expect to inherit family property – land particularly. The aristocracy's affected already, with stately homes being turned into schools and so on to pay death duties. The Thirzahs of this world want it both ways – and that just isn't on. Times change.'

'But people don't – well, not much. Are you sure you won't come with me to see Beth and Elyot? What have you got planned to do, once I'm out of the way?'

'I must write half a dozen letters,' he lied. 'Then if I feel like it, I'll walk down to join you.' So Fran went by herself. He took care to be doing nothing when Sophie brought his coffee into his study, but she got in first.

'If you ain't got nothing better to do than just sit there looking for Sunday,' she said, 'you might come and tell me what to do with them things as you brought back from Cambridge. I just bundled the clo'es into the wardrobe, but them old cardboard boxes full o' musty ol' bits o' paper I never was told what to do with. Are you ever likely to wear them things as I 'ung in the wardrobe again? 'Cos if you want 'em kept proper, you'd better let me put some camphor-balls in with that black thing with the white stuff on it. Don't, it'll be ate by moths. Same with that dolloping thing like a red dressing-gown. Shall I jus' roll 'em up with moth-balls in a old sheet?'

So much for his academic garb! There was no telling whether he might ever have use for them again – but he didn't fancy stinking the Senate House out with moth-balls. 'Leave them to me,' he said. 'I'll deal with them. And to tell you the truth, I don't know what's in those boxes. I don't think I've ever sorted them out since Jess sent them to me when our mother died. I'll go up now and sort them, and throw out the rubbish.'

The telephone rang. It was Fran, ringing from the Old Rectory to say that she had been invited to stay to lunch and that he was invited to join them if he hadn't anything better to do. Did he mind if she stayed, whether he went or not?

'Of course not,' he said. 'Thank Beth for me – but I'm going to be busy. I'm going to sort the stuff I brought home from Cambridge. If I get it finished, I'll walk up and join you. If not, I'll tell Sophie not to bother about lunch here, and we'll eat when you get home.'

'Don't expect me too early then,' she said. So he drank his coffee, and told Sophie he wouldn't stop for lunch and that he'd rather not be disturbed till he'd got the stuff sorted. He went along to the fourth guest bedroom, the one least used. Sophie was absolutely right, of course – he must do something to protect his robes from the ravages of moths, but rejected camphor-balls. Big plastic bags would serve temporarily.

He regarded the boxes, faded with age, with reluctance, but it had to be done. He sat down by the window, piled them at his feet, and took up the nearest one. He untied the knotted string that bound it and lifted the lid.

A photograph, its back towards him, lay on the top and he turned it over. A man in the khaki uniform of an infantry officer of the First World War, bare headed, holding his soldier's cap in his hands, looked back at him.

The face was a younger version of his own. He stared at the hands holding the cap, and his own holding the photograph. They were identical. His own began to tremble as he disengaged the photograph from the rusted paper-clip that held it to a thin sheaf of other yellowing papers. He turned it towards the light and studied the face, especially the eyes – and his heart turned over. He had met his father.

He gazed at it till he could have sworn the eyes were answering him; then, swept by a huge wave of emotion, he raised the photo to his cheek and held it there. He sat back, held it close to him, and let the unbidden tears come.

Fran never visited Beth and Elyot without a feeling of enormous satisfaction for her own part in their metamorphosis – from a parson's daughter heading for miserable spinsterhood and a stiff-as-a-ramrod retired naval officer already over fifty, into this delightful couple simply glowing with happiness and shedding it all round them like a shower of gold. But for her taking a chance on asking the shy bachelor ramrod to her own fiftieth birthday party, the six-month-old baby he was at present tossing up and catching would never have been, nor would Beth be singing as she prepared to take the baby from him and hand it, covered with kisses, to the girl who stood waiting – Emerald Petrie.

The girl was part of the scene. She had always had a lot of social poise, even when half-starved and thinly clothed in spite of the rigours of winter in the draughty, unheated, comfortless house Danesum unrestored had been. Good living and the warm atmosphere of the Old Rectory over the past year had matured her into a striking young woman, though the pre-Raphaelite ethereal quality she had always had was still there. Fran did a rapid calculation – she must be eighteen now, or very near her eighteenth birthday.

Emmy thanked Fran for letting her and her younger sister go to their party. 'It was wonderful,' she said. 'We'd never been to a party before. And Professor Burbage danced with me!'

'I don't wonder,' Fran said. 'You and Ammy looked like a couple of princesses strayed in from fairyland.'

'Yes,' said Elyot, 'we were proud of you – both.' Fran noted the stress on the last word, and wondered what lay behind it. She would probably find out when Emmy had gone with the pram for the baby's morning outing. Beth asked which way she was going.

'If you don't mind, up to Castle Hill. Mrs Bellamy asked me on Saturday evening if I would go up again soon to make sure Jade and Aggie don't forget me, however happy they are. Daddy wanted us to keep together more than anything else. I wish he could know what has happened to us.'

131

'You mustn't take it for granted that he doesn't, you know,' Beth said. She looked after the girl pushing the pram rather sadly, and back again to Fran.

'We're having our first ever little bit of trouble with them,' she said. 'Ammy's sixteen and left school, and Emmy's being a bit difficult.'

Fran found that hard to believe. But, as she had just been thinking, Emmy was no longer a child. 'What's wrong? Throwing her weight about in the house? Staying out too late with boys?'

Beth laughed. She had the most infectious laugh, rather high-pitched and silvery, like tubular bells. 'Good heavens, no!' she said. 'Sometimes I wish she would kick over the traces a bit more. That's what I worry about. She's old before her time. She'd thought it all out before Ammy left school – that as her sister would be free to take over nursemaiding Ailwyn, she should start looking for a job. We'd been so good to them, she said, letting her and Ammy stay together, and having Wyn to look after had made the break from their little brothers easier to bear. But they had known it couldn't last very long, and the time had now come when she, as the elder, must look after herself. I was distressed and said all the wrong things. I asked her why she wasn't happy with us!'

'That's when she broke down and cried – and couldn't stop. I just couldn't comfort her. She was almost exhausted with crying when Elyot appeared. He took it all in at a glance, and just lifted her out of my arms and sat down with her on his knee as if she was no more than six. Fran – I was awed! He just hugged her close to him, holding her tight, and never said a word. After a minute she put her arms round his neck, and her head down on his chest – and the sobbing stopped. I knew just how she felt. He's so solid and strong – and safe. I think it was the first time she'd ever felt that sort of safety since she realized that her father – well, Mr Petrie – was going to die.

'I had enough sense to go away and leave them, so I was in the kitchen when Ammy came in. I kept her there with me and told her why. She knew what it was all about, she said. Then Wyn started grizzling, and I heard both girls rush upstairs to him, so I went back to Elyot – to be comforted myself. He went straight to the point. We'd made ourselves responsible for them – and we had to honour our responsibility. To all intents and purposes, we'd made them our daughters. He hadn't been prepared to find how fond of them we – well, he – had become, and though he couldn't answer for me feeling the same way, he guessed I might. What he would like was for them to go on just as they were, as part of our family. The daughters we might have had if we had met long before we did. I'd been thinking just the same thing myself – but I'd hesitated to suggest it. There's the financial aspect, for one thing; and for another, we hope Wyn won't be an only child. We wouldn't want them to think we were just making sure of two permanent nursemaids and babysitters!'

Elyot had come back in from seeing Emmy off for her walk. He picked up at once the gist of the conversation. 'What's your opinion, Fran?' he asked. 'I think I speak for Beth when I say they've got under our skins. In plain words, we love them – but can we expect them to feel the same way about us – enough to want to stay with us? I guess Beth has raised the cost bogey – which is nonsense. She'll never get used to the truth that I inherited all the de ffranksbridge estate – and am still making a lot of income from it because I had enough sense to reinvest it with Eric and Co. She, bless her, still thinks of money in terms of a poor parson's stipend, and how much is in the collection plate on Easter Sunday. She won't believe that I could almost fund an orphanage and not notice it.'

He hesitated a moment before going on. 'Besides – Beth, my love, don't get upset if I tell Fran the truth, will you? I do have a bit of an ulterior motive. I'm twenty years older than Beth. If nature takes its course, she'll be a widow for a long time. We plan another child – but it may be another boy. I'd die happier if I knew she'd have daughters to care for her in her old age. Is that very selfish of me?'

Beth had assumed what Fran called her 'terrier look'. 'And suppose, Fran,' she said, 'that I die producing our second child, is it selfish of me to think that Elyot would have someone to look after both babies and stop him from drinking himself to death on brandy and ginger ale?' She was so indignantly full of life that Fran burst out laughing. She looked from one to the other.

'If I were you,' she said, 'I shouldn't give such ulterior motives another thought. I should act on instinct, and treat them like the young adults they are. Just put it to them as you have done to me. And do it soon, before Emmy tells you she has got a job as Beryl Bean's live-in skivvy.'

They were about to start lunch when Emmy returned, earlier than they had expected her. She came in with little Ailwyn perched on her hip, and told Beth she'd take him straight upstairs and 'deal with him'. Fran remarked to Elyot that all the Petrie girls seemed to wear babies on them as other girls wore jewellery.

'She wanted to get away,' Beth said. 'Something's upset her. I wonder what on earth it can be?'

Emerald had set out, as she had said, intending to visit Castle Hill. It made a nice long walk, and she could be sure of being fed there while playing with her two little half-brothers, before setting off back. She had done it often before.

She had reached the spot, about 200 yards from the farmhouse, where the ways branched. The main one went on to the house; the other, one of many grass-grown tracks thereabouts, went up to the little church on the hill. At this point, a five-barred gate could be closed to keep cattle one side or the other of it as Bob Bellamy decreed. Today it was shut, and leaning on it, with his back towards her, was Nick.

Emerald didn't actually know Nick, but she knew who he was and quite a lot about him. At the awful time when her mother had deserted them, taking all the boys with her, and their 'daddy' had been in hospital, they had been cared for at Benedict's, where the Franks and the Bellamys were regular visitors. She and Ammy could not but hear and piece together the story of Jane, her son, and Bob Bellamy. But the son had been involved in an accident which had first put him into a deep coma, and afterwards left him with no memory at all of his early life. So he had not been much in evidence anywhere in the village since she and her sister Amethyst had been given shelter at the Old Rectory, after their father had died on the trip to Wales to try to find their little brothers. It was after that that Mr and Mrs Bellamy had taken the two youngest, Jade and Agate, and kept them. She and Ammy had been given to understand they were always welcome to go and visit them, and Nick had occasionally been there, but as he remembered nothing, not even who his best friend, Charles Bridgefoot, was, she had not spoken more than a dozen words to him.

It was not to be expected that he would remember them, even though they had been bridesmaids at a wedding at which he had been best man. He had had no eyes for anybody but the chief bridesmaid, Poppy Gifford.

She and Ammy had rather envied Poppy, and had been a bit disappointed that Nick had not come early enough to take part in the dancing at Saturday's party; they had also been aware that when he did come, Poppy had rushed away.

Emerald didn't know now whether to speak to him, or not. She slowed up to give him the chance to speak first, but when she got near enough, she saw that his head was down on his arms on the top bar of the gate, and that his shoulders were heaving. *He was crying.*

She had neither maturity nor experience to help her deal with such a situation. It didn't surprise her that a man should cry – in her sad young life she had caught her 'father' in tears more than once, and after he died she knew that Dr Burbage had wept for him. Those tears had added honour and reverence to other feelings she already had for William. She had thought him the most wonderful man in the world – matchless indeed – until the other day when Commander Franks had comforted her. But she had never seen the Commander cry. As far as she understood, in the ordinary course of events, men didn't cry. Especially modern young men. So what could be the matter with Nick? Was he ill? Had something dreadful happened on the farm, or in the house? If so, she shouldn't go on without knowing.

She pulled the pram to the side of the road, and waited. She didn't know how to address him. 'I beg your pardon,' she said at last, 'but are you all right? Can I do anything to help?'

He swung round as if he had been stung, and she saw his face, blubbered with tears, crease into a scowl as he recognized her. His voice was like hoar-frost and his eyes like ice. 'Thank you – I am quite all right.'

He turned away to lean on the gate again. But her ears were

135

sharp, and she heard him mutter as he did so, 'That's all I wanted. Another bloody Petrie!'

She was not a redhead for nothing. The blood flooded into her face till it almost matched her pre-Raphaelite hair. She jammed on the brake of the pram and left it where it was as she stormed down the grassy verge towards him.

'I heard that!' she said. 'What do you mean? What have you got against the Petries? What have any of us ever done to you? Whatever's the matter with you now isn't my fault. And who on earth do you think you are, to speak like that about my family?'

There could hardly have been words in the whole English lexicon more guaranteed to take the last remnants of his self-control from him than those she had uttered. Who did he think he was? He didn't know, and he was beyond thinking. A red flush of shame at his churlish behaviour rushed into his tear-blotched face, and then drained away again, leaving it very white and taut. He mumbled an apology.

The anger that had flared in her died at the sight, and she went towards him. 'Something awful must be wrong,' she said. 'I was on my way up to see your mother and my little brothers. Is anything wrong? Ought I to intrude? Please tell me.'

He had, at any rate, stopped crying. He dried his face, and didn't turn away from her again. 'I do think it would be better if you didn't go up just now,' he said. 'As a matter of fact, there's been the most God-Almighty row. Mum's crying up in her bedroom, my step-father's stumped off and shut himself in the church, and Grandfather and I have quarrelled – he's dreadfully upset and has gone back to our cottage to be by himself. Nobody wants me! Not even my mother. I seem to have lost her – to Grandfather and Bob Bellamy and to those two kids. That's why I was nasty to you. They're much more important to her than I am. I'm nobody, and nobody wants me. That's what the row was all about.'

'Because you were jealous of Jade and Aggie?' she asked, incredulously.

'Well, no – not really. It's all my fault, I suppose. I asked a question and they wouldn't answer it. I got nasty, and said a lot I ought not to have done.'

He was still very pale, and he looked round for somewhere to sit down. He sank on to the grass at the bottom of the gate, and leaned back against it. She took a look into the pram, saw that the baby was asleep, and went to sit down by him.

'Where do Jade and Aggie come into it, then? Was your question about them? Because if it was, perhaps I can answer it.'

'No, they really had nothing to do with it. Only – I had to be nasty to somebody about something. I just can't stand not knowing any longer. I asked them outright when they were all there – and none of them would answer me. They just won't tell me.'

'Won't tell you what?'

If she had not been so sure that it was something concerning her little brothers that had caused the row, she would have known better than to ask; but she had asked – and the one thing he needed most was somebody to tell. What did it matter if he told this girl who was a stranger, more or less, and hadn't known him when he was a child?

'Who I am. Who my father was. Why they won't tell me.' And out poured all his anxieties, though without any reference to Poppy.

Emerald listened quietly and sympathetically, because he was very much her own age and she knew how easy it was to get upset and worried when there was no grown-up you could talk to. She didn't, however, comprehend the reason for him being in such despair and bitterness.

She said so. 'Does it matter to you so much?' she asked. 'Compared to all you have got, I mean? I'm sure you can't really believe your mother doesn't love you or want you any longer. Look how she looked after you when you were ill! She's so happy to have got you back with her, as well as having your grandfather and Mr Bellamy. She's looking after my two little brothers out of gratitude because she is so happy, I think. Aren't you spoiling it for her by showing her how jealous you are? Why on earth should you be jealous? It just means you've just got more people to love and to love you.'

'Then why won't they tell me who I am?'

'I don't know – but I can't see why it matters to you enough to make them all miserable. If it comes to that, I don't know who my father is, either – but to tell the truth, I don't want to. Mr Petrie was the Daddy who brought us all up, and we loved him,

137

though none of us but Jasper is really his. I suspect all eight of us had different fathers, so it wouldn't be any good me asking – I don't suppose my mother would remember, anyway. At least you have a real mother – mine's a hippy drug addict. What on earth have you got to grumble about?'

He was shocked by her frankness, embarrassed that he had caused her to disclose what she had, and ashamed of himself. 'I'm sorry,' he said – and this time he meant it.

'What for? Everybody in Old Swithinford knows about us. Or did you mean you were sorry for asking and upsetting your mother? She'd have told you long before now if she'd wanted you to know. I can't see what good you are doing making such a fuss about it now – you can't alter it, any more than I can. You're only hurting your mother for nothing. You're you, whoever your father was. Like I'm me. As far as I am concerned, my father was the man who loved me, and I loved him. I've never had what you'd call a mother. If your mother had died, like my father has, I would feel sorry for you.' She got up. 'Thank you for telling me, so that I didn't go up to the house and make it worse for your mother. What are you going to do, now?'

'Clear off somewhere by myself. Go away till they miss me. Be by myself, and get used again to being a nobody.'

She gave him such a look of scornful disdain that he coloured all over again, and she turned the pram and strode off back to the Old Rectory. She was indignantly angry with Nick for making such a song and dance about something that could only stir up trouble. He'd gone down considerably in her estimation – and, into the bargain, had brought back her anxiety about her own problem, which had only been temporarily solved by Mr Franks's kindness to her. She was almost back at the Old Rectory when it occurred to her that if that silly boy went off and hid himself for the rest of the day, or didn't go home tonight, his family would go out of their minds with worry. She was the only one who had any idea that he was only proposing to take himself off to sulk. She had no option but to tell Mrs Franks about her encounter with him. Elyot had gone into his study, but Fran was still chatting to Beth when Emerald went down.

*

'I'll go up there and tell them,' said Fran at once. 'William isn't expecting me back yet. If he comes after getting his job finished, send him up to Castle Hill after me.' She turned to Emmy. 'I think you said Mr Bellamy had gone to sit in the church. He often does that when he has important things to think about. I shall go first to the church, to see if I can catch him.'

He was still there, sitting in one of the front pews, and communing not only with himself but with all the ghosts of the past that he found there, and which had soothed his troubled spirit many times before. He didn't turn round when he heard the creak of the door, expecting it to be Nick. He wasn't ready, yet, to deal with the boy. That was for Jane and her father to do before he interfered. His great soft heart was lacerated for them all, though especially for Jane, because he loved her most, and he knew that in the end only he would be able to comfort her. But not yet. Not until the cause for all the distress had been removed, and that he couldn't do. In this particular issue, he was still the outsider – and must remain so till he was called on.

Once inside the church, he had soon begun to feel the solace of the quiet, the beauty, and the silent presences that only he could hear. His fenland sixth-sense, always at its most keen when he was in any trouble, was also telling him that this was really no more than a ripple on the surface of their general content.

He was sorry for Nick, who after all had never really been able to go through the usual storms of adolescence. He had been too careful not to do anything to add to his mother's sorrow by complaining at that time when most boys have tantrums, or get themselves into difficulties and blame everybody but themselves. Nick had been far too mature for his age, then, compared with Charles or Robert, his two best friends. Before he had had the chance to absorb the shock and grief of Robert's death, he had been knocked out – and when he had found himself again, his whole world had changed. Bob was pretty sure that the scene they had had this morning was only a belated and accumulated tantrum from his lost adolescence. There was probably a girl in it somewhere, and who could that be but Poppy Gifford? Nick, he thought, had used the question of his illegitimacy as a peg to hang all the rest of his unhappiness on. He had been nasty and

139

belligerent and rude in a way no one had ever seen him before. And he had foolishly dared to ask who his father was. 'Silly young fathead!' Bob thought – but that's all it was. He was still so young.

Bob was angry only because of Nick's attack on Jane. He would deal as gently as he possibly could with the boy – but not at Jane's expense. And till she asked him to interfere, he would stay on the sideline, be there when she wanted him, and try not to let her see just how grieved he was for her. He was also irritated with Nick – from whom no other secrets had ever been kept – for throwing this fit just at the moment when he and Effendi were dealing with the last legal matters concerning the purchase of Castle Hill Farm. But then, wasn't that always the way? The sweetest things were always better for a pinch of salt.

His face lit up at the sight of Fran. He didn't stop to ask himself why she was there – he knew at once. He beckoned her to come and sit beside him, and took her into his arms and kissed her when she did. Since he had Jane, and she had now married William, neither of them had any inhibitions about it. Their friendship was of a very special kind.

She didn't waste time. She simply told him what she had come to say, and how she knew about what had happened.

'We knew already, from Charles and Charlie, that Nick was boiling up for this,' she said. 'It's all to do with Poppy Gifford, of course. But we had no idea that he would cause such an earthquake. I can't see why it matters so much to him, under all his other circumstances. William's more sympathetic, because he says he would have liked to know a bit more about his own father, who was killed just before he was three. I suppose people like you and Charles – and even me, don't bother much. We know, even if what we know isn't as good as it might be – which incidentally is what's wrong with Poppy Gifford, according to Charlie.

'But William thinks that what's really bugging Nick is his complete ignorance of who or what his father was – so there's a vacuum that imagination may be rushing in to fill with all sorts of fears and horrors. Bob – if William's right, won't such fantasies be even more real now that he has asked and an answer of any kind has been refused? Couldn't you tell him, and not let Jane or

Effendi know you had done? Or, at least till he settles down again, just tell him something.'

Bob shook his head. 'No, my pretty, I can't – and if I could, I wouldn't. It's Jane's business, and hers only. Even her father hasn't the right to interfere between her and her son. And I can't, because I don't know any more than he does. I've never asked and she's never told me. What difference could it make to me? I love her and she loves me. Why should I want to make her unhappy by stirring up things past? If it has to come out because of what Nick's doing now, I shall stand by her. It'll all come right in the end. Are you coming up to see Jane?'

'No. I should say too much – and it really isn't anything to do with me. And you're right, you mustn't. Jane just can't. That leaves only one other person who can. If all his diplomatic training can't help him deal with it, it's a pity. I'm going to call to see him.'

She stood up, and so did he, his head on one side, as if listening. Then he leaned forward and kissed her. 'Yes, you do that. They agree.' She knew what he meant. His sixth sense was satisfied with that plan. She believed entirely in that great gift of fenland feyness he had inherited from generations of his pagan ancestors. That he should come closest to them in a Christian church was just another mystery.

He told her he had a premonition that Nick would come to find him in the church first, so he'd go now to make sure that all was well with Jane and the boys, and if necessary, come back and spend the night in the church waiting for Nick.

She left it in his hands, and went briskly homeward by the road that would take her past the cottage which Effendi had rented for the summer.

Nicholas Hadley-Gordon, better known to all his friends in Old Swithinford as Effendi, greeted Fran with his usual suave courtesy, but she had no need to be told that beneath it was a very distressed man. She said she had just come from Bob, knew all about the trouble at Castle Hill, and was only reporting what Emerald Petrie thought they ought to know – that Nick had declared to her his intention of taking himself off 'for as long as it took' before going home again.

'My dear Fran,' said Effendi, 'how good of you. Naturally, we should have believed that he had run away – or worse. We didn't think anyone would know.'

'It's the village grapevine, luckily bearing fruit this time,' Fran replied. 'It won't go any further. It was absolutely by chance that Emmy met Nick, and that I was with Beth when Emerald came back and felt she had to tell to save you from worry. Beth shied away from any interference – but I knew Bob would understand if I went directly to him. He did – though he's just as adamant as Beth that he can't and won't interfere with what is Jane's business only. He said he doesn't know the answer to Nick's question, has never asked, and doesn't want to know now – unless it would make Jane happier. His concern is mostly for her, though he hates to see you and Nick in such distress. I'm just a messenger, Effendi. That's all.

'But I did know before today that Nick was upset, and why. Charles and Charlie know all about it, though not how to deal with him. They told us, and asked our advice. I'm afraid we're very much like Bob. We'd like to help, but don't know how.'

'Do come in,' he said. 'I'd like to talk to you. I can't disclose the answer Nick wants, because it's a quite impossible situation. So forget that part of it, and just turn your mind to the problem of how we deal with Nick under these circumstances.

'Jane, of course, understands him better than anybody else, because she knows what he endured as a child, being illegitimate and in such poverty. I'm glad I don't – but as it happens, I am in a position to guage what damage would be done to other innocent people by telling him the truth. That simply isn't an option. So he's hurt and angry, and ready to explode, and whatever he does is bound to blow all Jane's new-found happiness sky-high.'

'You've missed out one significant factor in Nick's distress,' she said. 'That he's in love.'

He shook his head. 'Jane hasn't. She's known about Poppy since he first met her. Remember how worried she was about Poppy being Charlie's bridesmaid, because it would mean Poppy having to come down the aisle with Nick when he didn't even recognize her? When he regained his memory in the very nick of time, we were all so overjoyed we felt the problem was solved, which was naïve and silly of us. What's happened between them now, we just don't know. Except that whatever it is has changed him again, this time into somebody we hardly recognize. A touchy, bitter, angry, even unstable young man. We're desperately worried what it may do to him on medical grounds. He'll have to go back to the clinic if he shows any more signs of mental imbalance. All our hopes down the drain.'

He sat back with his eyes closed. Fran saw him as an old man for the first time. A splendid athlete defeated as the tape came in sight.

'Do you know why Poppy has withdrawn?' she asked.

'Jane asked. Nick says she has another man – boyfriend or lover – at college. I'm pretty sure that isn't true. Nick's made that up because he can't bring himself to tell Jane what he believes to be the truth. He remembers his childhood all too well now. You know how cruel children can be. Then when he and Poppy were in their teens, her father made it very clear to him that he wasn't good enough for his daughter. Poppy was forbidden to see him – she daren't let her father know they even had a cup of coffee and a bun together in the school canteen. When she began to avoid him after Charlie's wedding, he jumped to the conclusion that it was because she's a Bridgefoot, and he, as far as this village goes, is only – forgive me for using his term – "a charwoman's bastard". Even Bob didn't meet Gifford's standard. That Nick's your grandson can't wipe out what people in this village knew of him before you turned up.'

'And *is* that Poppy's reason?'

'If it were,' said Fran stoutly, 'Nick would be well rid of her. But it isn't. The boot's entirely on the other foot. She may be one of the Bridgefoot clan – but she can't forget that she's also Vic Gifford's daughter and Pansy's – Pansy Bailey's – twin sister. She thinks *she's* tarred with the Bailey brush – and is simply not good enough for him now. She loves him too much to run the risk of dragging him back to where he was by any association with her. And I think, though I don't know, that she's also terribly afraid of being hurt more than she is already. Afraid that what he feels for her now may only be the remnants of calf-love, and that if she dares to let herself believe in it, he'll throw her over as soon as he's found his feet among the girls of the class he really belongs to. Yours and Jane's. Oh, Effendi – they're both so young! And love hurts so much then.'

'More than it does when you're older? You know better than that. But there's no way I can see that we can do anything to stop the pain for either of them.'

Fran sat silent for a minute or two, before speaking again. 'Effendi,' she said, 'I don't want to be told any details – but do you think you could go as far as explaining to me *why* it is that Nick may not be told what he wants to know?'

He got up and stood looking out of the window of the cottage, thinking of that dreadful time twenty-odd years ago. He spoke in a flat, deadpan voice, without turning. 'I was abroad, doing my job, when Jane's mother developed cancer. We knew there was no hope for her, so we got Jane out to be with her till she died. Then Jane refused to leave me to come back to England and Oxford. It was all my fault. I let her stay, but I couldn't adjust, even with her there. When the chance came, I left her – as I thought – safe with my deputy.

'When I went back, Jane had gone missing. They had assumed she had come to join me. I found a note from her – simply stating that she had found herself pregnant, so for my sake she would disappear. It's not very easy for a British citizen to do that, you know. Embassies in foreign countries exist largely to see that they don't, or to help trace them if they do. So of course I tried everything in my power – and got nowhere. What was obvious was that she must have had help, presumably from the father of her child, who in turn must have known the ropes. I guessed him to be one of our latest bunch of recruits – someone, in fact, on my own staff. That didn't make it any easier. Till I met Jane again and she told me, I had no inkling who.

'It's a dispensation of providence that life has to go on. Anguish, physical or mental, turns into a dull ache with the passing of time. One fact kept some hope alive in me: Jane knew how and where to find me if ever she needed or wanted to. The fact that she never tried was perhaps the worst of all to bear. I thought she blamed me. I certainly blamed myself. I'd begun to feel very lonely when I found Jane again, and Nick. I wasn't alone, after all. It had all turned out better than I had any right to hope for – until now. You and William may possibly work out for yourselves the reasons why we can't now tell Nick the whole of it. But we have to do something. If only I knew where to begin.'

Fran had listened with sympathy that amounted to pain, mostly because of her own helplessness. As always, in instances of this kind, she tried to hold off her own pain by thinking philosophically and recalling parallels. What struck her now was the thought that whatever people advised about putting the past behind you, in truth it could never be done. Memories, even repressed memories, find their own outlet somewhere. William's nightmare, Elyot's 'black dog', Eric's grief, Sophie's remembrance of Jelly, and the death of young Robert Fairey – which in fact had been the beginning of Pansy's association with the Baileys, bringing the wheel full circle. It wasn't fair! Hadn't Jane and her father suffered enough to compensate for any wrong or foolish act committed long ago?

He turned towards her at last, and sank again into his chair; she spoke with all her sympathy in her voice. She didn't propose to try to solve any mystery, she said – but she had an inkling of a course of action that might help. She, without thinking, had perhaps asked the right question. Not the same question that Nick had asked – the one he might be afraid to ask. *Why couldn't he be told?*

'Is he possibly letting his imagination run riot because something has to fill the vacuum in his knowledge? Making mountains out of molehills – or volcanoes out of smouldering bonfires? Imagining that his father may have been a serial murderer, or that Jane might have been raped by a terrorist – or that he may even be the result of incest? I think if you were to tell him as much as you have just told me, it would at least act as an antidote to such wild fantasies. There's mystery enough in the story to intrigue him, and explanation enough to make him see why his childhood was as it was. As I heard the story there was neither shame nor blame in it. His mother and you were both victims. She, young and innocent as she was, coped. A lot for him *to be proud of.* Why don't you try it?'

She didn't wait for a reply, but got up and left abruptly, and hurried home.

*

After the first great wave of emotion had receded, William still sat with the photograph of his father in his hands, as reluctant to put it down as he would have been to say goodbye to the living man. All sorts of feelings were revived in him. The first thoughts to break surface were that, though he had no memories at all of ever seeing his father alive, he knew him; not only because at twenty-five he must himself have been almost a physical replica, but because at that age they had been in similar situations – helpless against forces too great for them to change. At war, parted from everything they loved, and facing death from minute to minute. The expression and the eyes of the dead father spoke directly to his living son. And those hands, so like his own.

The photo was signed on the front – in writing that might also have been William's. '*T.m. D.L. Tommy*'. Which didn't make sense. His father's name was not Tommy, and there was nothing to suggest that it was a facetious reference to Tommy Atkins. The captain's insignia forbade that explanation, as well as the pose and expression. They were those of a seasoned soldier, well aware that this might be the very last time he could ever send anything of himself home. To whom? To his wife and his baby son? So Tommy was perhaps his nickname, or a pet-name or even a secret love-name used only between himself and his woman – just as he, William, left kisses in Fran's hand that nobody else in the whole world shared, or knew of their deep significance.

The woman must have been his mother. It was sad that he had no memory of her at all before she had become Mrs Henry Wagstaffe – tall, slender, bright, vivacious, purposeful, and still quite young. He reached for her in the deep recesses of his memory, but she didn't come to him in the same way as this unknown father did.

Jess had the family photographs, and he had seen them. Up-market photographs of couples named Wagstaffe – his mother and her civil-service husband, and Fran's parents, a brigadier and his wife. His mother must have been something of a social butterfly, in the immediate aftermath of the war, after her remarriage to a 'somebody' high in the civil service. Which could account for him never having seen much of her, especially after he had been sent to his first preparatory school – at Cambridge, luckily, where he was near enough to spend all his exeat weekends with 'Grandfather' at Benedict's, as well as all the long holidays.

A lot of middle-class children like him and Fran must have lost out on home life during those confused, strange, between-the-war years. Fran's father had been in the Territorial Army before the outbreak of hostilities, and had soon risen to the rank of brigadier. He had, no doubt, expected to return home and take his father's place, one day, but that day had never come. After the war, there was very little of the inheritance he had been brought up to expect for him to come back to. A small, run-down estate, an old house in a very sad state of repair, and nothing else much but the shadow of the next war looming nearer and ever nearer. After the Armistice, he, too had moved around a good deal, taking his family with him until Fran had had to be left where she could go to school. He could hardly be blamed for taking the good job overseas from which he had never returned.

It suddenly became very clear to William why all his cherished memories of childhood were centred on Benedict's. That was where family life had been – the stability, the freedom, the love, the companionship. Though perhaps their children had suffered a bit, the parents could hardly be blamed. The generation to which they belonged had dared to look neither back nor forward. No wonder they had become hedonistic, taking what they could for themselves with both hands while it was still there to be taken. Their children had grown up in a great gap left by the removal of a whole generation of men – either dead or frenetically seeking life wherever it could be found. For some the gap had been closed by grandparents. People like Grandfather.

William the historian saw the pattern of those years whole as he had never done before – children and grandparents trying to close the aching gap, in mining villages as well as country estates, in London's slums as well as in ancestral homes.

Was it at that time the Gainsborough had had to go – to help finance his own and Jess's and Fran's education? There were no boys, other than himself. Yet he and Grandfather had been almost as close as if they had been of the same blood.

Poor old Grandfather – he was the one who had had to square his shoulders, accept his fate, and be satisfied with second best.

147

And in spite of all he had done for them, his three grandchildren had in the end all deserted him, and left him to die alone. That was as much his doing as theirs, of course – because he had foreseen that the only real property he could endow them with, and of which they couldn't be robbed in future, was a proper education. He had made sure that all three of them had gone to a university, from which they had never returned, being in their turn as hedonistic as their parents, and for much the same reasons. Old England had gone, and in its place, especially in East Anglia, were airfields, prophesying another war.

William felt sorrow, but no guilt, that he didn't feel towards his parents the same love as he did for Grandfather – or for him whose photograph he still held in his hands.

Why had nobody ever told him anything about his father? 'Be fair,' he told himself. There was only one person who could have done – a war-widow left with a little boy to do her best for. He had never heard of her family, perhaps because she had none. The Wagstaffes must have reached a conscious decision that he should be brought up entirely as one of them.

He was suddenly very grateful to them that they had not changed his name. It was the only actual bond between him and this dead soldier. A bond that was tugging at his heart-strings. He wanted to know his father better. What could that inscription possibly tell him? '*T.m. D.L. Tommy*'.

He laid the picture down at last, and read the papers he had detached from it. The telegram from the War Office announcing Capt. Burbage's death in action; the usual letter from his Commanding Officer. Nothing more? Had 'Tommy' really been just another of the millions killed on the Somme? Finis – just like that?

*Finis?* No. There had to be more, or why was there as much as there was? What else was in this box, and the others? He lifted another layer from the box on his knees. Something square, wrapped in a man's handkerchief that bore brown stains. Untie the knot. A square presentation box which when opened showed him his father's posthumous Military Cross. The citation, folded in with it, told how he and the tiny remnant of his platoon had held a gun emplacement till the last of them was dead, but long

148

enough to enable many times their own number to retreat. William was filled with helpless anger. Why had nobody ever told his son about that?

He studied the pictured face again, his heart aching with love. It was not that of a man hardened to, or hardened by war. Not the sort who even in such a tight spot would have believed that it was right for him to think only 'Kill or be killed'. His eyes met William's with a message in them as clear as if it had been spoken. *'You know how it feels, don't you, son? You've been there, too.'*

William sat still, communicating with his father. There was a bundle of letters which were, he could see by the writing, those of his mother to her soldier husband. He unfolded one and skimmed through it, feeling guilty. Perhaps he had no right so to intrude upon their private life; yet after a few lines, he knew that that was not the reason. Intuition warned him that they would hurt him too much. So he left them lying, and glanced into the other boxes. From what he could see, all were filled with old papers, some handwritten, some typed. Business letters, probably. All the sort of things his mother would have had to deal with when she had made up her mind to marry again. He piled the boxes neatly on the floor of the wardrobe and shut the door on them, to give his attention back to the box whose contents did matter to him very much indeed.

He was glad, for once, that Fran was not at hand, so that he could not leave what he was doing to go and seek comfort or consolation from her. In his highly emotional mood, the sight and sound and scent and feel of her would have undone him altogether. Besides, he wanted to be alone with his father, to have his father just for the next half-hour all to himself. And he also wanted his father to have him, and only him, for a little while, too. He put all but the photograph back into the box, and put the box away with the others. Then he took the photo to his study, and sat down to commune with it again. And again. And again.

His watch told him that it could not be long before Fran was home again. He had never felt reluctant to share anything with her before – but in this case he must wait for the right moment. He picked the photograph up for one last look before putting it

149

into the locked drawer with Bob's book. His fingertips told him he had missed something: something tucked between the print and its mount. A small, thin scrap of paper. The last-ever message of love?

He used his ivory paper knife to ease it from its hiding place, and then, with gentle fingertips, smoothed the creases out. The handwriting was small and fine. Not a letter – a poem, *To My Dear Love*.

He read it again and again, his trained visual memory committing it at once to memory. Not that he could ever forget it. It was his father's heart, sent home from a shell-hole, in words meant only for one pair of eyes and to ring forever in one pair of ears.

William refolded it, and restored it exactly to the place from which he had taken it – behind the left breast-pocket of the soldier's tunic. Where the living heart had still been beating, hoping and expecting that the symbolism of his putting it there would be understood. The pain was almost more than William could bear. He knew now why he had been so reluctant to read those letters. His mother had never seen the poem, had never looked long enough at the photograph to have found it. She was not the same sort of woman as Fran.

Of course, to be fair to her, he had to concede that she might not have got the letter and the photograph until after her husband was dead. He had no right to judge her; she had been left alive, no lonelier perhaps after her husband's death than she had been for the past two years. Already, maybe, looking into the future rather than dwelling on the past. And yet – he had every right to think what it would have meant to his father, had he ever known. William's eyes sent a message to those other eyes. *'I'm like you in more than looks, Father. I know, too, what it means to love.'*

He locked the drawer hastily, hearing car wheels on the gravel, and went to the door to meet his own dear love.

Nick scrambled to his feet when Emerald left him, and stood for a moment watching her rather hurried but resolute progress down the slope that soon hid her from his sight. Then he turned back to the gate to lean on it again and think about their extraordinary conversation. Though she was more or less his own age, he hardly knew her, but that hadn't prevented her from being staggeringly forthright with him. In fact, she had jolted him several times.

For one thing, he didn't need her to tell him what his mother had had to endure, not only in all the lonely years of bringing him up, but also when his life had been in the balance and his future, if there was to be one, that of a brain-damaged invalid. Nothing he had so far suffered bore any relation to what she had had to cope with.

The remembrance of her as she had been when in his temper he had rushed out of the house an hour or two ago made him wish he was a worm that could crawl into a hole and never been seen again. After trying for a long time to keep her patience with him, her voice calm and her temper that of her usual reasonable and loving dignity, she had suddenly broken into a passion of tears and sobbed until Bob had taken the tear-sodden mass of her upstairs, and come down without her.

He had then tried to reason with Nick, in his usual sympathetic way – but whatever he said, Nick had silently and angrily ignored. The last straw had been that in his colloquial way, Bob had called him 'mate'. Nick's response had been one of fury that this rural tomnoddy, who had married his mother before she'd had time to take any advantage of what her father was prepared to do for her, should expect their relationship to include him in any sort of familiarity. Bellamy was not his father, whoever else had been, and need not think he would ever be regarded as a stepfather. At nearly twenty-one, he, Nick, could do without either.

Bob, reading and understanding him, had said no more. He had picked up the younger of the two Petrie babies, now almost a year old, kissed him and cuddled him, and set him down again, giving him a finger to hang on to while he tried a few tottering steps. Then he had picked Aggie up under one arm, taken Jade by the hand, and led them out. Jane was in no state to care for them, so he had bundled both into the car and taken them to the gamekeeper's wife who helped in the house, and whom the babies knew well and didn't mind being left with.

That had left only Nick and his grandfather together in the huge room, which seemed vaster and less comfortable to Nick than it had ever done before. But of all of those involved, the one who would best understand his feelings and sympathize with him the most was still there. He threw himself into a chair facing his grandfather.

Effendi, however, was no longer simply a passive observer. He had risen to his feet, and stood tall, stately, unsmiling, looking down on the fuming youth. Not Effendi now, but Mr Hadley-Gordon, the mature, seasoned diplomat well versed in dealing with upstart youngsters who were taking too much for granted. Before Nick could find his tongue, the elder man addressed him coldly.

'Stand up, if you wish to speak to me, and before you say anything, listen to what I have to say to you. The moment Mr Bellamy reappears, you will offer him a full apology for your behaviour. I only hope he will accept it.'

Nick got to his feet, his face suffused with shame and anger. 'Apologize to him? That – that yokel? What for?'

'For your unwarranted discourtesy, to any man, whoever he is, in his own house. For insulting one so much your senior, and especially one to whom you owe so much. By doing so, for demeaning your mother, who happens to be his wife. And for demeaning me, because as you are my grandson I expect you to behave like the gentleman you were born.'

The likeness between them in their anger was unmistakable. Nick's lip curled.

'Oh! So I was born a gentleman, was I? *Then why don't you tell me who I am?* Where were you when I was being dragged up as a pauper child in a bumpkin's hovel? Didn't working in the fields, half-starved, demean my mother, as you put it? You can't have it both ways. I may not know who I am, but till you answer my question, I shan't apologize to anybody, especially to that oaf! A fen-tiger who can't even speak the Queen's English and took advantage of my mother when she had nobody else to turn to. Do you think I don't know what the village people think of him – and her? You should just hear them. I have to. However rich and high and mighty you may be, to the village folk I am only Bob Bellamy's molly's bastard. If you know different, why don't you tell me?'

He was aware that he had gone too far, but had no idea now

how to retreat. The cold, proud disdain he read in the face on which he had never before seen anything but kindness and love told him what a fool he was making of himself, but he couldn't stop. Nor, having voiced such a challenge, could he now allow himself to be defeated.

Effendi's face and stance matched his voice when he spoke again.

'Very well. I will tell you – not who you are, but *what* you are – in my estimation. You are an ignorant young puppy who deserves a good whipping. An arrogant, ungrateful, callow, adolescent fourth-former. An unbearable young idiot I'm ashamed of ever having introduced to anybody as my grandson. An unmannerly cad who deserves to have his behind kicked –' He stopped, only because he had heard Bob's tread on the stairs, first going up, and then softly coming down again.

Bob put his head round the door, where one glance was enough to tell him what was afoot, and said simply, 'Jane's cried herself to sleep. Don't wake her. I'll be in the church if I'm wanted.'

Effendi gave Nick no chance to take advantage of the interruption. He went on, coldly. 'You realize, I suppose, that this may destroy the status quo and put an end to other plans that were being made? I need time to consider this new situation. So I shall now go back to the cottage – alone. My advice to you is to go somewhere by yourself as well and do a bit of thinking on your own behalf.'

He strode out, his handsome grey head held high, his step firm and unhurried. He did not give his shaken grandson even a glance as he passed him.

'Grandfather,' stuttered the boy. 'Don't go.' There was pleading in his voice, but it fell on deaf ears. There was no response. Nick in desperation followed him to the door, and watched him set off down the path towards the cottage. Then he began to blubber, having no idea whatsoever what to do next. He followed his grandfather at a distance until he reached the gate – but the older man never once looked back. At the gate, Nick gave up, and stopped. Leaning on it, he was just in time to see Bob take the key from its hiding place in the ivy, unlock the porch and go inside the little church.

Nick was now alone. He viewed the desolation his temper had caused, and was still sobbing helplessly at the gate when Emerald found him. His anger had left him limp, robbed of all energy. He had nowhere to go. When Emerald's back was out of sight he felt more isolated than he had felt in all his life. His feet simply would not lead him away from the spot which, however he had reviled it, still spelt 'home'. He blindly climbed the gate, lay down under the hedge on the other side, and went on crying.

Later, Nick watched Bob leave the church and make his way back to the farmhouse. He was excluded from there as well as everywhere else. There was no present, no future. There was a past – but that was too painful to recall, especially the bits that had included Poppy. He had neither will nor strength to get up from his ditch, so he just lay there in the tall grass for what seemed like an eternity. He wasn't hungry; he wanted nothing but for time, which appeared to be standing still, to go backwards. Exhausted, he dropped into a doze, from which he woke, stiff and cramped and cold, to find dusk already falling. His problems had not gone away. Soon it would be night, and he had to find shelter somewhere. Keeping to the other hedge of the field, he crawled as far as the church and only stood up when he reached the shadow of the porch. Then he tried the door, found it unlocked, and went in. Bob was waiting in the darkness for him.

'Come in, mate,' said Bob. 'Don't put the lights on. I thought if I waited long enough, you'd come.'

Nick stumbled down the nave to the end of the pew in which Bob sat. 'I'm sorry,' he said. 'Especially for being so rude to you.'

'Don't bother about me. It was your mother I was concerned about, and the way you were hurting her. I thought you loved her. She's all right now, and waiting for me to take you home. Your grandfather's there as well, and they want to talk to you. But I want a word or two with you myself, first, if you'll listen. And then I'll either come up to the house with you while they have their say, or I'll stop here. It's up to you.'

'What do they want to talk about?'

'The question you asked, and why it matters so much.'

'Do you know the answer?'

'Me? No, because I've never asked. I do my best to make up to your mother for all the pain some other bugger caused her. And though you may think I don't, I can see what it means to you – but I reckon it'd be better for everybody if you could be satisfied with just being yourself. Like we all have to be, sooner or later. I can't help being like I am – a lot of folks think I'm barmy because sometimes I know things that they don't – like I knowed tonight that I only had to sit here long enough and you'd come. But whatever I am, your mother loved me enough to marry me. I haven't got over that yet – I never shall. So now, why don't you tell me about Poppy?'

'You know that, too?'

'Of course I do. But I've got enough sense not to interfere just because I know what's happening sometimes before it happens. There's always a chance I may be wrong. And while you're young, there's a lot to learn. One thing is that there ain't many things worth having that you don't have to pay for somehow. Love worth having costs a lot, and you have to pay for that with pain. If the pain don't come early, it catches up with you sooner or later. I'd rather get it over first. That's how it was for me and Jane, and for Charles and Charlie. I think it's how it may be for you and Poppy. But as I say, you don't have to believe me, though I hope you will.

'Now – do you want me to go to the house with you, or not? Because, though I'll do whatever I can to help you, with me your mother comes first. She won't feel better till she's set eyes on you again – so don't keep her waiting. Go by yourself if you like, or I'll come with you – but I won't have her upset again tonight, even if I have to take my gun to you.' Nick felt, rather than saw, the smile as Bob made his unlikely threat.

'Please come, Mr Bellamy,' he said, in a very shy and humble tone.

Bob reached out, and pulled the boy towards him, holding him for a long moment in a strong clasp against his solid shoulder in the soothing darkness.

Nick staggered as he stood up, and Bob was quick to catch him. 'You're wore out,' he said. 'What you need is a hot bath and some grub inside you before anything else. There's more ways o'

155

killing the cat than choking it with butter – or blowing its head off with your gun. Come on, old son. We'll find a way. Let's go.'

It took more than a bath and a meal to take from Nick's face the ravages of the day, but the time came when his entry into the sitting-room where his mother and Effendi sat making uneasy conversation could no longer be postponed. Bob went in first, going over and kissing Jane to reassure her.

'Here's your lost lamb,' he said. 'He hadn't even strayed out of the pen, but he's been feeling lost all the same, so go easy with him. I reckon it won't do any of us no harm to have a glass of brandy. Sit still – I'll go and get it.'

Having neatly removed himself, he stayed out long enough for the first difficult minutes to pass. Nick went to his mother to be hugged and kissed. He turned to find his grandfather standing with outstretched hand. The lump in Nick's throat almost choked him, but he stood firm, and before he took the hand he said, 'I have apologized to him, Sir. And I'm sorry.'

The handshake was warm and lasted longer than usual. 'Good,' said Effendi. 'Now as soon as Bob comes back, we have quite a lot to discuss. What happened this morning's over and I hope may soon be forgotten. Unfortunately, we can't dismiss what happened twenty years ago quite so easily – but what concerns us all now is the future. Come in, Bob. Both Jane and I want you to hear all that there is to hear.' The drinks were passed round.

'Jane and I agree that Nick has a perfect right to an answer to the question he asked – but there are reasons why we can't – not won't – tell him the truth. We owe it to him at least to tell him those reasons.

'Before I say anything more, I want you all to believe that the greatest blame for all that happened must fall on my shoulders. If I had been stronger – if I had been less selfish and more sensitive to Jane's need of me – if I had been as wise then about human nature as I am now, none of it would have happened. It has been pointed out to me that perhaps what is worrying Nick most is not who his father was, but why we won't tell him. Naturally, he is imagining some terrible shame or scandal about it. Will you take my word for it, my dear boy, that there is neither?'

Nick could only nod.

'Then I will tell you as much as I'm able.' Succinctly, Effendi outlined the background to Nick and Bob as he had done to Fran. 'So you see, when I returned, Jane had gone – pregnant. In spite of all my efforts to find her, she had disappeared into the blue. I waited for her to make contact with me. She didn't. She thought she had disgraced me for ever, and that I should disown her. Only one thing was clear to me. I deduced that whoever the man responsible was, he had to be one of my subordinates, someone I knew, who had used inside knowledge to smuggle her out of the country and thereafter block all my attempts to trace her. We were up against a complete wall of silence. Time went on – awful weeks, dreadful months, dull, aching years. There was nothing more I could do but wait in the hope that one day I might find her again and learn the truth. When I did, it was worse than anything I could have imagined.

'Nick – I told you this morning that you were born a gentleman. It does, of course, depend on how you define a gentleman. You must make your own mind up about that. If you think it means blue blood, then your father was a gentleman. From a collateral branch of an ancient aristocratic family with everything but the means to support an aristocratic lifestyle. That's why this man was in the diplomatic service. He was a very able man, and worthy of promotion. That doesn't, I fear, make him a gentleman. He was an unprincipled blackguard who seduced an innocent twenty-year-old motherless girl, and then got rid of her as soon as he understood the threat to his career, and thereafter abandoned her. Because he was so able, he was the agent I chose to help me in my search for her. When at last, in her distress about you after the accident, Jane appealed to me and I learned the awful truth of what she had been doing for those twenty years, I asked her to tell me who the man was. I wonder the shock didn't kill me. I was glad that he was already dead. I had grieved for him sincerely, and had done my best for his family of boys, all a little older than you, Nick.'

He paused, his face for once not completely under control, for all his long training and experience. 'You must never, never blame any of *them*. He deceived them as badly and as skilfully as he

157

deceived me. They still regard me as a substitute father, though their mother has married again. The boys are still in and around London. You may even have been in their company without suspecting it, though it is not very likely. All are either at university, or heading for one, as I hope you are. Though I can see a family likeness now I know, I think no one else will. You take after our side.

'But I think you must see why I can't – won't – tell you his name. You don't carry that, anyway. The name you bear, thank God, is the one you have every right to. It is too late to put any of the past right – and I wouldn't be party to visiting the sins of an unprincipled father on his innocent children. If you must blame anyone, blame me.'

Nick sat, looking bewildered and unbelieving. Jane had begun to cry quietly. Bob crossed to her, lifted her out of her chair, and sat down again with her on his knees. Effendi stood before all three.

'I can only ask you to forgive me, and believe that I shall spend the rest of my life trying to make up to you and your mother for all you have suffered. In return, if you can forgive me, Nick, I beg you not to use any clues I may have given you to try and satisfy your curiosity. It would do you no good, and perhaps cause a lot of harm. In any case, there's no proof. What you choose to do now with your own life will affect only those who love you. Remember that, through thick and thin, your mother brought you up by her own standards, to be a gentleman. I hope you will always act like one.

'It has nothing to do with blue blood. It's a quality born in some people, and not in others. It is almost built into the way of life here in Old Swithinford. You could have landed in many a worse place, my boy. As I, in my old age, could have done. It is one of the greatest blessings I have now to count, though of course you may think differently. When you have got over today, and reflected on what I've told you, let us know what you want to do with your immediate future. What you decide may affect my future plans – but that's perhaps the price I have to pay.'

'No!' said Jane, vehemently. 'I don't agree. There would be no sense in that. If Nick lets what he has forced us to tell him change him, or his life, we can't help it, though I can't see what possible difference it can make to him. He's still Nick, isn't he? Nick, alive and well, when it could have been so different! Isn't that blessing enough for him to count? He has a right to decide his own future – but I don't give him any right over mine and Bob's or over little Jade's or Aggie's. Most of all over yours, Effendi.'

She sat up, still on Bob's knee, and addressed herself directly to her son. 'So it's your turn to tell us a few things. First, what caused you to make such an issue about this? And what's the problem that knowing what we can't tell you would have solved? Why should any of us change our plans for you if you won't come clean with us?'

'I remembered too much. I wanted to know who Nick was. And I had a reason for wanting to know.'

Bob spoke, slowly and gently, reluctant to interfere in what he still felt was a family matter that excluded him. 'What he means is that he had to know *which* of the Nicks it was that Poppy Gifford didn't want to have anything to do with. Ain't that right, mate?'

Nick nodded, struggling for words. 'I went up to see Charles and Charlie, and she was there. I couldn't bear it. I'd never been jealous of anything Charles had and I didn't in the old days – but what he's got now – what Mum's got with Bob – what so many others round here seem to have got – not even Grandfather's money or prestige can get me. Poppy loved me when I was a complete nobody. She doesn't want what I am now, and I can't go back, even if I would. Besides, she loves somebody else. She doesn't even like the new Nick, or want the old one back. I thought if I knew who I was I might be able to find another Nick she might like, or even love again, one day. And one that I myself could be happy with, even if she wasn't. I'm grateful for what you have told me, but I still don't know who the real Nick is. Mum's right, though – I haven't any right to spoil any plans for you just because I haven't any of my own. What were your plans, Grandfather?'

'It all happened while you were in the coma. I wanted to give Bob this farm as a wedding present. He wouldn't have it. But he did agree to let me lend him the money to buy it. In a few days' time it will become his legally. In the ordinary way what I lent him would have been on the same terms, more or less, as a mortgage; but that was before I found Old Swithinford and a lot of friends here. So we agreed on a new plan for me to become Bob's sleeping partner, taking an interest in the everyday running of our farm. I want to live here. The cottage isn't big enough, even if it was for sale.

'So I've made Eric Choppen a bid for Dr Henderson's house when it is fully restored and Dr Hardy no longer wants it. I think we all expected you would make your main base with me for the next year at least, while you were preparing for university. I shall keep on the flat in London for the time being, so you could have been there or here, as you wished. I believe Bob and I both hoped you would develop a family interest in the farm, some day – you were brought up a countryman, and we thought Poppy would be a major factor. It seems we were wrong. We still have three days left in which Bob and I can go back to our first plan. I don't want to – but I feel I still owe you a great debt.'

Nick burst into vehement speech again. 'I've told you I don't know what I want! You've got to give me time to find out. But I do know two things I don't want and won't do. I won't go near any university – looking at every other student and wondering if he's my half-brother, and hating them all, just in case. I'll do anything but that! Before the accident it was all I did want, because I thought it was the only way I could make myself good enough for Poppy and her family. Till I got my memory back, I did what I thought you wanted me to. The other thing I can't and won't do is to stop around here, where everything reminds me of Poppy. Meeting her relatives at every turn, everywhere I go reminding me of the last time I was there with her – especially during that lovely time at Charles's wedding when I thought I stood a chance – and the awful possibility of meeting her with her new boyfriend, or even perhaps her husband. I can't! I can't, and I won't.'

Jane was clenching her teeth to stop herself from either flying at him or crying. Bob heaved her off his lap. 'Don't cry, my beauty,' he said. 'I'm going to have my say.

'That's enough, old son. If you go on much longer like that, you'll find yourself back in hospital. Do you think you're the only one who's ever felt like you do? Most of us go through it some time or other in our lives. I did – not so long ago. When you had had your operation and we knew you were going to live and be all right, the flags were out for everybody – except me. What it meant to me was that your mother would soon be leaving me, and I should never see her again. The farm was being taken away from me, and Charlie had found her man and so was going to leave me as well. I had nobody – and nothing. I had to face up to it, though how I was going to live without Jane I didn't know. I was a middle-aged man. I had to go on. So I made up my mind to do just what you said you want to do. Find myself – the Bob Bellamy I had never had the chance to find before. I was going back to my house in the fen – to live all by myself, except for my animals. I had nobody but myself to work for, so my time would be my own. I could use it just as I liked, to do all the things I've always liked doing. Watch the clouds all day, if I felt like it. Spare time to see a butterfly come out of its chrysalis and try its wings for the first time. Look for rare wild flowers and birds' nests. Sit in my old flat-bottomed boat and spend all day fishing. Tame an otter pup – I've always wanted to do that. And in the winter, skate when there was a chance, and paint pictures when I had to stop indoors. And everything I filled my time with would be done thinking of Jane and the time when she'd had nobody but me to look after her. That would have been my greatest blessing – the memory of her. But it didn't turn out that way. Instead, I got all I'd ever wanted.

'Now there's you. You haven't so far had a much better childhood than I did – no chance, I mean, to do all the things you dreamed about. But perhaps that's still to come. Poppies bloom in their own season. I never had the chance to paint or go fishing. What didn't you have a chance to do? Read? Go to cinemas and theatres? Museums? Picture galleries? London's full of 'em. Get yourself a job in London – you'd be by yourself there better than here, where everybody knows you. Clear out, be by yourself, but remember we love you. You'll be welcome when you want to come back. If you'd only believe me, I could tell you that one day, sooner or later, your dream will come true.

'And now I've had my say. I'm going to leave you with your mother and your grandfather. There's a clear sky full of stars and a full moon. I'm going to stand under them while I have the chance, and count my blessings.' He stood up and walked away, to do just that.

The others, shaken to the core, stared silently after him.

It was Nick who came round first. His voice was awed. 'How did he know what sort of things I've always wanted to do?' he asked.

'Will you follow his advice?' asked Effendi. 'I can't think you will ever be given better.'

Jane said nothing, but her eyes sparkled like the stars in the Milky Way.

'Where would I live? In your flat, Effendi?'

'No,' said Jane decisively. 'That wasn't what Bob meant at all. You'd just become an idle young man about town, a social waster, a handsome spare pair of trousers for hostesses giving dinner parties, a bare field with nothing growing in it. Forbid it, Effendi, please. Help him to find a one-bedroomed flat where he has to be by himself among millions of other people who have real troubles. That's what Bob meant.'

'If you're game, my boy, we'll try it for six months. I'll make you an allowance that will keep a roof over your head – but like Bob, I suggest a part-time job for the rest. It's a challenge. Can you meet it – as your mother met hers when the man who fathered you left her to face everything alone?'

'I'll do my best to prove myself her son,' Nick said, 'and your grandson, Effendi.' For the first time, there was a hint of self-esteem in his voice.

'You'll do,' said Effendi, 'if you'll only try to be either of those. But if I say what I really think, I guess you have to prove yourself worthy to share your mother with that Greatheart who is standing out there talking to the stars and listening to the moon.'

When Fran left the Old Rectory, Emerald went upstairs and sat down to think about her encounter with Nick. She'd been angry, both at his rudeness and because she had no sympathy with a whinger who in her estimation had so little to whinge about. Far less than she had. The conversation with Nick had been too close to what was on her mind already. She'd spoken the absolute truth

– but hearing herself saying it hadn't done much to settle the problem of her own and Amethyst's future.

It was not yet a year since their family had been broken up. Once the worst of their grief and fear had subsided, they had lived from day to day, uncertain in every way about the future – though, till now, it had turned out better than they could ever have hoped.

The last months had been beyond their dreams. She and Ammy had been given what amounted to a self-contained flat in the back part of the Old Rectory, to their eyes furnished like a palace. They'd had food in kind and quantity such as they had never known before, and pleasures such as a radio at their disposal, and books always at hand, with time and peace to make the most of these new pleasures. Their previous lifestyle had been too precarious for them to take it for granted that such luxury could last long, but until now they had not looked the gift horse in the mouth. It had been almost too lucky that, so far, she and Ammy had not been parted at all, and they had also been in a position from which they could keep in touch with the younger ones – all 'parked out' with one or another of William Burbage's friends, pending the Welfare Officer's decisions. It had begun to appear that the welfare people had seen the sense of letting well alone. While their drug-addict mother kept out of the way, everyone was, it seemed, content. Jasper, the oldest of the three smaller ones, was the pampered darling of Jess and Greg, who had made him 'their own'. Though Bob Bellamy and his wife were above the legal age to be adoptive parents, they had applied to be allowed to keep both the youngest boys, and had meanwhile been accepted as the children's foster-parents. All satisfactory, till now.

Emerald, being the oldest, had always believed that she would have to be the first to leave the comfort of a family and set out on her own. It was all very well to have put a brave face on it to Nick, but her days of comfort and security under the Old Rectory roof were now numbered. For the first time, all that it was going to mean had come home to her. She wished she had told Nick still more of what she thought of him. What had he to grumble about? Till now, she and the sister who was so close to her in age had not been parted. What *would* they do without each other?

When Ammy arrived 'home' soon after Fran had left for Castle Hill, she found Emmy upstairs in very low spirits, in tears for the second time that week. She went to tell Beth, who had already foreseen that the disintegration of the Petrie children into units would mean that they might lose touch with each other.

She and Elyot, of course, had made up their minds that it must not happen, but hadn't so far found or made the opportunity to open the painful subject again with the girls themselves. Beth now reflected that only earlier on this very day Fran had said that they had better do it soon, or they might find Emerald had acted on her own initiative. She wished Fran hadn't left. She felt the issue too delicate for her to broach with the distressed girls unsupported. It occurred to her that if she kept a look-out, she might be lucky enough to catch Fran going homewards, and ask her to help at least till Elyot got home. She set Ammy to watch for Fran, and went to find Emmy.

The girl was now crying quietly, anger having given way to a sort of leaden desperation and resignation. She told Beth that her talk to Nick had made her see quite clearly what the situation was, that the change was inevitable, and that the sooner she made it, the better for all of them.

Then Ammy, deserting her post as watcher, rushed to hear what was being said and gave way to the tempest of tears, clinging to her sister as if she would never again let go of her.

Beth rather helplessly left them alone. How very much alike they were – though Ammy's gorgeous hair was a little darker shade of auburn, and had more tendency to spring into curls round her forehead. Beth found herself thinking that they were, if anything, more alike than the twins were. She thought they must have had the same father – there were only thirteen months difference in age between them. They had never before faced separation from each other. Well, they didn't now – but Elyot had said they must be very tactful. Two such intelligent and mature girls might actually want to be allowed to make their own plans and be independent.

Beth was no weakling, nor a moral coward. It was unlike her to shrink from any task. But the truth was that she had suddenly discovered how fond she was of the two waifs whom in the first instance they had only taken in to help out an overwrought William and an overburdened Fran, and to satisfy her own Christian conscience about caring for the poor and needy. She kept remembering the sight last week of Emmy clinging to Elyot, and wishing helplessly that what was past could be changed. If only she and Elyot had met during the war, and these two marvellous girls had been their daughters! It was herself, not the two girls, that she was crying for. Angrily, she shook off her tears. Wasn't she satisfied with the miracle that had happened – soon enough for her to give Elyot one son and not too late for there to be others? If that were still to be, then she would be even more in debt to that Somebody she believed in so firmly. He had shown her how she could show Him her everlasting gratitude.

Beth was facing up to the task of setting the situation before the two girls unaided, when she caught sight of Fran hurrying past the house on her way home. She rushed to the front door, and called.

Fran turned, somewhat reluctantly, because what she wanted now was to get back to William. She had a lot to tell him. But it was clear that she was needed here.

Beth, the strong-minded and capable, had for once lost her self possession, and wanted Fran to stop and help her. For once Fran was reluctant to have to put her finger into somebody else's so very personal pie. William had once told her she liked being the village wise-woman. She'd replied tartly that she did – it must be her bumpkin mentality. He had at once been contrite, and told her she couldn't help it any more than a magnet could help attracting iron filings, of which he was a good example. Where she led he followed. Hadn't he got himself up to his neck with the Petrie family to the point of being the worse of the two of them?

She didn't mind being the recipient of other people's confidences if and when she could help; but there was, she thought, a great difference between soothing a ruffled Sophie, and poking her finger into the business of a couple like Elyot and Beth Franks.

She was about to say so, as firmly and as kindly as she could, when the door opened, and Elyot came in. He took in his wife's tears, handed her his handkerchief, and said, 'What's all this flap about? Come on, bear a hand there. You as well, since you happen to be aboard, Fran. It looks as if we may need you.'

She was trapped. This was not Elyot the gentle, calm and easy neighbour; he had reverted, as she had seen him do in moments of crisis before, to the naval officer who expected everybody, including her, to take his orders. After her first moment of surprise, she endured the awful moment of wanting to laugh when she knew she mustn't. She beat down her too-ready reaction to the ludicrous side of the situation, and explained to him what the 'flap' was about.

He strode to the bottom of the stairs, and called an order to the two rather scared girls to come down at once. They came, but the sight of their frightened, wan faces sent him 'full astern' in an instant. He became his ordinary gentle self again. He led them over to where Beth was sitting, and told them what he had to say. Within five minutes the storm was over, and the sun shining on a very bright blue sea. Fran was amazed. She never stopped wondering how complex and of what infinite variety human nature was.

As she got up to leave, she heard Emerald saying shyly, 'We just don't know what to say, Mr Franks. It's just too good to be true.'

'You can't go on calling me "Mr Franks", now, you know. So what are you going to call me?'

The girl was ready with an answer. 'What we always have done, between ourselves, if you don't mind. What you are – "the Commander".' Fran could see how much that pleased him.

'And what about me?' asked Beth in a small voice. 'I don't want to be Mrs Franks any longer, either, but I refuse to be a modern plastic pseudo-aunt. I'd rather be just Beth to you than Auntie Beth.'

Elyot pulled her up, and stood with his arm round her. 'If I am to continue to be the Commander,' he said, 'you'll have to learn the chain of command. The safety of the whole ship is my job. The welfare of the crew is delegated to the Master-at-Arms – the Chief Petty Officer, the Buffer. The real boss – as you are. So you decide, Chief.'

'We'll think of something,' Beth said. Then, turning to the girls, she said, 'I'm sure you want to escape and talk it over with each other. I'll be up to see you and Wyn when I've said good-bye to Mrs Cather – to Mrs Burbage. Will that do?'

It was Amethyst, greatly daring, who set them on course. 'Aye aye, Buffer,' she said. Fran left with Elyot's laughter ringing in her ears. That little matter had been settled.

It was already dusk, and Fran had been away a very long time. William had not gone down to the Old Rectory to join her, because he hadn't wanted company – not even hers, until he'd had time to recover. As he sat waiting for her, he wondered how much he should tell her. It was rather a delicate matter. He owed such a lot to the Wagstaffes, but . . . since this morning, he'd doubted their wisdom in keeping from him knowledge that was surely his birthright. He felt aggrieved that he had never been told any details of his father's death, or of the heroism that had won him the Military Cross.

The Wagstaffes had not adopted him outright, or changed his name. He had sometimes wondered why. He had long had reason to be grateful for that, not least because it had established in their childhood that though he was kin to Fran, he was not a close blood relation. Such things mattered in a village community.

He was sure that the Wagstaffes had done what they had considered best. He was not finding fault with what they had done – only with what they hadn't. That brought him up against something he didn't want to have to admit: that that sensitive man who had been his father, and with whom he had at once felt such complete rapport, had neither been understood nor appreciated by the woman he had loved so desperately. She had had no conception of the depths of his love for her.

It was a shock to find himself making a comparison between her and Janice, but to that thought there was a corollary. If he was identifying himself with his father, did that mean that he had once loved Janice in the way his father had loved his mother? In the way that poem had made so clear? He knew that compared with his love for Fran, what he had felt for Janice was a glow-worm to a star. But if he told Fran that, would she be able to believe him? He shrank from telling her. It would be prudent to keep

167

quiet, at least till he had gone right through the yellowed hoard upstairs.

As the dusk deepened and still Fran did not come home to him, William debated with himself till he was wrought up again to a dangerous level of tension – the sort that caused their few but devastating quarrels. Janice, though dead, had been too much to the fore of his consciousness in the recent past. He had better keep quiet about anything that might raise any doubt in Fran's mind, just when the barometer of their compatibility seemed to be so steady on 'set fair'.

His other reason for deciding not to say anything yet surprised even him. Would revealing his own doubts about his mother be tantamount to betraying the father who had written the love-poem that she had not understood? Wouldn't it be better to leave the myth untouched by truth? That hurt. In finding his father, he had lost his mother.

He saw her now through a man's eyes, not those of a lonely little boy. If she had returned his father's love, she would not have become the woman he remembered, able to abandon him and his little son so soon, and apparently so callously, for the material advantages that her new husband's social and financial standing gave her. Better say nothing, lest he said too much. And here, at last, was Fran.

He went to meet her putting his thoughts and feelings firmly behind him. If he gave her the least inkling of them, she would read him so accurately that he would be forced to break the resolution he had just made. He was lucky that she had so much to tell him; he said he had been busy till it was too late and he too tired to go to meet her.

They ate the supper Sophie had left ready for them at once, because, Fran said, apart from the fact that she was starving and he had confessed to having skipped lunch, she'd better not start on her tale till they were safely *à deux* in the sitting-room.

'You do look tired, my darling,' she said. 'Washed out. What on earth have you been doing all day?'

'Turning out those old boxes I brought home from Cambridge. Crawling about the floor, stooping and sorting and peering at faded old bits of paper. I found it physically tiring. I'm not so

168

young as I was once. There comes a time when one has to admit it.'

She eyed him a bit anxiously, though with the scorn she felt such a remark deserved. 'What makes you say that?' she asked. 'Just when we're all set to go forward again. We've been at a still point, but on Monday we step into a new dance. Roll on Monday! We both need to be up and doing. Shall we not wait even till then?'

'Let's leave it to the gods,' he said. 'They may have got it mapped out for us. Come on – I want to hear what it is that has kept you all day, and sent you home so fired up.'

'You can't fool me,' she said. 'You're just as impatient to start work as I am. I can almost hear the wheels turning. We're simply waiting for each other to give the word. What's happened today?'

He suddenly felt much better. He decided he would play the matter of his father by ear. If the right moment arose, he would tell her. 'My darling,' he said, 'I can see that your sabre's drawn. So you shoot first.'

Her laughter rang out – and immediately all was right with his world. 'Really, Professor!' she said. 'I think it's quite time you either got a pen in your hand or stood in front of an audience again. Your command of language is slipping. I had no idea that you could shoot anybody with a sabre.'

They took their coffee into the sitting-room, and he found some liqueurs. The comfort of having her with him again, and in a fairly light-hearted mood, was straightening out his fears. He wanted to hear her tale.

'I wish we knew what's happening up at Castle Hill this minute,' she said. 'After what did happen at the Old Rectory, I'm afraid to think. There simply couldn't be two such happy endings on one day, could there? I wondered whether I ought to tell you about Nick being so nasty about little Jade and Aggie. If it's a choice between Nick and them, of course Nick will win. If Bob and Jane had been able to adopt them, Nick's tantrums would have been too late – but foster-parents can change their minds. I don't want you to have to start worrying again about them. It's so unlike Nick. I can't think what's come over him. But you don't have to worry any longer about Emmy and Ammy. They're Elyot's and Beth's from now on.'

'Not an entirely one-sided bargain, either, if you ask me. I'm sorry about Nick, though. And for him. The more I think about it, the more I sympathize with him. Whichever way you look at his story, he's had a pretty raw deal. It's like an old-fashioned "exemplar" type nursery tale – Cinderella without the happy ending. Suppose the slipper hadn't fitted Cinderella when the prince found her? Suppose she'd dropped a flat-iron on her big toe and her foot had swelled so that the slipper wouldn't go on? That's what's happened to Nick. Rags to riches is one thing. Rags to fairy-gold that won't buy you what you want's another. So he's jealous. Isn't that natural? It's envy – wanting what somebody else has got – that's the sin. Jealousy's one of the same family but a much more natural one. Haven't you ever been jealous? You know I have! And it's awful – especially when you're ashamed of yourself for being so petty.'

'Yes, I know,' she answered truthfully. 'When I thought you might be bringing Janice back with you, I was almost out of my mind with jealousy.'

'Sweetheart, you had every right to be. What you hadn't any right to do was to mistrust me.'

'Any more than you had a right to be so stupidly jealous of Bob,' she said.

'That's what I meant,' he said. 'I knew how stupid it was, but I couldn't help it. Nick's got a built-in jealousy. Compare his lot when he was growing up with that of the Petrie children. They had far more than he did, because as well as John, they had each other. Nick's eggs were all in one basket – his mother. For twenty years, each was the one and only thing the other had to love. Which is why he began to feel wicked as he grew up, intelligent enough to know that sooner or later there would be another woman in his life besides her. I think it never entered his head that he might ever have a rival for her love. Then came the accident that knocked him out.

'When he came round, he might as well have been on another planet. His whole firmament had changed. His polestar had moved, and there was nothing to take bearings on. His mother had acquired a father, a husband, and two babies – all male, and all apparently taking what he had thought was his alone. Then there's Poppy. His raging jealousy of her supposed lover has focused itself on what he regards as Jane's rejection of him. He's had as much as he can take. I'd be very worried if it weren't for Bob. He sees through convention to human nature, besides having a natural empathy with all young and dependent things. When he has to, he'll put his spoke in and set Nick right. As I said, Bob feels where most folk only reason. He understands.'

Fran listened, and wondered. He was right, as she had been right in her instinct to find Bob instead of Jane. 'And what you mean is that you understand too. Why's that?'

He got up and went to take his favourite place on the floor at her feet, his head against her knee. That way, he didn't have to look directly at her while he spoke.

'Because I've been in Nick's place, to some extent. I know I was only three – but people make a huge mistake in imagining that young children don't get hurt, or "forget". Till I was three, there had only been my mother – not even my father to share her with, because he was at the front. She married again. Nobody considered me old or intelligent enough to understand what it meant. But I was, and I did. Everyone was very, very kind to me – but later on, when I read David Copperfield, I cried myself to sleep, remembering. And when she and my step-father drove away together after dropping me at my first prep-school, I can't tell you the agony of jealousy I endured. That was the day the bug of jealousy bit me, and left me with it in my blood, like malaria, to keep recurring.

'I concluded that my mother no longer wanted me. Nobody but Grandfather did – certainly no other woman. Women looked after me, as Kezia did, but they didn't *want* me. I'm pretty sure that's why I married the wrong woman, and I wonder how often that happens? I'd had to accept that I was not the only pebble on the beach for my mother, so I married the first woman I thought wanted me as my mother had done once.

'I was still flying when I first found out how wrong I was about Janice. After that, all I wanted was to be killed before the next morning. I was out on my own, far more than Nick is. When Roland was in the same fix, he had a mother still whom he could come to – and he did. Lucky Roland. I hadn't anybody.'

Fran couldn't bear it. She had to stop him, somehow, without making him think she wasn't listening and suffering too. She turned, as always, to words, and quoted:

'So some of him lived, but the most of him died.'

'Yes. Kipling knew. It happens to a lot of men. Like Nick now. So he wants to kick everything and everybody, especially his mother, because she has other concerns and in any case can't cure his pain about Poppy. He sees her loving Bob and Effendi, and soothing Jade and Aggie – but he's at odds with her because he won't let her show she loves him, and jealousy stops him from showing how much he still loves her. I was a lot older than he is. I decided I could do without women. He's too young, too inexperienced in life, to do that, thank goodness. Poor young thing.'

Both of them were too moved to speak. All those empty years, and yet he had still remained the man he was. The silence grew long. He forced himself to go on. 'But Benedict's was still here, and it brought you back to me. I didn't dare let myself think you could want me – especially under the circumstances. I couldn't believe any woman would ever want me, and me only. A part of me didn't want to risk it.'

He paused and waited, though she didn't think he expected a reply. She was giving him her whole attention, her face full of love, and he was reading her correctly.

'But then,' he went on, looking up at her, 'on the night of Mary's horkey, my will not to risk it failed me, and I kissed you. Though you tried to hide it, from that wonderful moment I knew that there was one woman who did want me, and always would. If only I could wait long enough – but the knowledge made my bouts of malaria-like jealousy worse. Do you understand now, my darling, why I feel so strongly for Nick? Don't blame him. He can't help it. And don't despair, either. Bob will know and understand. There was no Bob for me. Just for a while, there was Mac

– but when he was killed I was utterly alone, inside. Nick isn't. It'll come right, somehow. It has to.'

He got up and went towards the kitchen, ostensibly to make their last drinks of the evening. She sat thinking of the past, and particularly about her aunt, William's mother. She hadn't known her at all well, because, as he had said, she hadn't been there in holiday time. Now she knew why she hadn't liked what she had known. Her own closeness to William then had probably been because she had picked up on his loneliness, and given him what he had needed most, even as he had given her the same. Thank God for Grandfather, and Benedict's. They had both been wanted here.

They, too, had been war orphans in their way; victims of what two wars had made of society. Could William be right about deprivation of parental love causing so many unhappy marriages? Of course, it depended on the people concerned. The more sensitive they were, the more they suffered. As Kipling had, and Dickens. Dickens had married the wrong woman. Kipling had suffered the agony of being deserted by his parents.

As William had said, Bob would see to it that Jane understood, perhaps even Nick too. They weren't her primary care. William was. Memories were hurting him too much.

They were both unusually silent as they lay in bed, his long arms round her, measuring his length against hers, their faces touching. She wanted to beg him not to go on thinking, giving himself yet more pain, but she was afraid to interfere.

He began to stroke her hair, to run the tips of his fingers over her face and gently up and down the curves of her, like a blind man learning something he couldn't see but wanted never to forget. Then he turned her face towards him, and began to speak, in a voice of such tenderness that she almost stopped breathing lest she break the magic.

> 'Had I the music of the south,
> The golden song of birds,
> I could not teach my eager mouth
> The cadence of your words.

Had I the blue of sleeping seas,
The grey of twilight skies,
I could not match the harmonies
That mingle in your eyes.

Had I the hope of old days fled,
And all-forgotten zest,
I could not wish more than my head,
Pillowed upon your breast.

Had I the very power divine
To mould the world anew,
I would not lift a hand of mine
To change a line of you.

She listened entranced, in a state of almost spiritual ecstasy, to ordinary words so exquisitely wrought into poetry, especially as William's voice was more than usually charged with emotion. When the last line fell like a stream of silver into silence, each felt the other's quivering response. Fran found her voice first, and said, 'Darling, where does that come from? I don't know it.'

'It must have been the last poem my father ever wrote, I think, before he was killed. I found it today. I didn't know he was a poet.'

'He must have been a wonderful man,' she said, 'to be able to love like that, and to say so in those words. I should have loved him.'

'I'm not sure my mother did,' he said. 'I don't believe she ever found that poem, even. If she did, I don't think she understood it, or him.'

Fran heard the tears in his voice, and couldn't answer. But she was there, already in his arms, when he whispered, 'Comfort me then, my precious one. You always understand.'

Fran woke early next morning, while William still slept. She looked down at his sleeping face, loving it; relaxed though it was, it still showed the strain of yesterday.

She looked back on their time together, and was appalled to realize what a long, unbroken period of high tension it had been, right up to and including yesterday. His capacity for loving made him extra sensitive to being hurt, and all the time there had been that other pain which, till last night, he had never mentioned, and she had never suspected. The little day-to-day niggles she had thought were upsetting him had only been like tiny scratches on the surface of a huge, deep, double wound. Until three months ago, though he had been happy, he'd always been too vulnerable to memories.

And what mountains of emotion he had been climbing recently! She had thought she understood him – but never as well as she had done last night; never loved him as much as she did this morning. Her heart was almost bursting with contrition. She should have known. He half roused, half smiled, instinctively reached for her, and went back to sleep. She lay still till, remembering what day of the week it was, there arose inside her a sudden flood of optimism.

This was Saturday. Monday, Michaelmas Day, would change the pattern of the dance. From this time forward, William could be wholly a countryman, however far his scholarship still stretched. And she? Well, she had never stopped being a countrywoman at heart, however ambitious she might have been. She still loved what she called her 'work', but she wasn't forced, now, to put it first. There was no need for her to be anything but William's wife, if that was the way he wanted it. If he needed her.

How clever Dr Hardy had been to diagnose at once that William's temporary breakdown had not been physical, but only the result of so many years of emotional stress! The last straw had been the wrench of leaving Cambridge, especially, as she now knew, with the feeling that even his *alma mater* didn't want him any longer.

Her mind went back to that marvellous love poem he had quoted to her last night. The last poem his father had written to his mother, he had said. She schooled her impatience to know more, cuddled down beside him and continued her meditation about the poem till she fell deeply asleep again, and only woke when he, washed, newly shaven and dressed, brought her a cup of tea and stroked her face to rouse her.

It was over their late breakfast that she asked him about the poem. He told her about his discoveries yesterday, and fetched both the poem and the photograph to show her.

'He must have been killed very soon after sending her that,' William said. 'Maybe he had a presentiment that it was the last poem he would ever send to his "dear love". I hope that included me. I've had to wait for fifty years to find it – or this.' He handed her the medal, and the citation.

Fran read it and inspected the medal in silence.

'I think I feel very much as Nick does,' he said. '*Why didn't they tell me?*'

She heard the pain in his voice and answered gently, 'We have no way of knowing, or finding out, now. But it may have been best in the end. The gods decreed that your father should tell you himself. They knew what they were doing – keeping something in reserve for you to find at the right moment. Something for you to live up to at the crucial point of change. Are there any more of his poems?'

'I don't know. There's a bundle of letters – hers to him. Darling, I wish I hadn't found them. They were just duty letters, written by my mother to her husband and my father – they weren't love letters. How they must have hurt him! You'd have put more of yourself into a note to the milkman than she did to her man at the front. I wanted to stick them in the Aga there and then. And a lot of other stuff. Shall I go get it?'

'Yes, please. But don't get upset again, or be too hard on your mother. You're only hurting yourself. Sweetheart, women did have to harden their hearts in wartime. They had to steel themselves against losing their men – and keep going for the sake of their children. She may have been desperately lonely – that's when other men become a danger. Don't keep hurting yourself. Think what could have been the case. Suppose he'd survived and come home maimed or blinded to a woman who'd stopped loving him? If he had to die, wasn't it better that he should die still loving her and believing she loved him? Though how she could have stopped loving the man who wrote her that poem to swap him for a man like my Uncle Harry is beyond me!'

He left her holding the photograph, showed her where he had found it and told her of his conviction that his mother hadn't bothered to find it. He was a long time gone upstairs, and her heart had gone with him. If he was finding it all too much for him again, up there by himself, she was in no state to help him. She would only upset him more if she went to him, so she sat reading and re-reading the poem till she knew it by heart. Then she picked up the photograph and communed with the man who wrote it.

He was no stranger. She had met him before, on the last occasion she had seen William before they had lost each other. Though this man was wearing khaki, and William had been wearing airforce blue, it was the same man. The face, the stance – and those hands – when this photograph was taken, he must have been five years or so older than that jaunty, debonair, devil-may-care young RAF officer who had given her a cousinly peck that had been goodbye for more than twenty years. But those same hands had stroked her, made love to her only last night. She would have known he was William's father by those hands. The eyes, too, were alike, especially the wistful, yearning look in them, one she had seen in William's far too often, and for far too long. How could she have been able to keep him waiting all that time? Tears were slipping down her face when he returned. He put down the box, and rather hesitantly held out a hand to her.

'Darling – why are you crying? Has it brought back memories to you of being the woman left alone? Of Roland and Kate without a father? Forgive me. I'm sorry.'

She looked up, her eyes bright through the tears. 'You're still intent on hurting yourself, aren't you? I was thinking only of you – not at all of Brian. I haven't stopped loving him – I never did stop loving him – because, as I told you on Hunstanton beach, I didn't know what love was till you came back to me. I don't know if he really loved me – he never wrote love poems to me, or even letters that I wanted to keep. He was satisfied, anyway, and if that was love, he died believing it to be returned. God knows what might have happened if you'd reappeared then instead of twenty years later.'

'And Roland and Kate? Do they know him?'

She had to be truthful. 'Of course they know of him, because his parents talked to them constantly about him, but I have an idea they don't think of him as ever being real. More like a character in a play. If they did have a gap where he should have been, they've now filled it with you. I promise you that if ever they ask, I'll be honest with them. I won't keep anything from them – even what I have just confessed to you.'

He rose and went to stand over her, gathering her up to him without words, and attempting to take the photograph from her. She hung on to it. 'No, please don't take him away from me yet. I want to get to know him.'

When she spoke again, it was in her normal, Saturday-morning tone. 'I've been thinking about it being Michaelmas Day on Monday, and what it means, especially this year. It's always brought changes, I suppose, but there are a lot this year besides business transactions. Some personal ones, and others that affect everybody – us, and Bob and Effendi. Then there's Elyot and Beth, and those girls – and young Nick, whatever happens. Most of all, perhaps, dear old George – the first Bridgefoot ever to give up the reins before, as he says, they plant him.

'Then there's having to face the future without old Henderson – nobody's going to like a posse of new medics who don't understand them as he did. And every major change drags others in its train. Daniel Bates is having to change a lifetime's pattern of work to tiffle about at the Old Glebe, and Thirzah's putting herself out about that.

'Sophie told me that Nigel's going to take the services here on Sunday – I guess to please George, though he won't be inducted till next month at the earliest. I think we ought to attend. We've come to the end of another phase – but it's the beginning of a new one as well. I've become sort of superstitious about it. Isn't that why we are deliberately waiting to start work – because we feel we must see the old out with respect before we rush into the new? Let's stick to our bargain, sweetheart.'

'So what shall we do till Monday, then? It's beginning to hang heavy on my hands. I want to get at Bob's book, if only to help me to forget all the things I found out yesterday. If I read seventeenth-century history, I shall be jumping the gun.'

'Yes, I'd thought of that. I know you. Look – I went round the old village yesterday, and visited some of our friends, but not all of them. You need fresh air and exercise. Why don't you finish the round? Go to see George, and then on to Eric and Nigel. Then we'll go to church tomorrow morning, and on Monday we'll buckle down to work – though I haven't yet settled on any idea for mine.'

'That sounds a good idea. I take it you are coming, too?'

'No, if you don't mind. What you need is men's company just at present. But don't go anywhere near Jess. She's your mother's daughter, if she isn't your father's. Don't worry about me. If you'll let me, I would like to spend my day with your father, and get to know him through his poetry. I love him already. After all, he gave me you.'

William gathered that Fran was of the opinion that he had been wallowing in a morass of indecisive emotion long enough. It was time he snapped out of it and accepted the change that had overtaken him, for her sake as well as his. She must have foreseen that when it came to it, there would be some sort of emotional crisis, and that to make a firm *terminus ante quo* to one life and an equally firm *terminus post quem* to another was essential. He therefore submitted to her, and set off alone.

At the end of the avenue of trees, where their private drive met the road, he had another decision to make. Left towards the village, or right towards the hotel where, Saturday though it was, he would be most likely to find Eric, and possibly Nigel? Towards the old or the new; towards the past or the future? The past would always fascinate him, but he had no option but to go on living in the future if he went on living at all. Past and future met in the present. What had Fran called it? 'The still point of the turning world.' The rest of today and tomorrow was the long chord played by the musician to warn the dancers to be ready to step into the next dance.

This Michaelmas was not merely the end of an agricultural year, as in the past, a time of leases running out and rents due, of evictions when the breadwinner failed, of new terms between masters and men and housewives and maids. As far as Old Swithinford was concerned, it was the end of an era.

The age of technology was well and truly established, and there

179

was no going back. The contemplation of what it could mean in the future almost frightened him. Well, thank heaven that both he and Fran were old enough to remember the past as it had been, and still young enough to cope with the future. Nothing, at any rate, could prevent them from keeping the past alive for themselves – he because of his love of history, and Fran because she could always find words in which to conjure it back.

Somebody was in the churchyard. Nigel, probably, making sure everything was set for tomorrow. William thought he would, at this moment, perhaps rather meet Nigel than anyone else he could think of. A man who spanned and dominated all worlds, physical, intellectual and spiritual, and sat in judgement on nobody.

It was not Nigel. It was George Bridgefoot with Daniel Bates, working together cleaning and tidying up graves. As he went up the long path towards them, he noticed how the graves on one side of the path were all tended and cared for, while those on the other were neglected and overgrown. On the cared-for side lay past Bridgefoots, running back to where Wagstaffes predominated. George and Daniel were busy with the neglected side.

George straightened up as William approached, his face breaking into a smile of welcome. 'Dan'el, my boy,' he said to his companion, 'it's time we knocked off for a little while. Get you off home for your dockey, and see as Thirz' is all right. I'll meet you back here in about an hour's time.' To William, he said, 'Will you come back to the Glebe, or shall we go and sit in church? This job's a bit hard on my hip, stooping and such, and I should be glad of a bit of a sit-down.' They went into the church.

'Why are you doing it, then?' William asked. 'It isn't part of your job as a churchwarden, is it? Can't you get somebody to do it on a regular basis?'

'No – though it is our job to look after the churchyard, I dare say it will come to having it all cleared soon. Gravestones all rooted up and put in a row down the side o' the church, and all the humps and bumps levelled like a cricket pitch and grass sowed and kept cut. Seats put up for strangers to sit on to eat their picnics – and leave their beer bottles and crisp packets round. I know that's what Kid Bean's got in mind. But he won't get all his own way while I'm alive, and 'specially now we're going to get a proper rector again. But to tell you the truth, I had to find myself a job o' some sort today – partly to keep myself out o' Molly's sight, and partly 'cos I daren't let myself sit and think.

'I know as I've done what's only right and proper, to give up and let Brian take over, but there's only the rest of today and tomorrow left for me to be what I have been for the last fifty year. Since my father died and I had to take over whether I wanted to or not. Died of cancer, he did, and took a long while about it, so I'd had some warning. But while he still had breath in his body, I should never have thought o' crossing him, or doing anything different from what he wanted. That was the way of it, then. I was chuntering a bit about being more or less forced to give up afore I had to at breakfast time this morning, till Molly couldn't stand it, and squared me up. So I come down to Father's grave, to tell him why I was letting him down, like. I'd got to do something, d'you see, William, to stop myself from being too sorry for myself.

'By the time I'd got here I'd remembered all as I'd got to be thankful for – how lucky I am to have a son and a grandson to follow me. And there was all them graves on the other side o' the path in such a mess. Why? 'Cos there either ain't nobody left to see to 'em, or if there is, they don't – for their own good reasons, I daresay. All them Thackerays laying there, my family's best and dearest friends, generation after generation. There's as many generations o' them as there is of us Bridgefoots, till they come to grief in that fire. Michael's still alive, with a son of his own – but he never comes near the place. Can't face it, I reckon, with his father and mother and his brother and that boy as caused their deaths all laying there side by side. Then there's the Faireys – you'd think Tom and Cynthia would want to see that Robert's grave was kept tidy, at least, but I wonder, if it had been Charles, whether I could have come near? And I've got other grandchildren, even if they are all girls – but Robert was the only Fairey left after nigh on four hundred year. I can understand how they feel. And dear old Miss Budd lays there among 'em – her grave's never neglected, and won't be while your Soph' lives. Miss Budd herself wouldn't have cared – except about the untidiness. Well, to cut a long story short, by the time I got here I were downright ashamed of myself. So I went and collected Dan'el and some tools, and both of us were glad to have something to do as needed doing. Thirz' is taking it bad that he's coming to muck about with me, instead o' stopping on to be Brian's right-hand man. There never was no likelihood o' that, only in Thirz's mind. Brian don't want such as him – he's a cow man, not one o' these new-fangled know-alls as won't call theirselves farm labourers. But Thirz' had made her mind up, and what she thinks has got to be right. So poor old Dan's getting the blame for it at home. Thirz' all'us has been a awk'ard character. Takes after the Tibbs side o' the family – there's one o' them in every generation as is different and has to be handled careful. Dan knows which side his bread is buttered on. He'll enj'y being with me. I like a farm to be a mixed farm, you see, crops mixed with looking after animals and such. I plan to buy a bull and a couple o' cows o' one o' these new breeds, and raise a special little herd for Dan to look after, and keep some sheep and pigs and poultry. I don't care if we don't make a lot o' profit on what little bit o' land I kept for myself. I shall get more pleasure out of it than money could buy me any other way, I reckon. I kept about half-and-half pasture and arable. When we're all got used to it, we shall be happy enough.

'Charles has got what he wanted – except a son to follow him, and that'll come. Brian's got what he's been wanting – the reins in his hands. He'll sell off all the land Vic used to farm for development, so there'll be no need for him or me to worry about any of them not having more money in the bank than they need, even when the time comes and farmers ain't wanted no more, and live on government grants and subsidies and such instead o' the sweat o' their brows. Marge, bless her, is my only real worry, and she'd be all right if it weren't for them gels of hers. She's worried to death about both of 'em. Ah – here's Dan'el back. I'd better go and get on with my job, or he'll tell me off. Give my love to Fran. Where is she?'

William pulled a face. 'Like Molly is with you. There's too much change in the air. Women are better than we are when it comes to taking whatever comes. She sent me out to walk my blues away – and meeting you has done the trick. We've got to face things

- 182

as they are. But we'll see you in church tomorrow morning – by Fran's decree.'

George's face lit up, and when William had gone, he sat down again to put his head on his hands for a minute on the top of the pew in front of him. Then he went out to take his orders from Dan. As it had always been: if Dan knew best, George let him.

William turned his steps towards Monastery Farm, and was lucky enough to find Eric and Nigel just about to leave for the hotel to have lunch there. He was invited to join them, and after asking if Jess was there, he accepted. Jess was at home, so it suited him well to lunch at the hotel. He rang Fran to tell her where he was, and Jess wasn't.

He told his two companions where he'd been earlier, and what George had said. Eric nodded, looking concerned when William reported the bit about Marge.

'I know,' said Eric. 'She tries hard not to show her anxiety, but it's there, all the same. It isn't fair that both her girls are causing her such worry. My opinion – though I shan't express it to her – is that Poppy is just being bloody silly. It's Pansy who worries me.'

'I'm beginning to think that we're lucky to be middle-aged,' William said. 'I've got a lot of sympathy for young Nick on his own behalf – and some for Poppy as well, but they're being as selfish as most young folks are. They don't stop to think how miserable they're making other people. Love may be the greatest thing – but when you're their age it can be the cruellest thing, too. Bloody awful, in fact. I remember.'

'So do I,' said Eric. 'Marjorie keeps her thoughts to herself – and I'm glad, because at the moment I shouldn't have much comfort to offer her with regard to Pansy. I don't know about Poppy – but in my opinion Pansy's heading for trouble.'

Nigel was being very silent, and William picked up the clue. 'I see,' he said. 'You think Poppy and Nick's difficulties are in Nigel's field, but Pansy's are in yours, and you know something we don't. Can't we be let in on it?'

'No – I don't *know* anything. But I can read straws in the wind in business matters. There's something fishy going on in the Bailey camp. I told you I'd heard a rumour that Casablanca was on the market, and the Baileys wanted to go back to Swithinford. Well, the first bit's true, and the white elephant, as Bob nicknamed it, is on offer – to Terence Hardy. But as I read it, Lord Arnold and Lady Norah have no intention of living in Swithinford. The latest rumour is that they've bought a villa in Spain, and intend to winter there before deciding where to settle. Now what does that mean? That he's making plans to be out of the country if he needs to be? His Clerk of the Works would only have to step on to a ferry at his back door and be in France next morning. His son – and Pansy – live in rented accommodation. Where? At Deal – about as close as they can be to stepping across to the continent. And Jess says Beryl Bean's having kittens about something, and Ken is going round with his head down, growling and slavering like a mad dog. There. Now you know as much as I do. Put it all together.'

'Bailey overreached himself?' asked William. 'Going bankrupt?'

'Possibly. But I've got a devious mind and, after all, we're both in the development line of business. We can't help our lines crossing now and again. My guess is that he'd bluster his way through any threatened shortage of money. The smell in my nostrils is of a full-scale scandal or back-handers big enough to be criminal because of their source. I shouldn't have thought Bailey a big enough fish to be in on anything like that – but as the old proverb says, it's the rotten twig in the hedge that cracks first. I should merely be interested to see how near my guess is if it weren't for Pansy being mixed up in it.

'But for God's sake, William, don't go telling anybody about my fantasies – I'm only surmising, putting two and two together and probably making a baker's dozen. I really shouldn't have given a thought to where Bailey was going or what he was doing, but for Pansy. Marge has spent most of the last two evenings trying to ring her, but there's no reply. Well, she's probably only gone to Brighton for the weekend. It's none of my business.'

'Nick Hadley-Gordon told Fran yesterday that he was hoping to buy Henderson's house from you,' William said. 'I thought you were afraid Bailey would be after that.'

'Another straw in the wind,' Eric replied. 'I tried to get in first, as you know. Casablanca, going very reasonable for a quick sale, was too good for Hardy to pass up, so I made Mrs Henderson an offer direct and it was accepted. She's officially moving out on Monday. Effendi wants me to restore it for him, so that he can make a permanent home here, near Jane. Terence has to have a base while Casablanca is being converted to house all three doctors. So in the meantime, we compromise. The Henderson house was once three cottages, so the plan is to restore it all, but to make two separate dwellings of it, the bigger one for Effendi and the other – the end Old Henderson used for his surgery and offices – for Hardy. When he finally moves out, we can put it back together to one large house, or leave it separate for Effendi to do as he likes with. Terry'll stay on here at the hotel for the time being. But he says he wants a home of his own, away from his younger partners, in case his children want to come and stay.'

'His children? I thought he was a bachelor.' William was genuinely surprised. 'Is he married then?'

'No,' said Eric. 'As far as I gather, not at present. But he has been at least three times.'

'Well! Strike me pink!' said the Emeritus Professor Elect of Medieval History, Ph.D. 'No wonder he said he was no expert on affairs of the heart.'

'Conversely,' said Nigel dryly, 'it could be said that practice might make perfect.'

'I don't see what right we have to judge,' Eric said. 'Nigel's never tried marriage at all, I've tried it once, and William twice. If there are rules about marriage, we don't seem to know them.' It was too sore a point with Eric for his friends to dwell on.

'I must go,' said William. 'I didn't really intend to leave Fran alone for quite so long.'

They went to church for morning prayer next day, and were glad they had made the effort. There was a very good congregation, including quite a lot of people Fran knew by sight but couldn't put a name to. She was delighted to be part of it. It seemed so right for them to be there on that particular day, a day outside normal time, a special Sunday.

She guessed that a lot of those present had come out of politeness to the new rector, although he had not yet been inducted, and a lot of the others because they had already fallen for Nigel's charm and charisma, or, conversely, wanted to sample him and compare him with his predecessors. She had no qualms on that score. She was slightly anxious that one face was missing – Thirzah was not in the pew beside Daniel and Sophie. But as Sophie didn't seek her out after the service was over, she concluded that there was nothing for her to worry about.

They walked home soothed and contented, and spent the rest of the day going through and sorting the rest of William's father's manuscripts and typescripts.

'As I haven't yet decided on what to do for my next series,' she said to William when, towards dusk, they had begun to make some order out of what they had found, 'and tomorrow is the day we have decided to start work again, I think I couldn't do better than to type up all the lyric poetry. Those scrappy bits of paper are too easy to lose. I don't suppose there's even a millionth chance that any publisher would be interested in them, but we could have a few copies spirally bound for anyone – Jess and Greg, for example – who might enjoy them. And we'll have one bound properly and beautifully, just for ourselves. Is that a good idea?'

'Splendid,' William answered, stooping to the floor. 'Look, you've dropped one. He must have just scribbled things down whenever the idea struck him. This is a page torn out of a notebook. It's a wonder it didn't get thrown away with the rubbish.'

Fran took the crumpled piece of paper from him, smoothed it out, read it, and handed it back to him.

*Song of Nothing Much*, he read aloud, and went on:

> Sweet as the lark's song,
> Clear as the call
> Of tumbling streams
> By the waterfall,

186

Soft as the down
On the wren's breast,
Bright as the sky
In the glowing west,
Clear as the first star
Piercing the blue
Hazing the gloaming,
Sweetheart are you.

'He's said it all,' William added softly. 'All I ever wanted, and still want, to say to you.' He stopped to give her a long, lingering kiss and went alone to his study. When she had finished clearing up, she followed him there. He was sitting at his desk, with Bob's book, still closed, lying before him.

'I'd intended to start on this first thing tomorrow,' he said, 'but having heard just how well words can be used, I'm afraid. Whoever wrote this was, I think, a wordsmith like Father. I can't hope to do justice to him. Oh, I can translate it all right – but you know how awful most translations are! I've seen enough of this to know he had something to say, and knew how to say it. I'm afraid of spoiling it, if I can't match his style.'

She went and fetched the photograph. 'I had plans for sneaking in here and hanging this over your desk for you to find tomorrow morning,' she said. 'But let's hang it now. It's your talisman. Darling, don't you see? You have his genes.

'Till now you have only written academic history, but your books wouldn't have sold as they have if they hadn't been a bit different from the usual dry-as-dust stuff most academics write. Nobody could accuse you of writing popular history, but there's a difference, all the same, between yours and those of academics who write only for each other – not even to please themselves. As if they were members of some exclusive club, intended to keep the ordinary interested reader of history out. Yours aren't like that, because you clothe history in – in *humanity*. Yes, that's what it is. You make history real. Of course you can do it! Do it for your father. He could have made the dullest bits of history sing, I think. Don't let him down.'

He swivelled his chair to look at her, and she knew she had

won. They hung the photograph, and there was a jaunty purpose in his stride as he went to their library to collect his Latin dictionary and a few other things he felt he might need. In his absence, Fran looked up at the pictured face and blew it a kiss. She could have sworn that he winked back at her.

Monday, Michaelmas Day. By nine o'clock they had finished breakfast, and were both ready to plunge into their studies to 'work'.

'Sophie's late,' Fran said. 'Don't wait for her if you don't want to, though I will. She's bound to want a bit of a chat about church yesterday. I can't disappoint her.'

'No – fair's fair,' he said. 'I shall wait till you can go to your study, too.'

'Here she comes,' Fran said, head cocked on one side, listening to the heavy footfalls. 'Heavens, I don't like the sound of that tread. Something's wrong.' It was indeed a very glum Sophie who came in. Fran asked at once what the matter was.

'Thirz' took to 'er bed again. Didn't you notice she wasn't in church yist'day?'

'Yes. Oh, I am sorry. Same trouble as before?'

'If you mean is she as awk'ard as she was afore, and all'us is, only more so, the answer's yis. She ain't complaining o' no pain, as far as I know, nor yet no shortness o' breath – well you wouldn't think so if you could 'ear 'ow she goes on at Dan'el. She vows as she'll never rise from 'er bed no more till 'e puts 'er first, seeing as it's 'er as 'as been 'is lawful wedded wife for thirty year or more. Never stops chuntering at 'im for a minute, once 'e comes into 'er sight.

''E don't bother to try and answer 'er no longer, only to tell 'er again and again as 'e 'as never gone back on 'is word to nobody in all 'is life afore as 'e knows on, and 'e ain't gooing to now, to please 'er nor nobody else. I don't know as I blame 'im! If that's the way to keep 'er abed and out of 'is 'earing, at least 'e'll get 'is

188

meals in peace. And Aunt Sar'anne all'us was a good cook. Be a nice change for 'im.'

'Aunt Sar'anne?' William's eyebrows registered his bewilderment. 'What has she got to do with it?'

'You're forgot,' said Sophie reprovingly. 'Though I did tell you my own self when we got back from Cousin Tilda's fun'ral. 'Ow Tilda's 'usband said come Michaelmas 'e were a-gooing to turn Aunt Sar'anne out. Dan upped and told 'er then that she was our kin when all was said and done, and sooner than she should goo to one o' them old-folks's 'omes, if it come to it and she 'adn't got no other roof over 'er 'ead, she'd be welcome at their'n till she found somewhere else to goo. And tha's what's happened.

'Seems she went out Sat'day morning as usual to draw 'er old-age pension, and stopped with some other old women as she knowed for a cup o' tea and a bit of a chat, and when she went back, she found the door locked against 'er and all 'er belongings in dustbin bags outside on the doorstep. 'E'd gone. Poor old soul, she didn't know what to do, Sat'day afternoon an' all. Then she remembered what Dan'el 'ad said, and she 'ad two weeks' pension in 'er purse, what just paid for a taxi to bring 'er 'ere. Got to Thirz's about tea-time, and it were lucky for 'er as Dan were at 'ome. He told 'er she was welcome, but Thirz' put 'erself about till Dan told 'er to 'old 'er tongue, so by that Thirz' said as she was a-going to bed and wouldn't get up never no more till Dan 'ad got rid of Aunt Sar'anne. What'll be the hend of it, I'm sure I don't know.

'Dan left Aunt Sar'anne by 'erself while 'e come to fetch me, and I went back with 'im. There ain't no way she can come to mine, 'cos I'm only got one bedroom and I won't share that with nobody only my Jelly when I say my prayers at night, even if she'd be safe trying to get up and down my twisted little old stairs. But I done the best I could, for the time being. I said if she could sleep and keep 'er things in their spare bedroom, she could come up mine and set there during the day, while I were 'ere at work, like. But Thirz' is that nasty, and Dan's so put out as there's no peace there at all, and Aunt Sar'anne don't like being left all day by 'erself, and I don't want nobody there every time I goo 'ome come evening. I don't know whatever is to be done, that I don't.'

Fran and William both understood that though they were not being expected to help, they were being asked for advice, as well as sympathetic understanding and support. Fran said soothingly that she didn't see how they could offer much help or advice, until they knew a bit more about Aunt Sar'anne. 'From what you say,' she said to Sophie, 'she appears to be in very good shape for somebody well over ninety. I suppose there are some old folk's homes in Swithinford?'

Sophie sniffed, and didn't reply. Fran could see that she had pulled the wrong string, and tried again. 'Where is she now?' she asked.

'By 'erself in my little 'um,' Sophie replied. 'So I can't stand 'ere a-talking, 'cos I shall hev to get 'ome soon as ever I can to stop 'er from being too miserable. Not as she is miserable – but she does so 'ate being be'olden to me or anybody else, and she can't abide not heving anything to do. But what else to do with 'er only leave 'er there, I'm sure I don't know. It's early days, yet.'

Fran cast a glance of mixed aggro and humour at William, and found exactly the same feeling registered in his face. Both knew that their plans had already been thwarted, before they had actually begun.

'Go and fetch her. We'll talk to her and see what the possibilities are,' William said.

Sophie heaved a great sigh of relief. That was more than she had hoped for.

While she had gone, and William and Fran were consoling each other that this was exactly the sort of thing they might have expected, Greg arrived. He was still in the habit of dropping in most mornings, to satisfy himself that he had not dreamed he had painted *The Burbages at Home*. He often didn't come to speak to them, but they left him alone with the picture until they heard him expressing his renewed delight in it on the piano. He went on playing till after Sophie had arrived back with Aunt Sar'anne in tow.

She proved to be as unlike what Fran had expected as was physically possible. Fran realized she had been visualizing a clone of Kezia, only grown older, tougher and more bitter. Kezia had been tall and raw-boned, and her character hardened by the poverty of her long widowhood and her struggle to bring up her three girls in the fear of the Lord, according to her own lights. Sophie had inherited her stature, but little else. Neither of the other two looked anything like her, though Thirzah outdid her in toughness, morality and the determination never to be 'set down' by anybody else. Hetty might as well have been a cuckoo in the nest. Kezia, however, had been so strong a character that she had imprinted something of herself on all her three daughters, and her personality still overshadowed them. Fran had imagined another Kezia, in character as well as looks. She could hardly have been more wrong.

Aunt Sar'anne was as small as Kezia had been large. Where Kezia's hair had been, like Sophie's and Thirzah's, thick, black and straight, parted in the middle and drawn back into a bun, Sar'anne's little head was snow-white, her curly hair cut short and fitting her bright, bird-like face so well that she resembled a midwinter robin peeping out of a snowball. Her eyes were black and bright, her small face clean-cut and thin. Fran noticed with awe that all her front teeth were still her own, yellowed a bit and parting slightly with age though they were. Her thin, short little legs protruded from below a skirt of a far later style than Sophie's, and her tiny, work-worn but agile hands stuck out from the sleeves of a nylon two-piece far more modern than Fran had ever seen on any of Kezia's two oldest daughters.

When Greg decided to look in on them that morning, Aunt Sar'anne was sitting at the kitchen table with William and Fran, looking as completely at home there as Sophie did, her little head cocked sideways and her eyes bright with interest in everything.

'Hold it!' said Greg from the doorway. 'William, where can I find some paper? In your study? No, don't move – any of you. Just sit still. I'll get it.' He returned with a pile of white paper, and from the doorway made sketch after sketch of the porcelain-like head of the old lady, talking to her all the time to keep it turned his way.

'Book me some sittings with her somewhere, somehow,' he whispered to Fran before leaving. 'She's the absolute essence of beauty. Like a tree in winter, stripped to its bare essentials and

191

shaped by all the winds of life. If she isn't hanging in next year's summer exhibition, I'll eat my paintbrushes.'

William and Fran were enjoying her, too. She was as bright as a new-polished button, as lively as a cricket, and as voluble as a chattering magpie.

'And to think,' she was saying, 'as I should ever be a-sitting in this old 'ouse again! I remember well enough the first time as I ever see it, when I come 'ere to my first place in service when I were only 'leven. Eighty-one year ago, that'll be, come Swithinford Statis. Not as I was hired at a statis – folks had give up sich ways o' doing things by then, but it were still kep' up as a bit of a holiday, like.'

('Statis?' asked Fran, seeking information from William. 'Sh! Corruption of "Statutes" – hiring fair,' he whispered back.)

Sar'anne was not in the least put out by the interruption. She added her own explanation. 'It were the time o' the year as us gels and boys were took on as farm boys or maids in the big houses. We all'us knowed where we were with our wages, paid from that day by the quarter. Five pound a year and my keep, I got. My mam arranged it all with ol' Miss Wagstaffe, as was your grandfather's mother.'

'You mean you came to service here?' asked William, unbelieving.

''Course I do. Ain't Soph' never told you? We was all born 'ere and we went to work soon as we was big enough. My Mam and Dad had ten on us in that two-roomed little ol' cottage as used to stand down Ringles Lane. The big'uns had to go to a job soon as ever they could to make room for the littl'uns. Aunt Marthe – as was Soph's Grandmother Berridge – wanted the place 'ere for Kiz, and never got over me getting in fust. She put 'erself into such a puggatery about it as they fell out, and never 'ad much to do with each other afterwards. Tha's what's the matter wi' Thirz. She's just keeping it up and won't have nothing to do wi' me. I don't want to hev to stop with 'er no more than she wants me. Soph's as diff'rent as can be. She takes after 'er Dad.'

She looked around to find Sophie, who was standing behind her at the sink.

'Soph!' she ordered, her voice with a rising inflexion meant to be obeyed, 'Do you let that washing-up be! I'll do it afore I goo, for old times' sake. I'm done it often enough before – though this kitchen were a lot different then from what it is now. It used to seem such a big ole place to me after our little rooms at home – specially at six o'clock on a winter's morning when I had to slop it all over on my knees afore anybody else was up.'

It took a good deal of cajoling on Sophie's part to stop her from seeing what else she could do before Sophie left early to take her back to her own home. Fran and William watched them crossing 'the front cluss' till they were out of sight.

'What would she do in a geriatric home?' said William, looking troubled.

'Die,' said Fran. 'We can't let that happen if there's any way we can prevent it. Greg's right – he must paint her while there's a chance. And I want to record her life. She's a walking, talking history book of our family, for one thing. She and grandfather must have been very much of an age, so they would have grown up together. I wonder if he ever kissed her on the sly in the pantry? She must have been very pretty, then.'

'We'll talk to Sophie,' William said. 'It really isn't anything to do with us, but I can't bear to think of her being shuffled off to a home just because Thirz' is still carrying on a feud inherited from her mother all those years ago. Dan's got plenty of sense, and so has Joe. George will remember her, and perhaps he may even have a bit of influence on Thirzah. But we can't interfere. They'll have to find some solution for themselves.'

'Doubtless the Lord will provide,' said Fran, rather bitterly quoting Thirzah. 'He usually seems willing enough to oblige Thirzah.'

'Not this time, 'E ain't,' said Sophie, reappearing after getting Sar'anne home. ''E ain't obliging Thirz' now. She can't abear Aunt Sar'anne being the holdest in our family, and letting things out as is been 'ushed up, like, for years. She'll likely come round, do none on us don't take too much notice. But I hev to say it, though she is my sister – she's got a nasty ungiving way with 'er as comes out now and again in anybody kin to the Tibbses. There's been too many o' them as 'as ended up in the 'sylum, through not being able to get their own way with everybody. Mam see to it, though, as we all knowed our duty, so p'raps Thirz'll remember that if she lives to be as old she won't have nobody left close kin to 'er more than Aunt 'as. And Aunt Sar'anne's 'ad six child'en, all dead now, though Thirz' ain't got a single one. It's to be 'oped she'll get over 'er temper, and do as she would be done by. But there, them as lives longest'll see most.'

Time slipped along reasonably enough for the next few days. Thirzah did not relent in her attitude towards Aunt Sar'anne, with results which might have been predicted. The situation soon ceased to be of interest to the other members of Kezia's family. Rural philosophy dictated that what couldn't be cured had to be endured. It was hardest on Daniel, who was otherwise very satisfied with his new lot in life. He could have asked for nothing better than to be always at George's side, going along with the old ways that he understood, and being the cow man he had always been.

So Thirzah stayed in bed every morning till both he went to work and Aunt Sar'anne had gone to Sophie's, and took care to be back in bed before they returned. Dan had taken to having his dockey with George and Molly, and Aunt Sar'anne her lunch at Benedict's. Her life had taken on a pattern with which she, too, was satisfied, though she was too wise in the ways of the world to expect it to last long.

Greg had been quite serious about wanting to paint her, so Sophie escorted her to his studio in Southside House each morning for a 'sitting'. Mid morning she poddled alone up to Benedict's, giving Sophie a lot of help and instruction she could have done well without, and finding herself little jobs to do till Sophie served lunch to William and Fran in their breakfast-room, and got her own and her aunt's in the kitchen.

William had started work in earnest on the book, and apart from the day when he had to leave to go to do his lecture in Cambridge, became absorbed in what he was doing. Fran was not quite so dedicated, but things were going well for her, too. It took her very little time to reduce Burbage Senior's lyric poetry into neat type, and once she had done that, she inveigled Aunt Sar'anne into her study, where she had set up a carefully concealed tape recorder. Aunt Sar'anne's eyes, though, were too keen to miss it. 'What's that there thing, then?' she asked. Fran, crestfallen, explained, and let her hear the conversation that had been recorded.

'I was afraid you'd mind, if I let you know,' Fran said. 'But it would please me a lot if you'd go on talking to me about your life, so that we have a true record of them.'

'What sort o' things?'

'Anything and everything, from your childhood right up till today,' Fran said.

'Tha's no worry to me,' said the old lady. 'I all'us did hev a good mem'ry, and besides, I'm kep' a little book ever since I was married, with dates and such in it. So I can tell you to the very day when folks were born or got married or died, and suchlike. Where do you want me to start?'

'As far back as you can,' Fran said happily.

It took about three sessions before Aunt Sar'anne really began to let herself go – and a walking, talking history book she proved; but what she told was more than that. It was the story of a life so full of drama and feeling that by Friday Fran knew quite well where her new series was coming from. She said no word to William, who appeared to be as much absorbed in his new challenge as she was in hers. It was not until Sunday morning, lying in bed and enjoying their usual review of the past week, that Fran disclosed her plan.

'I'm going to do a sort of "annals of a village" series, based on Aunt Sar'anne's life,' she said. 'If that sounds ordinary, you can take my word that it won't be. For one thing, because she remembers tiny details about how and why things happened as they did, so you can see them happening as she tells you. She told me one day this week how she had been boiling a sheet in the three-legged pot hung up the chimney on a pot-hook on the hearth, and when she went to lift the pot off the hook, it slipped out of her hand. The water put the fire out, and scalded the cat. That went yowling across the floor, and her old father-in-law, who lived with them, tripped over the cat, and to save himself from falling he grabbed the rickety old table, and that fell over and shot all the children's tea, and the old man, into the ashes on the hearth. And while she was helping the old man up, her husband came home bawling for his tea, which she hadn't had time to cook. "It was herrings," she said, and he put himself into such a temper because he'd been looking forward to them so much that he started swearing at her, and flung himself out and went to the pub. Then she didn't see him again for two days. It turned out afterwards that he'd been in bed with the wife of the chap who kept the pub most of the time, and when the woman's next baby was born, her husband wouldn't own it and took it along for Sar'anne to bring up. And she did – but the "poor little mite", as she called it, toddled out by himself one day when he was about two, and got "drownded" in a dipping hole in the river. And all because a pot handle had slipped in her hand when she was lifting it from the pot-hook. And if that isn't drama, I don't know what is!'

'Oh dear,' said William, gasping with laughter, 'you'll have to deny the viewers the bit about the baby being drowned – because it's all high farce without that.'

'Yes, my darling, but good drama with it. "Make 'em laugh – make 'em cry." And it's history, too, real history. It's my job to turn it into something worth watching. If it does come off, I have enough already for at least three series. So now you tell me what you've been finding out.'

He'd been so reticent that she'd begun to fear he was finding Bob's book a great disappointment. He was silent for a moment, and then, his mind made up, began to explain to her. He was well aware that what he had to tell her would stun her credulity.

'I suppose what it boils down to is that for the first time I am really understanding what time is. Learning its philosophy. Historical roots go deep, and keep flowering. In this particular case, ancestral roots, I think, as well. The place is St Saviour's Church, my darling, and the roots, I'm pretty sure, are yours. The man who wrote it was the parson there during the Civil War. And his name, my sweetheart, was Francis Wagstaffe.'

They were silent, till the shock of his disclosure had worn off. Then he went on, gently warning her not to expect too much. 'I think he must be somehow blood-related to you, but of course he lived three hundred years ago, and he may be of a collateral branch of the family. I haven't got very far with it yet. But his ancestry till then is set out fairly clearly, and one thing certain is that Francis and Frances are family names.'

'Grandfather's second name was Francis,' she said. 'So was my father's.'

'Yes, I knew that. And that's a cogent point. What it means is that if the rest of the book proves him to have been your direct ancestor, I need have no further worries about declaring it, or letting anybody else in on it. If it had come down directly from father to son, it would have come to you. You can claim it as yours by hereditary right, if anybody ever asks. I have no idea what the law about such things is, but I doubt if anybody would question your right to it. Bob would be tortured before he'd let on how we came by it. Especially when he knows what it is.'

'It's marvellous. I can't believe it! So what will you do with it?'

'That, my sweetheart, is the question. Unless there's more fact to it than the book itself so far provides, I can't call it research. Of course the bit in code may be different if I can decode it – but at the moment there isn't enough documentary evidence for me even to call it history. But the narrator has such an engaging style that you forget it's history. It reads more like a novel. Honestly, he actually states that the first bit was written for something to do and because he loved writing – like you do. But then, you have his genes – and, incidentally, Cromwell's. His grandmother was a Cromwell. I always said you were a Puritan – though in fact, according to him, few of the Cromwell family were. Most of them were royalist cavaliers. Well, so he declares. But it may all be fiction. I don't know, yet.'

'Based on fact, though. Most fiction is. Like mine is based on Aunt Sar'anne. So . . .' She lay silent thinking. He knew her too well to interrupt the flow of her thought.

She sat up and looked down at him. 'William,' she said, intent and serious, 'you don't have to stick to historical fact absolutely, do you, now? You've always said that to be a good historian you have to use a bit of imagination. Why not stretch that element a bit more? You know all the historical background, anyway. Now you have the bones of a story which could have actually happened.

It only needs the details added from your imagination. Why not turn it into an historical novel?'

'It's a fascinating thought,' he said. 'I should have to have a pseudonym, though. William Burbage might write a modern whodunit, but not tangle with history proper. Can you think of one for me?'

She knew he was only half in earnest. 'It's what your father would have done with it – because for fiction you need to be a wordsmith. You are tied to nothing but your own imagination and your skill with words. He wrote novels. I think that is his legacy to you. What did you say his full name was?'

'Jonathan Ross Burbage.'

She mulled it over, trying it this way and that. 'You'd have to discard the Burbage, of course. Why Ross?'

'I don't know, darling. Your guess is as good as mine.'

'Maybe a family name from your mother's side. Ross of Benedict's. Benedict Ross. That's it! Benedict Ross.'

It pleased him. 'Done!' he said. 'Amen. So be it.'

When Eric Choppen put his hand to the plough of business, things tended to get done quickly and efficiently. His intention had been to 'develop' Old Swithinford in a very different way from that of Arnold Bailey. His object had been to preserve it as a 'show' village to which he could encourage townfolk and tourists to come for nostalgic country holidays, and make very successful commercial ventures of the extra facilities and attractions he intended to provide. During the process, the rather ruthless businessman doing his best to substitute work for the adored wife he had just lost had been 'tamed' by the friends he had found in this new environment. They included his present partners in Manor Farms Ltd – the composition of which company had changed very considerably since its inauguration. He was himself one of its larger shareholders, as well as its managing director. The biggest shareholder of all, now, was Elyot Franks.

Since William and Fran's 'wedding', Eric had finally ceased to be a 'furriner' eyed suspiciously as somebody likely to exploit the community for his own ends, and had become genuinely accepted as a member of it. The catalyst had been Nigel Delaprime. That he should have been the person responsible for ensuring that the parish had a new rector – and such a one – had settled his status there once and for all.

Michaelmas over, Eric got on with the business of restoring the old surgery for its new owner, Nicholas Hadley-Gordon. As Manor Farms Ltd now owned such a large part of Old Swithinford already, especially all the small cottages they had restored in the first instance, Eric kept at his disposal a team of building contractors, always at the ready for any large task between his own additions to the hotel and sports centre, and constant maintenance and repair of the firm's cottages.

His reputation for honesty and efficiency stood him in good stead with the local authorities, as did his complete grasp of their functions. Nobody attempted to take Eric for the sort of ride which less knowledgeable people were subjected to by planning committees and their officers. He got what he asked for with the minimum of fuss by knowing where he stood with them and letting them know that he knew.

Nick had gone to London, and his grandfather had gone with him to see him settled into a pad of his own, the agreement being that he should be left to his own devices for six months, with an option to continue the experiment for another six months if by Easter he had not yet made up his mind what it was he wanted to do. Effendi really no longer needed his luxury flat in London, but until he had tried out being a permanent resident in Old Swithinford, he felt it would be foolish to get rid of it. He thought it unwise to encroach on Bob and Jane too much while the old surgery was being restored for him, but he felt it was selfish to hang on to his lease of the cottage, knowing that Anthea Pelham wanted it when his lease ran out. He gave it up willingly to her at once, and agreed wholeheartedly to Eric's plans for the conversion of the old surgery, so that Dr Hardy could occupy the smaller part of it while awaiting the completion of his plans for Casablanca.

Eric would not undertake any alterations there – for one thing because time was of the essence for the doctors, and for another because he wanted no dealings, however vicariously, with Bailey. He still believed there was more to Bailey's departure than met the eye, but he kept that to himself. There was no need to add to Marjorie's worries.

Nigel, though not yet inducted, had taken over the tenancy of Church Cottage down Spotted Cow Lane, and was furnishing it with treasures of his own taken out of store, and other antique bits suitable for so modest a dwelling. In the arrangement of his new home he had an excellent ally in Marjorie, and while waiting he lived with Eric at Monastery Farm, where Marjorie took him under her wing as well as Eric. Apart from worrying about the twins, she was happier than she had been for years.

So, as they moved into autumn, the group of Church End friends settled into a new pattern, with some temporary gaps, and one addition, Dr Hardy.

Terence Hardy had continued to make the hotel his base, rather to everybody's surprise, even after Eric had moved heaven and earth to get his part of the old surgery habitable. Some of them – Fran for one – hoped it didn't mean that he would, after all, move out to Casablanca when he could. They were getting increasingly fond of him, and as living in the hotel meant he was in close personal touch with Eric, he was often also to be found at Monastery Farm, another unattached male gathered under Marjorie's wing.

Fran sensed Hardy's restlessness, however, and remarked on it to Beth. Beth ventured to suggest that perhaps, after all, he felt Old Swithinford a bit of a dead end after living so long in a town. They went out of their way to make him feel one of them, inventing reasons for social occasions they could invite him to, such as informal dinner parties. All very nice, fine and large for those who had nothing better to do, said William, which made Fran laugh. He was about the last person to deny his company to anyone who wanted it.

They all agreed that Hardy was a social asset to them, as well as proving himself to be a good doctor. He made excuses to visit Benedict's, dropping in mid morning, sometimes coinciding with Greg taking a break from his now almost continuous painting.

The daily sittings with Aunt Sar'anne were coming to an end, which meant that she was often parked in the kitchen with Sophie while Greg and Terence occupied the sitting-room, where Fran and William joined them out of courtesy, albeit on William's part sometimes uncharacteristically grudgingly. He was becoming more and more immersed in his task with Bob's book.

Fran found time for the doctor partly because she liked him, and partly because he soon opened up to her, as most people did. On one of the few occasions on which they had been alone together, he had sought her advice about how to handle the different sorts of people in his rather widespread, three-in-one new practice. He knew from experience how to deal with the Lane Enders, who were very much like any other modern suburban people. He found the displaced villagers who now lived in the Hen Street semis and council housing more difficult. As he told Fran, they were much like the estate-dwellers until they were ill and needed him. Then they became a different breed of people that he couldn't categorize as fish, flesh, fowl or good red-herring.

'I should go for fowl,' Fran advised him, laughing aloud. 'Why do you think the place is known as Hen Street?' But she tried to answer him seriously, all the same. 'I think I know what you mean,' she said. 'It's probably due to the change in their social status. They don't consider themselves farm labourers any longer, though some of them were born to be just that. But neither are they "middle-class", because they're still truly rural at heart. I imagine being ill causes them to revert without knowing. In remote rural areas like this, from time immemorial the parson and the doctor have had a sort of mystique it is now difficult to explain to outsiders. Reason tells postwar generations, such as those you're speaking of, that it was – is – old fashioned nonsense that they want no truck with. But it's there, in their bones. Such dyed-in-the-wool feelings take a long time to eradicate. So if they're a bit truculent, I'd guess that it's because they feel the mystique you carry with you, and hate to have to admit it.

'Go easy with them. William would tell you that it's because in this transitional period from a hierarchical system to a classless society, nobody knows where he stands. We don't feel the change nearly as much as they do – but then, it's always easier to travel downhill than up. How do you get on with the few real villagers still left – people such as George Bridgefoot or Bob Bellamy, or those like our Sophie and Ned?'

'I've never classified Bridgefoot or Bellamy at all,' he replied, rather surprised at her intuition. 'They don't belong to any class, do they? They know who they are, and expect other people to take them or leave them. Either of them would only be himself, wherever he was or in whatever company. I can't say that so far I've had much to do with the Miss Wainwright sort – they don't seem to be ill.'

'What you mean is that they don't send for you before it's absolutely necessary,' she said. 'What you have to be careful of with them is never to tread on their pride.'

He was beginning to enjoy his new surroundings, and had made up his mind to stop in Church End. Then there would be room at the Casablanca Health Centre for both his married partners, and a block of consulting rooms. It had also occurred to him that it might be of advantage to him as the senior partner to be a little removed from the others, and in a different social milieu. His life was at a crossroads, both professionally and personally. He felt he had to choose carefully the path he followed from now on.

So far, the personal side of it could hardly be called an unqualified success, but the stability he sensed in Old Swithinford attracted him more and more. He didn't want to make a mess of this chance to start again but he was in unknown territory.

He had imported a young locum to help him with the large practice till his partners should be installed, and this gave him a bit more time for social activity, though he was still rather overworked. He enjoyed these short spells of freedom thoroughly.

It was in one of these intervals, when he been hoping to be able to 'socialize' with his new acquaintances, that it was borne in upon him how hard they worked. None of them had the luxury of a locum. All of them worked, in their own way, morning, noon and night – according to the season, or the weather, or whatever was driving them.

The exception, he discovered, was Elyot Franks. Most of them, as far as he could judge, were quite comfortably off, even the farmers. Of the rest, with the possible exception of Nicholas

Hadley-Gordon senior, Elyot Franks was by far the wealthiest. It didn't take Terence long to diagnose that Elyot was the one with time on his hands. He had become a magistrate, and was on local committees here and there when he felt there was any obligation for him to serve. But before unexpectedly inheriting the Swithinford Hall Estate and the fortune that went with it, he had spent his life in the Royal Navy – and after the first novelty of being suddenly very rich and equally unexpectedly, happily married had begun to wear off, his continuous inactivity irked him.

He lacked hobbies. Having spent his life at sea, he was no gardener. He did not write, as William and Fran did, or paint and make music, as Greg did professionally and Bob did as an amateur when he was not out at work or enjoying some aspect or other of the world of nature. The many facets of Eric's job left him very little spare time; Nigel had undertaken the very demanding job of pulling the church and the parish back from the brink of extinction. Yet all of them still found time for each other, and for him, the newcomer. Hardy appreciated that. He marvelled at the way they all seemed linked to a private intercom system, so much on the same wavelength that what affected one affected all. He had never met quite the same thing in any town, though of course people sorted themselves into groups or cliques according to their circumstances, wherever they lived.

He began to feel at home among them, and looked forward to invitations to formal dinner parties as he had never done before. Yet he enjoyed even more being able to drop in for no reason other than that he could spare the time. It was by dropping in on Elyot and Beth that he began to strike up a special friendship with Elyot.

He had always loved to use his hands. It had been that fact that had led him into medicine because someone had once told him he had surgeon's hands, and from that moment his great ambition had been to be a surgeon. He hadn't achieved it – but the reason for that was something he didn't particularly want to be reminded of. He had, instead, become a GP. But before any of that had happened, he had enjoyed making models, especially ships. He was consequently knowledgeable about ships and naval matters.

One day when he called at the Old Rectory, he found Elyot there alone, accompanied only by bottles of brandy and ginger ale. When offered a 'horse's neck', he broke his own rule never to drink on duty, and accepted it.

'I don't usually drink alone, these days,' Elyot said. 'Beth doesn't like it, for one thing, and for another, when she's about, I don't need to. She somehow seems to find me things to do, so time doesn't hang on my hands so much. But I'd got into the habit of it – rather badly – between having to part with my ship and finding Beth. That's why you caught me out today. She's taken both the girls and the baby to Cambridge, and they won't be back till fairly late because they're going to have tea with Monica and our two girls' twin sisters. I expect you've heard the Petrie story.

'But I hate days when there's nobody here but me and I have nothing special to do. My thoughts go back to my days at sea. I sometimes wonder what on earth would have happened to me here if Beth hadn't taken pity on me – I should probably have drunk myself to death. A lot of naval men do. They invest all their finer feelings in loving their ship, and when the inevitable parting comes, they can't take the loneliness. Any more, I suppose, than a lot of widowers can. I'd had some pretty difficult years before I inherited all this – and Beth. I would have said no woman could ever take the place of my ship – but one lives and learns. I know better, now.'

'Tell me about her – your ship, I mean, not your wife.'

Elyot hesitated. He would very rarely tell anybody about his last command. The memory was still too painful. Hardy was quick to notice, and went on himself instead of waiting for an answer. 'I used to make ship models, when I was a boy. I was crazy about war ships. What was she? What class? And what happened to her?'

Elyot ignored the last bit of the question and answered the rest. He found his listener very interested, and was surprised how much they had in common.

'So when did you stop making models, and why?' Elyot asked.

'When I married the first girl I fell in love with, without giving any thought to anything but getting her into bed. She wasn't much

204

of a success as a wife, but I can't blame her for that. She had no time for a man whose ambition meant he had to work when she wanted to be out at parties, or who had a stuffy hobby she didn't share. She was no happier than I was. As a marriage, it just didn't work. That kind of calf love's like a virulent fever – you can't help getting it, or acting like an idiot while your temperature's running so high. When it was too late for me to go back to what I had intended to do with my life, I could see how hopeless it all was. She was bored and I was miserable. I left her. I was twenty-six. I've never made a ship model since.'

'I don't suppose you would care to begin again?' Elyot asked. 'I've always wanted a scale model of my last ship – and I could share all the plans for construction and provide details that only somebody who'd sailed on her could know. We could investigate all the new commercial kits to see if it would be possible to adapt one, or we could start absolutely from scratch – expense no object. As it happens, I'm a relapsed ship-modeller, too, so you'd find me a reasonable sort of apprentice. But I know how much time such a project would take to complete. That may be the worst snag. You've just told me you were twenty-six when you broke with your first wife. I was already fifty-six when I met mine. Suppose you find you want to marry again? Or I slip my cable? We might have to leave our model half-finished.'

Hardy was immediately hooked on the idea, and said so, smiling a wry smile.

'I don't think you need worry very much about me trying matrimony again,' he said. 'I did make two further attempts at it, both just as disastrous, if for totally different reasons. The voice that breathed o'er Eden never reached me. I think the needle must have got stuck somewhere round here. You can still hear an echo of it, though I'm not the only one to have missed it. Eric and Nigel, and Hadley-Gordon, who'll soon be my next-door neighbour. Gosh! Is that really the time? I must go! But I promise that I'll give that model project a lot of thought. It's probably just what I need, and come at the right time, too.'

'I shall keep you up to it, so don't worry,' said Elyot.

Beth found her husband in a much more relaxed mood than she had expected when she got home. She soon found out why, and in her usual way, did not forget to record her thanks for another blessing, though not to their new GP.

If there was a cat among the pigeons, it was Aunt Sar'anne. As October slipped along towards November, and the days grew shorter and the evenings longer, the problem of what to do with her became more and more acute, but so far there had been no other solution to the problem of where to house her. There didn't seem to be any solution, and in the way such small matters grow like pimples into abscesses, so the shadow of what to do with her grew darker daily to those most closely involved, while a penumbra formed round others not directly involved but made to feel uneasy.

Thirzah had remained adamant, but found Daniel as determined as he had ever been. As mornings grew darker, she had to stay in bed later, and as evenings drew in, to go to bed earlier. The resultant inactivity was beginning to tell on her health; because she spent most of the middle of every day alone, she was bored, chagrined and bitter, especially at Dan's holding out against her, and ate more and more to comfort herself, thereby gaining a lot of weight. Sophie did her sisterly duty, visiting her morning and evening, reporting truthfully to Fran and William – but the situation was beginning to eat into her, too.

'It's all very well for Dan to be as he is,' she said, 'but after all, it's Thirz's 'ome as well as 'is, and 'e ought to think about 'er more than 'e does. If you ask me, 'e thinks a lot more of them two Jersey cows as George is set 'im up with to breed from than 'e does o' Thirz'. Pure-bred they are, both in calf, and I reckon Dan would sleep up at Glebe to be with 'em if George let 'im. 'E 'ardly ever sets eyes on Thirz', only in bed, 'cos by the time 'e's got 'ome, so 'as Aunt Sar'anne, so Thirz' is a'ready gone to bed.

'Aunt 'as to goo 'ome while it's still daylight, else I hev to turn out to goo with 'er, and to tell you the truth, I'm glad when she does hev to goo. I want my 'ouse to myself sometimes, same as other folks do.'

The last thing Fran and William wanted was for anything to upset Sophie, or the routine at Benedict's that depended so heavily upon her. They discussed her outburst later with anxious seriousness.

'Nobody in his right senses could possibly have expected the arrangement to last as long as it has,' William said. 'Especially anybody who knows Thirzah. But apart from the fact that I can't see any other solution to the problem, I rather suspect Dan's part in keeping it going. I think he's having the time of his life! He's been what Sophie would call "a toad under a harrow" with Thirzah all his married life – and has suddenly found out what it is like to be unbridled and go his own way. Working side by side with George, and with two beautiful cows to look after in the hope of raising more till he's got a little herd, he must be in a sort of seventh heaven. It's an ill wind that blows nobody any good.'

Fran smiled. She had had such thoughts herself, but had been careful not to voice them. 'Unbridled?' she said. 'I told you you needn't worry about not being able to find the right words! You make him sound like the Tiber when Horatius was keeping the bridge. You mean he's *"Burst the curb, and bounded, Rejoicing to be free"* – exchanging his anything-but-docile wife for a couple of gorgeous Jersey heifers? Why Jerseys, I wonder? They're out of fashion, in the doghouse for producing too much cholesterol. I'll bet George let Daniel choose, and psychology suggests that he went for something as unlike Thirzah in looks as well as temperament as he could. I must admit I have got a soft spot for Jersey cows – but if George sends us cream and butter, I shall soon begin to look like Thirzah, so you'll have to keep your eye on me.'

'I always do,' he said. 'But not because I worry about you putting on an extra pound or two. It is all a bit like a Whitehall farce, if there weren't such a serious side to it. It's beginning to worry a lot of people – George for one. He's obviously in Daniel's confidence. He took it on himself to go and see Eric to ask if there was any chance of a cottage being free. As it happens, there are several – but that could only be a temporary solution. For one thing, Eric is getting lets over the Christmas period this year. But that wasn't the real objection. She wouldn't have been safe, and though George was offering to pay the rent, it wouldn't have been fair moving her for such a short time. Eric said he felt that George was relieved that he had to refuse to let him a cottage. The case is too close to home for George. He blamed himself for what happened when old Esther Palmer was made homeless, and he can't forget the consequences. George is worried about both women – Aunt Sar'anne and Thirzah.'

'As I am about Sophie. It isn't fair on either of them – but what alternative is there? We can't exploit Aunt Sar'anne – as Greg and I have been doing – and then condemn her to a geriatric home, can we?'

'No. Eric has an uneasy private conscience about such as Aunt Sar'anne. He told a lot of old people like her when he first came here that he paid taxes to make sure there were places for them to go to, and he did turn some out of their homes. Then he had occasion to go to a geriatric place – about Aunt Esther – and it has haunted him ever since. He's wondering about a private home – paid for by contributions from all of us who could afford to contribute, as he had to fork out for Aunt Esther till she gave in and went to Temperance Farm.'

'That's absolutely out of the question!' said Fran, her voice almost brittle with horror. 'Eric can't know what he's talking about! In the first place, she declared from the start that she wouldn't be put in the "union". We might as well sign her death warrant and be done with it! And it would be such an insult to Sophie and her family, so damning to their pride, that they would never hold up their heads again, or ever forgive Eric for putting his oar in, or anybody else like us for ever contemplating such "charity". I'm sure George squashed that idea before it was ever hatched.'

'Yes, he did, and in the same sort of terms as you have just done.' William got up and walked about – a sure sign to Fran that he was disturbed, however lightly he seemed to be taking the matter. 'But you haven't put forward any other options, have you? What Eric saw was a geriatric hospital ward into which people who shouldn't have been there had been put to die. One would hope that old people's homes would be a lot better than that. But they aren't and we know it. Just sitting. Sitting from early morning till they are put to bed with the fowl, and then sedated so that they cause no trouble during the night.

'I was talking to Elyot about it – Beth was born with a social conscience and has nudged him into taking notice. One of his fellow magistrates happens to live next door to one. Every sound, and apparently a lot of smell, gets through. I shan't tell you half the horror stories I heard at second hand from Elyot, or you won't have any sleep. It's just another example of the Welfare State as Beveridge envisaged it not being able to cope. It was a good idea that didn't work in practice. Except, of course, that anything which doesn't work in practice wasn't a good idea in the first place. In this instance, I'm not sure the criticism applies. It *was* a splendid idea – but how could Beveridge or anybody else have foreseen the future as it has turned out to be? There must be hundreds of Aunt Sar'annes. Their very numbers numb our sensibilities about them. It's only when we get one of them literally on our own doorstep that we start to give the matter any proper consideration. And, my darling, they are not all Sar'annes, with all their buttons on at ninety-plus, or half as lively physically as she is. The great majority who submit to becoming cabbages are kept alive more to soothe our communal conscience than for any other reason. It will work out in time, I suppose.'

'In time for what, though?' she asked. He didn't answer. Neither needed telling what the other was thinking, but both hoped the other wouldn't put it into words. Of all their circle, they were the only ones who had rooms furnished but not occupied. They feared they would, in the end, have to submit to conscience again. Fond of Sophie and willing to relieve her of her encumbrance as they might be, they didn't want anyone living permanently under their roof.

Nigel moved into the cottage a week before his induction at the end of October. It would be an occasion made the most of by two sets of people – his friends, who were so glad to have him permanently among them, and the faithful congregation, who had been so long starved of what they hoped for and expected from their rector. Sophie openly rejoiced that it might possibly mean they would see Eric in church oftener than he went at present, which was only for special occasions. Fran doubted it, and told her so. Eric was no church-goer, though very willing to pull his weight as a businessman wherever his particular expertise might be of use.

Nigel's induction would, as always in the past, have to be accompanied by a social gathering after the service. This caused the first rumblings of disquiet in Sophie. Where would it be held? Before the short spell of Beth's father as rector, when the 'Old Rector' had occupied the Old Rectory, before its restoration 'a big old barn of a place', where the octogenarian bachelor occupied fewer and fewer rooms as the years passed, church functions were held there, especially as congregations continued to decrease. But the Old Rectory was now the rather grand home of Elyot and Beth Franks, and the old school, which had been kept to act as 'parish room', was brought back into service. There had been little if any use for it since the new hotel offered suitable facilities for almost any kind of social occasion.

Sophie, whose feathers were already ruffled by the trouble with Aunt Sar'anne, raised the question with Fran. 'It's to be 'oped,' she said, 'that the new rector being so thick with Choppen won't mean they'll 'old the reception after the service anywhere but in the old school. It wouldn't be right to ask the bishop to go to a pub. The old school belongs to the church and what were good enough for us once still ought to be, though I daresay it'll fall to me to get it ready. If they call a meeting about it for such as us, I shall 'ave my say, and tell 'em what I think.'

(Standing in for Thirzah?) Fran was disturbed by Sophie's air of truculence, and tried a bit of verbal soothing syrup. 'The school would be very bare and musty, after all this long time, and evenings in October can be very cold. Besides, you can hardly describe the hotel as a "pub".'

'It's no place to 'old church do's in. Whatever would the bishop think?'

'My dear Sophie, bishops are men of the world. They always have been, especially the Lords Spiritual – those who sit in the House of Lords, you know. And as it happens, our bishop is an old friend of the Reverend Delaprime. They were at school together.'

210

Sophie's sniff and set lips said so very plainly 'Now try pulling the other one' that Fran laughed aloud. 'I don't think we need worry, Sophie, honestly. The new rector and George will sort it out sensibly without much fuss, I'm sure.'

'And what about Kid Bean? 'E's still the other churchwarden, be 'e who and what 'e may. Time was when there would ha' been a vestry meeting, so as people like us wasn't left out altogether.'

'Will Thirzah be there?' asked Fran, in an attempt to turn the conversation.

''Ow should I know?' replied Sophie huffily. 'That'll be between 'er and Dan, I daresay. No business o' mine, as far as I can see. Beryl Bean knows more about what goes on there now than I do. Aunt Sar'anne don't say nothing, and I don't ask 'er. But it can't go on as it is a lot longer.'

For once Fran felt annoyed by Sophie's silliness, and let her go to get on with her work without more ado, telling William that they might have known somebody or something would spoil even as innocent an event as an induction.

William raised his eyebrows, and said, ''"*As it was in the beginning, is now, and ever shall be*". Forget it, my darling. It'll sort itself out, and it won't affect us at all.'

Fran wasn't so sure, but she let the matter drop.

Two days later, Greg having asked Aunt Sar'anne to go for one final sitting, they expected Sophie to be late and arrive alone, which she did, but in a great state of flurry.

'Thirz' took bad,' she said, sitting down on the nearest chair and with every appearance of being about to burst into tears. 'I'm been there trying to persuade 'er, but hev that new doctor she will not. Do, she say it ain't the doctor as can do nothing to 'elp, it's only George and Dan'el and the new rector as can do that. She wants me to goo and get Kid Bean to interfere, which I will not, even for 'er.'

'Whatever's the matter with her?'

Sophie, incapable of answering, shook her head so vigorously that she sent huge tears from her cheeks alternately to one side and the other.

'It don't bear thinking about,' she said at last. 'George warned

Dan as 'e feared it might 'appen, if she were crossed like she is being for much longer. Goo right off 'er 'ead, I mean.'

Having begun, she poured out her tale. Last night, the bell-ringers, who had been out of practice since the New Year, had had a long practice session with a full ring. George had gone down with them to help, though he could no longer ring, and Dan had gone as well, instead of going straight home. Sophie had delivered Sar'anne back to Thirzah's house before it was dark, so Thirzah was already in bed when the bells began to ring. The sound of them, going on and on had 'druv Thirz' silly'.

'Seems she squealed at the top of 'er voice for Dan who wasn't there, but wouldn't go downstairs 'cos Aunt Sar'anne was there, so she set about stopping the sound o' the bells from reaching her as best she could.

'She got out o' bed and locked the door, do Aunt might try to get in to 'er, and by the time Dan got 'ome, she'd stuffed every crack with rag – she'd tore up pillowcases and Dan'el's best Sunday 'ankerchiefs into strips and shoved 'em down the cracks round the winders and the door.

'When Dan 'ad broke the door down 'e still couldn't get in, 'cos she'd pulled the feather-bed off the bed and were laying underneath it, right up against the door, rolled up in blankets and the eiderdown. And she'd stuffed 'er ears up with candle wax, and wrapped 'er 'ead in a towel. Dan thought she 'ad smothered 'erself, but she come round when she see 'im, and called 'im such names as you'd never ha' thought she knowed.

'Dan set about righting the bedroom, and got 'er back into bed. Then 'e told 'er as 'e was going to fetch me, and get the doctor. But she wouldn't let 'im leave 'er, and it were nearly daylight this morning afore she started to snore, and 'e slipped out and come to mine. As far as I can make out, she's 'erself again now except as she keeps a-saying as *she will not hev them bells rung never no more* – and ordering Dan to go and tell the new rector and George so. 'E don't know what to do.'

'She must have the doctor, of course,' said Fran, quite horrified by the tale. 'Whatever the outcome is. It sounds quite serious.'

Sophie had by now given way to tears. 'It is, and more'n you know,' she sobbed. 'George could see it coming, the way she's

212

been just lately. You see, our Grandmother Berridge was sister to old Billy Tibbs, as weren't in 'is right mind, and never 'ad been. Folks'll tell you that there's all'us one o' the Tibbs fam'ly in every generation born like that or goo like that. Mam used to worry about it when we was little, and she prayed and prayed as none of us three would 'ave it, but when Het started heving 'sterricks Mam was feared it was the Tibbs blood in 'er coming out. That's why she made us promise as we'd all'us look after 'er. But it seems it weren't Het as 'ad the Tibbs blood – it were Thirz'.'

'Oh Sophie, don't say such things! She's just showing off. You know how she acts to get her own way. She's been bottling up her temper about Aunt Sar'anne till it's got the better of her, that's all. I suggest we get Dr Hardy to her as soon as ever we can. He'll give her something to calm her down, and she may be quite different after a good night's sleep. She won't want to miss the Rector's induction, I'm sure.'

'That might ha' been so if it 'ad been old Dr 'Enderson, but she's took agin the new man. She don't reckon a lot to a man as is a'ready 'ad three wives by the time 'e's forty.'

'How on earth does she know that? And what's it got to do with him as a doctor? She can't have Dr Henderson back, whatever sort of a state she puts herself in. Here's William. We'll ask him to ring Dr Hardy and explain the case to him. Perhaps it would be a good idea if I came with you back to Thirzah's, to be there when the doctor comes.'

The relief on Sophie's face was evident, and William was sent to call the doctor. He went to use the study phone, and came back saying Dr Hardy would make it his first call after he had finished his morning surgery, in about half an hour's time.

As a consequence, it was a very anxious group that sat round the kitchen table at Benedict's at mid-morning. It had been a strange experience for them all. Daniel had been at home when they all got there, and had done his best to persuade his wife to see the doctor, but she had reacted so strongly and unreasonably that in the end Sophie and Dan had had to hold her down to allow Dr Hardy to administer an injection to sedate her. She had sworn and screamed and fought him off, her references to his past private life being little short of obscene.

He had asked if there was anywhere he could have a consultation alone with Dan, so they had all gone back to Benedict's, where Dan said he wanted Sophie, as well as Fran and William, to hear what the doctor had to say. William was called, and asked to ring Greg, telling him to keep Aunt Sar'anne out of the way as long as he could.

The doctor was grave. He listened to a very garbled version of the chance of there being hereditary derangement, was told of Thirzah's recent tendency to have 'turns' if she couldn't always get her own way, and the whole fantastic situation with regard to Aunt Sar'anne.

'I really can't believe it is anything much more serious than what she has brought on herself by getting into such a temper, made worse by her self-imposed imprisonment,' he said. 'It could be that there is a slight hereditary tendency towards hysteria, especially as I understand there is another sister prone to it. But I'm pretty sure that a day or two of sedation, followed by some exercise after being cooped up for so long, will put her right. Of course, the thing most necessary is for the initial cause of her anger to be removed. Would you like me to try to get the other old lady into a home?'

It was Dan who answered. 'We don't want that, Sir, if there's any other way. I know Thirz' better 'n most folks, and I'm in be'opes that when she comes round she'll be ashamed of 'erself, and be peaceable. I reckon we ought to give it a try, like, afore we put poor old Sar'anne into one o' them places. I'll stop at home more to look after Thirz', 'cept for an hour morning and night when I hev to go and see to the cows. If you was to ask me, I should say as she'll be as right as rain a week from now.'

Aunt Sar'anne appeared at this point, and Hardy, taking in at a glance how utterly capable she was, decided on the spot that if anybody had to go into a home, it would be Thirzah. He took his leave, asking them to let him know at once if Thirzah had another fit of hysteria; if not, he would call again tomorrow.

'I fear we haven't heard the last of that,' William said ruefully to Fran as they prepared to return to their respective studies for what was left of the morning.

*

At six o'clock that same evening, Sophie, in deep distress, burst in upon them in new trouble. When she had taken Aunt Sar'anne 'home' to Thirzah's for the night, they saw at once that Thirzah had seized the chance of Dan being gone to see to his cows to throw all Aunt Sar'anne's belongings out of the back door. She had then locked the door on the inside, and barricaded it.

Sophie had left Aunt Sar'anne sitting on the dustbin bag into which Thirzah had pushed all her clothes, and had gone to fetch Dan. George had insisted on going back with Dan to see if there was anything he could do, and was now helping Dan to break the door in. Thirzah was shouting at them to stop, 'cos she was quite all right, but wasn't going to let nobody in till 'that old bitch' had been found somewhere else to go to. Dan had sent Sophie to ask Joe, Hetty's husband, to bring his van and help to pack Sar'anne's things in it – though where they were going to take them, nobody knew.

Fran looked at William resignedly. There was only one place Sar'anne could be housed there and then, which of course was why Sophie had been sent to test the possibility. The part of Benedict's they called Eeyore's Tail was a self-contained set of rooms, but for the fact that William's study was situated there.

'She can't and shan't have your study,' said Fran, firmly.

'She won't want it,' Sophie said. 'Do you don't mind heving 'er for a little while, she'll be as 'appy in that kitchen there as she would be anywhere. The bed's all made up ready, and she can get up and down them stairs as well as I can. If you don't want to see 'er about, you needn't. Just keep 'er in 'er place.'

Fran had no faith that any such injunction would have the slightest effect – the old lady was too lively to be kept in her place, whatever they might want. Like it or not, the privacy of their sanctuary had been invaded yet again. But short of sealing Eeyore's Tail up, Fran saw no help for it but that from time to time it would become a refuge for some waif or stray with nowhere else to go.

William was having difficulty in repressing his desire to say 'I told you so', and seemed to think it all amusing rather than annoying. Fran, who usually saw the funny side of things, was less cheerful, not because she minded doing a good turn to Sophie or Sar'anne, but because she objected to having been so cleverly manipulated by Thirzah. She was angry, and could not help but show her irritation, which both William and Sophie noted with some dismay.

But when Joe had gone to fetch Aunt Sar'anne and her belongings, Sophie sat down with her hands folded together in her lap, dropped her eyes, and offered her thanks silently to ''Im Above'. Then she looked up to where William stood close to Fran with his arm round her, trying to induce her to accept the inevitable philosophically.

'A friend in need is a friend indeed,' said Sophie simply. 'Thenks.'

Her dignity covered Fran with a great sense of shame, and she left William's supporting arm to go to Sophie to give her what comfort she could before the homeless outcast should arrive.

While there was general concern about Thirzah in the village, to Beryl Bean the story was a godsend. She had been deprived of any new topic for gossip since William and Fran had proved that there had been nothing in the least scandalous about the silence regarding their marriage. Once she had vented her spleen on the stupidity of the second ceremony, 'as only such fools as them with more money than sense would ever have thought of', there had been a dearth of topics worth talking about. She had said as much to her husband, who had snapped back at her that it might be a good thing if she did have to keep her head down and her mouth shut for a little while.

She took umbrage at his daring to suggest he had a right to tell her what she might do in the shop, but disgruntled and frustrated as she was, there was something in Kid's manner that made her, for once, obey him enough to bridle her tongue a little.

'Kid' (official name, Kenneth) was and had been subdued and moody lately, but Beryl thought she knew why. Things hadn't gone well for them recently. Their high hopes of making a lot of money, and of being 'somebody' because of their association with the Baileys, had been doused when Bailey had failed to secure Castle Hill to develop, and had lost the backing of George Bridgefoot's son Brian and Vic Gifford, who'd had a fatal accident.

According to Beryl's reasoning it had all been 'done a-purpose' to prevent them from getting on. She had been very bitter to anybody who would listen about the way she and her Ken had been cheated by 'them two from Benedict's, and them Bridgefoots, and that stuck-up lot at Castle Hill as was only a ignorant fen-farmer married to a charwoman who was now pretending to be rich and posh, though as she, Beryl, knowed for certain, her father was nothink only a undertaker from London.'

She had embroidered the details of that story till she had worn it threadbare; but in the present dearth of anything new, had tried to make it over. To her surprise and displeasure, Ken cut her short on it. Any mention of Bailey was like a red rag to a bull to him now. He went about silent and morose, lying as low as he was able, saying little.

Beryl urged him to stand up for his rights (and hers) against the new parson, but he lost his temper and bawled at her to keep her trap shut. Especially, he told her, about what had happened round last Christmas and New Year. That was more than she would take. She went red with anger, puffed out her chest like a pouter pigeon, and turned on him.

'That new rector is as thick as thieves with all them as robbed us,' she expostulated, 'but they can't get round it as you are the other churchwarden, and you're got to stick up for yourself, so as him and George Bridgefoot don't have things all their own way. From what I'm heard, they're making all the arrangements for the rector to be introduced or whatever they call it without so much as asking your leave. I don't intend to put up with it even if you do. If you don't go yourself and tell that new chap as you expect to be treated properly, I shall!'

'You bloody well won't! You keep out of it, d'you hear? It's my affair, and nothing to do with you. You ain't a member of the church, and never have been. I'm been church all my life, but till Arnold got me made a churchwarden, you'd never been near the place. You don't go nowhere, now, neither church nor chapel, as far as I know.'

'Yes I do, then! You don't know everything. I went to chapel only last Sunday while you'd gone somewhere as you wouldn't tell me, and who should be there but that old woman as is upsetting Thirz' Bates. She's been chapel all her life, and still is. That's one in the eye for Soph' Wainwright, that is! That woman I never could abide, seeing how it was her who done us out o' Jelly's money when he got killed. He wouldn't ha' left her all that for nothing, you may be bound. All'us on 'er knees in church, she is, pretending butter wouldn't melt in her mouth. She's got need to be, if you ask me, carrying on the way she did with Jelly. But it's coming home to roost, what with Thirz' going off her head, same as Hetty all'us has been. Serve 'em all right. I shall get to know from the old woman as Thirz' won't give houseroom to what's going on. You'll see.'

'You won't do nothing o' the sort. You'll do as I say, and keep your mouth shut about me and Arnold. And if anybody comes here asking questions, you tell 'em you don't know nothing.' Then he slammed himself out of the house, leaving his wife with her mouth as wide open as usual, though for once with no words coming out of it.

When Beryl was told that Aunt Sar'anne had found refuge at Benedict's, her frustrated indignation knew no bounds – not because the story itself lacked potential, but because of Kid's embargo on her tongue. All she could do was to produce dark hints.

In the event, Kenneth was consulted about the induction, and took his part in it as instructed, as his wife said, 'as meek as a sucking dove'. Beryl would not grace the ceremony with her presence, and neither, it appeared, would Thirzah.

As Dr Hardy had predicted, once the cause of her indisposition had been removed, Thirzah had become her normal self. Daniel, perforce, had had to do the same, somewhat sadly subdued after his short spell of freedom; but life had to go on.

Thirzah showed no signs of having another 'turn' till the very morning of the induction, when she again raised with Daniel the question of the bells. Was they, or was they not, intending to ring them that night? Yes, they was, he said. Wasn't that what they had been practising for, the night she had throwed such a fit about 'em?

She was beetroot red with anger. Hadn't she give him orders *that she would not have them bells rung ever again*?

Realizing with dismay that she had 'flipped' again, he rushed out to consult George. George, who had plenty on his plate that evening, didn't want Thirzah added to it. He tried suggesting that this time they should just let her get on with it. She was only trying it on, he thought, to see whether or not she was going to be able to lay the law down at church in the future like she had done in the past. She'd draw her horns in, he said, once she found out where she stood. The thing to do was to take no notice, and not give in to her. Dan went home in trepidation to say George had been no help.

Thirz' told him that if he was willing to go on licking George Bridgefoot's boots, she never had been and wasn't going to start now. She wouldn't be going near the church never no more. She was going to stop at home; and stop at home she did.

Sophie did all that was required of her that evening with a glum, set face that told its own tale. Next day, in answer to Fran, she agreed that it had been 'very nice', though Thirz' not being in her pew beside Daniel had left her with more than one pair of hands could do. She wasn't used to them new ways of doing things, neither. If Thirz' had been herself, she would have stood out against the bishop having to go to the 'pub' after the service. Fran judged it best to let the matter drop, though she told William that she was sorry at the effect the situation was having on their usually placid Sophie.

'Poor old Sophie,' William said. 'She's being pulled both ways by this family feud – like the Goths used to pull their prisoners to bits between two teams of horses. Don't you remember what Aunt Sar'anne said about her? "Soph's different," she said, "she takes after her father." The feud's on her mother's side. It may go back centuries. It may even have begun when

> Thurstan and Thorkill from Jutland came
> To harry our homesteads with sword and flame.'

'You don't really mean that, do you?' Fran asked, surprised at William taking such interest in it. 'I just wish we hadn't had to be involved in it.'

'I didn't want us to have to be involved in it, either – but we are, and now it fascinates me. We have two of the protagonists under our roof – though neither of them would keep the quarrel up if it were left to them. But as I see it, it's in Thirzah's blood. Not the tendency to hysteria Terence Hardy diagnosed, but the blood feud. Sophie will never be happy while Thirzah lives, because Thirzah won't let her forget it. We live in the territory of the East Angles, after all. Thirzah and Sophie's ancestors are probably lying in those barrows down at Danesum. Their genes – and their feud – are still with us.'

'William, that's nonsense, and you know it. You're pulling my leg.'

'No, sweetheart, I'm not, honestly. I'm on my own ground, literally and academically. I know this village inside-out and I am still a medieval historian. The basics of life here are still what they were in the Middle Ages.'

'The Angles were before the Middle Ages.'

He was visibly shocked. 'Darling! Surely you know better than that! The Middle Ages began with the fall of the Roman Empire in the fifth century, and lasted a thousand years, approximately. But such terms are only used for the convenience of historians. History is really seamless. Look – let's find a bit of common ground. You must have read some of the Icelandic sagas – *Njal's Saga*, for example.'

'Of course I have. As literature.'

'You can't separate history from literature. *Njal's Saga* simply tells what went on in Iceland after land-hungry Vikings and other Scandinavians discovered it. The various tribes only fell out with each other when greed got the better of common sense; then violence crept in. But tribal characteristics passed down with the tales, and go on being passed down. People like Thirzah are to their Anglo-Saxon ancestors what that rowan tree at Danesum is to the one that was first set there at Dane's Holme to keep evil spirits away. I'll bet Sar'anne lapses into genealogy all the time, doesn't she? I'm just incredulous at the thought that I may be witnessing in Thirzah's behaviour the last remnants of a blood feud which may have begun centuries ago as the result of a quarrel over a bit of land or something. Add a few of the unstable Tibbs genes and we get Thirzah. We can look for real trouble if Thirzah ever imagines she's got a genuine cause for jealousy!'

Fran went straight to their library and took down *Njal's Saga*. Reading it as history, in the light of what William had said, gave her goose pimples. She lost some of her resentment at having to house the sprightly old lady. It was Sophie who suffered. She was, as William had said, torn between her duty to her sister and her aunt, and she no longer had the consolation of long chats alone with William and Fran. She had always to keep a guard on her tongue, whether visiting Thirzah or working at Benedict's. She also felt a burden of guilt for landing Fran and William with Sar'anne. There was no alternative in sight yet and she worried about the immediate future. Fran's birthday fell in November, and in the last years or two Sophie had looked forward to the party as much, if not more, than the guests. She loved the catering for it and the serving up – with Thirzah at her side. But Thirzah wouldn't be there, or at any church affair for any occasion, Christmas included. She would not breathe the same air as Sar'anne.

Sophie broached the subject with Fran, who begged her not to start worrying till the need arose. With so much going on among their friends, they really couldn't make plans. They went on to discuss how other people's plans were progressing, and Sophie, for once having Fran to herself, cheered up a good deal. Fran led her cleverly to talking about her family, and afterwards was able to report gleefully to William that she had discovered other bits that sounded Anglo-Saxon.

'Oh, don't tempt me any more,' said William. 'Here I am, sunk deep into the seventeenth century and getting more and more involved with it every day – and suddenly the old Vikings and Danes pop up and beckon me.'

'I told you,' said Fran, laughing, 'that you needn't fear becoming a hopeless old dodderer, didn't I?'

'And as usual, my darling, you were right,' he said, dropping a rather casual kiss on the end of her nose.

'Get back to your Latin,' she said. 'The Angles and Saxons will wait.'

'Wrong for once,' he said, gloating. 'Your scribbling ancestor has abandoned Latin for his native tongue – I guess he couldn't get what he wanted to say down fast enough. You show your genetic inheritance as much as Thirzah does.'

'Do you want your ears boxed?'

'No. I wouldn't mind being kissed, though.'

November is rarely a popular time of the year, though this year the weather was good and the leaves clung to the trees, flaunting their autumnal beauty till a brisk breeze removed them. But the weather still continued fine, even sunny, and work went ahead with such urgency that there was even less socializing than there had been earlier.

All the farmers were ploughing, cultivating and drilling as long as light would allow them to work. For once, even they had little to grumble about. As Jane, playing with Jade, sang:

> First the farmer sows his seed,
> Then he stands and takes his ease.
> Stamps his feet and claps his hands,
> And turns him round to view his lands
> Waiting for a partner.

In Bob Bellamy's case, the old rhyme was this year literally true. He was waiting for his partner, Effendi, to come back to Old Swithinford, though it could hardly be said that he was taking his ease while doing so. He did, however, have good reason this autumn to view *his* lands with satisfaction. They were his.

Brian Bridgefoot and Charles were in the same boat. Old George, having come to terms with being retired, was enjoying himself a great deal, going his own way without fear of interference or contradiction, and with Daniel beside him.

Eric was doing his best to get Dr Henderson's house restored and ready for occupation by Effendi, who was still in London. Terence Hardy was pressing his firm of builders to get on with the alterations at Casablanca, hoping to get his partners installed there by Christmas. Till they arrived, he was on call too much to spend as much time as he would have liked with his circle of new acquaintances. Comfortable and pleasant as the hotel was, he also began to wish for a place of his own, like they had. He rather surprised himself. His idea of 'home' had so far hardly been somewhere you couldn't wait to get back to – as it seemed to be to most of his new friends, who were all so busy anyway that he occasionally felt lonely.

Nigel was facing up to the less attractive sides of his new incumbency, particularly the sad state of the church tower, and the equally sad state of any finances with which to tackle the urgent problem of restoration. He was genuinely very glad of Eric's practical knowledge and expertise. The cleric and the tycoon made strange bedfellows, but their friendship was close and deep. One way or another, at the present time Eric appeared to be involved, as Sophie remarked, 'at every verse's end' in the affairs of the village – though he had plenty of routine work as well, as the hotel began to gear up to Christmas. Consequently, he was more likely to be found in his office than anywhere else, and to him there went the rest with their problems – or for a pleasant chat, knowing that they would be likely to find other friends doing the same including Terence Hardy when he did have time on his hands, though he now had a new and absorbing interest.

Elyot had lost no time in following up the ship-modelling proposal, clearing one of the downstairs rooms of the former servants' quarters at the Old Rectory to act as a workshop (with Beth's complete approval). There the somewhat unlikely friendship between Elyot and Terence ripened fast, as together they designed and installed work-benches, searched commercial catalogues for the latest equipment and materials, and pored delightedly over plans and diagrams, with Norman Ough's *Royal Navy Warship Drawings* as their bible.

After such sessions, Terence went back to his hotel room

reluctantly. Elyot had a real home. Beth did not intrude on them, though whenever she did appear she showed intelligent interest. It was after just such an interruption that Terence first became aware of a twinge of 'homesickness', or to put it more accurately, a desire for what Elyot had and he hadn't: the bit of his life that centred round Beth.

He noted the lift she gave to Elyot, the change in his voice as he addressed her, the instinctively covert caress of her arm as she set his tea down, the kiss she blew him from the door as she left. The doctor had never experienced that sort of marriage.

He recalled Eric's quip that day he had been called to William – that in his first new patient's case it was no use him quoting the old adage that marriage was the cure for love. He had found out what Eric had meant the very next day, when he had visited Benedict's again after Fran's return and had observed them together.

Then there was Greg and Jess. He saw a good deal of Jess, who since Anne's dereliction had been forced to spend more time at the hotel. He thought Jess by far the most fascinating of the women, and didn't wonder at Greg's slavish devotion to her. Then, in conversation with Elyot, he heard the story of Jane and Bob – a very unlikely couple of married lovers, he judged. He was looking forward to meeting them.

All this made him inclined to look back, review and assess his own experience in the matrimonial field, where three times marriage *had* proved to be the cure for love. More, perhaps, his fault than that of any of his wives. Medical men were reputedly bad husbands. They knew too much of female anatomy to be excited by it for long.

That could only be a partial explanation, though. Young Mrs Charles Bridgefoot, on her way to becoming a vet, must be as well aware as any young doctor that human beings at mating-time were animals in the same class as cats and dogs or hedgehogs – yet whenever he had met her with her husband he had noticed an aura of something else as well as sexual attraction, young as they were.

So what was the missing ingredient in his relationships with the other sex? He was only forty-three, and he still had the same kind of interest in women as most healthy men did. Well – there was plenty of opportunity for sex while he remained in the hotel unattached, but so far he had taken no advantage of it. After being in the company of any of the couples he had just catalogued in his mind, he felt that 'a bit of sex on the side' would be like eating sawdust. Ship-modelling would satisfy him far better.

At social gatherings to which he was invited, there were always at least two other couples besides the hosts. As he had no partner, the hostess usually balanced her table by inviting the other newcomer, Anthea Pelham, with the intention of making both feel at home among them. Very pleasant, too. It could not be denied that Miss Pelham was exquisitely beautiful. About thirty-five, he guessed, with black curly hair like a cap framing a strikingly handsome and intelligent face in which, he thought, every perfect feature fitted to make a perfect whole.

Yet she didn't attract him sexually. He was beginning to think experience must have disillusioned him completely, if a woman like that did not even stir something in him. He felt better for observing that she didn't seem to have much effect on any of the other men either – not even Greg. It was at Benedict's that he reached the conclusion that she was a woman entirely without sex appeal.

It was at a party to mark Fran's birthday, only a small, intimate gathering this year, and the other guests besides himself were Jess and Greg, Beth and Elyot, Jane and Bob, Eric and Nigel, and Anthea. The atmosphere was one of relaxed, gentle compatibility, in which he felt totally at ease; yet the group was made up of people from very diverse backgrounds.

There were five women, very different from each other – yet four of them nevertheless had something intangible in common which the fifth lacked. He tried to diagnose what the difference was, and soon did.

Anthea was the youngest of them, and by modern standards by far the most beautiful. Her figure was exactly the slim silhouette modern fashion dictated. Her hands were beautifully kept, her make-up expert. Her clothes were fashionable, though almost always, he seemed to remember, with high necklines, as if in deliberate contravention of the prevailing emphasis on the female

225

bust and the impossibly low cleavage which drew attention to the little it did conceal.

He looked round at the other four women – and with a sudden flash of insight, spotted what he was looking for. Fran was too plump, Beth too tall, Jane, though elegant, rather plain; Jess was slim, but her figure was too boyish to be fashionable. Yet they all gave out in their own way something so essentially feminine that if it wasn't sex appeal as that was understood, it was something very near it. Anthea, on the contrary, gave out no feminine signals at all. He was by this point clinically interested.

Fran, in her role of hostess, glowed with both light and warmth, providing her guests with a beacon by which to navigate safely in new social waters. Beth, tall and stately, flamed gently and peacefully like candlelight in church. Jess was a firework, lighting up at a touch or a word and positively sparkling with animation, while Jane – it was the first time he had been in her company for more than a few minutes – Jane was a night light. Safe, steady, unfailing, comforting, constant. Lucky Bob. But Anthea was the moon, cold and distant, whose light, however beautiful, gave no warmth. She was not, like the other four, lit from the inside. Any light she gave out was no more than reflection.

His psychological training now suggested to him that her lack of feminine charm must be a deliberate act on her part. She had been switched off, and had resolved never to be switched on again. It was her own decision not to have her bulb replaced or the fuse mended. Hurt desperately, he guessed, by a broken relationship.

She had a habit of avoiding physical contact wherever possible, even drawing back from shaking hands, if she could without offence. So very different from Fran, who had been bear-hugged by Greg, done the bear-hugging herself with a kiss added to Bob, kissed Eric and Elyot warmly, receiving equally warm salutations in return, and turned invitingly to Nigel, who had promptly responded. She had held out both her hands to him, Terence, which he had taken and held, wondering how long it would be before he, too, was expected to kiss her.

William was just as happily saluting all the women (other than Anthea) in the same way, finishing his round of welcome back at

Fran's side, and bestowing on her the warmest kiss of all, to the amusement of those who knew them well and were used to it.

It was during the next visit Hardy paid to the Old Rectory that the subject of Anthea arose between himself and Elyot. Beth had brought drinks for them, and stopped to greet the visitor. Elyot escorted her back to the door, giving her a quick surreptitious kiss behind it. Turning back, he knew that his visitor had seen it.

'Sorry about that,' Elyot said, rather shyly and flushing a little. 'I never expected any of this to happen to me, you know, and I still can't get over it. I apologize. A man of my age shouldn't behave like that in front of other people.'

Hardy smiled a little ruefully. 'It seems to be endemic in Old Swithinford,' he said. 'William Burbage seems to have no qualms about it. I don't think it can be catching, though, because Miss Pelham and I both seem to be immune to the disease.'

Elyot replied much more seriously than Terence had expected. 'Fran and Beth are concerned about her,' he said. 'Jess, of course, works with her, and declares that her air of cool aloofness is deliberately put on to hold off too much brash male attention, and guesses there may be a jealous husband or lover somewhere. I'm no judge. She certainly doesn't invite male attention – but then I don't either look for it or offer it. I never have had much interest in women, since my callow days as a raw naval cadet – well, that is until Beth sailed over the horizon. So I'm nothing to go by. Neither, for very obvious reasons, is William, however many women fall flat at his feet. But she doesn't even attract Greg, to whom beauty in any form is like honey to a bee, female beauty particularly. She leaves him absolutely unmoved. He says she's like a marble statue, good to look at but not what a man wants to take to bed.

'He swears she's actually on the alert to repel any hopeful boarders before they get near enough to grapple. William told us that when Jess first introduced him to her and he was only being normally courteous, she stood him off with unmistakably polite firmness. Jess noticed, and laughingly warned her that she would find quite a number of attractive men about these parts. She had replied, apparently, that she approved of handsome men – *at a*

*distance*. William took it as intended as a warning to stand off.'
Elyot grinned. 'She really needn't have bothered to warn William
off! But one does wonder why she takes that attitude.'

'I was thinking the same thing the other night at Fran's party,'
Hardy said. 'I thought of her as being "switched off", and not
wanting anything or anybody to switch her back on again. So,
of course, she interested me clinically. There must be some
psychological explanation – but she isn't my concern. Sexual
relationships or marital breakdowns are hardly my speciality. Miss
Wainwright and Mrs Bates would say "Physician, heal thyself" if
I attempted to put my oar in. You must have heard how my
reputation as a gay Lothario has cast its shadow before me.'

Elyot suspected that he had introduced that subject on purpose,
and felt obliged to respond, though it was hardly 'up his street'.
'How old are you, Terry?' he asked.

'Forty-three. Still young enough to want a woman in my arms
in bed, if that's what you're asking. But I'm not looking for a wife.
Three's enough.'

'You told me about the first,' Elyot said. He was out of his
depth, and heaved a sigh of relief when Beth appeared, and the
conversation halted abruptly.

'Don't let me interrupt,' she said, taking the hint. 'I'm going,
anyway.'

'No, please stay,' said Hardy. 'I want somebody to know the
truth about my marital escapades before garbled versions wreck
me before I'm given a chance. I'm not at all proud of myself –
but neither am I the black-moustachioed Victorian-music-hall
villain Mrs Bates believes me to be. Elyot's already heard about
my first go at marriage.'

'Yes, and he told me,' Beth said, catching on quickly and
prepared to rescue Elyot from his embarrassment. 'So tell me the
rest yourself. What happened to the next?'

'She was one of my patients, older than I. Out of the top drawer
socially, and very wealthy. I suppose the truth is that she caused
the breakdown of my first marriage, because she was offering me
all the chances my first wife was taking from me. I was flattered,
too, of course. (There was a rather long pause.)

'We had two children – a girl who's fifteen now, and a boy a

228

year younger. I thought I was in clover till I began to suspect that I'd been bought, and was expected to behave as a bought slave should. And I was as helpless as a slave, because she held all the cards. But I couldn't take it – especially having no say in anything concerning the children. I had to re-establish myself as a man who still had ambition to be something other than a gigolo. I walked out again. It didn't do my professional reputation any good. I'm not excusing myself, but it suited her book to put all the blame on me.

'I could see how she had manipulated me to give her what she hadn't got and her social image required – married status, a presentable husband, and children. She had no use for *me* other than that. What she showed off as an ideal marriage was in fact no marriage at all, once Nathan had turned out to be a boy and the son and heir her family had demanded she produce. I couldn't stand the charade, and left her to it – but I wasn't prepared for the aftermath. I'd spoilt her carefully built-up image, and you know the clichés – she played it by the book – "the woman spurned" and all that. Only her pride was hurt, honestly. She was angry – she'd misjudged me and made a bad bargain. She didn't really care any more than she would have done if she'd picked out a wrong'un at a blood sale at Newmarket. I didn't care either, though I love my children. I fought for legal access to them, which I still have. Not that it does me, or them, much good now. And the fault was mine, not for leaving, but for ever marrying her. It left me bitter and disillusioned.' His face twisted into a grimace of self-distaste. 'I stayed single for almost a year – and then went and did it again. Do you really want me to go on with such a sordid tale?'

Beth put out her hand and touched his sleeve. 'Yes, go on,' she said. 'We shan't sit in judgement on you, you can be sure of that. What happened then?'

'The worst bit. Judy was a lovely girl, the daughter of one of my colleagues, pitch-forked by fate into my orbit just at the time when I was missing all the comforts Marcia's money and social position had supplied. Poor child – she fell in love with me. But I should never have married her. I was angry and cynical, taking my fun where I found it, even after I married her. I fell heavily for a

Danish glamour-puss, who was prepared to make the most of her chances for a good time with me. I had no desire for a faithful loving wife or another batch of children. I'd become completely callous about women's feelings by then, and when Judy had had as much as she could take, and protested, I walked out on her as well. The affair with Dagmar didn't last – it was never intended to. Judy would have taken me back, but I knew it would be no good. She would only have been hurt worse the next time. I was ashamed, and vowed I'd never again let myself be tempted into any relationship likely to end in marriage. I felt the most despicable cad – and I still do. I comfort myself by hoping that by now Judy's forgotten me and found somebody worthy of her.

'It's my guilt about her that's making me tell you all this. Punishing myself, perhaps – risking all that your friendship means to me by making sure you know what sort of a snake you are harbouring. It's up to you to make up your minds whether I'm your friend or only your doctor. I know what a multitude of sins a stethoscope can cover, but the truth is that where women are concerned, I just don't make Old Swithinford's grade.'

He looked up at Beth, trying to read her expression. Elyot was wishing he was somewhere else. Looking at Beth, who was returning Terence's look steadily, he saw that his wife's eyes, full of kindness and sympathy though they were, showed the ghost of a twinkle. 'Poor Terry,' she said gently. 'You really have been putting yourself over the jumps. Like The Bolter in *The Pursuit of Love*. Chasing an ideal called love, falling, running away and trying it all again. I know. I'm much the same age as you. I couldn't bolt – but not because I didn't want to! I wanted to bolt *into* a marriage of any sort that would get me away from home and church duties. You could bolt because you were a man with a profession. I had to stay put, because I was a woman and a parson's daughter. We were in the same boat, though, with a lot more just like us. Rebelling against the old ways but unable to cope with the new. I had to stay put so long that the tide turned, for me. You weren't so lucky. And I was made to learn to make the distinction between sex and love. Men tend to find that more difficult than women, I know, especially medical men, or so I've heard. Did you learn the difference? Have you ever been truly *in love*?'

'How on earth should I know? I don't know what love is, except for the bouts of fever that ended by finding myself manacled in marriage. I didn't think about it, till I landed myself here, up to the chin among people who treat love like spring rain – expecting it to do good even if they occasionally get wet. But that's where we came in. What I want to be sure of now is where people like me and Anthea Pelham stand with you, before I burn my boats behind me and decide to live here. Wouldn't it make more sense for me to be just one of the new doctors from the new health centre? I've got cold feet, or I wouldn't have put you through all this soul-searching this morning.'

Elyot excused himself, lest his presence should embarrass the distraught doctor. He saw that Beth approved. She let Hardy collect himself a bit, before answering. 'Don't run away again with your tail between your legs, Terry. Stay with us, and be one of us. Maybe our sort of love is catching. If it isn't, it's still comfortable to be with. And you can't know till you give it a chance – like Elyot had to.' She took a deep breath, but went on resolutely. 'I think what you need to learn is that love is greater than the sum of its parts, and sex only one of the parts – important as it may be. There's plenty of sex without love nowadays – and some folks have to be satisfied with love without sex – like poor old Sophie. But try to believe those of us who know that love and sex really go best together. Even that old misogynist St Paul came to that conclusion in the end.'

She thought it better to paraphrase than quote direct from the Epistle. 'As he wrote, Love doesn't give up easily, and goes on believing and hoping, however grim things get. And love very rarely fails anybody, in the end.'

With Christmas once again in sight, things began to move quickly. The news of Dr Hardy's decision to take up residence among them in part of the restored old surgery was greeted by the Church Enders with relief and pleasure, pouring a soothing balm over

231

their anxiety. They wanted their doctor to be close at hand, knowing their names and recognizing them as individuals in the way they had been used to for at least two centuries, until one thundery night this last summer.

There was more to this than the comfortable feeling of having medical help 'on tap'. In a community which, until the end of the Great War, had been hierarchical in structure for countless generations, the few professional people whose callings brought them continually in touch with high and low, rich and poor, old and young, church and chapel, and all the other variations and permutations of a village, had had a significant social role to play.

When the old order had begun to break down in the first half of the twentieth century, and the finely graded hierarchy to give way to distinct class-consciousness, the social ladder had two ends, but no middle. With the land-owning squirearchy gone for ever, the successful farmers had moved upwards to occupy the top rungs, while the farm labourers and artisans, sticking together, had become a recognizable social group lower down. This caused a 'them and us' situation which threatened the vital interdependence on each other that had previously been the strength and the hallmark of remote rural communities.

It fell to the doctor, the parson, and above all the schoolmaster or governess to make both ends of the ladder meet in the middle. They acted as links and as buffers, and kept the community whole. It was to them that their rather bewildered country neighbours turned for support among the many changes to their traditional way of life, especially those caused by government decrees geared to the urban majority, and to them appearing nothing better than incomprehensible 'foolery'.

'British Summertime' or 'Daylight Saving' in 1916 was an example. It was, said the government, 'a good thing', especially for the working class – but what about those whose working day started at 5 a.m. summer and winter alike? How to explain to the cows why milking time was an hour earlier at both ends of every day? Or to huge cart-horses standing asleep at their mangers, to prevent them from being so startled by the horsekeeper coming to bait them an hour before expected that they lashed out with both huge hind hooves, killing him? What could either farmer or labourer make of such foolery, or do about it? Did they have to toe the line and go along with such nonsense as 'that old hower'?

It affected them even on 'the Lord's day'. A few old folk, unable to understand, ignored it, and continued to attend chapel 'by God's time', going through the pattern of the normal service and leaving again 'by God's time' just as the appointed preacher for the day and the more amenable members of the congregation arrived 'by gover'ment time'.

That story, handed down from father to son, had become a regional 'folk-tale'; but a residue of bitterness was left with the humour. It was only one example.

Old Swithinford had suffered in the name of progress like all other small communities. It had lost its school, two of its three pubs, and its rector. Till lately, it had kept its own old-fashioned doctor – but he had dropped dead in summer this year.

How were they now going to cope without him, who had lived among them so long that he knew their families backwards, and regaled them when visiting with memories of the day he had struggled to bring their first bouncing baby into the world, or patiently urged a poor aged parent out of it. Dr Henderson's death had seemed like the trump of doom – but then, is not the darkest hour always before the dawn?

In spite of the odds against it, they had got a new rector. And though he was young and modern, they were still going to have a doctor living where he should, in the doctor's house. Terence had picked up, mainly from chats with Fran, some of the lingering feelings on this particular point. It had been a factor in his decision to share the old surgery with Effendi, now that it was restored to the point of occupation. It was a charming old property, with the advantage of being close to the Old Rectory, where Elyot and his new hobby could be found when he had time to spare. He made up his mind that as far as it was practicable he would look after the old village himself, and leave the new estates and the rest to his partners. It was a wise choice.

Nigel Delaprime and Anthea Pelham were already established in their cottages, and the new health centre would be opened in the first week of the New Year.

Yet, promising as it all appeared, Fran began to detect pin-pricks

233

of unease, especially in Sophie. So much had changed since last Christmas.

The end of the Michaelmas term was in sight, and William had done his last lecture. He and his wife had been invited to farewell lunches, both in his own honour and for the retiring Master. It gave him enormous satisfaction that at the very last gasp Fran had been recognized, and he was looking forward to having her by his side at these functions; but all the same he wished it was over and done with. He could have done without any official farewells. He had left – in fact, if not officially – when his year of sabbatical leave had begun, a year and a half ago. By now, he did not miss anything of it. He had settled wholly into his new routine, in which there was time for his wife, his household, his friends and his book.

He was, in fact, a supremely happy man, and showed it. Fran rejoiced, and acknowledged that a great deal of it had been due to the discovery of his father. She often looked up at the photograph hanging over William's desk, and gave thanks. Always, it seemed to her, she received an answering smile from those Williamish eyes. How pleased he would have been with the son who was now her husband.

William *was* himself again. He whistled, he sang, he chatted. He was found by Fran early one morning piloting Aunt Sar'anne round the kitchen table to the tune of 'The Cock of the North', which he'd had no idea he was whistling till she had joined in and sung in her rather creaky voice the words she had always associated with that tune:

> Chase me Charlie, chase me Charlie
> Lost the leg o' me draws,
> Chase me Charlie, chase me Charlie,
> Kindly lend me yours.

Fran had collapsed in laughter at the sight and sound, and had been made to let him change partners, and polka briskly till his breath gave out. Long might this mood last!

Only Sophie did not respond to it. She was, she said, worried about arrangements for Christmas. Fran had not till then bothered to think much about it, yet. She, too, would have to give it some thought.

'What am I got to do?' Sophie had asked her, miserably. 'There's Thirz' saying as she expects me and Het and Joe and young Stevie up at her place as usual for Christmas dinner. What about Aunt Sar'anne? She won't ask 'er – and I shan't be 'appy thinking o' that poor old soul heving 'er's by 'erself, when she could ha' been enj'ying it with me and mine. But none of us dare cross Thirz', in case she goos off 'er 'ead again. And there's them bells. They start her off, like, and me and Dan 'ev to 'old ourselves ready to deal with 'er whenever she 'ears 'em. But come Christmas morning, they'll be going on and on, a full ring like they all'us used to. There's a lot o' folks coming to the 'otel to spend Christmas and the New Year 'ere because they 'ad such a good time last year. Neither me nor Dan'el 'as ever missed a Christmas morning service as I know of, but we don't know as we dare go this year and leave Thirz' to be by 'erself with them bells ringing. We should likely find 'er with 'er throat cut when we went 'ome.'

William and Fran took time off to stroll down to Southside House. They found Greg alone, but busy. Christmas was in the air there as never before. There was an Advent calendar at a height Jonce could reach to open one little window each day; there were sketches pinned here and there of Father Christmas negotiating their chimney with a bulging bundle on his back; there were scribbles – Jonce's messages to the red-cloaked, white-bearded old man Greg had depicted, which all parents are so adept at reading – lying everywhere. It would have been difficult to decide whether the adults or the child here were having most pleasure on this run-up to Christmas. Neither of them had ever experienced it before. How different it all was from the dark patch last Christmas had been! Fran had a lump in her throat as she remembered Sophie's tale of last Christmas Day at Danesum, with eight youngsters and their dying father being so pathetically grateful for sausage and chips and a bought mince pie, with a whole orange to call their very own as well. William was just as sadly recalling how very nearly Greg and Jess had come apart for ever just at that time.

Greg came out to greet them wearing a traditional artist's smock, which he showed off with his usual panache. 'Present from Jess,' he said as he kissed Fran, 'after your wedding day.'

William recognized it for what it was – Jess's acknowledgement that the husband she had so nearly written off as a loser had proved himself the exact opposite, once they had got their private misery sorted out. That smock was Greg's equivalent of his own doctorate robes.

'Come and look,' Greg invited, leading them towards his studio. And there, still on his easel awaiting its final touches, was the portrait of Aunt Sar'anne. They stood awed before it, not only because of the splendid likeness he had achieved, but because of what it was – an outstanding work of art. Fran gasped, and Greg heard her.

'I told you, didn't I?' he said exultantly. 'I knew the moment I saw her that this was my chance. I'm going to submit it for the Summer Exhibition. Of course, it's a chance in about ten thousand that the judges will do more than wave it away, but I shall be satisfied if they even hold it for their shortlist. You never know what may take their fancy.'

'They know real art when they see it,' said Fran. 'You'll submit three, won't you?'

'Why do you ask?' he said. 'You're reading my mind.' He looked quizzically at them. They both spoke at once in reply – of course he could have *The Burbages at Home* – for as long as it was needed.

'And the third?' asked William.

Greg took a covering sheet from another easel, and again Fran gasped. She recalled that evening last year when her birthday party had been held at the Old Rectory, and Jess had refused to accompany Greg to it. He had been so wrought up that he had drunk too much – but it had sharpened all his perceptions, and she had witnessed the effect the two oldest Petrie girls, who were acting as baby-sitters, had had on him when they had come together through the door, each carrying one of Monica's twins. He had been making sketches of the girls from the moment he had first seen them, and the whole experience had now gelled into a world of beauty and feeling. The picture was only in its first rough stage, but Fran thought privately that it was set fair to outdo the others. The two girls, in all their ethereal pre-Raphaelite youthful beauty, were coming through a door, beyond which lay dark shadow, into light that caught them full in its beam. To those in the know, its symbolism doubled its effect. Emerald was slightly in front, her glorious copper-coloured hair hanging over one shoulder, while she wore a sleepy baby over the other. Just behind was Amethyst, her curly hair a darker shade of red, her slightly sturdier figure adorned by a baby carried on her hip. Fran's expression told Greg just what she was thinking.

The copy of Gainsborough was a triumph of technical skill, but the other two pictures outshone it wholly as art. They not only pleased; they dug deep into the realm of human emotion. The same difference, Fran was thinking, as that between good literature and immortal prose or poetry. But then, of course, Greg knew. He'd probably made his own comparison in terms of music.

'Let's have a drink on it,' Greg said, pleased by their reaction. 'May I ask you to keep my plans a dark secret?'

They drank a toast to his success, and left him to go back to his painting.

Being so close, they called at Monastery Farm in the hope of catching Eric at home. They were unlucky, but they did encounter Nigel outside his cottage, and were asked in.

'I wanted to see Eric,' William said, 'though I know how busy he is. It can wait.' They took their opportunity to tell Nigel of Sophie's dilemma about Thirzah and the bells. He had already heard of it, and was unperturbed. 'Thirzah's just trying it on to see what it feels like to be God,' he said. 'As I understand, she's got poor old Dan and her sister where she wants them, but that's where she must be stopped, for her own sake as well as for ours. Forewarned is forearmed, and we have been warned. The bells will be rung, and my guess is that Sophie and Dan will find nothing worse than a burnt dinner when they get home. My concern's for the other poor old woman who'll be left out.'

'Don't let that worry you. She'll have her Christmas dinner with us,' Fran said. 'We take it that you'll be with Eric – though you'd be welcome if you have no other plans.'

Nigel thanked her, but said he would be with Eric. 'At the

hotel, probably. Eric had considered asking Dr Hardy, but he's been invited to the Old Rectory, and Miss Pelham's going to the Taliaferros'. So as far as can be foreseen, all's well. Perhaps that's a bit too optimistic – it depends on what Eric and Marjorie find today.'

Fran pricked up her ears, but William asked bluntly what he meant.

'It isn't really my business to bruit it abroad,' said Nigel, 'but I'm sure Marjorie wouldn't mind you knowing. Poppy's coming home for Christmas, but there's no word from Pansy about anything. Marjorie has worked herself into such a state about it that Eric decided somebody had to act. He's taken today off to escort Marjorie to Deal, to see Pansy and find out where she'll be for Christmas. Marjorie wrote to tell her they were going, and Pansy rang back asking them to meet her for lunch at a pub. Marjorie interpreted that to mean something amiss, but Eric cajoled her into thinking it was a good idea. I believe he knows more than he's letting on to Marjorie. Those girls spoil things for her, but she won't admit it to her father or her brother, so Eric has to stand in for both. She looks after me like a daughter, and like a sister after Eric. They're very good for each other.'

Fran and William left him and walked towards home disturbed by what he had said. If Pansy was being difficult, the whole Bridgefoot clan would be upset. Then there was also the question as to whether Nick would come home while Poppy was in the vicinity. Poppy wouldn't be happy one way or the other. They hoped they would soon hear from somebody what had happened on the trip to Deal.

In fact, they didn't have long to wait, and they heard it then from the primary source. Eric came to Benedict's that very evening on purpose to tell them, uncertain as to what he should tell George, and wanting Fran's opinion.

He reported that they had been a little early for their rendezvous with Pansy. Marjorie was very edgy because she was still offended at not being invited to Pansy's home. Eric had tried to make all sorts of excuses why at such short notice it might not have been convenient, suggesting that Pansy's husband could have objected

238

to his presence. But Marjorie had grown increasingly uneasy until, more than half an hour late, Pansy had finally appeared.

'I'm not a sentimental sort of chap,' Eric said, 'but I was shocked myself at the sight of the girl, and watched Marjorie take one look at her and virtually shrink. She barely recognized her own daughter. I'd remembered Pansy as the bigger of the twins – tall, broad and well-covered, and with a lot more go, especially since Poppy lost her vivacity after her split from young Nick. Pansy seemed the hard one, the brash one, the one always set on having a good time. Dressed and made up to give that image.

'The woman who came to our table wasn't that Pansy at all. She was very embarrassed, apologized for being late, and began to explain it was all because her hairdresser had made a mix-up of her appointment, and that in the end she'd had to come away to meet us without getting it done. She need hardly have told us that! It looked as if she hadn't been to a hairdresser for months, or as her mother said afterwards to me, "as if she'd been dragged through a hedge backwards".

'When I'd last seen her she was a rather brassy blonde – obviously out of a bottle. It has now grown out, so that she is more or less piebald. She used to have such thick bouncy hair, which though it was worn in a short, bobbed fashion always looked smart and healthy. She's let it grow now so that it's almost down to her shoulders, and caught it up in a pony tail. I think we were so used to seeing her in riding gear that we were both jolted to see her in a skirt and blouse with a huge chunky sweater to keep out the cold – and I'd forgotten she was pregnant – which she looked. It showed more because she's lost so much weight. And she was tense and nervous – which wasn't surprising. I left her with her mother and went to order drinks and our lunch, leaving them together. They had both been crying when I got back and I took them into the dining room.

'"So you're quite sure you won't come home for Christmas, and let us coddle you?" Marjorie said. "Poppy would be so pleased to have a bit of a share in the baby. When is it actually due?"

'"End of March or early April," Pansy answered. "I go to a clinic at the local hospital, and they can't be quite sure. But

Mum – I can't make any plans, because the chances are that Darren and I are going to move again soon. In fact, he's away now, looking for somewhere for us to move to, which is one reason why I didn't want you to come to our flat today. His father has got some urgent business on, and we have to have the new architect living with us. It's a bit of a shambles by your standards, or by those of Casablanca this time last year."

'Marjorie asked her if she was looking after herself, eating properly and so on. She said she hadn't much interest in food – she thought it was mainly because she felt so cooped up in a flat in a town, and wasn't allowed to ride. She missed that terribly.

'"Wouldn't Darren agree to you coming home till he's found you somewhere else to live?" her mother asked.

'She shook her head. "Don't ask, Mum. I shall be all right. I should love to come and see Poppy and Granny and Grandad, but it really wouldn't be wise. I'll come when I can. And I must go now, before Darren gets home. Walk with me to the gate, Mum."

'She might as well have asked me outright to let her speak to her mother alone – I should have had enough sense for that in any case. She thanked me coolly, much more like her old self, and they went off together while I paid the bill and got the car out of the car-park, and hung about a bit to give them time to talk. Then I saw Marjorie waiting by the entrance alone, looking like death. I thought she'd collapse before I got her home. When she began to cry, I stopped the car and made her tell me what the matter was. I guessed Pansy's marriage was on the rocks – nobody ever expected it to last. I was wrong.

'I'm afraid it points to something a good deal more serious. I feel a heel, giving away Marjorie's confidences to me, but I think I must. She said Pansy had asked her to do something "unthinkable". I made her tell me.

'The twins are twenty, so their next birthday at Easter-time brings them to twenty-one, when they'll each get the ten grand George has settled on all his grandchildren. Pansy pleaded with her mother to ask him to let her have it now – because she needs it urgently, though she wouldn't say why. And that's where my anxiety's got out of bounds, so that I have to tell somebody else

240

what I suspect. I can't let George get dragged into a national scandal to save the skin of any Bailey.'

William refilled Eric's whisky glass, and he sipped while choosing where to begin. 'It starts at high government level – where somebody crooked is using confidential knowledge on what is fundamentally a good plan for the redevelopment of derelict industrial areas in some inner cities to feather his own nest. From that Whitehall level the corruption goes down to an equally bent tycoon who has one of his fingers in the construction business – and he in turn diversifies the chain of corruption through lesser developers, builders' merchants, architects, local councils, planning officers, inspectors – anybody and everybody willing to take risks to get a good rake-off. The net's cast far and wide, with the intention that if anybody gets caught it'll be the small fry, while the big boys have time to slip away, or at least to hire solicitors and barristers as crooked as themselves to get them off. Approaches to people a long way down the list, like me for example, are tentative and very subtle, with no details given if the bait isn't taken and swallowed immediately.'

He smiled, answering Fran's anxious look. 'My dear Fran, I wasn't born yesterday! I was just interested enough to keep my ears and eyes open, though I didn't think there was any site round here worth the big boys bothering about. But when the Bailey faction suddenly all made for the south-east, I began to smell a rat. My guess is that they've been in it up to their necks somewhere along the line and have now got the wind up. They want every penny of ready money they can lay their hands on to do a bunk before the enquiries get as far down – or up – the line as their level. Pansy's probably being got at morning, noon and night to get hers from her grandfather before it's too late, and what she said about moving fits. She may not have a clue what it's all about.

'And it's only surmise on my part and I haven't told Marjorie. She thinks Pansy wouldn't have asked if it hadn't been something entirely above-board, and I don't want to disillusion her. What I'm afraid of is that George would take that same line, and hand out the cash. I can't let him – can I? I'd take a bet that it will be headlines in the press within weeks, unless my inside information is way out; and if local newshounds got so much as a sniff that anything George did was connected with it, they'll have a field day. It would kill him. So put your thinking caps on and advise me what to do for the best.'

There were so many aspects to be considered that the discussion went on a long time. In the end, it was Fran who gave her verdict first.

'You'll have to persuade Marjorie not to do anything. Let sleeping dogs lie as long as they will. There must be so many others in the same boat as the Baileys that they haven't much to fear except what guilty consciences do to them. By my bumpkinish standards of morality, telling George would be a greater sin than robbing the taxpayer.'

'You're taking it for granted that I have a lot of influence over Marjorie. I haven't. I'm only a friend, but Pansy's her daughter. She'll probably tell me to mind my own business – which I am very glad to be able to say this is not. I have no right whatsoever to interfere in what Marjorie does.'

William agreed with Fran, but added some thoughts of his own. 'Nigel was saying only this morning how fond he is of Marjorie – and to anyone brought up as she was, the cloth means a lot. Let Nigel in on it, and then leave Marjorie to him. If anyone can persuade her that to keep her head down and say nothing is the best policy, it's him. He could suggest that at least she ought to ask what Pansy wants the money for before she worries her grandfather about it.'

Eric was relieved, both to have voiced his suspicions, and to have allies including Nigel. William's advice to bring Nigel in was very sound.

The sleeping dog lay quiet until two days before Christmas, and it was Sophie who brought the news that it had broken its chain. She came in breathless, pale and tense.

'Whatever will it be next!' she said, sitting down in the first chair she reached without attempting to take off hat or coat. 'It'll be all over the place by dinner-time, and my Jelly's good name'll be fly-blowed as bad as Kid's, 'cos 'e was Kid's brother. What might ha' been my name, do I 'ad married 'im! We never should ha' lived such a disgrace down. I dunno as I shall as it is –seeing as that Beryl knows very well as some o' Jelly's money come to me. She's 'ad plenty to say all the way along about that, telling folks as I stole it from them as 'ad a proper right to it – but till now nobody's ever said as it were stole in the first place. Whatever shall I do if them police come a-questioning me?'

That idea was too much for her, and she began to cry, boo-hooing loudly like a frightened child. Fran, though very concerned for Sophie, was nevertheless puzzled. Sophie had never before made such an exaggerated show of her feelings.

'What's Beryl been saying to upset you like this?' she asked.

The noisy lamentations ceased so abruptly that Fran's suspicion that they were not wholly genuine was confirmed. Sophie was going to enjoy telling her tale.

'She was outside the shop when I come by, squealing out like a stuck pig and running after a car as 'ad just druv off, trying to catch it up, like. When she see as she couldn't, she turned round making such a to-do as I knowed something must be the matter. Do I never 'ave no more to do with 'er than I can 'elp, I felt in duty bound to stop and ask 'er if I could do anything.'

Sophie dropped her voice. 'She come to me roaring out loud as she should never see Kid no more 'cos the police 'ad just took 'im away to gaol to hinterview – no, that weren't the word – hinderrogate . . .'

'Interrogate?' suggested William, afraid Fran might not be able to stifle her hiccups before he had got the whole story.

'Ah. Tha's it. To question 'im, like, at the police station.'

'Was it a police car?'

'I dunno. I only see the back of it while Beryl was running after it and squawking and I never see no policeman. But there weren't nobody else for 'er to tell, only me, so she bluthered out as a policeman 'ad been asking Kid a lot o' questions about wheer 'e'd got them things such as doors and locks and toilet seats from as 'e were putting into them 'ouses being built atween Lane's End and Hen Street. I stopped with 'er as long as I dare, but I were late as it was. It weren't till I'd got nearly 'ere as I thought as 'ow Jelly was Kid's partner once, and very likely they'd think my Jelly 'ad been in it an' all. I know as 'e 'adn't, and so do you, but there's no telling what tales Beryl'll think up, 'specially about me. It's only since Kid got in with that there Bailey as 'e's been led astray. I feel like gooing back straight away and telling Beryl to leave my Jelly out of it, 'cos 'e never 'ad nothing to do with it. Praise be to 'Im Above, 'e was dead and buried afore we ever 'eard of them Baileys.'

Fran had another fit of coughing which required her to go to the tap for a drink of water. Righteous anger had driven fear of the police from Sophie's face, on which two red spots had now replaced tears. William decided it was time both women were brought to their senses.

'Make Sophie a strong cup of tea,' he instructed Fran in a voice that was so nearly a command that it caused another fit of strangled coughing while she filled the kettle. William sat Sophie down at the table beside him.

'Now, Sophie,' he said. 'There's nothing for you to get upset about. Jelly has nothing to do with it at all. Everybody knows that what money he left you was part of his premium-bond win. And Beryl has no cause for alarm either, if it's to do with what I've already heard about.

'It seems that hardware shopkeepers and small builders are likely to be asked about where they buy their goods, because it seems that a lot of government supplies have gone missing. All the police will be concerned about is whether Kid bought any of these stolen goods, and if so where, and whether or not he had any idea that they were stolen in the first place. Routine questioning. So if it was a plain-clothes man in an unmarked car, nobody but you and Beryl need ever know. She'll wish she hadn't told you, and will probably deny it once she comes to her senses. If you don't tell anybody, that'll be the end of it. Kid will be back home by lunch-time.'

Sophie now looked offended at his implication that she would ever dream of telling anyone. Looking distinctly disgruntled, she replied that as far as she knowed, she wasn't noted for 'heving a loose tongue', and if 'e didn't know by now as she never repeated nothing, 'e ought to. If tales got about, it wouldn't be 'er doing.

'My dear Sophie, isn't that just what I was saying?' he said soothingly. 'Just forget it.' She drank her tea and went off to work mollified.

But William and Fran were not nearly so sanguine when they discussed it after Sophie had gone home. It was a shot across Bailey's bows, whatever eventually happened to Kid. William rang Eric to inquire if there had been any further moves on the Pansy front.

'As you thought,' Eric replied, 'Nigel was a great help. He's so unflappable – that's his great strength. He pointed out to Marjorie that George wouldn't be likely to keep that amount of money in an old sock under his bed, and that wherever it was invested it would take a few days to withdraw it. As Christmas was so near, it wouldn't be possible for him to let Pansy have it till after the holiday even if he agrees, so there wasn't much sense in her spoiling her father's Christmas by saying anything to him yet. Besides – it would give her, Marjorie, time to write and ask Pansy what she needed the money for, because apart from her father's feelings, there was Poppy to be considered. If it was only that Pansy wanted some money of her own to buy baby things with, he felt sure she would get more than enough in Christmas presents.

'So Marjorie's written, but so far she's had no reply. Post does get delayed just before Christmas – though I find it odd that Pansy's phone's always engaged.'

'We may be putting two and two together and making five,' William said. 'It's so easy to do when you know a little but not all.'

The incident of the visit of the police to Kid was not mentioned by either party. Nevertheless, William had a feeling that Eric knew. There wasn't much in the business world that escaped his vigilant eye.

In spite of her anxiety, or perhaps because of it, Sophie made preparations for their Christmas at Benedict's with even more than her usual thoroughness. She assured Fran over and over again that there would be nothing left for her to do 'a-Christmas morning' but put the turkey into the oven early enough, and see that Aunt Sar'anne set the table. Fran knew how Sophie hated not to be there to do it for them herself, but Christmas to her was 'an 'Oly day' like the Sabbath. She hinted that as she had left so little for them to do she hoped she might see them in church.

'And seeing as 'ow we shan't 'ave nothink to stop us,' Fran said to William, 'perhaps we'd better show up.' He was quite happy to do anything she wanted, and when Christmas morning turned out to have been copied faithfully from a Victorian Christmas card, they were glad to have a reason to go out into it.

There had been a sharp frost overnight and everything from the grass under their feet to the huge wellingtonias in the garden were pantomimed with hoar-frost. The sun shone clear in a pale blue sky, lending sparkle to everything, even the iced-over puddles. Fran thought she had never before seen a wintry country scene more beautiful.

They enjoyed the service, too, and greeting their friends, especially George Bridgefoot. Marjorie, Poppy, Charles and Charlie were all in the Bridgefoot pews, but Effendi sat alone. Fran noticed that only Sophie and Daniel were in the Wainwright pew, and deduced that Hetty and Joe were 'on duty' to keep their eyes on Thirzah. The bells were still to come at the end of this service, so it was no surprise to her that Sophie and Dan didn't hang about to exchange Christmas greetings.

Their lunch being safe with Aunt Sar'anne in charge, there was no need for them to hurry home, especially while the bells were still making such joyous clamour.

'Let's go and see what they are doing at Southside House,' William said. Fran agreed happily, guessing what prompted the suggestion. He wanted to share Jonce's first ever proper Christmas. As they strolled along, a car hooted, passed them and then stopped. Terence Hardy called a Christmas greeting.

'Are you on duty?' William asked in surprise.

'Have been – as part of a conspiracy set up by Nigel. Mrs Bates has been hinting darkly what the bells will do to her, so I paid her a solicitous visit like the caring doctor I am, careful to be there with her when they began to peal. She could hardly throw a fit with me actually at her side, and I made excuses to hang about till her family arrived home – ostentatiously administering a placebo in their sight. It may not have been ethical practice, but I'm learning a lot in these backwoods. It is a good medical ethic to believe that prevention is better than cure, though – and what I was doing at Nigel's instigation could be said to have prevented an attack of self-induced hysteria. So having performed my good deed for the day, I'm off home till lunchtime. Come in and have a drink with me.'

'Sorry, but we're heading for Christmas drinks with the Talia-ferros. You come with us instead. They'd be so pleased.' He agreed, but said he'd catch them up. He was officially on call, so he'd have to go home first to see if there were any messages.

They opened the door to a Christmas wonderland. Jess's sitting-room had been subjected to a complete transformation to make room for her Christmas present to Greg – a beautiful old upright Broadwood piano. She'd been saving up for it since their reconcili-ation last year, and Fran learned afterwards that William had been in on the secret, promising to make up himself any deficit if, when she found the piano she wanted, it was more than she could afford. In the event, she had not needed his help.

Greg's joy threatened to overflow into tears as he showered kisses on Fran and hugged William. Jonce, clutching with pro-prietary little hands the model fire-engine for which he had shouted polite requests up the chimney to Father Christmas, flung himself at William and climbed on him the moment he sat down. Jess went into the kitchen to indulge in a few private tears of happiness and Fran followed. They were at one again, as they hadn't been for a long time till this past year.

'Can all this last, Fran?' Jess asked. 'I'm so happy today that I'm frightened. It's what I've dreamed all these years come true. I keep telling myself I mustn't hope for too much, and that it can't last.'

'Nonsense. This is no time for your tragedy-queen act to spoil a minute of it, for Greg and Jonce – or for William and me. Accept it. Grab it with both hands and hold on to it. You've got Greg, he's got all he ever wanted, and you've both got Jonce. So put on a happy face, because you're going to have another visitor in a minute – Terry Hardy. I can hear a car now. That's probably him.'

'It's more likely to be Anthea,' said Jess.

'Actually, it's both,' called Greg.

'Coming,' Jess replied, hastily refurbishing her face.

Two cars were lined up at the front of the house, Terence waiting till Anthea had got out of it to pull his car alongside hers. Looking very smart in what was by now almost a uniform of a well-cut tartan suit with high-necked lace blouse, she took her time, sedate and dignified as always. There was never any joyous abandon in her movements, which always seemed to be under the same rigid control as her face. Terry, impatient, watched her with an interest that was not all professional. She had never unbent towards him, however many times they were paired by their hosts, nor given him the least sign that she enjoyed being in his company. He was not used to being so completely ignored by women, and had been piqued enough to turn on his charm. There had been no response whatsoever, unless it was to withdraw from him more than from others. She was cool towards everybody, but he felt that the permafrost of her behaviour was reserved for him personally. She froze him out before he ever got near enough to her to be more than normally polite.

As he watched her now, he was conscious for the first time that he was letting her get under his skin. 'Damn the woman,' he said to himself. 'That's the last thing I need. I'd better watch it. If she thinks that running away is the best way of getting me to run after her, she can think again.' There was no doubt about it – if she had shown the least feminine charm towards him, he could be in danger. But however lonely and susceptible he was he had no use for a snow queen. Experience had at least taught him that.

Her arms being full of parcels, she pushed the car door open rather clumsily with her foot. Then she made rather an ungraceful effort to get out. He had let in his clutch and was easing his car gently forward when she stepped on to an iced-over puddle, slipped, and fell heavily. She lay with parcels round her, making no attempt to rise.

Quick as he was to react, Greg and William reached her first. Her face was very white and set, as if she were in pain, and both men were reaching down to lift her up before the doctor could join them.

'Don't move her!' he called. 'She may be hurt.'

She made what seemed a great effort, and sat up. 'I am not hurt,' she said. 'I'll get up when I'm ready.'

'No – don't try to move yet,' Terence said, preparing to get down to her level.

Her face contorted into what might have been interpreted as a grimace of pain, except that the way she spat out her next words made it seem more like the snarl of a trapped animal. 'Dr Hardy, I have no need of your services, thank you. When I do require your attention, I am quite capable of asking for it. What you can all do for me at present is to give me a chance to collect myself. Just leave me alone.'

William and Greg, for once unsure of themselves, withdrew, shepherding Fran and Jess before them into the house. Terence still hovered.

From her sitting position, still on the broken ice, she looked straight up at him.

'I was not aware that you had the misfortune to be deaf, Dr Hardy,' she said, in a low but tense voice. 'I do not wish for your attention, medically or in any other way.'

So the rebuff was purely personal. He felt the colour seeping into his face, and wished stupidly for a hat to raise before turning away. Instead, he made a stiff little bow, and retired to his car with every intention of driving away. He was surprised to find Fran at the gate before him, blocking his exit. She came to his side window, which he courteously wound down to speak to her.

'I sneaked out round the back,' she said. 'Please don't go, Terry. I'm asking you not to – not for myself, but for Jess. She was in such euphoria when we arrived that she confessed to having a premonition that it would all be spoilt for her. This silly little incident is quite enough – it used to be Jess herself who could turn into a cat with its claws out ready to spring at nothing, till we found out what made her do it. I know what you must feel, but honestly, it's Jess and Greg's happy Christmas Day I'm trying to save now, not your gentlemanly feelings. Don't let the silly little spitfire win! Please, just ignore her, for all our sakes. I think she is hurt, and in pain, but it's part of her act not to let any feelings show. Come on – be magnanimous.'

249

William appeared at her side as Hardy still hesitated. He grinned. 'You're on trial, Terry,' he said. 'If you can resist my wife in this mood, you're a better man than most of us.' He put his arm round Fran and squeezed her, and she got his message. She leaned inside the open window, and kissed the astonished doctor – who, to his own surprise, responded heartily. William opened the car door, and Terry got out.

Jess had taken Anthea to the bathroom, given her a chance to make her face up again, and settled her into a comfortable chair. She was still very pale, with her jaw set and her lips a little too firm.

'Brandy for Miss Pelham, I think,' said Greg. 'What will the rest of you have?'

They were all trying so hard to act normally that in their anxiety they had overlooked Jonce. Fran had once assessed him to Greg as a little pitcher with very large lugs and a high intelligence quotient. He had also been through more emotional experience than most children of his age. In contradiction to what most adults would expect, he had observed the incident that they were now all trying to ignore. It was he who noticed Anthea wince as she put out a hand to take the drink. He got up from where he had been sitting among the unopened presents still under the Christmas tree, and went with large, sympathetic, solemn eyes to her side.

'Does your hand hurt you very much?' he asked. 'Would you like my fire-engine to make it better? I never had a fire-engine before. It's my very, very favourite thing.'

He tried to put it in her lap, leaning against her knees. She attempted to accept it, but with a glass in one hand and him in the way, she could only whisper thanks and smile at him. Hardy, who had been keeping a professional eye on her from a distance was the only one to notice – and to register how much the smile transformed her.

'Poor pretty lady,' Jonce said, picking up his toy from her lap, and stroking gently the arm closest to him. 'Poor pretty lady.'

Fran had persuaded Greg to let them hear him try his piano. The rest closed round him, but Terence, looking at his watch, asked to be excused. He was about to go without speaking to

250

Miss Pelham, but thought better of it. When he reached her and looked down, it was to see tears dripping from her cheeks, making her irresistibly beautiful. She looked up at him, and though she said no word, he read the apology in her face – and something he had hoped never to feel again tugged at his heart.

'Damn and blast,' he said. 'Thank God there'll be no women with Eric and Nigel. I'm not safe to be let out!'

They all agreed after it was over what a strange Christmas it had been in comparison with the excitement and drama of the previous two. The round of visiting each other's homes in the week between Christmas and the New Year had been less formal, and as Fran commented rather sadly, less fun, if less dramatic.

'A different sort of play with a different cast,' William said, summing it up for her. 'More humdrum – but then we're all getting older, and we must expect and accept some changes. I seem to remember that in prospect we rather welcomed the thought of staying quietly at home and doing as we liked. And whatever you say, we've either been out somewhere every evening, or entertaining friends here. I suppose what you really mean is that we didn't roll up the carpet and dance. It wasn't on the cards this year.'

'No. That is what I meant. There wasn't that sort of spirit about. But why? We're the same people, with a few newcomers added, but we all seemed to lack "gump". And I felt uneasy, as if I knew there was something nasty lurking in the background. Do you think we're getting too smug to enjoy parties? Or too middle-aged? I should hate to think that! Your retirement – and us being relegated to being "only grandparents" – isn't a signal of senescence, is it? I won't let it be! We can't stop the next generation's children growing up, and wanting their Christmases at home, but that's as far as I'll go. Like Martin Luther, I say "Here I stand" for at least another twenty years. I shall still want to dance, whether I can or not, when I'm eighty. But I wasn't thinking about the future. I was asking why we've been such a dull lot this year.'

251

Seeing how much she meant it, he gave her his full attention, and thought out loud. 'I suppose,' he said, 'we haven't yet got used to the changes that we've had to accept. Nagging little problems add up and most of us have had some.'

'Problems? What problems have we got compared to those we had last year? We've had a wonderful year. Do we honestly have problems we can't solve?'

'If you want a truthful answer, yes, we do. Silly little ones, perhaps – but the sort that get at you once you notice them. Sophie's one of ours. She isn't happy. We didn't throw the sort of party you like this year mainly because Thirzah is *hors-de-combat*. Sophie had no heart to tackle it alone, and she's miserable about the family feud, anyway. I fear, my precious, that she and Aunt Sar'anne together are putting a damper on us! For one thing, to misquote somebody or other, like the poor they are "too much with us".'

With sinking heart, Fran acknowledged the truth of what he said. Sophie was such an integral part of their household that the change in her had affected them. She asked him where Aunt Sar'anne came into it.

'Darling – do I really have to spell that out to you? We had no choice but to let her come to live in Eeyore's Tail – as a temporary measure. If we don't look out, it will become permanent, and – I hate to put this into words, but like all other old people in her situation, she's begun to encroach on us, and on Sophie. To put it bluntly, I don't care for a third party who is no proper part of our household being continually under my feet. Sophie knows how I feel, and thinks it's her fault, which just adds to her distress. And there's no end to it in sight.'

Fran was appalled that she hadn't noticed how much he was feeling what she was herself. He must have been at pains not to let her know so as not to upset her. She had tried hard not to show her feelings because, as he said, there was no alternative.

'I'm glad we've both admitted it,' she said, 'but what is there we can do about it? We can't honestly consider ourselves hard done by if that's all we have to grumble about. Let's hope and believe, as Thirzah would, that the Lord will provide another place for Aunt Sar'anne some day before too long.'

'I dare say he will,' William said, smiling rather sardonically, 'considering that she's already in her ninety-third year. But if we have to wait till he does, we shall probably both be too old ourselves to care whether we can dance or not. I shall be a nasty old curmudgeon and you a frustrated and cantankerous old hag. There's really nothing wrong with her, any more than there is with the water that one drop at a time for long enough will wear a hole in a stone. But the hole's still there.'

He fetched them both a brandy. Fran said she wondered whether, if as he said other people also had problems, they were as small and as irritating as their own was.

'Well, take them household by household,' he said. 'It can't have been as happy up at Castle Hill as they hoped it would, because of Nick. He came home, but only just for the two days, and then pleaded arrangements in town. Effendi was hurt because he was looking forward to having Nick with him for a few days in his new home. Jane's inclined to be angry – she hasn't really forgiven Nick for his treatment of Bob, and thinks he's got too big for his boots with all the pampering he's had. She believes he won't come home to be a member of Bob's family. Bob gets nearer to the truth, but he's wise enough not to say anything. So he keeps quiet, and Jane's afraid he's offended.

'Poppy's been very dull and listless, according to Eric. Becoming an old-maidish bluestocking, he says. Eric thinks she resents the rest of the family's preoccupation with Pansy. It was all very well for Pansy to write sweetly to Marjorie, telling her not to worry Grandad about the money because the urgency was past and plans had been changed as to where she and Darren might be going to live. She gave no indication where, and there's been no word since. It didn't serve to make Marjorie's Christmas a particularly happy one. Nor Eric's. He can't and won't tell Marjorie that he suspects Pansy's precious husband is in hiding from the law. No doubt the news of Kid Bean being questioned caused the sudden change of plan. So Eric's concerned for Marjorie, as well as being short-staffed at the hotel at their busiest Christmas ever. His own Christmas Day was only a stag party, because Monica and Roland wanted their Christmas in Cambridge.

'Grandparents were invited, but we couldn't go because of

leaving Aunt Sar'anne, and Eric was too busy. Marjorie and Poppy dutifully attended dinner at the Old Glebe, however miserable they felt, so all the company Eric had was Nigel, with Terry Hardy thrown in at the last minute.'

'Beth says that Terry really does get on well with Elyot,' Fran put in, 'and he loves their ship modelling. But she thinks he hides there from Anthea. It was pretty pointed that she didn't accept Beth's invitation, and he didn't accept ours. I don't know what Anthea's got against him, but I can't say I blame him, after the way she treated him on Christmas morning. I'm disappointed in him that he lets her faze him, all the same.'

William agreed that it was unfortunate that they should have taken such a scunner at each other. It upset the balance, as well as defeating hospitable intentions.

'That only leaves Nigel, and Jess and Greg. Thank goodness somebody's happy.'

'My sweetheart – there isn't a happier man in all the United Kingdom than I am, and you know it. You asked me why the general atmosphere wasn't quite what it had been last Christmas and I tried to answer you truthfully as far as I could. I don't know about Nigel. It's a case of many a mickle making a muckle.'

'If you're happy, so am I,' she said. 'We've had our little grouse, and cleared the air. Has Nigel any particular grouse?'

'As a matter of fact, yes. All the new interest being shown in the church since he came has made the matter of the restoration more urgent. Bailey's promise of a largish sum to give the restoration fund a push-off has gone down the drain, of course – and set things back a lot, because what they get in grants and such is matched against the parish's own efforts. The sort of chicken-and-egg situation one might expect from a board of trustees, or whatever they are. But with Eric around, I'll bet they'll find a solution to the church's problem easier than we do to ours.'

She laughed, quite herself again. 'Our problem?' she said. 'We haven't really got one – well, no bigger than a pimple on a round of beef, as Aunt Sar'anne would say.'

'Aunt Sar'anne? Not Sophie?'

'Sophie's early life didn't include rounds of beef. Aunt Sar'anne, here with Grandfather in pre-war times, was accustomed to whole sides of beef, never mind rounds. "Times is changed", as both of them would sadly agree – even at Benedict's.'

As soon as the new health centre was set up and his married partners installed, Hardy took a week off and went away, leaving his locum to cope with the old village end of the practice. The locum had rented rooms in Hen Street, but had agreed to house-sit for Hardy and hold a surgery there, as Terence did, twice in the week. Fran wondered how much Beth had influenced their new doctor's decisions in such matters. Beth had had to learn the ways of village life herself the hard way, so he couldn't have had a better mentor. The surprise was that he was so willing to learn. As Fran and Beth agreed, his coming had been a great boon to the elderly, of whom there seemed to be more and more. They clung to their old homes, not wanting to move to new houses with all mod. cons. on the Lane's End or any other estate; but they were, naturally, those most likely to need medical attention, as well as those least likely to own a car to get them to the health centre. Their nostalgia for Dr Henderson and his ways was rapidly waning because Hardy understood their problems. Nevertheless, it would have been untrue to think that it was for their sake he had chosen to make his home in Church End.

He liked it, and he liked having such a cultured, friendly man as Effendi as a next-door neighbour. Both were working themselves into the community with greater content than either had ever thought possible. Effendi's commitments to London and his friends there were growing less and less, as his interests in his agricultural environment grew greater. Though hurt, Nick's family made every allowance for his age, the conditions of his adolescence, and the effects of his accident. They had offered him freedom, and couldn't with any justification grumble now if he took it. It took a good deal of persuasion by Bob to induce them not to enquire too often or too soon what his future plans were. 'Give him time,' he would say, over and over again. 'You can't get your harvest in till the corn's ripe.'

'I'll give him till Easter, as I promised,' Effendi said. 'But I shan't hold the flat for him. I want my own things here. Home to me now is where Jane is.'

It had been cold and frosty ever since Christmas, but once the temperature rose a little it began to snow, and kept on snowing.

'February fill-dyke white, this year, and no mistake,' said Sophie, stamping snow from her boots. 'All very well for them as don't hev to goo out in it morning, noon and night.'

There was an edge in her voice these days that in the past had never been heard. Fran sighed. Sophie's pointed remark had been two-edged. She not only had to go out of her way, whatever the weather, to check on Thirzah, but the days when she used to come early to work on purpose for a chat with Fran – and William when he was there – at the breakfast table had been precious to her. Now there was always Aunt Sar'anne, who since Christmas had taken liberties that irked them and offended Sophie to her very soul.

The old lady took it for granted that the kitchen was now her domain as much as it was Sophie's, and always found some excuse to be there when Sophie arrived. William, letting it irritate him more and more as the days passed, got into the habit of making for his study as soon as he heard Aunt Sar'anne's light footfall, and Fran stayed only long enough to greet Sophie. William commented that at any rate it was good for work, so he didn't care how long this weather lasted. His was going well, and so was Fran's; but they agreed that if the price was alienation from Sophie, it was too high.

Time trudged on. By the second week of February they were really feeling the stress of the uneasy state of affairs at Benedict's. The snow melted, leaving cold slush, but William suggested it would be a good thing if they made an effort to go out.

'Let's go and see Eric and Nigel,' he suggested.

'I was rather hoping for a long chat with Beth,' Fran said.

William raised his eyebrows at her. 'Can it be that we're sick of the sight of each other?' he asked, wickedly. 'We've been cooped up here together now for nearly six weeks. Do you mean you'd rather go alone?'

'Fathead!' she said, scooping Cat out of his arms to occupy them herself. 'Let's compromise. I'll come as far as Nigel's with you, spend a few minutes there and then leave you with him while I go to see Beth. Then if Eric's gone home, give me a ring at the Old Rectory and we'll go on together to visit Eric. Three birds with one stone.'

'All stone dead, no doubt,' he said. She laughed, and had the pleasure of hearing him laugh, too. Spring couldn't be far away.

It really was a pleasure for Fran and Beth to be alone together for a chat. Emerald was upstairs with Ailwyn, and Elyot in his workshop with Terence.

'That means Terry's back,' Fran said. 'I'm glad to hear it. Sophie's been as glum as a glow-worm under a bucket while he's been away. Thirzah's an unexploded bomb for all of us at Benedict's, lately. Sophie's patience with Aunt Sar'anne is being stretched to the limit, too. Something will have to give, sooner or later.'

She told Beth about her own and William's feelings with regard to being landed with the old woman – as far as they could foresee, till she died. All because Thirzah had to be handled like a hand grenade with the pin out. 'But Terry seems to have got her measure,' she said. 'So I feel safer to know he's back.'

Beth, setting the tea-tray down, closed the door firmly behind herself.

'I wish I did,' she said. 'I'm worried about *him*. I know I oughtn't to say so – but I think he's heading for a nervous breakdown. I don't want to tell Elyot, because he and that ship model seem to be Terry's lifebelt just at present. Better that Elyot doesn't suspect anything's wrong. Do you mind if I tell you – in absolute confidence – what happened yesterday? I do need advice – and I can't go to the doctor!'

She went on without waiting for any reply. 'I noticed a difference in Terry after Christmas. He's been acting oddly ever since – refusing invitations and making excuses for not being sociable. I

257

remember saying that he came here to hide from Anthea. Now I'm almost sure. He'll hardly go anywhere else. I thought perhaps that he'd got too tired, and was glad when he took a break. He came back yesterday, and called here almost at once, while Elyot was out. O dear! It was awful!'

Fran's face registered her disbelief at the interpretation she put on Beth's words. 'You mean he made passes at you?' she asked incredulously.

Beth sat down, gurgling with laughter. 'That'll be the day!' she said – and instantly became sober again. 'What's the trouble between him and Anthea? Do you know?'

Fran told her of the incident at Southside House on Christmas morning. Beth listened soberly, looking down at her hands clasped in her lap. 'Fran,' she said, looking up, 'I'm afraid we – you and I – may have got hold of the wrong end of the stick. But let me tell you about yesterday first. He was quite obviously not himself when he arrived. He'd hoped that Elyot would be here, but I told him there was no reason why he shouldn't go into the workshop and play by himself. Instead, he asked if he could talk to me.

'I ought to explain that once before he had insisted on telling us – for several reasons – all the grisly details of his three broken marriages. Mainly, I think, because he wanted somebody to know the truth as he saw it, to counteract Thirzah's tales and Beryl Bean's gossip. He was transparently honest, and took more than his share of the blame, though by no means all of it. He was very ashamed of himself about the last wife, who had apparently loved him deeply; but by that time he'd become disillusioned and cynical – and confessed to being blatantly promiscuous, and, though not deliberately cruel, uncaring. He said he was happier feeling free to go his own way.

'Not, I thought, the sort of man to be enclosed in a little tight community like ours, where everybody knows everybody else's every move. But he made it plain that what he was up against was his own assessment of it, which was that he was not worthy to accept the friendship we were all offering. And it was clear to me that, whether he knew it or not, he was feeling a sort of jealousy. Of me and Elyot, of Jess and Greg, of you and William, of Bob and Jane – even of Eric's memories of a happy marriage and his easy friendship with Marjorie. Without actually saying so, he somehow made me realize that he found here something he'd never before experienced, and didn't understand.

'And he asked me, seriously, if I thought it was right for him to stop here. What on earth could I say? I begged him to give it a try. I even joked that our sort of love might be catching, but he assured me cynically that he was immune to any variety.

'So back to yesterday. He'd told us before that by his second wife he had two children, now teenagers – whom he loves but very rarely sees, though he does have access.

'Well, in the week before last, he heard of the death of the deputy lord lieutenant of the county, whom when he had been married to his second wife – a typical "county" sort of woman – he had known well and liked very much. He had arranged some time off, so he made up his mind to go to the funeral, and while there, see if he could arrange to take his children out for the day.

'All his family were at the funeral, but he found himself completely ostracized, not only by them, but by all his former friends. He said everybody just looked through him. His children didn't appear to recognize him. He spoke to a man who had been a near neighbour, and was frozen out.

'So he sought out another, who had been a close friend, and said, "Look – what's this all about? Anyone might think I had just been released from Broadmoor." And apparently, the chap actually shook his hand off his sleeve as if it might have been a tarantula and replied, "According to Marcia, that's where you ought to have been."'

Beth's face crumpled, and she paused to wipe her eyes. 'Fran – he just broke down and cried. It seems that his former wife has set up a virulent, sustained hate campaign against him, to make sure he keeps out of the way and has no influence at all on the children – especially as she is contemplating marriage again to a titled widower. Her tales are full of half-truths on the surface, but no truth at all as she interprets them. A case of a dog with a bad name. He's devastated – knocked out. He kept saying he'd be an outcast wherever he went, and the sooner he acknowledged that he wasn't fit for civilized society and got out, the better.

'Oh, I can't tell you how awful it was! He was so terribly hurt!

259

I wanted to cuddle him – I felt much more for him than I ever did for Father in the same state. I know about nervous breakdowns, remember. And from what you say, it looks to me as if it might have been Anthea's brush-off that's pushed him over the edge. Whatever made her do it? And why does she matter to him? The rest of us take him as we find him, and as far as we know she had no previous knowledge of him. It doesn't make sense!'

'She's a very strange woman – especially for one so utterly beautiful on the outside,' Fran answered. 'Any man might fall for her, but she seems repelled by all men, and Terry more than most. I thought it was just an unfortunate case of "diamond cut diamond" – that both of them must have been too hurt in the past to feel very much yet, one way or the other. She appears as hard as nails, and anybody could see that he was studying her clinically – she might as well have been a specimen under a microscope sometimes. Perhaps she resents that, though I think she asked for it first. Or it may be that it's just his male self-esteem that's suffering, fearing his lack of effect on her means he's lost his attraction for all the opposite sex. I suppose it's just possible that he's regretting his reputation, which he admits isn't all exaggeration, and remorse is catching up with him. That he finds it difficult to face her, knowing what he's done to other women who hadn't her will-power to withstand his charm. So he's mad because he likes it here, but if she's going to stay, he thinks he'll have to cut and run yet again.'

'Well,' said Beth, 'that's exactly what I'd worked out, till you told me just now about Christmas morning at Jess and Greg's. But we've got it wrong, Fran. I'm sure we have! I believe the real trouble is that he's fallen head over heels in love with her. It's she who's running – and the faster she runs, the more he wants to chase her. But he's no fool, and can see it's hopeless. All men are anathema to her; him more than most.'

Beth began to cry again. 'Sorry, Fran, but you see I know just how he feels. Father had rubbed into me that I was a menopausal old maid having sexual fantasies till I half believed him – and then the only man I'd ever really loved or wanted told me he never wanted to set eyes on me again. I know what Terry must be suffering.'

Fran went to Beth, but Beth was far from needing comfort.

She looked over her handkerchief at Fran with eyes, as Fran had once said of them, 'as big as mill wheels', bright with determination and hope. The tears were only those of overwhelming emotion. 'And just look what happened!' she crowed, waving her hand around to indicate the room, her husband usually happy messing about in his workshop, her baby upstairs, and all the blessings that had been showered on her.

Fran understood her completely. 'Ssh!' she said. 'I can hear them coming. I think your diagnosis is probably spot on. We can't do much but watch and pray. Let's leave it to the gods. After all, they didn't let either you or me down in the long run, did they?'

In a damp, cold, slushy February, every day seemed as long as a month of Sundays. Under the circumstances, William found it useful. There was little incentive to leave his study, which during the daytime was a refuge from three women, two of whom were visibly on edge. The outcome was long days of solid work on the book. For the moment, he was intent on getting the gist of all that the author had to offer. So far it had been easy to deal with, and he had become absorbed in it. He was so gripped by the narrative that when he met references to characters, procedures or events that he did not immediately or wholly comprehend, he made notes for himself to look up at his leisure and went on reading.

This was history – there was no doubt about that – but history in a different guise. 'Story' was now the operative part of the word. It was surprising what a sense of release and freedom that gave to him. He'd finished the first Latin section, and the next longhand English, but the writer had then taken to homemade shorthand. As far as William could judge, this was to save himself time and paper. It wasn't difficult to read, but it slowed the reader down. William turned another page, only half filled, and was stopped in his tracks. *The rest of the book was in code.*

He had met codes before, many times, and thought this might

not be too difficult to break *'if he had world enough, and time'*. Well, wasn't that just what he had got? For the first time ever, his time was his own.

But he was impatient. The point at which the code began indicated that what was to come concerned one of the most dramatic periods in the whole annals of England, and the writer had somehow been personally involved. There had to be a good reason why he had broken away from his fascinating memoir so abruptly and sought safety in code for what he had next to tell.

William was professionally excited, but it wouldn't do now to let historical fact overwhelm what his imagination had made of the characters. They were alive to him. He had begun to believe in himself as a writer of fiction as much as Fran believed in him. He couldn't and wouldn't be put off now, whatever the obstacle that stood in his path, but he was nearly maddened by frustration, all the same. As far as he could discover, the author had left no key to the code.

He said nothing to Fran, but spent several days setting about breaking it in schoolboy fashion, and got nowhere. He read everything he could lay his hands on about ways and means of conveying information secretly, but letters written in lemon juice, invisible till subjected to heat, had no relevance to him. What confronted him was not invisible writing but incomprehensible gibberish. He discovered that most codes of the period had been numerical. This one was aggravatingly, blatantly literal. All he needed was one key word. As well try to find a needle in an acre of haystacks! By the end of the week, having lost confidence in himself, the book, and the whole project, he decided to consult Fran.

She had been rather miffed that he had said so little to her of what he had found so far, but had forborne to ask because she put his general air of impatience, frustration and irritability down to Aunt Sar'anne's constant presence. In fact, she gave him credit for not bothering her about it until she had succeeded in shaping some of Aunt Sar'anne's stories into first drafts of scripts, but she was still miffed. Didn't the idiot man know yet that if anything could put her out of her stride, it was to keep her in the dark? It was the one thing likely to cause iconoclastic rows between them.

262

He was aware that he was on dangerous ground, and sensibly delayed any mention of it to her till Saturday evening, when after supper they went to the sitting-room to relax. He got up from his chair to go and sit at her feet with his head against her knee. Both felt guilty that of late they had lost the habit of enjoying such close, casual intimacy. He said so, taking her hand and printing a kiss on the palm before closing her fingers over it, as he had done so many times before.

'What's the matter with us?' he asked. 'Is it all my fault?'

'No. Just when we thought we had solved our biggest problem, Cousin Tilda "took and died", and threw us out of kilter. We know how silly it is to let Aunt Sar'anne being here upset us, but it's no use denying that it does. Why do we mind so much?'

'Because we're selfish, perhaps? Or because we're afraid that so far we've only seen the tip of the iceberg of that silly feud Thirzah has raked up? While I've been translating the Latin part of Bob's book, I've come across tags I'd either never read before, or had forgotten, and they've stuck in my head like poetry sticks in yours. Our Teutonic ancestors didn't invent the blood feud by a long chalk. I came across a very pertinent bit of Tacitus the other day. "*Accerrium proximorum odia*" – "*Family rows are the worst*".

'I'm absolutely hooked on what I've been reading, but even so the sound of Sophie's voice wrenches me away from it. She's instinctively afraid of something, though she doesn't know what. The submerged iceberg. You quoted once something you'd read about a historian being a prophet with his head turned backwards. Because I know so much about the past, I see a little way into the future – and don't like what I see.

'Aunt Sar'anne's only one fly in the ointment, but in thirty years' time the ointment will be thick with Aunt Sar'annes – nonagenarians nobody wants or knows what to do with. She's also a straw in the wind . . . who's going to care for us when we're ninety? Our family? They may be willing, but as helpless as everybody else is. Actions speak louder than words. Consider Moses!

'"Honour thy father and thy mother", he said, and look where that's got Sophie! He was no longer young himself by then, and was probably getting the wind up. What have nomadic tribes always done with their old folk? Left them alone to die in the desert as soon as they were too old and feeble to keep up with the sheep and goats. Family feuds have existed since Cain and Abel fell out. The Old Testament's full of blood feuds, and the one thing time doesn't change is human nature.'

'But what do you mean by human nature?' she interrupted.

'The basic instincts that are the common denominator of the human race. Infinitely varied by whatever genes we happen to inherit and by tribal experience and custom. Nature combined with nurture. Like me, for example. Burbage by nature, Wagstaffe by nurture. I know what the Wagstaffes made me – but all I have to show me what they had to work on is a photograph and a few scraps of writing.'

He turned the course of his argument. 'It's a gut feeling, to want to know what lies behind you, but in future there won't be many who do! Promiscuous sex, broken marriages, bitter divorces, extra-marital affairs – is anyone going to know who or what they come from? Families won't count, because by the turn of the century most mothers won't be able to tell their young with any certainty who their father was. Actually, there's nothing much new about that, especially in aristocratic circles who till now have been those who have upheld "the family". We shall soon all be equal in that. The luck will be not in who you are born to, but how you fare in whoever it is that brings you up.

'But I'm old-fashioned. I want to know as much about my own folk as I know now about yours – but I'm afraid I may not discover much more. I'm stuck. Come to a dead end, unless somebody can throw me a lifeline. Who should I turn to but you?'

She stroked back the wavy white hair from his forehead, and smoothed the creases in it. 'I thought you didn't want to let me in on it,' she said. 'So I haven't asked – but not because I didn't want to know.'

He hesitated. 'It was silly and selfish of me not to have shared it with you, and with Bob. I ought to have told him weeks ago.'

'So what? Is it too late now?' she said, seizing on the pragmatic lest emotion defeat purpose. 'What's the trouble? Why are you stuck? You know as well as I do that you were born to be a creative writer. Stop being so introspective and get on with it. Prove to yourself that you can, not that you can't.'

She had sat up, stiff-spined in her chair, and moved her legs out of his reach. He was reminded of Cat, who when startled raised her neck ruff, spread out her tail like a stiff bottle-brush, and yowled. He laid his head on her hands, and began to laugh. 'My gorgeous Penthesilia,' he said. 'You look just as you did when you flattened Archie Marriner with your tongue! I never expected to see you look like that again – "*all furnished, all in arms*". But it's your brain I need this time!'

With the tension broken, he explained to her his predicament about the code. She offered the first bit of advice that came into her head. 'Go and see Bob. You ought to tell him, as you said, in any event – but don't forget his sixth sense. Put me into the picture just a little more.'

'It's a sort of memoir of the years previous to and continuing into the Civil War – a startlingly vivid picture of what rural life was like then. But it breaks off suddenly, in mid sentence. He scribbled something, and left it. When he began again, it was in code. Inaccessible, unless I can find the key to it.'

'What did he scribble, as you put it?'

'A sort of goodbye. A well-known tag they often used on gravestones. "*Vale, sed non aeternum*" – "*Farewell, but not for ever*". Or as Tommy Handley would have said, "TTFN" – "Ta-ta for now".'

She laughed, but her quick mind, fresh to the problem, had seized on the association of ideas. She said aloud, 'Bob. Church. Gravestones. They go together. Go to see Bob as soon as you can. Not tomorrow, though, because I've promised Nigel we'll be at church in the morning – it's the last before Lent. I shan't go in Lent. I can't bear the church all cold and bare, and told him he needn't expect to see me there again before Easter. Go to see Bob on Monday, and at this minute to get us a drink.'

He went, stopping to kiss her *en route*. 'A journey of a thousand miles begins with one step? Yes – I know that's Confucius. You told me. Your literary education is a ragbag of priceless stuff. All

265

right, don't fluff your tail up again. I'm going. "*Cara valeto. Cara, vale, sed non aeternum*".'

She was able to translate that without his help. 'Ta-ta to you as well, but you'd better not make it for ever. I want that drink.'

They sat up late, and caught up with a lot.

They had both noticed Sophie's extra tetchiness in the last few days. She had begun to unburden herself to them one morning, when Aunt Sar'anne's uninvited intrusion into the kitchen had shut her up like a clam. But they had heard enough to know the genesis of her complaint. What she had had time to say was that for as long as she could remember it had been the custom for the church to hold some function or other, in aid of church funds, on the evening of Shrove Tuesday, before Lent put an end to such worldly frivolities as whist drives or jumble sales. Such events had been held in the old school and it had always been Sophie and Thirzah's jealously guarded privilege to see to the refreshments on such occasions.

It had slipped from them when the shame of an illegitimate child in the family had stopped them from 'putting theirselves for'ard', and it had never been recovered, because the death of the old rector and the unhappy period of Beth Franks's father's incumbency had intervened, when taken-for-granted old ways had been dropped. Sophie had been entertaining secret hopes that all would be restored by the coming of the Revd Nigel Delaprime, but she was doomed to disappointment. The old school had deteriorated, and had been deemed unsuitable for the new rector's induction. Sophie had been deeply distressed and offended, mainly because to her it was a shrine sacred to the memory of her beloved teacher, Mary Budd. That whist drives could no longer rival television as a source of entertainment, or that Thirzah was no longer willing or able to help, were secondary matters in comparison to the slight that she felt was being done to the memory of Saint Budd. She was also aware that the new rector, welcome as he was, had ushered in a different age, in which she and her like were liable to become as outdated as whist drives and jumble sales.

She had launched into that morning's 'maunch' by saying that she couldn't be in two places at once, and would 'hev had to set with Thirz' anyway to let Daniel goo', but that she didn't ''old with the way things was going'.

'The schoolroom's the place as we're all'us 'ad church do's in afore,' she said, 'and wheer else does 'e think we're going to get all that money from to do the tower up if we don't do it little by little with whist drives and fêtes and such? What was good enough for us in times gone by ought to be good enough for 'im now. There's one thing, if 'e thinks 'e's going to get me to 'elp with things 'eld in a pub, 'e can think again. But there, Dan'el went to the vestry meeting, and said afterwards as it was as plain as plain could be that such as us wasn't wanted no longer.'

It was at that point that Aunt Sar'anne had appeared and cut the diatribe short. Fran and William recalled it with sympathy. 'It is hard on them,' Fran said. 'They've been the ones who've kept the church going till now. They can't accept changes.'

'They won't try,' William rejoined. 'They regard any change in church affairs as sin. Sophie's got more sense than most, but she's too vulnerable just at present to use it. She has to let herself go about something to get her real grievances off her chest. She knows a Shrove Tuesday whist drive or a jumble sale won't do much to raise the sort of money that's needed now. I wonder what steps Nigel will take? Perhaps we ought to get up and go to church tomorrow morning, while we still have a chance. The tower will be declared unsafe if something isn't done pretty soon.'

'We shall have to get up early, church or no church,' Fran retorted. She didn't need to explain to him why. He laughed, reading her mind and concurring. 'In that case we'd better go to bed now, hadn't we?' he said.

Sundays had always been special to them. They had become extra-special since Fran had given in, thrown convention to the winds, and let William share her bed. They often rose late on Sunday, secure in the knowledge that not even Sophie was likely to find them still 'abed'. Though they had not exactly said so in so many words, they had last night acknowledged that of late they'd felt inhibited by Aunt Sar'anne's presence in their house, even though she was supposed to be confined to Eeyore's Tail. They discussed it in bed next morning.

'We're a respectably married couple now,' William said, 'and were before we'd ever heard of Aunt Sar'anne. Why on earth should we care what she thinks?'

'We don't, do we? Not really. We're reacting to our upbringing, just as Sophie would about any church do in Lent, or any open mention of sex. The funny thing to me is that Aunt Sar'anne's so different. Perhaps it's because she's been exposed to real life in a way Kezia's family never have been. She made no bones about it when she was telling me about her own life with "her Perce". She "had" to get married. "I knowed very well", she said, "as he didn't want me. It was me as wanted him. I made my bed and I had to lay on it. It weren't no use me grumbling about him all'us having another fancy woman somewheer. I didn't expect no sympathy from such as cousin Kezia, and I didn't get none."

'She did have a lot to put up with, like when the little boy from next door was playing with her own children, because, she said, he "didn't need no swearing". He was the spit and image "her Perce". "His mother blamed him on poor Billy Pratt as were simple, and saddled him with herself and a whull hustle o' child'en she had by other men. I don't know how many more of 'em belonged to my Perce," she said.

'I asked her why she'd stopped with him, to go on having babies that she had to work herself to feed and clothe. She didn't mince her words about it. "Ain't I just told you?" she said. "If he didn't want me, I still wanted him. You and your man know how it is, don't you? If God ever made anything better, he kep' it for hisself!" Honestly, I was so surprised I found myself blushing! If Kezia's ghost was listening in, it must have needed treatment for shock!'

'Crude, but she'd got it right though, hadn't she?' he grinned, gathering her even closer to him. 'So if we intend to be at Morning Prayer, we'd better get up this minute.'

They were glad they had. Fran always felt a bit of a hypocrite in church, because she had such grave doubts about a lot of Christian dogma, but loved the ritual aspect of it, especially on days such as this last Sunday before Lent when the church looked beautiful, with hothouse flower arrangements sent by Effendi, and she could wallow in the beautiful archaic language and Beth's choice of music. Then there was that stately, upright and handsome old figure in his long cassock and snowy surplice – washed, starched and ironed with devotion by Sophie. Daniel wasn't present; he and Sophie took turns to stay at home with Thirzah. Fran was glad it was Sophie who was there to hear what Nigel had to say that morning. He didn't preach, in any sense of the word. He took the opportunity to talk to them, and as he said, 'to put them in the picture' about what must be done, and soon. Once Lent and Easter were over, it had to have priority.

He explained the stark choice they had of raising a great deal of money, or letting the tower be condemned as unsafe. They would need every penny, every widow's mite that could be raised locally, but they couldn't hope to raise in such traditional ways the large lump sum they needed before work could be started, even if those who could afford to were willing, as he hoped they would be, to donate some of it direct. It was his task and his responsibility to raise that lump sum in whatever way he could.

In this, he was relying on them to back him to do what he had to, even if it went against their feelings. If they would allow him the freedom to act unhindered in the main, he in his turn would help in whatever way he could to further their traditional ways of fund-raising efforts. It was in the raising of such small contributions by working together in goodwill and neighbourliness that gave them the reason for bothering to keep the church alive. Without that, they might as well let the tower collapse and the church be condemned as unsafe.

Fran suspected that somebody, probably Beth, had warned him of possible opposition from die-hards of the Sophie variety, though it wasn't necessary; but she gathered that he was going out of his way to reiterate his fear that some steps he might be forced to take would probably be unpopular, but that under the circumstances, he could not allow that to deter him. Force was no choice.

'I ask you to let me do it unhindered and as far as possible in my own way. If we work together, faith may move mountains. During Lent, we can do no more than set the ball rolling, but once Lent is over we must all work with a will.'

William and Fran went home amused by his strategy. The

aristocratic, war-seasoned, man-of-the-world Nigel they knew had quite deliberately and effectively donned the role of a nineteenth-century village parson with his cassock that morning. He had, in his charmingly forceful way, told them gently but firmly who was in command, and what he expected of his troops. Fran said she thought he'd taken exactly the right line. They'd been too long without leadership, sadly lacking since their old rector had declined into senile inactivity and during Beth's father's didactic and uncomprehending ministry, though any rector was better than none. Since he had left, they'd all feared that St Swithin's would be held in plural with St Crispin's in Swithinford. She calculated that now, for every carping critic or interfering upstart like Kid Bean, there would be three or more docile sheep gratefully content to follow their new shepherd.

William agreed. 'But I wonder what it is that Nigel's got up his sleeve? He took trouble to warn the Sophies and Thirzahs among the faithful that what he had in mind was something they wouldn't like. He was softening them up to accept it whatever it is before they object. He also gave the wink to folks like us that he expects us to cough up. Who but he would have dared to remind Elyot and Effendi and the rest of us to our faces that from those to whom much has been given, much will be expected? I'll take a bet with anybody that the church tower won't be allowed to fall.'

'We shall have to be prepared to help Sophie with her little money-making events as well,' Fran said. 'She can, and will dish out a donation from Jelly's legacy, but she'll want to be seen doing something on her own account, once Lent is over. Nobody can do anything till then, as Nigel said. I think that's just plain silly – but then, I'm not a proper orthodox Christian. I'm only a religious heathen. I can't see much sense in wasting six weeks when money's so badly needed and time's so short, just because it's Lent! As far as I understand, there's no proof at all that Jesus rose from the dead on the first Sunday after the first full moon after the 21st of March! Who's idea was that, anyway?'

'The Synod of Whitby's, early in the seventh century.'

'How and why does the full moon come into it?'

'My darling, I don't know. I'm not a walking version of the *Encyclopaedia Brittanica*! Something to do with fitting the church's festivals as close to those pagan ones that already existed as they could, I suppose.'

She stopped and stood still, a picture of female scorn for male chicanery. 'Well, all I can say is that there's no sense in it now. It's just keeping folks like Sophie in their place to let such as her go on believing that God wrote the Bible himself with a quill pen, and that it's sin to "goo against" what has always been. Honestly, I do sometimes think the C. of E. is one of the last of the dinosaurs. Huge, frightening, noisy, but with very little brain. Just look at the mistakes it's made during this century – and it wonders why its congregations are dropping! It doesn't affect me, because I shall please myself whether or not I conform to its shibboleths, as Bob will. He'll give generously enough, pagan though he is, but he won't pretend he'll please anybody by denying himself simple pleasures because it's Lent.'

William had stopped walking to wait for her, gazing delightedly at her expression of belligerence. 'Don't worry,' he said. 'I think Nigel's quite well aware that most of those he hopes will get out their cheque books aren't much better Christians than Bob is, as far as dogma goes. He has to think of his parish as a whole. Sophie's at one extreme, and Eric's at the other – he's the nearest of us all to being an atheist. We fit somewhere between. Nigel knows well enough that we shall all fork out.'

'And what about Nigel himself? Where does he stand?'

'I haven't the faintest idea – except that he knows what he's doing.'

William began to stride out again. 'I'm sure he has his reasons for upholding the Christian faith, even if he doesn't always go along with its shibboleths. I don't suppose he cares a brass button whether or not Sophie deprives herself of sugar in her tea during Lent – but he does care that the church still goes on helping to keep a community like this together. On a larger scale, what is most likely to keep any society from disintegrating is the centripetal force of an established religion.'

He saw that she was a bit startled and he was immediately contrite. 'Sorry, my darling – but you will invite history lessons, and I get carried away.'

'You answered the question I asked. I think as much of Nigel as you do and I go along with him, in all but bits of dogma. I can't forget Beth's father during Lent two years ago, when I had to challenge him. Nigel would have put Beth and Robert Fairey's grieving parents before anything else, Holy Week or not. Archie Marriner wouldn't, if I hadn't made him. That's where I part company with orthodox Anglicanism this morning. Just at present, I could do with a bit of cheering up, not a period of forced abstinence from simple innocent pleasures like flowers on the altar.'

'So could I. I feel much more like indulging in a few high jinks now than I did yesterday, before I laid my problems at your feet. I could go home and kiss Aunt Sar'anne.'

She stopped again, this time to let her laughter free. 'Be careful – or I shall tell on you to Nigel, as they would have done in Cromwell's time. If you get on well with Bob tomorrow, we'll have a celebration – though if we want Sophie to help or Beth to attend, it will have to be before Wednesday. Tuesday would still be OK. Even the Puritans made the most of Shrove Tuesday. Isn't that why it's Pancake Day?'

He raised an eyebrow lopsidedly at her. 'Am I hearing you aright – that you connect pancakes with Puritans? I thought we had decided they were the food of love.'

'So they are on Shrove Tuesday or at any other time, providing the right people eat them together. You give me ideas.'

'Not the same as those you give me, I'll bet. What's your idea?'

'Wait and see,' she said. 'Only till Tuesday.'

The weather next morning matched William's optimistic mood. The clouds were higher, here and there thin enough to give promise that the sun might peep through. He set off for Castle Hill without ringing Bob first, fairly certain that the land would still be too wet for work that would take Bob far from the farmyard, and relishing the thought of a walk if he had to go to look for him out in the fields. As it happened, he came upon Bob emerging from one of the outbuildings.

272

Intent on what he was doing, Bob didn't notice him. He was standing on the steps of the barn, leaning on a long-handled two-tined hayfork, and looking behind himself.

'Hello!' William heard him say, 'I *am* glad to see you again. It's been a long while since I did.' William didn't think Bob was addressing him, but could see nobody else, so he moved forward, and watched a slow grin spread across the farmer's face. 'Hello, William,' he said. 'I'm glad to see you, as well.'

'Who were you talking to, if it wasn't me?'

Bob settled his old pork-pie hat firmly on his head, and said, 'My shadow. I ain't seen him for more than a month. I didn't expect anybody to hear me.'

William laughed, his spirits lifting. Bob usually had that effect on him.

'You're just in time for 'levenses,' Bob said. 'Jane'll be pleased to see you. Nobody's wanted to leave the fireside lately, but being shut up with two lively littl'uns like she is all day's enough to wear anybody out. Aggie's into everything now, as well as Jade. Not that Jane grumbles, bless her, and she will have more company when her father gets back later today. Was it the fine morning that tempted you out?'

'No,' said William truthfully. 'I needed to talk to you. But let's go in and see Jane first. Then I'll tell you. It's about the book.'

'Well, in that case, we'd better nip in for a quick cup of tea and then go and talk in the church. We shan't be able to hear ourselves speak for Jade and Aggie playing trains, and they'd want us to play as well, like I had to before I came out.

'"*We're all off to London, Early in the morning, To see the little puff-puffs, All in a row,*"' he sang. 'It caps me why they love it so, 'cos they've never seen a "puff-puff" in their lives. I suppose they like Jane blowing the whistle. But perhaps they'll be had enough by now, though.'

The game had changed. Jade was holding Aggie astride Bonzo's broad back while Jane, flicking her duster as she moved round the big room, was teaching them to say, '*If I had a pony, and he wouldn't go . . .*'

*

William had never stopped wondering at the rightness of that incredible love-match. Half an hour later, he and Bob were seated side by side on the front pew of the little church, as William told of his great interest in the book and how he had run into a brick wall when he had come upon the coded section.

'But we knowed all along that the end part was in code,' Bob said.

'Yes. The trouble is that I'm not half so clever as you think I am. I didn't expect the book to be what it is. I thought I *knew*, where you stood by what you *felt*. What I knew was that by the seventeenth century a lot of folk could read and write, and keeping diaries was the fashion. The same with codes – they were popular with ordinary people because they were so much in use for all the political intrigue and religious manoeuvring – plots and counter-plots going on all the time.

'When ordinary men took to code it was more often than not to keep secrets from prying wives – about money matters, or their latest bit of philandering with the pretty new maidservant. I thought it wouldn't take me above ten minutes to get the hang of the code. But I was wrong, on both counts. The book's a tremendous find, Bob – a bit of genuine history – and thanks to you, nobody else knows anything about it. You stopped me from handing it over, and am I glad you did! I changed my mind fast when I found that the chap who wrote it was the vicar here during the Civil War, and that his name was Wagstaffe. I'm not a bit worried now, except that I feel a bit guilty about your share in it. You found it.'

'I knowed as you were the one meant to have it, though,' Bob said calmly. 'Why did folks as different as you and me get on so well together from the start? That was meant. I reckon we'd better start putting our heads together over that code. Tell me again what you made of the first part of the book.'

William knew Bob to be quick on the uptake, but he had done no more than sketch briefly a very vague outline of what he had learned when Bob interrupted him. 'Cromwell?' he said. 'I never reckoned much to him as a man – folks from round here, and 'specially from round Ramsey, know too much about the Crum'ells. When I first come here, one o' my men told me that if I made a go of it I should be the first as ever had done, 'cos some o' the Crum'ells lived here once, and the church put a curse on all such places as the first Crum'ell had stole from them. I half-believed him, 'cos I'm a fenman anyway, and I had good reason then to believe in any curse.

'"Bugger the church," I said, "if it's that's what's at the bottom of all I'm having to put up with." I used to lean over the wall and wonder why anybody in that graveyard should have got it in for me as hadn't never done none o' them any harm, but I never set foot inside till that day as found you here with that Starchie-Archie parson. He thought I was crazy, 'cos I was so surprised at how I felt once I got inside that I said so out loud. He didn't know what to make of me.'

'I remember,' William said. 'What you said was that "the ghosts liked you".'

Bob nodded. 'What I *meant* was that I felt welcome here – and I reckon as my luck began to change from that very day. Now you're telling me as that old book as I found here is to do with Crum'ell.'

'Not much, though it is about events that happened in his time. Why do you call him "Crum'ell"?'

''Cos there ain't no "O"s in our ol' fen twang – they're all pronounced like "U"s. We say "dug" for "dog", and "uvver" for "over" and suchlike. And "W"s ain't sounded at all, no more than in Norwich or Harwich or Benwick. But go on.'

'What's puzzling you?'

'I wonder what made the chap stop writing sudden, like he did. Did something scare him, do you reckon?'

'Everybody was running scared then, parsons 'specially. They were all having to keep their heads down. But I get the impression that it was something extra urgent that stopped him. He must have been actually sitting writing when it happened, because he stopped halfway down the page, scribbled something underneath in a hurry and left it to go wherever he'd got to go. The coded part starts on the very next page, and my guess is that it tells where he went, and why. We shan't know unless we find a key to that code. That's what's so infuriating.'

Bob was sitting with his head cocked on one side, as he usually did when listening to his 'silent voices'. 'What was it he scribbled?' he asked.

'The first thing that came into his head, I imagine. A few words to all intents saying, "So long, I've got to go now". It's in Latin – but it was the sort of thing people would recognize because it was put on gravestones. Like R.I.P., for instance, is still used. That stands for the Latin words "requisciat in pacem" – "rest in peace".'

'Write 'em down for me to see, them Latin words as he wrote.'

William took his diary out of his pocket, found a clean page, and printed VALE NON SED AETERNUM.

Bob shook his head, disappointed. 'No – that ain't the same. I don't know no Latin, but I know it ain't that.'

'What do you mean?'

'There's some words chiselled on the slab o' that old vault as is fell in, down that bit o' the graveyard as nobody but me ever goes to. As I say, I'm welcome there. It's one o' them tombs as used to stand proud o' the ground, like a box, only this one's collapsed so as the sides have fell flat outwards, and the grass is growed over 'em. But you can still make out bits of what used to be the top slab. They ain't them words, though.'

William had sprung to his feet. Any lead was better than none. 'Take me to see it, please – now.'

Bob looked dubious. 'You can't go in them clothes. It's been raining non-stop for a fortnight till yesterday, and you'll get slared up to your hocks with mud getting across to it, let alone near enough to read what's on it. It's all covered with lichen, anyway. We shall need some tools. Come again when it's dried up a bit, and we'll take a proper look.'

'No,' said William firmly. 'There's no time like the present. For some reason I can't explain, I think you're on the track. I'll sacrifice an old pair of trousers to the chance. Don't bother about my clothes.'

Bob didn't argue. They set off round to the wild part at the back of the church, struggling through brambles that clawed and held them, sinking into pools where ancient graves had left hollows, finding their feet entangled by sodden long grass that hadn't been moved for years, falling over tussocks that hid small footstones, until at the very edge of the bare piece where there were no gravestones, they came to the altar tomb.

It was indeed in a ruinous condition. The side slabs lay as Bob had said, face downwards and overgrown with matted grass and weeds. The end slabs still stood, festooned with brambles and old man's beard and convolvulus, leaning drunkenly inwards, and what had once been the top slab now lay flat on the ground, covered in moss and lichen. Bob pulled the brambles and weeds away to let William near enough to it to examine it. With Bob's shut-knife they cleared enough of it to reveal an inscription, and with growing excitement went on scraping till individual letters were legible. Some were defaced by time, some chipped by frost, or broken by the collapse, but here and there enough remained for William to guess what the words had once been.

### EUDO MONAR RAMSIEN

'Eudo, monk of Ramsey,' William translated. 'That makes sense.'

'There's more farther down,' Bob said, getting down on his knees in the long grass and working with a will. This inscription had fared better.

### DEUS DET NOBIS PACEM

'May God give us peace,' said William, his voice just a fraction deflated. Nothing, so far, was likely to be of help to him.

Bob was lugging at a twisted clump of convolvulus and bind-weed that was still obscuring the bottom end of the slab. It came away suddenly, all in one piece, and a third inscription was revealed. Just one word. Both were on their knees next minute, cleaning one letter at a time till the whole was visible.

### RESURGAM

William stood up, his face suddenly tense. 'That's a real possibility,' he said. 'A literal translation would be, "I shall rise again." But put colloquially, and in the context, you could say it means "I'll be back", which is what he meant to convey, I think. But – no. It's no good.'

'Why not?'

'Too easy, unless – wait a minute, let me think. How stupid can you get! I jumped to the conclusion that the Latin tag must be a clue to the key, but it couldn't have been – *because at that point there was no code*. Nor, as far as he knew then, any reason why there should be. There he sat, scribbling away, when something or somebody made him stop.

'When he got back to it, he had something very secret to set down as to where he had been and what he'd been doing. But no time to do it in. I'm only guessing, of course – but that would account for the Latin tag and the code. It was his way of telling whoever might find it that he had been forced to leave the first part in a hurry, though he hoped not for ever. Its association with gravestones was intended as a hint that if he never got back to it, it would be because he'd be in his grave.

'That was what sent us here, wasn't it? It could be that somebody was after him, so he hadn't time to invent or use the usual sort of difficult numerical code. He had to use one he was familiar with – easy to write and easy to break if you knew the word it was based on. All he was banking on, I think, was to stump anybody who found it from reading it for long enough for him either to get away himself, or for some friend he had helped to escape. So he got it down in code as fast as he could, and to be on the safe side decided to hide it. He did all he could to preserve it and then hid it, here in his church. He wouldn't dare take it with him if he had to make a run for it himself.

'I may be absolutely off-beam, but it's a possibility. Now I'm a historian – if I wanted a code word in a hurry, I should probably think of some historical term first. You'd be likely go for a fen dialect word that people like me wouldn't know. A priest who was as much at home with Latin as he was with English would be quite likely to seize on a Latin word. Anyway, I'm soaked to my waist and getting cold, and can hardly wait to get home to try "Resurgam" out. But don't be too hopeful. I still think it is too obvious.'

'Come across to the house,' Bob said, 'and I'll run you home. I told you it was too wet to go crawling round graveyards this morning. I shan't half catch it from Fran if you die of pneumonia.'

'Now that would make a good code word,' William said. 'It's

got all five vowels in it.' Bob drove him home, both in complete silence. William had a one-track mind at the moment.

William went round to the back door to take off his shoes. They were so clogged with mud that he doubted if they would ever again come clean enough to be wearable. Neither would his trousers. He was damp to his waist, as far as his knees soaked, and covered with bits of grass, leaves and burrs; above knee level his trousers had suffered several jagged bramble snags. He was fond of those trousers – but he didn't care much about such mundane matters just then. He couldn't get to his study fast enough to try out his hunch that they had found a possible key to the code. Nevertheless, he couldn't sit down in this state. He'd go through the kitchen to the downstairs cloakroom, strip there and go upstairs for a quick warm bath before eating. He looked at his watch. Past two o'clock! He was very late for lunch, but at least it meant that Sophie would have gone home, so he was safe to leave his trousers downstairs. He went towards the kitchen, calling 'Fran! Fran darling, where are you?'

A rather croaky old voice, raised to a high pitch, answered him. 'She ain't here, and Sophie's gone home. I'm here, a-waiting for you.'

William's feeling of elation dropped like a hard dumpling to the bottom of his stomach, round which he was holding up the top of his sodden trousers. He always hated having to come home to a house with no Fran in it, especially if he hadn't known in advance that she wouldn't be there. On this occasion, the disappointment was made considerably worse by the fact that Aunt Sar'anne was there. He clutched his trousers round his waist with cold hands, and padded across the floor in bare feet, having left his wet socks in his shoes.

Aunt Sar'anne was sitting comfortably by the side of the Aga, as complacently content as Cat curled up on Fran's lap. She cackled with laughter at the sight of him.

'Wherever hev you bin to get yourself in a mess like that?' she asked. 'In a ditch under a 'edge wi' some gal? I shouldn't ha' thought you'd wouldn't have had no need for that, when you'd only got to come home to your wife for a bed and a woman as soft and warm and bouncy as any man could want. 'Specially after all that rain!'

William stopped, anger and revulsion rising in him till he felt unable to speak. Fran had told him that Sar'anne had none of Sophie's Victorian prudery, and no man who had ever been in the armed services was embarrassed by any reference to sex, even from a woman. But the sight of her, and the vulgar familiarity of her greeting, offended him. He was affronted at the personal application of her remark to himself and Fran, and suddenly, senselessly, overwhelmingly infuriated by her.

There was something so intrusive about her. She was ensconced by the side of *their* fireside, in *their* kitchen, robbing them of what they surely had a perfect right to expect, privacy in their own home. She was taking everything far too much for granted – settling herself in little by little, day by day, like an old hen making a nest. He could foresee just what would happen, when everybody else, other perhaps than Sophie, would forget, and be only too happy to let well alone. Except that it was not 'well' – and he saw that the longer it went on, the harder it would be ever to winkle her out.

He retained enough self-control to be able to reason that none of it was her fault – as old women went, she was really rather a delightful specimen, who had not asked for the shelter that he and Fran had offered. Nor could he blame her for making the most of it. But it had never been meant to become a permanent arrangement, and she was, however unintentionally, encroaching on their privacy and getting up their noses more and more.

He was conscious of his bare feet getting colder on the bare flags of the kitchen floor, and the puddle that was forming round them as water dripped from the sodden ends of his trouser legs. This was no time to resolve that knotty problem, but his jaw set square in a rather white, unsmiling face, as he told himself that this situation must end – and soon. Nobody else was likely to take any steps to end it, so he would have to, even ruthlessly, and whatever Fran said, if necessary.

'I see Sophie put your dinner in the oven,' she said. 'Fran told her to, if you wasn't home by one o'clock, and said she'd left you a note on your desk. Soph' was for waiting till you come, but I said there was no need for that, 'cos I could see to you as well as she could when you did come. D'yer want your dockey straight away?'

She made to get up, but William was roused from his temporary abstraction, and replied rather curtly that he must have a bath before he could do anything more, and would read Fran's note before eating in case she needed him. He then stalked away, with as much dignity as a man in his state of undress could, and left her still sitting in great content between him and his lunch.

His warm bath and a fresh set of clothing restored a lot of his good temper, but induced a feeling of lassitude in which he decided that the code would have to wait till he could bring a somewhat clearer mind to it. The next thing to do, obviously, was to read Fran's note, lunch or no lunch.

It lay on his desk, along with the mail that had come by the second post. That, too, could wait, including the letter marked 'Private', which told him it was from Robin Drake, who still reported at intervals on the progress – or lack of it – of the lawsuit in the USA. As he was completely indifferent to its outcome, he ignored that letter as well as all the others. There was nothing of any consequence. Whatever it was that Fran wanted of him was much more important.

Darling,

I've waited as long as I could, but I promised to be at the Old Rectory by two, so I'm off now. I hope your being late means you've had a happy and successful morning with Bob.

Your lunch is in the Aga, and if, when you've had it, you could join Beth and me, we should be glad of your help in hatching a plan for a bit of fun tomorrow evening. Bring the car. We may need you to play the part of messenger to the gods.

Always, your Fran

He smiled, wondering what she was up to this time, and feeling cheered by her light-hearted tone decided that he was quite hungry. When he went back to the kitchen, it was, mercifully, to find that

Aunt Sar'anne had retired; so he ate a large and succulent lamb chop surrounded by the first offering of purple-sprouting broccoli from Ned's vegetable patch and mashed potato, with his favourite bread-and-butter pudding to follow. As he drove away towards the Old Rectory, clean and warm and satisfied, he felt more optimistic about everything – code, book, and their unwelcome pensioner. It was silly of him to get into such a state about something that couldn't be altered. He began to whistle, reminding himself of Autolicus:

> 'A merry heart goes all the day.
> Your sad tires in a mile-a'

Fran's habit of finding apt quotations must be catching.

Fran and Beth were as merry as he had expected them to be; both, he noted, with mischievous twinkles in their eyes. They were setting up something extraordinary with very little time to spare, he guessed. That's why they had called on him for help. He had picked up from Fran's note that she was in a merry mood, intent on defying the looming presence of Lent and conjuring up a happy ending to their winter's tale. Well, for once he would get his quotation in first, and remind her that he wasn't a complete ignoramus where literature was concerned.

'"*Is this a meeting of the petty gods, and you the queens of it?*"' he asked as he went in.

Fran was on to it like a cat pouncing on a mouse, and replied, as pat as if she were playing a part, '"*Apprehend nothing but jollity*".'

'But I'm afraid we do need your help. We're arranging the first event for the restoration fund, here, tomorrow night – throwing a love feast for as many of our friends as we can entice to come. It is, after all, Pancake Day. We shall eat very little other than the food of love – which will be made by the men and offered by them to the ladies of their choice. And you, my darling, will be the master chef, with Elyot as your assistant. You will demonstrate how to make and toss a pancake, and one by one all the other men will take their turn at trying their hands.'

'With a fine of 50p for every pancake they drop while tossing it,' added Beth, 'and an entrance fee of a pound for each couple. We ought to make a fiver for the fund, and have a lot of fun.'

'Who are you planning to ask? It's jolly short notice.'

'That's why we need a Mercury with wings on his heels. We want you to be our Mercury, now, this very afternoon, if you will. Would you mind taking invitations round? To Jess and Greg, Bob and Jane, Charles and Charlie, George and Molly, Eric and Marjorie, and Nigel – who'll have to be the odd man out. He won't mind.'

'He needn't be an odd man,' William said. 'Effendi's coming back tonight. But Charles will want longest notice because he'll have to fetch Charlie from Cambridge.'

'Good,' said Beth determinedly. 'But Fran's missed out the two most important, who gave us the idea in the first place. Terry Hardy and Anthea Pelham.'

William whistled. 'Whew! Is that wise?'

'We don't know till we try. But when the gods set out with good intent, they usually achieve something. We may induce those two to get as far as speaking to each other again. As far as they are to know, it's just an impromptu Shrove Tuesday party, though it was thinking of them that gave us the idea. Will you play?'

William would have had difficulty in refusing either of them singly; combined, they were irresistible. Besides, his cares were somehow slipping off his shoulders. 'As long as you won't be too disappointed if Terry and Anthea both decline your invitation,' he said, 'I don't mind being the messenger.'

'And the master chef too?' asked Fran, in a wheedling tone.

'There's no fool like an old fool,' he said. 'You wouldn't ask me if you weren't sure of the answer. Have you got the invitations ready?'

'Yes. Here they are,' said Beth. 'Take your time. We've got to get round Elyot yet, but we'll manage that by supper-time. It's only cold ham and salad, I fear, but you'll be very welcome to share it if you'd like to. Will that do?'

'In the absence of the true food for the gods, it will be manna from heaven,' William said, kissing them both, and setting out on his round with a much lighter heart. He had given up any thought of trying to work today. The code would have to wait. In fact, he was reluctant to try it, in case it depressed him and spoilt Fran and Beth's fun.

He told Fran later about his visit to Bob, and his irascible reaction to finding Aunt Sar'anne there instead of her. 'It threw me,' he said, 'till I read your note. But I may have got a promising lead. Don't set your hopes too high – either on me and the code, or on your matchmaking. Matchmaking never works.'

'Really? Then may I ask what you are doing in my bed, Dr Burbage? Forget that old book and let's enjoy ourselves. Support me and Beth – it's her idea. She thinks Terry's already fallen for Anthea, but is scared. We have to teach him that faint heart never won fair lady. He should try the tactics of your father's little *Rondeau*.'

'I don't remember it,' he said. 'Tell me.' He knew she could – and she did.

> If I should ask a little kiss –
> No, don't be coy, but tell me this,
> If I should ask, would you be fain
> To give my kisses back again,
> And so increase my hope of bliss?
> Or would you turn with eyes of pain
> And stare in hauteur and disdain
> Refusing me with emphasis
> If I should ask?
> But then (this in parenthesis)
> Suppose if asking prove amiss
> Taking should prove the way to gain?
> Would courage plead with you in vain?
> I think I should deserve to miss
> If I should ask!

'Good for him,' William said. 'He knew what he was talking about. I shan't ask.' And promptly proved his father's tactics to have been right.

Early next morning he remembered to warn Fran that Bob and Jane had said they couldn't accept unless they got a baby-sitter; but Effendi had phoned just now to say he thought Jane needed an outing, so he had volunteered to stay at home to let her and Bob come. 'But you'll be disappointed that Eric and Nigel can't be there, or Marjorie. I didn't tell you while we were up at the Old Rectory – but there is a good reason. They'd arranged an urgent session together about the church finance. I thought it diplomatic to say nothing to you about it in front of Beth. What it amounts to is that Nigel naturally consulted Eric about ways of raising a lump sum big enough to ensure a good grant from the Church Commissioners. Eric said the best way of raising money in a hurry is to sell something else – and Nigel said that was fine so long as you had anything to sell. Eric, who isn't hindered by sentiment as Sophie and Co. are, said that he had been doing a bit of snooping, and thought the church still owned a saleable piece of property in the old school. It may not look to be worth much as it stands – but in this field Eric does know what he's talking about. The site itself is worth quite a bit, and the building has possibilities for conversion to a dwelling. Victorian buildings were built to last. Converted well, it could still last a lot longer than Bailey's estate houses. Eric's advised Nigel to get it on the market. Spring's always the best time for property sales.'

'Sophie will have a fit!' Fran said.

'I'm afraid she'll have to, because that's what Nigel was preparing them for on Sunday. He hasn't got a valuation yet. Eric says it would be higher if the conversion possibilities are pointed out. He won't touch it himself, because he's too close to Nigel. They've got to be seen to be keeping it all above board.

'And speaking of that – that national scandal Eric forecast has broken. Headline news everywhere, apparently, with a government minister out on his ear, and a lot of bigwigs all over the country caught in its coils. But as far as he can discover, there's been no mention of the Bailey outfit in it so far. He's hoping for Marjorie's sake that they may have got away with it. She's had no word at all from Pansy since Christmas – but if this blows over, all may turn out to be OK. If so, they're luckier than they deserve. Kid Bean's been very nearly round the bend, so Eric says, but the effort to keep her mouth shut was too much for Beryl. Of course, in her version of it, her poor simple husband had no idea in the world that he was being offered "government surplus" that had never been paid for. Anyway, now you know about the school, keep a weather eye out for storms from Sophie's quarter. It makes a lot of sense to me. The old school building as it is is nothing but a liability. The sooner it's sold and converted, the better. What's our programme for today?'

'Beth's going to prepare her kitchen and get in all the ingredients we need,' she said. 'But somebody must go to Cambridge for other things. I rather hoped you'd drive me in, and give me lunch.'

'I should love to,' he said, 'if you really need to go. Or is it just a ploy to keep me out of my study till this evening's over.'

'Both,' she said, 'as well as getting me out of the house while Sophie glooms and Aunt Sar'anne gloats. I can't stand it much longer, any more than you can.'

It turned out that all Fran needed to buy in Cambridge was a butcher's apron and some comic paper chef's hats of different sizes. They had a long and leisurely lunch, browsed round Heffer's bookshop, and then the second-hand ones. They were home while it was still daylight, feeling better for taking a holiday.

By seven-thirty, they were ready for the fray at the Old Rectory. Beth and Emerald had prepared gallons of soup and bought fresh rolls and butter to go with it. The kitchen table had all its leaves out, and there were twelve places set with nothing but knives, soup spoons, dessert-spoons and forks. There was no sign of either William or Elyot when Anthea Pelham made a rather late, shy entrance. Beth ran to welcome her.

'I didn't know whether to come or not,' she said in a low voice to Beth. 'Dr Burbage said it was a party, and I didn't know quite what that meant. I'm afraid I'm not one for playing boisterous games – or anything of that kind.'

286

'Nothing at all like that!' Beth assured her. 'So don't worry. As far as I know, you won't be asked to do anything but talk and eat. Come and sit down.' She guided Anthea to one of the still-empty chairs, with a rather anxious glance at Fran as she did so. It was all-too obvious that the other guests were seated in couples. Fran signalled back a 'can't be helped' shrug, as sorry as Beth was that Hardy had not turned up; but as she went to make sure that William and Elyot were all prepared, she heard a car, and waited by the door.

'Am I late?' said Terry. 'It's this weather. I had such a full surgery I didn't have time to put on my best bib and tucker. I hope you don't mind.'

'All the better,' Fran said, and in her relief and delight did the most natural thing in the world for her – leaned forward and kissed him.

'Well!' he said, 'I don't remember getting a greeting like that for a very long time.'

'Then William can't have explained what you have let yourself in for. It's a love feast, thought up on the spur of the moment. You'll see why.'

He followed her into the kitchen, where at the table only one chair was still vacant. Apologizing, he sat down and greeted Anthea. She had coloured furiously, but returned his greeting. Beth heaved a sigh of relief, and taking a cue from Fran that she should begin, stood up to welcome the assembled company.

'Thank you all for coming at such short notice – to what, most of you have yet no idea. What you all do know is that today is Pancake Day. I hope you haven't eaten a lot already, because you've been invited here to eat more. All you're going to get is soup and pancakes – but with a difference. You see, it's always been a joke between us and William and Fran that pancakes are the food of love. We thought of eating them together tonight, but we decided that we could make it into a love feast by inviting other friends we love, too – and in doing so perhaps give the restoration fund for the old church the right sort of push-off. I've had word from the chef that all is now ready, but I'm still a parson's daughter, you know, and I think it would be rather nice if, before we begin to eat, we acknowledge with gratitude a meeting

287

of so many in such warmth and friendship as this. So why don't we borrow a custom from the Society of Friends? When Elyot has taken his place at the head of the table, will you please make it an unbroken circle of friendship by all holding hands round the table?'

Elyot appeared, sat down, held out his hands each side, and said 'Welcome'. By that time the circle of handholding was complete – except at one place. Anthea had given her right hand to Charles with no fuss – but she did not offer her other to Terry. He had put out his to take it, but her left hand lay flat on her knee, her fingers beating a tattoo.

Hardy had had too many such insults in the last week or two to take another, so utterly unprovoked, and in front of other people. He pressed the hand of Jane, who happened to be next to him on the other side, to show her that in turning away from her he intended no disrespect. She returned his gentle squeeze, and held fast on to his hand. He then looked the woman on his right side full in the face, his eyes angrily bright with interrogation. To his amazement, he saw that she was not only blushing, but struggling to keep back tears.

Hurt and doubt battled inside him, and hurt won. He wasn't going to let her get away with it, this time. He turned himself square to the table again, and dropped his right hand over hers where it lay on her knee, picked it up and held their clasped hands high to show the others that the circle was complete. In the ensuing half-minute, silence reigned. He held her hand tightly and looked towards her. A tear was sliding down her beautiful nose, and after a moment he felt a slight tightening of her fingers round his.

'Thank you,' said Elyot. 'We're ready to eat now, William.'

William appeared, clad correctly in a complete chef's outfit (supplied by Eric), carrying a huge silver bowl of soup in his hands. Under cover of the laughter that greeted him, no one except the two principals gave any further thought to the incident. Hardy did not let go of the hand he had picked up, nor did she attempt to withdraw it. Instead, to his astonishment, she squeezed his gently before releasing it, leaned towards him, and said, 'Thank you so much. I'll explain – some other time.'

There was no more time for talking, then. Elyot had slipped out of the kitchen, while all the others tucked into a spiced vegetable soup well laced with sherry and cream. By the time it was finished, he had reappeared, clad exactly like William, though with a slightly less impressive hat. Between them they carried in a table piled with plates, bowls, pans and other utensils, and put it in front of the cooker, leaving ample room between. Elyot banged a spoon on the table for silence, and William explained the nature of the feast. He would now make the first pancake, to show them all how it should be done.

'Then, in turn, you men may all try your hand at it or pay a fine of one pound into the church fund for your cowardice. If you drop a pancake when tossing it, the fine will be fifty pence each time it lands on the floor. Here we go.'

He tossed a pancake expertly, caught it, tossed it a second time and caught it on a warmed plate substituted for the frying pan. Then he made his way solemnly to Beth, raised his chef's hat a fraction to her, went down on one knee, and presented it to her. She took the plate, put it on the table, leaned towards him, and gave him a spanking kiss.

'Now you, Elyot,' said William. 'You've had plenty of practice before.' The spirit of the evening had got into most of the others already. Elyot's expertly made pancake went to Jane. Greg fumbled his on purpose, demanding several tries, till at last he produced a really splendid one for Fran. Bob, with the spirit of mischief alight in his eyes, declared his was for the most beautiful woman in the room – and went down on his knees to Molly Bridgefoot. Charles didn't do too well, and cost himself four fines before he managed to get one on the plate, at which in relief he declared that as it was a love feast, his would, of course, go to Charlie. Jess said loudly that unless George did better than his grandson, she wouldn't get one at all. In fact, he did prove most unhandy – as Fran said afterwards, men of his generation thought the kitchen was a woman's place, and never soiled their hands with anything like cooking. But in the end Jess did get a rather thick and uneven pancake, and the heartiest kiss of the evening.

'Is that everybody?' asked Elyot. 'Because if it is, William and

I will supply a second one for everybody – as they should be made. Terry – are you scrimshanking, or have you decided to pay the fine instead?'

'No,' said a feminine voice, loud and clear. The doctor stood up, and went forward. He knew how to use his hands, and performed perfectly; then, taking his pancake back to Anthea, he went down on his knee before her, head bowed, not uplifted. But she put her hand under his chin, turned his face upward, leaned forward and kissed him.

William was alive to the ripple that ran round the table. He broke the tension deliberately. 'That's the end of the first round. Line up if you want another, and we'll do our best.' They all did their best, too, till they could eat no more.

Then they retired to the sitting-room, for coffee, liqueurs, and talk.

'What about the washing-up?' asked Molly. 'Let me do it.'

'No, of course not. The girls are going to do their bit. They want to.'

'How much have we made?' asked George.

William counted the notes and coins in the basin they had used for the purpose. 'Just about enough to pay for one of the bottles of port we've emptied,' he said. 'But that was only the excuse. What we were after was the friendship and the fun.'

'And for which we all ought to be willing to pay extra,' George said, producing a five-pound note and tossing it into the basin. Other contributions followed thick and fast. Terry was the last to add his. 'No amount of money could pay for all that I have been given tonight,' he said. Nobody looked to see what he had put in – but when it was counted again, the sum had reached more than ten times the 'fiver' Beth had hoped for.

'I think,' said William as they went home, 'we can honestly say a good time was had by all.'

'I hope it's only the beginning,' Fran answered. 'But that's too much to hope for. Still, you never know. I shan't forget Anthea kissing Terry.'

He didn't answer. Instead, he began to whistle softly to himself. She knew he had no idea what he was whistling, but it was familiar, and she recognized it.

'If I should plant a tiny seed of love
    In the garden of your heart –'

'Very apt,' she said. 'Where on earth did you dig it up from?'


Next morning, the rain was back, but with a difference. It was softer and gentler. Yet though it gave promise of spring, it warned that winter was not over. Or so Fran thought, as she waited in bed for her morning cup of tea. She watched as two languid, globular drops landed on the window, ran slowly towards each other, and became one so large that it glissaded downwards propelled by its own weight, as unshed tears do when they are too big to be held back, and slide dripping from the chin.

Why so gloomy? Because it was Ash Wednesday? Hardly likely! It had been her rebellion against Lenten dolour adding to the gloom of a dull, dark February that had sparked off last night's nonsense. She had declared roundly that she would *not* be made to feel sad to order; and the few tears shed last night that had not been tears of laughter had not been of sorrow either. There had to be a reason for her mood this morning. She was still digging for it when William appeared with her tea. He was already dressed, and sat down on the side of the bed and handed her her tea.

'You're up early,' she said. 'Why? It's a miserable morning, by the look of it.'

'I want to get at that book,' he said. 'I came home from seeing Bob on Monday full of it – but things haven't exactly been conducive to work since then.'

'Oh, William – have you grudged the time you gave to Beth and me? You certainly didn't let it show! Wasn't last night's fun worth it? What was wrong with it?'

The disappointment she felt showed on her face, and she took on the slightly belligerent expression that meant she was truly upset. He was quick off the mark to put it right – if he could. 'Sweetheart, nothing was wrong with it, and a lot was right. But something's missing. I don't quite know what, but it was the same at Christmas. It's just gone on and doesn't seem to get any better. Do you really mean you didn't notice it?'

'No,' she answered truthfully. 'I did feel it – and asked myself just now what it could still be. I came to the conclusion that it had to be that Sophie and Thirzah weren't there. Is that what you think?'

'Not entirely, though it did make a difference. But there's a sort of worm in the bud with everybody. Didn't you sense it?'

'Yes,' she said. 'I don't want to have to admit it, but things aren't quite what they were. Go on. Tell me what's the matter.'

'Same as before, I think. Niggles everywhere. Take Effendi. He would have loved to be there last night, because he loves a bit of bucolic fun. He stayed at home baby-sitting to let Jane come. And that was because they're not happy about Nick.

'Things were going so well when he threw that identity spanner into the works. It's left them doing their damnedest to solve a problem they know they can't. All they can do is wait – and the strain's beginning to tell on them. Bob's matter-of-fact enough to accept that Nick's only twenty, and that there's a girl at the bottom of it. His tantrums about his father are real enough, but he's using them as a cover-up. I don't suppose he has an inkling what misery he's causing. He thinks they don't care about him. *Romeo and Juliet*. Star-crossed lovers making everybody else suffer. And it washes out over the rest of us. We all feel bad because we can't do anything to help.'

Fran nodded. 'Making it worse,' she said, 'like fish-hooks dragging other things than fish up.'

'Yes. Charlie links them at Castle Hill with the Bridgefoots, who've got troubles enough of their own. George braced himself to give up before he was ready – and found he didn't mind. But his family comes first. Pansy's the real fly in their ointment. The black sheep of the family who's sold her Bridgefoot birthright to the Baileys. Married a Bailey, become a Bailey herself – so that George's first great-grandchild will *be* a Bailey! That's like a cancer gnawing away at Marjorie, so all the rest suffer twice.

'And Eric's involved. Why wasn't he there last night? Meeting with Nigel? He sees Nigel every day of his life! He didn't come

292

because Marjorie couldn't face it – and he's too fond of her to leave her alone, or let her be conspicuous by her absence. Between you and me and the gatepost, Eric knows a lot more about Bailey's involvement in this scandal than he wants her to find out. That isn't surmise. He told me – in confidence. He's pretty sure the Baileys have cleared out, gone overseas, and presumably Pansy is with them. She daren't let her mother know where she is, because a chance word might lead the police to them. Eric says the case may drag on for years. He won't tell Marjorie till he has no other option. Pansy might just as well be dead, as far as her family is concerned.'

Fran reached for his hand. 'How absolutely awful!' she said. 'Especially for George and Molly. No wonder George couldn't toss pancakes! So what else? Who else – besides Thirzah?'

'Well, Jess and Greg are happier than they've ever been before – put them in the balance on the other side. And Elyot and Beth, I suppose.'

'And us?'

He was silent too long, and her fear showed in her face. He leaned forward to take her empty cup from her, and hold both her hands in his own. 'You don't really need to be told that nothing – but *nothing* – can possibly change what we mean by "us",' he said. 'Except, of course, the passing of time. No doubt there will come a day when, as Rupert Brooke wrote, "*Love has turned to kindliness*", but darling, that's where we stood when we met again. I don't honestly think we need worry yet about that wheel coming full circle. If or when it does, it will mean we have been lucky enough to live to be old together. We've got all we ever hoped for – more than I did, and more than I deserve. All the same, I shouldn't be as truthful as I try to be with you if I said that I'm not aware of feeling edgy. Not all Aunt Sar'anne's fault, either. I don't know why. I wish I did.

'Take this morning. I woke early, and instead of cuddling up to you and counting my blessings, I thought about what we've just said, and I had to get up to snap out of it. I go to work to stop myself from getting more uneasy. Then I neglect you and feel guilty, and that makes me worse. But sweetheart – let me go now. If I don't, I shall get caught by Sophie and her sainted aunt, and I don't feel up to it. There, I've confessed. Are you all right?'

'No – but better for talking to you. Incidentally, Sophie won't be here yet. As it's Ash Wednesday, she'll be going to church before she comes, though her sainted aunt won't. They eschew things of that sort at the chapel. But off you go.'

He left, and she went downstairs to a kitchen that seemed colder and less welcoming to a new day than usual. Aunt Sar'anne was already there, and so was Ned. A flush of irritation that was almost despair swept over Fran. For once she ignored the old lady, and said, 'Hello, Ned. Is something wrong?'

'Not much. Let's say as there's something as ain't quite right. I stuck a fork through my foot one day last week, and didn't take no notice of it at the time. But I reckon it must be gathering, 'cos it's swelled so as I can't get me boot on, and it throbbed so last night as I didn't get no sleep. I don't know as I could walk as far as the surgery, even if there is one today. Do you know if there is?'

'I'll soon find out,' Fran said, 'and take you in the car if there is. You must see the doctor. You shouldn't have left it as long as you have. Sit down while I go and phone.' He hobbled towards the old Windsor chair that always stood by the Aga.

'Don't set there. Tha's my cheer,' Aunt Sar'anne said. 'I were just a-gooing to set down when you come. I don't know what men are coming to, that I don't, making such a hormpologe about a bit of a sore toe, and wanting to be druv in a car to see a doctor. If you'd had to pay him, like we used to hev to, you'd doctor it yourself, same as we should ha' done. All it wants is a scalding-hot bread poultice. I'm never knowed a gathering as a bread poultice wouldn't clear up overnight if you put it on hot enough.'

Fran was back in time to get the gist. She took the situation in at a glance, and the wave of anger washed up again. 'Ned,' she said, in a somewhat brisk, 'mistress-of-the-house' voice he hardly recognized, 'I told *you* to sit down.' She pulled the Windsor chair towards him.

'Tha's my cheer,' Aunt Sar'anne told her.

'No it isn't. It happens to be my husband's chair, as it was once my grandfather's. He doesn't normally mind you using it. But if there is a chair in this house you may claim as your own, it's the other side of that door. So please let Ned sit down now until the doctor comes. He'll call and see you here as soon as he can, Ned. Let me know what he says, and whether you need a lift home.'

Ned sat down obediently, while Fran stood and waited for Aunt Sar'anne to go. She felt mean and guilty and in another moment would have given way; but she caught Ned's eye instead and saw his eyelid flicker. She managed to control her tongue until the door to Eeyore's Tail closed behind a very offended old woman.

'Give 'em a inch and they'll take a yard,' Ned said. 'It didn't matter to me where I set, but I can see very well how the land lays with her. They're all alike when they get as old as she is. My mother-in-law were just the same, till I didn't know which was her house and which was my own. But she were Eth's mother, when all was said and done. This one ain't got no claim on you, nor anybody else, from what I can see of it. But she will have, if you don't look out.'

His observation of what Fran knew was only too true made her more depressed than ever. She wanted a shoulder to cry on, but she would *not* disturb William. She went to her own study instead, trying to be calm. Reflecting on the morning so far, she came to the conclusion that she and William were in a predicament very similar to that of the Bellamys and the Bridgefoots. They, too, had an insoluble problem.

It was the best part of an hour before Hardy arrived. He went to the door of Fran's study, and she accompanied him back to the kitchen.

'I need Ned down in the surgery,' he said. 'It may have to be lanced to give him any relief, and he must have an a.t.s. injection. Then antibiotics and a rest should do the trick. Can you bring him down, wait till he's ready, and take him home? I'm due somewhere else very soon.'

'Have we got time for coffee first?' asked Fran. He gladly consented.

William appeared just as the coffee was ready. He had gone to his study genuinely impatient to test his hunch that he and Bob might just possibly have hit on the key word to the code. Having been forced to leave it for two days had deflated him and he had lost some of his confidence. For one thing, he felt he had allowed himself to be unduly influenced by his belief in Bob's sixth sense.

*He* was a trained researcher. He had to *think*, not feel. This morning he wasn't very good at thinking, except what he had said to Fran. Had he upset her? Had he let her know too truthfully how unwilling he'd been to leave his own concerns for hers? She'd been determined, almost aggressive, to get her own way – which wasn't like her. Were they getting out of kilter with each other? They'd agreed that something was wrong, and then he'd left her. She'd more or less told him to go.

He forced his mind back to the code. Secret information spelled danger; so why had Francis Wagstaffe risked it? Up in the graveyard with Bob, he'd been hopeful, but he wasn't at all so sure now. He was preparing to begin on it all over again, when he heard the wheels of a car scatter the gravel in front of the house. Good God – Terence Hardy, carrying his doctor's bag! What had happened to Fran while he had been deliberately neglecting her? Damn the bloody code, and to hell with the book! He left them where they lay, and rushed kitchenwards.

Much relieved, though concerned for Ned, he offered to be the chauffeur, which was just as well, for as he went out with Ned, Sophie arrived, and found Fran, alone, still in the kitchen. One glance at Sophie was enough. Something was very much amiss. She was wearing her second-best, which like her Sunday attire was mostly black, except that in deference to this day she wore a plain hat without any flowery decoration, against which her normally rosy cheeks showed up drawn and bloodless. She still wore her everyday black woollen stockings and her laced up boots. The heaviness of her tread added to Fran's apprehension.

Fran waited while, robot-like, Sophie took off her outdoor coat and hat, put on her overall, and tied her apron over it. Then she came towards the table, and groped for a chair. Fran sprang to her feet, guided Sophie to the chair, lowered her gently on to it, and sat down facing her, both hands reaching across the table to clasp Sophie's.

'My dear Sophie, what's the matter? Are you ill? Let me catch Dr Hardy before he leaves home again.'

Sophie found her voice with an effort. 'They're a-gooing to sell the old school!'

Fran had thought Sophie would be a bit upset, but she hadn't expected her to react to that bit of news as to the trump of doom. The well of her sympathy this morning was not very deep. 'Yes, I had heard a rumour that they might have to consider raising money that way. I think that's what the rector was hinting at on Sunday. It's a case of "Needs must when the devil drives". And the school isn't much good to anybody as it stands, is it?'

'Not to such as you it ain't, I daresay. You didn't goo there and be teached by Miss like we did. They ain't got no right to interfere with things as mean so much to folks like us without as much as asking our opinion.'

Fran's social equilibrium was definitely off-balance. She felt exasperated and irritated by the prospect of having to deal with yet another storm in a tea-cup. She let go of Sophie's hands, and said, in a rather firm, practical voice, 'I think you'll have to make your mind up which matters more to you, the church or the school. I shouldn't have thought there was much comparison.'

To her dismay, Sophie leaned forward over the table, and began to cry in earnest. This was not just a case of injured feelings at Nigel acting without calling a vestry meeting. These tears were from a reservoir full to the point of overflowing, and of which the news about the school had broken the dam. Fran sat still, hardly daring to show any sort of feeling till she had heard more. Sophie's voice was raised to a high pitch of misery.

'I don't know what I'm done to deserve that everything should be took away from me,' she wailed. ''Specially up 'ere! We was so 'appy when first you come back, and then 'im, and everything. Now it's all gone! Fust Wendy, then Jelly, then Miss. But I still 'ad Thirz' and my fam'ly, and I 'ad you and 'im, and whatever else was wrong I could look for'ard to coming to work and you being 'ere for a chat with me. Even when Miss Franks's father was the rector, and I couldn't say as I enjoyed going to church no more, I could look to the next day being Monday, so as I could come and feel at 'ome 'ere with you and 'im, and talk to you about old times, and Miss, and Jelly. And after Het and Joe went to live in the school 'ouse, it seemed to bring Miss back nearer to hev my own sister living in 'er old 'ouse, so's I could look out o' the window to see the dear old school. Now it'll be pulled down, so they say, for some council 'ouses to be put there, or a new public-'ouse, or something. On top of everything else, I don't know as I can abear it.'

'What else, Sophie? Don't cry.' Fran's voice was softer now, but it only made Sophie sob more.

'Well, Thirz'. She's a-getting worse. I 'ate to say it, but she is going like the Tibbses, not knowing what she's doing or saying. Me and Dan'el hev to take turn and turn about to be with 'er – Het won't be left with 'er no longer 'cos she's frit. And Thirz' is took agin me. She's that nasty, you'd never believe – and me 'er own sister. She goes on and on at me about Jelly – seems as if 'er mind runs all the while on that – you know, men and women going together, like. She says as 'ow she'll be a blessed angel when I'm crawling about the floor of 'ell, 'cos I'm been such a bad woman – or else she's asking me questions about Jelly as I shouldn't ha' been able to answer do I'd been married to 'im as long as she 'as to Dan'el. When I hev to sit with 'er to let Dan goo to church, she keeps on and on like that till I feel as if I'm 'ad a bucket o' pig-swill throwed over me, and shan't never come clean no more. And she's so clart with it, never lets nobody else 'ear 'er talking like that. So if I try to tell 'em – Dan or Het and Joe – they don't believe me, and say as it's me going off my 'ead. You can't blame them, 'cos she talks to them as if butter wouldn't melt in 'er mouth, she does, and tells 'em she couldn't repeat the filthy things I'm been saying to 'er, and that they ought to hev me put away. Oh, Fran, what am I got to do?'

It was, indeed, a great deal more serious than Fran had ever suspected, and she simply didn't know what to answer. 'We must do something – but what I don't know!' she said. 'Why didn't you tell us before?'

''Cos I never 'ad no chance. I wasn't going to say nothing in front of Aunt Sar'anne. She's all'us 'ere when I come – and you and 'im ain't 'ere, not now, not no more! I don't come pleased to be coming, like I used to. I only come 'ere to work now. Nothing's like what it used to be. I don't 'ear you a-laughing afore I open the door, or 'im a-whistling, or both of you fooling about, like it was once. You're lost all your dossity, and the 'ouse ain't the same. Wheer is she?'

'Who? Oh you mean Aunt Sar'anne? In her room. We had to get the doctor to Ned's foot, and I had to ask her to go away while he examined it.'

'Well, I don't wish Ned no 'arm, I'm sure, but it were a good thing as I found you by yourself when I come. I feel better just to ha' been able to tell you. I don't blame Aunt 'cos I know she ain't doing it a-purpose, but it's never been the same since Tilda died. It's as if she left all her megrims be'ind 'er, just to make us suffer.'

Fran went to her study very subdued, and wished William would come home. What on earth could he be doing, to stay away so long without letting her know why?

He was getting a much-needed breath of fresh air. When Hardy had finished with Ned and William had driven him home, the rain had stopped and a slight breeze had sprung up, moving the clouds enough to let a ray or two of sunshine through. He overtook Eric and Nigel, on foot, and stopped to offer them a lift.

They declined, saying they had felt a walk might do them good. 'We're only off to take another look at the old school,' Nigel said. 'The news is out and I'm not very popular with my congregation – well, some of them. So I asked Eric to come with me and point out any possibilities the school has that might prove to be a shot or two in my locker – both to get the best price, and to smooth ruffled feathers. Park in that gateway and come with us. A walk wouldn't hurt you, either.'

William agreed. There was a telephone kiosk by the school. He would ring Fran from there if he thought he needed to, but as it chanced the kiosk was occupied, so they all went on to inspect the school, and he had no further opportunity.

The school building was like most village schools dating back to the Victorian age, erected either by the Church of England as in this particular case, or as 'British schools' by their Free-Church rivals: one very large classroom, one smaller one, and a porch at each end. One entrance for girls, one for boys. The playground surrounding all was of asphalt, with a paved area before each porch, which had at one time been divided into two by a row of spiked, solid iron railings, that even small hands could pass between only with difficulty and danger. There must be no contact, physical or verbal, between the sexes. Miss Budd had in her time got rid of that particular dire warning of what God had been up to in creating them male and female, though others were still in evidence. It was a large playground, now that the red iron rods had been removed. There was a high wooden fence from front to back down one side of it, put up between it and the house provided for the teacher, which, before Mary Budd had retired and bought it, had been part of the school premises.

Time, and a garden with fruit trees behind the house, had turned the schoolhouse into a pretty little dwelling. Time had also allowed to grow to their full height some rather splendid trees which had been planted in the first instance to hide and to separate the two lots of 'offices' at the bottom of the playground. End-on to each set of lavatories were two large open-sided oblong buildings, facing each other at the extreme outer edges of the playground, backed also by trees. These sheds had paved floors, having been intended for the infants, segregated by their sex, to play in on wet days. How to get them there in pouring rain without them getting soaked to the skin first was a mystery even Mary Budd had never solved.

The general effect was of a large, open site, treed at the bottom end, and with one side pleasantly softened by the schoolhouse and its garden. On the fourth side was an unmade by-road, hedged on the far side, which eventually wound its way round to rejoin the main village street a hundred yards or so from the church.

Nigel produced a large key and opened the door beneath the porch marked GIRLS in dark-blue brick set among the red. Past a row of cracked, First-World-War style wash-basins and a forest of wooden free-standing rails with hooks at three different levels for outdoor wear, was the door into the 'big room'. A big room it certainly was, not only in its floor area, but in its overpowering height, with huge windows of a vaguely Gothic variety with pointed arches reaching up into both gabled ends. The lower half of every wall was of solid brick, lest any young eye, or even that of the teacher, should stray from the primers to the wonders of a sunlit world outside.

William, who had never attended such a school, but was ever and always a historian, created in his imagination the experience of many of his contemporaries, and their fathers and mothers and grandparents. The awe, amounting almost to fear, of that space above, had surely been intended to suggest the all-seeing eye of the Almighty up there. The serried rows of children – sixty or seventy of them – had sat in tiers before the dragon-like keeper of this example of God's zoo, armed against the ferocious beasts he had charge of with a cane stuck up his jacket and in view as it curled over his collar, and from where it could descend with a terrifying swish at the least provocation, perforce on the very youngest because they sat in the front, and causing the unearthly silence which was the rule to be broken by cries of pain, fear, and distress. No wonder Sophie always spoke of God as ''Im Above'. After more than twenty years of being unoccupied, the smell of 'school' – Victorian school – still rose to the nostrils. The smell of young humanity herded too closely together, of damp clothing drying on them, and above all, of evil-smelling ink spilt and splashed on the floor and removed again and again by some breath-catching chemical. Surely, memories that no one cherished and wanted to keep? Yet it had been in this same atmosphere that one woman, by love and the power of personality, had not only kept order and imparted knowledge and philosophy, but generated such admiration and devotion that she still had a hand in village affairs. It was no wonder that there were still those who resented this monstrosity of a memorial to her being lost to them for ever.

'It's well built,' said Nigel, breaking into William's thoughts. 'It will be a pity if whoever buys it will have to demolish it all and start again.'

'I'm surprised,' William said. 'I'd never realized before what a valuable site it is – right in the middle of the village, but nowhere overlooked. The trees are a marvellous asset, especially that huge oak and the old walnut. It could be made into a pair of semi's, each with a ready-made car-port. It has far more potential than I had believed possible.'

301

Eric was giving the roof space a lot of his attention. 'It would make one large house or two smaller ones,' he said, 'but either would be a bad bargain. Think of the cost of heating all that height, right up to the roof.'

'False ceiling?' asked Nigel hopefully.

'Possibly. Then the space would be wasted. A false ceiling and dormer windows in the roof, and it could possibly convert to four smallish flats. But it isn't nearly so hopeless an asset as you were trying to pretend you had on your hands, Nigel. I'll give it more thought, now I've actually seen it. But not now. I must go.'

'Heavens! So must I,' said William. 'Fran will be having kittens thinking I've had to take Ned to hospital. And I've got work to do!'

'Well,' said Nigel, 'I hope you're right, Eric, and that it may convert. I think it would be a lot less painful to some of the older church members if it could rise again like a phoenix from the ashes of the old rather than be swept away altogether to make way for some dreadful lopsided or asymmetrical bit of modern architecture. What has to be will be – but if I could I would like to raise the money without depriving the village of a bit of its history. Thanks for coming, Eric. And it's good to have had you, too, William.' He held out his hand to William.

'Don't let it get you down, Padre,' William said. 'We'll just go on trying to think of ways of making sure it will rise again.'

Fran had sent a distraught Sophie home, so that in her present state she need not come face to face with Aunt Sar'anne. Ned was being taken home. She sat alone waiting for William to return, becoming more and more depressed. Aunt Sar'anne was obviously sulking, and for that at least Fran was grateful; but she needed an outlet for her feelings, and William wasn't there to be talked to. In all their time together again since they had first set foot in Benedict's, she could not remember any other occasion when he had left her, and then, apparently, forgotten her. That's what it must amount to, and if so, Sophie was right. Something *was* different. A light had gone out.

No – she hastily rejected that image. The light had not gone out of their relationship; but it had been, or was being obscured by things outside their control. 'Put under a bushel', as the Bible had it – where, if it were allowed to remain, it would either burn out, or in time actually go out for lack of oxygen.

She gave herself a mental shake. Getting herself into a morbid state about it was the worst thing she could do. '*The cure for this ill is not to sit still*' – thank heaven for Kipling! Nobody but she and William could put it right, so they'd better start, as soon as he came back. She'd try, anyway. But when he came in, he found her still sitting with traces of tears on her face.

Guilty, contrite, and apprehensive, he pulled her up from her chair, and held her. Contact was better than words, and she responded at once. So they stood silent, she comprehending his contrition, he her depression. For a few hours only, they had been out of touch with each other, stumbling in the dark.

'Lunch is ready,' she said – but she didn't pull herself away.

'Let it wait,' he said. 'Let's go and have a drink together.' In the sitting-room, for the first time for weeks lit by sunshine, he prepared the drinks and sat down in his chair, pulling her on to his knee.

'Now tell me what caused those tears,' he said. 'Was it me, and what I said?'

She smiled through new tears caused by his caress and his unspoken apology. 'There isn't any "you",' she said, 'or any "me". We're "us", as you said. But . . .' She went on to tell him all that had happened in his absence, and all that Sophie had said. 'And darling, she was right. That's exactly what we were complaining about earlier this morning. I expect it's what made me feel that I had to do something silly last night to stop the rot. We haven't changed, the house hasn't changed, and if our circumstances have, it's for the better. Our friends haven't changed – though a lot of them may have personal problems. Instead of sharing them with each other, we've all picked each other's up, and everybody's been carrying the lot. We've infected each other with anxiety. It's no use complaining about it now – that won't do any good. We've got to find a way of snapping out of it. I was just thinking so, with Kipling's help, when you came back. We've got to "*take a large hoe and a shovel also*" and do something about it. What, I have no idea – yet. But we mustn't let the gloom get worse. However busy we are, however we feel, we've got to make an effort to keep in touch with the rest. Invite them to come here, whether we want to or not, if only to keep Sophie busy and sane. Am I right?'

'When weren't you?' he asked. 'I expect a lot of it's the awful weather getting everybody down. There's nothing wrong with me except that I can't get on with the book till I can solve that bloody code. I was irritable this morning because I hadn't found time till then to test a hunch I'd had on Monday, and when I did, it didn't work.'

'Tell me,' she said. She took her head from his chest, and moved her weight from his knees to the arm of his chair. He explained his theory that her namesake, if not her ancestor, must have found himself in danger and in need of a code at very short notice, and had had to use an easy one, but dare do no more than give vague hints as to the key. Yet if what he had to tell were worth his trouble to set down, he must have wanted somebody, some day, to decode it and read it. Not immediately, though. He must have hoped that one day somebody would have enough nous to find the key to his home-made code if he didn't get back to it. Simple though the key might be, he had used it intelligently enough to delay the decoding of what he had written, and that was probably the most important issue at that point. He didn't want his adversaries, whoever they were, to be able to decode it till he and others had time to do what they had to.

'Like the Germans when they suspected we were getting on to their Enigma code? Didn't they change the manual it was based on, or something? I can't see any other way for you but to stick to your hunch till you prove you're barking up the wrong tree. Let's go and have lunch.'

He pulled her back on to his knee. 'I intend to,' he said. 'There's really no hurry, other than my impatience. But I do think you're right that we have to do something quick about what Sophie called "Tilda's curse". I think she's on the ball. Aunt Sar'anne hasn't meant to, but it is she who has involved us in this epidemic of insoluble problems. We've got to find a way out of our own before we can help anybody else. I haven't been pulling my weight. So from now on, as your husband and the man of the house, I shall take it on myself to do so, before bothering about that code.

So – will you please stop worrying and leave it to me? As I see it, what it amounts to is that we've been left holding a baby that isn't exclusively ours. I'll remind the others of that, and see what a bit of combined civilized thinking can do. Trust me, sweetheart?'

She turned her head to meet his kiss. Actions speak louder than words.

'Now do let's go and have our lunch,' she said, springing up. 'I'm starving.'

Beth the parson's daughter remained too good a member of the church to take quite the same casual attitude towards its calendar that the more sceptical Fran did. Beth couldn't ignore Lent, though she didn't make much of it at home. For one thing, Elyot had withdrawn from orthodox belief for reasons of his own before he ever set eyes on Beth, though finding her had shunted him back a bit. He'd go along with anything she wanted – or didn't want – purely for her sake. If it suited her not to engage in much social activity for a while, it didn't bother him one way or the other.

Fran, who would usually have taken Elyot's line too, was afraid that the six weeks to Easter was too long a period to risk the encircling gloom thickening round Sophie. Anything which was regarded as part of her job, Sophie would do, providing it didn't require her to work on the Sabbath or any holy day, whatever the season. In fairness to Nigel, Fran thought it wise not to involve Beth or any of the Bridgefoots.

That was rather a pity, because the Shrove Tuesday frivolity had appeared to give hope for the rehabilitation of Terry Hardy. Whatever William said about matchmaking, there was no need for Terry to consider himself a social leper. It would be very sad if the little seed sown that night died from six weeks' neglect just because it was Lent. It was no use trying to force false *bonhomie* on Jane and Effendi, when they were in no mood for it. But Greg and Jess could be relied on to cooperate.

Ned had played into her hands by sticking a fork through

his foot. He was the sort of man who was only miserable or bad-tempered when forced to be idle. He had been told to keep his foot up for a couple of days, but he had appeared at his usual time at Benedict's, 'tiffling about' to keep himself busy, which had resulted in a conscientious doctor calling to see him at Benedict's. Hardy seemed in such good spirits, full of his hobby of messing about with Elyot and their ship model, that Fran felt she needn't worry about him yet; but she was sorry about Aunt Sar'anne, who had taken her rebuke more seriously than she had meant it, and was pointedly keeping out of their way. In consequence, she had an uneasy conscience.

'Poor old thing,' she said to William. 'I do feel bad about her. She's had such a rotten life. I know more about it than either you or Sophie – because till Tilda died they'd had so little to do with each other. I can't help thinking how I'd feel if I'd had six children and was still left all alone without a soul who cared twopence what happened to me when I was ninety-two. Two of her sons were killed in the first war, and another died of lockjaw. Then the one who was left was blown up in the Blitz driving a lorry-load of potatoes to Covent Garden. Her two girls, who were born about as close together as they could be, were a sort of second hatching, because "her Perce" had been away. Doris, the elder one, was a GI bride, and from what I gather, was never heard of afterwards, which only left Tilda. Fancy living on to be ninety-two after a life like that! I feel mean because we've got all she's never had, and grudge her the chance to make the most of what she's got left now. Old people do tend to get selfish as their world gets narrower, and she's hurt now because she doesn't know or understand how she's offended us.

'Our difficulty is that we've got Sophie on our plates as well. She's losing heart, and blaming herself for us being lumbered with her aunt, whatever I do or say to assure her it isn't her fault. She's beside herself with worry and anxiety about Thirzah. But whatever I choose to say, I can't deny that we do find Aunt Sar'anne's intrusion into our lives very galling. Exasperating. Debilitating. It's getting me down and affecting my work.'

William admitted to feeling much the same, and finding it difficult to keep his mind on what he ought to be doing. He didn't say that apart from sharing her feelings, he was also coping with his own guilt. He was all too conscious of how near he'd come to making things worse. His freedom from his legal obligations to Janice, and from the University, must have gone to his head. Then finding out about his father, and the prospect of emulating him by writing only to please himself, had made him forget that it hadn't always been like that. He accused himself of having begun to take Fran and Benedict's and all the rest of it for granted in a way he would never have thought possible. Well, thanks to whatever gods there were, he'd seen the red light in time.

If Fran thought that all he wanted at present was to sit at his desk and plod away at the code, she was wrong. What he needed most just now was to keep her in view, to make sure yet again that she wasn't holding anything against him; so he made constant excuses to visit the kitchen, or her study, or wherever she happened to be. Terry Hardy's visit to Ned gave him a good excuse to knock off and join them.

Greg, now possessing a piano of his own, didn't call as often as he used to – but he was there that morning to set up arrangements for removing *The Burbages at Home*. The three pictures he was allowed to submit for the Summer Exhibition had to be delivered by the first week in March. The others, he said, were all ready, but he'd been busting himself to finish a replacement for theirs big enough to fill the space. He was very apologetic about asking to be allowed to take it, but Fran cut him short.

'Stop bleating like a lost sheep,' she said. 'You know how chuffed we shall be if they do hang ours! Let's leave the space empty till we know, and then we can have a hanging party for the new one, or a re-hanging party for our Gainsborough.'

'How long before we know?' asked William. 'And which others are you sending?'

'One thing you can say for that selection panel,' Greg answered, 'is that they get on with it. First round, they take one glance at each picture as it's carried by them. They do take a bit longer over the shortlisted ones. I'm submitting the Petrie girls, and Aunt Sar'anne, as well as yours.'

'And if they do hang ours,' William continued, 'what's our substitute to be?'

'Castle Hill – the church against the elms in flower and the rooks "playing breakneck", as Bob calls it. Do you mind?'

'*Mind?*' said William. 'I'm loaded to the gun'les with superstition and omens, all connected with that church. If that picture isn't another good omen, I'll eat my hat! What's the matter, Fran?'

'Don't make such rash statements, darling. To my knowledge, you only possess one hat – your topper. I refuse absolutely to let you eat that! But it *is* a lovely thought, Greg. I can't wait to see it. We'll have that party – for whichever picture, and the artist.'

She got up and kissed Greg, then William, and couldn't leave Terry out. It pleased him, and made her feel as she did in a theatre when the lights began to go up.

William went back to his study feeling a lot better. Fran, to say nothing of Sophie, had been chuntering at him for days for leaving it so untidy. Piles of unanswered letters, bits of paper with notes on, books and things lying about everywhere. It might be a good idea to clear it up now, and then make a fresh start.

He was reassured that Fran was herself again. He had promised to take command on the Aunt Sar'anne front, and thought perhaps he ought to deal with that, too, before he tackled the code again. There was no time like the present. He'd tidy up a bit till lunch, and go to see Nigel and Eric again afterwards. If he tackled outstanding correspondence tomorrow, he'd be free to get back to the book.

He didn't get much help that afternoon. Nobody had any solution to the problem of Aunt Sar'anne; the only one put forward was a repetition of the former one that they might all contribute to the expense of a place in a private nursing home, which William squashed flat on the same grounds as before. 'Besides, we – Fran and I – can't just post her somewhere else as if she were a parcel, even if we have to keep her till the end of her days. But the fact does remain that the old lady's not really our problem any more than anybody else's, and it does seem to me that as a community we ought to be able to deal with it somehow. The trouble with the DHSS is that it can't any longer think in terms of individuals – and if ever there was an individual, Aunt Sar'anne's it. But we'll cope as long as we have to. Just bear it in mind if ever you do have a cottage to let permanently, Eric, or anything else helpful crops up. I think Fran and I would feel better if it isn't taken for granted that we are wholly responsible for her. Sophie is our responsibility, and we have to prevent her from going under.'

He reported back at tea-time, and then went back to his study till supper. Fran spent her time planning a party – whether or not Greg got 'hung'. A small dinner-party, with herself and William, Greg and Jess, Terry and Anthea. She told William as they ate supper. 'And once Easter's over,' she said, 'we'll have another, real party, if you can spare the time. Have you got any further with the code?'

'No. I haven't tried.'

'I'm intrigued,' Fran said. 'I want to know what a country parson could have been up to, to need to write in code.'

'I think he was a man in a tight spot, not just a parson playing politics. His head may have been in danger,' William said.

'And he may have had other people to think about,' she answered. 'A wife and children, perhaps – must have had, if he really was my ancestor.'

'He didn't, darling – I know that. But he did have a sort of family all dependent on him. Go on imagining. You're better at it than I am.'

'More experienced, that's all. Let's forget him, and listen to some music.'

A cold blustery wind and a heavy shower woke William early next morning.

'I'm going to get up,' he told Fran, 'to go to tackle that pile of letters. You cuddle down again while you can.' She was quite willing. Their mood had changed, and she was happy and contented again. She tried to remember which seventeenth-century divine it was who had written, '*God made man to lie awake and hope, but never to lie awake and grieve*'. She thought he had been right, and drifted back to sleep.

Meanwhile, William began to sort out his correspondence into piles: bills, letters, miscellaneous bumpf. There was that long legal envelope from Robin Drake still unopened. He would file it with the rest in Drake's file, but he supposed he ought to glance at it first. He slit the envelope, pulled out its contents, and read. And read again. And again.

*It couldn't be true! He didn't want it to be true! He had never wanted it to be!*

But there it was. The verdict of the court in the USA had been that on what medical evidence there was, and the difference in their ages, the elder of the two principals had been deemed to have died first, making Mrs Burbage's will the effective one. The accompanying note from Robin Drake told him that as soon as he, Drake, could finalize the matter, a cheque for the amount in question, $250,000 less all expenses, would be paid into William's bank. He estimated that including his own charges, it should amount to something in the region of £100,000.

William sat staring at the letter. He had thought it all done and finished with. Did one never get to the end of paying for past mistakes? The only thing he was sure about was that he wouldn't mention it to Fran till he had to. It was absolutely the wrong time. They didn't want the damned money, nor any reminder of Janice.

He was incapable of doing anything till the shock wore off. Without Fran, he'd be completely alone on this moral desert island. Drake wouldn't be any help. He'd only tell him he was barmy. He looked up at the photograph over his desk, and the eyes seemed to be looking straight back at him. His father would have known how he felt. He'd died young, but he'd died wise, as all his writing, especially his poetry, proved. It was the only support William had directly to hand, so he reached into the drawer where Fran had deposited a typed copy of the lyric poems. Looking for a sigil, William supposed, contemptuous of himself. Looking for anything to counteract the shock and his own distaste of himself. He turned the pages of typescript to the end, to bits he had never bothered to read before.

Lines from a 'Sonnet, Written in Maturity' caught his eye, and held it. '*How like a reeling drunkard goes my thought . . . Just impotent and to no order brought . . . Freed from absurd debate and baseless fright . . . And into golden cadence to be wrought . . .*' William exploded into ironic laughter, and threw the sheaf of paper back into the drawer, looking back to the photo.

'God damn it, Father! That's just what has happened! A shower of gold I didn't ask for. Likely to kill all I hold dear, if not me into the bargain. What am I to do?'

He put his head in his hands, and tried to think. His father couldn't answer, but – hadn't he asked advice once before from another made wise by experience of war, when what was now reality had only been a threat? On the occasion when he had been ill, he'd asked Nigel what he was to do, and Nigel had said that if he had to have money he had no ethical right to, he should accept it and find a good use for it. If only he could!

The shock was slowly wearing off, and his thoughts were becoming ordered. Into the silence, broken only by the gusts of wind on the still-dark window-pane, he heard Eric's voice speaking as if into his ear. '*It might possibly convert into four flats.*' He reached for the telephone.

'Eric, I must see you – soon as possible. And Nigel. You want to see me? God – what a blessing. No need for me to lie to Fran. Eleven o'clock? Right, I'll be there.'

The relief restored a bit of the courage he needed to be able to act normally to Fran and Sophie. He announced that at Eric's request he was going to the hotel to have a mid-morning drink with him and Nigel. Fran, noticing how pale he was, put it down to a restless night, and gave the jaunt her blessing.

Two hours later, at the hotel, the three friends sat in Eric's private room.

'Well,' said Eric, 'who's going first?'

'Me, I think,' said William. 'It concerns both of you. How far would £100,000 go towards buying the old school and converting it into four furnished flats for elderly or disabled people?'

'Why do you want to know?' asked Eric bluntly. William told them.

They sat silent, too stunned to take it in.

'Look,' said William rather sharply, 'you both knew there was a possibility I should get the bloody money.'

Eric could see that he was in a very wrought-up state. So, he thought, would most people have been, though for a very different reason. 'It's a bit difficult to give you anything but an informed guess,' he said. 'I would say not quite as much as would be enough to do the job really well, but it would be the bulk of what would be needed.'

'It's beyond my belief,' said Nigel. 'And you're forgetting something, Eric. My immediate object is to get the church restoration fund off the ground. To raise the lump sum we need to get help from elsewhere. Calculate the cost of the restoration, Eric, as near as you can, and subtract that figure from £100,000. The remainder is the price of the old building as it stands to William. It will provide me with what I need to push the restoration fund off the mark. And a good investment it will prove to be for William in the long run, I don't doubt.'

'Investment?' William's voice rose almost to a squeak. 'I don't want you to sell the bloody place to me! I want to *give* you the whole damned lot – on a few easy conditions. That the flats shall be what almshouses used to be, for the elderly or the disabled, at subsidized rents, and that I have the choice of tenant for one ground-floor flat while I, or Fran, shall live. Say fifty years. It's what you advised, Nigel! You said if I got the verdict and had to have the money I had no right to, I should take it and give it to somebody who needed it. That's what I want to do. Keep my name out of it. Let me be an "anonymous donor". But I want one flat at my disposal – for Aunt Sar'anne now and possibly for Sophie in the future if at any time she should need it. Will you accept it?'

'Gift horses should never be looked in the mouth,' Nigel said, serenely. 'My dear fellow, it is the answer to many prayers.'

'Will you do the restoration, Eric?'

'If you are really mad enough to mean it, yes. I should need a good architect in the first place. I could use Roland – your stepson and my son-in-law. Keep it in the family.'

'Then let me ring Fran, who knows nothing about it yet, and say that you need me this afternoon as a witness for something or other. I want you both to go with me, here and now, to see my solicitor and set it all in motion. Can you? Will you? I think there'll be no difficulty in him finding time to see us. He won't know till we get there what it is I want with him – and that sort of money talks. You will? That's settled, then. I'll go and ring Fran and Drake.'

'He's obviously mad,' Eric remarked to Nigel after his retreating back. 'We'd better go along with him, I suppose.' Nigel didn't bother to reply. Instead, he began to ask Eric what to do about planning permission.

'And now,' said William, when he came back from the phone, 'what was it you wanted so conveniently with me today?'

'Advice – though we can talk about it on the way. There's no better place for secrecy than a closed car on the move. It may be Fran we really need, especially as at this precise moment you may not be quite your clear-headed self. Nigel suggested you as more likely not to be swayed so much by sentiment. He says he's no judge because he hasn't been here long enough, and I'm involved personally – with the Bridgefoots in general, and Marjorie in particular.'

William looked from one to the other. 'You know I'm not mad,' he said. 'I don't need this money or want it. It isn't mine, except in legal terms, to give away. Just thank your lucky stars it may do some good here. So forget it, and tell me what's wrong with the Bridgefoots. They're my friends and this money business won't cloud my judgements where my friends are concerned.' They argued no longer, and Eric explained.

One evening recently George had visited Marjorie, which Eric had feared might bode trouble, so as soon as George had left, he'd made an excuse to go to see Marjorie, and found her in utter despair. She had refused to give up hope that as soon as her baby arrived, they would hear from Pansy, and all would be well. Now, it seemed, George was forcing the issue.

The twins would be twenty-one on Easter Monday, and he and Mother had been hoping for the great family party they had been done out of at Charles's twenty-first. Besides, he wanted to give them cheques for what he had settled on them. It would be his and Mother's last chance to share a grandchild's coming-of-age. They couldn't hope to last to see Georgina's.

Marjorie confessed to Eric that she'd never told her parents how complete her ignorance about Pansy was. She'd kept hope alive by being circumspect in what she'd said about it, which, as Eric himself confessed, is exactly what line he'd taken with her. But Beryl Bean, despite her husband's specific embargo on her tongue, had not been able to resist throwing out hints that had reached Marjorie's ears, and she was too intelligent not to be able to put two and two together to make four. She had asked Eric outright if it meant that the Baileys were in any way mixed up in the government supplies fraud.

'I told her that, never having had any direct dealings with the Baileys, I knew no more than she did, which was only as much as the media revealed. A lie, of course – but what was I to do? Break all their hearts by telling them what I do know? Let George part with ten grand to Pansy to put in Bailey's pocket? Tell them of my suspicion that all the Baileys may have skipped overseas, and it may be that they will hear nothing more from Pansy till the case is all over, maybe years? What would Fran say I ought to do, William?'

'She loves George,' William answered. 'She'd want to shield him, but I don't see how she could. To her, he's at the very heart of Old Swithinford, and she'd say that for any of his family to be involved in such a scandal would hit him very hard. But how sure about Bailey's involvement are you? His business round here is still afloat, isn't it?'

'Nothing out of the way about that. It's good cover. He's got a very competent manager, and is perhaps still hoping to get away with it if he keeps his head down. Do we let him? And should I risk my own reputation if it ever comes to light that I knew things I didn't tell the police because they never asked me? Or do I harm George and sink the Bridgefoot name – and by association the Bellamys' – in Beryl Bean's sort of mud? I never thought that such a decision could hang on a birthday! Or that I'd be personally involved – because it's absolutely nothing to do with me, except that I'm fond of Marjorie and would like to help her if I could. Nigel says honesty with discretion is the best policy. I want to let sleeping dogs lie. We need an arbitrator, William. What do you say?'

William got up and looked out of the window. From the hotel, the village was visible, a bit of old England clustered round its church as it had been for seven hundred years. Was it really possible that a man like Bailey could bring it crashing down into the worst aspect of the present century? All because of a silly girl?

Without turning, he said, 'If we were all sure, it would be much easier to make judgements. Till we do, I'd say keep quiet and play for time. Take care not to make things worse by telling any fairy tales to Marjorie. She'll know sooner or later. Take her wholly into your confidence, Eric – tell her the worst, and say that for all her family's sake, it's up to her to keep up her act. She's had to keep plenty from her parents in years gone by, and still kept her own head up. I think it's more than likely that Poppy would refuse to have anything to do with a party just now, in any case. Persuade Marjorie to get in first, and announce that until Pansy's baby is born, the party will have to be postponed. Marjorie's a strong enough character to be a good conspirator, especially where her young are concerned.

'That's my advice. You asked for it – as I asked for yours. I'm taking yours, Nigel. I suggest, for everybody's sake, you take mine. We're now conspirators in both issues. I think that's just what Fran would have advised, that we share the load. So not a word to anybody but Marjorie – not even to Fran. Pansy's baby's a wonderful excuse for not celebrating the birthday on the actual day. Give the gossips the sale of the old school to talk about, instead of a missed Bridgefoot birthday. I'm sure that will be enough to mollify George for the time being, when he hears about it. So now let's go now, this afternoon, to see Drake and put that penny in the slot. Who can tell what may happen before the summer's out?'

'We ought perhaps to go on to see about the planning while we're about it – find out when the next meeting is, and so on. That's where I may have a little bit of clout,' said Eric. 'I've never had much trouble with them yet.'

'It's just possible that we can get some sort of charity status,' added Nigel. 'Even clergymen occasionally have a bit of clout, too.'

Eric and William, looking suitably admonished, led the way to the car.

For the next ten days or so, nothing much happened, except that Fran told Sophie she intended a small dinner-party as soon as Greg heard about his pictures. Time seemed long to William, who was keeping his secret, and he spent a good deal of it in his study, partly because his telephone was there, but mainly because of the temptation to tell Fran everything when they were together. So he pretended to be still struggling with the code, though in truth he had very little interest in it till he should hear from Drake, Eric and Nigel that all was going well with their project for the old school. Sophie was in better spirits because Thirzah had been less aggressive of late, and Ned was back at work. Aunt Sar'anne began to appear in the kitchen again, where even Sophie welcomed her. Fran felt that order was returning to what had threatened to be lasting chaos, and soothed herself by going to work at her type-writer again.

It was into this peaceful routine they were beginning to re-establish that the whole Taliaferro family erupted one morning. Greg was lugging a huge framed picture wrapped in a sheet, and yelling for Fran and William at the top of his voice. Everybody within hearing, even Aunt Sar'anne, flocked into the hall to see what the fuss was about, but neither Fran nor William needed any telling.

William went to help with the picture, saying, 'Greg, my dear chap!' and holding out his hand in congratulations. Fran hugged Jess, and bent to kiss little Jonce. Then she turned to Greg, who had set down his burden. 'They're going to hang it!' she cried, flinging her arms round him, almost in tears.

He could only hug her in return, and shake his head. 'No,' he said. 'Not it. Them. *All three.*'

Everything else was forgotten, even the new picture, till Ned broke in to ask if he hadn't better go and fetch a pair of steps so as to hang the new picture up.

'No,' Fran said. It should be properly hung with ceremony on

Saturday evening, at a hastily arranged little dinner-party 'specially for Greg. Only two days ahead, but that was enough notice, wasn't it, Sophie? Fran had the feeling that the grey veil with which Sophie's face had been covered of late was suddenly discarded. Her depression was not proof against the prevailing excitement.

'That'll be all right with me,' she said, 'do that be over by midnight.'

'Lovely,' said a delighted Greg. 'But oughtn't you just to take a look at this first, to make sure you want it up from now till the end of August?'

'What do you take us for?' William said. 'The only difficulty is where we're going to put it till Saturday.'

'In the cupboard under the stairs?' said Jess, and then sat down, a bit overcome with happiness and pride. They had once hidden one of Greg's pictures from her there, and her deliberate reminder of that unhappy time was the signal for another round of congratulations, embraces, and general delight. Then, with the whole gathering watching, William and Greg made room for the picture in the coat-cupboard, and the women began to plan Saturday's party.

'Who's coming, besides us?' Jess asked.

'I want to talk to you about that,' Fran answered.

'Drinks all round first,' said William, backing out of the cupboard. 'Come into the sitting-room.' Fran obeyed, calling over her shoulder to Sophie to find Jonce and the others some cake to go with their coffee in the kitchen.

While William and Greg went in search of 'something suitable for such an occasion', Fran told Jess what she had been planning with regard to Terry and Anthea. 'It's short notice,' she said, 'but we have a perfectly valid reason, now. Have you any idea how things stand between the two of them since our pancake party? Will they both accept, do you think, if each knows the other has been invited? I think I'd rather not risk it. Look, as far as we're concerned, it's a family occasion, a get-together to celebrate Greg's tremendous success, being held here because of hanging the picture. I'll ask Terry to be our guest, and you ask Anthea to be yours. You're not to know who we're inviting, or the other way round.'

'OK – I'll let Anthea think your choice is Effendi, because when you get your own picture back, he's going to buy this one. I agree it's wiser not to ask for trouble,' Jess said. Satisfactory all round, Fran thought.

As far as William knew, matters with regard to the school were proceeding reasonably well. With one party so anxious to sell, and the other so willing to buy, any delay would be for Roland as their architect to prepare and submit plans, and the usual delays attendant upon solicitors for legal conveyancing, and by local planning committees. William's unalterable decision to remain anonymous would also perhaps be a bit difficult, but Drake proposed that William should appoint a board of trustees to whom he could make a deed of gift of the property.

William hit on 'Mary Budd Close' for the address of the flats, and named as trustees the rector, the rector's warden, and one other resident, to be co-opted by the two ex-officio members – which, for the present, meant Nigel, George Bridgefoot, and Dr Hardy, if he agreed. Now all William could do was to wait.

He applied himself with some determination to breaking the code. All would be well again, code or no code, once he could come clean with Fran. He decided, if Fran's party went off well, that he would risk telling her all about it afterwards.

Saturday came, and so did the guests. Jess and Greg had insisted on fetching Anthea, as she was their guest. Fran had asked Sophie to prepare enough food for herself, Ned and Aunt Sar'anne to have their meal together in the kitchen, and invited all of them to come in to watch the new picture being hung – with Ned's help. Terry Hardy had accepted his invitation with the proviso that at such short notice he might not be able to get there in time for pre-dinner drinks, because till then no other doctor was free to cover for him. Fran began to think the gods were on her side. The pre-meal drink was the time most likely to be difficult.

They were actually in the dining-room by the time Terry arrived and was shown in by Sophie. He had taken a lot of trouble with his appearance, being smartly dressed and groomed, every inch the perfect professional gentleman. Fran wasn't at all sure she was pleased. Formality was the last thing that would help her cause tonight. But it took only his pleasant greeting all round, including Anthea, to show Fran that he had put on his social charm with his best attire. How different those three men were, she reflected: William, the perfect host; Terry, the perfect guest; and Greg – well, he was always Greg, but tonight he simply sparkled as the perfect artist. Jess was at her scintillating best. Anthea, Fran thought, looked more at ease than she had ever seen her before. Her 'uniform' was much as usual, but more than usually feminine, the high-necked blouse tonight being a froth of frills right up to her chin, and the skirt and jacket made of heavy, dark-green silk. It suited her to perfection, and even Jess was outshone. Well, that wasn't much to be surprised at – Anthea had the better part of two decades' advantage over herself and Jess in the matter of age. A few years younger than Beth, Fran judged, though much more classically beautiful than Beth had been till happiness had put such an extra gloss on her. Fran saw, in a moment of sudden revelation, that that was what was the matter with Anthea. Sad and oppressed as poor Beth had been when they had first known her, she had never worn such an air of determination never to be made happy again as lay beneath Anthea's fixed smile. She could, and would, enjoy the present as it passed – but no more; her set mien, though pleasant enough, was that of someone with a terminal illness, aware that for her there was only the present. Fran conjectured that the most likely reason was a broken relationship, a true love-affair ended by some awful tragedy. In which case, William had been quite right. She had no right to be playing at matchmaking with anyone whose past she did not know. She could only hope that what she had intended tonight to have a happy outcome would not end by pushing Terry deeper into a hopeless love for a woman who could give him nothing but a deeper wound than he had ever known before.

She felt William's eyes on her and knew that he had noticed her momentary abstraction; so she pulled her thoughts back to the present. There was no doubt about it, tonight's event was already going with a swing, and everybody, including Anthea, was enjoying it. So be it. 'Sufficient unto the day'; let the future look after itself.

The meal finished, they were asked to remain where they were for coffee and liqueurs till summoned to the sitting-room by Greg, who had disappeared with Ned. When in due course the summons came, they were handed glasses of champagne at the sitting-room door by Sophie and Aunt Sar'anne, went in – and there it was. Very different, but just as beautifully satisfying in that room as the picture it replaced. William called for silence and asked them all to raise their glasses to Greg, and his future as an artist, which from now on nobody could possibly doubt.

In the minutes of euphoria that followed, Fran found herself observing William. He could hardly take his eyes from the picture, and she saw how his head came up, his back straightened, and his face lost the intense, drawn look it had worn for the last few weeks.

Whatever it meant to the others, to him the picture had special significance. At Fran's suggestion, Greg went to the piano, and played for them. If any unhappiness was lurking, it lay outside the windows, while they sat inside a capsule of beauty, peace, content, and love. Fran, ever the practical philosopher, spared a moment to give thanks to she knew not what or whom, for the gathering together of friends who all had the sense to make the most of such times as this when they knew they were happy. It was an insight not given to everybody. It was a few minutes to midnight when Sophie came to say goodnight, and they all, regretfully, rose to go. At the door, William and Fran stood to watch them depart, and heard Terry offer to see Anthea home. William came to a swift decision that good news would be all the better for keeping. Fran was already overflowing with content.

Hardy drove in bemused silence, which his passenger did not attempt to break. They were still caught in the enchantment of the evening, unable to return to the ordinary world outside, like children stumbling out of the theatre when the curtain has come down but the magic still remains.

It was all too short a journey for Terry, who was trying to bring his thoughts to bear on what it was that he had been given a glimpse of tonight, but thought kept retreating behind feeling. He, an outsider, had been gathered into an atmosphere that he

320

had never experienced before, or if he had, had never properly appreciated.

The setting and the appointments of that lovely house were no better in any way than those he had shared with Marcia – yet how different. They were as different from each other as an Eskimo's igloo from a Tuareg's tent. So warm and homely. So unpretentious. So comfortable. It had been the people who mattered, and the friendship. There had been a sensitivity to beauty, to which he had reacted in a way that had surprised him. It had been there in everything within sight – in every sound, every scent, every taste, every touch. Greg's fingers on the piano shared his euphoria with them, making each one of them part of his success; Jess's vitality as she had watched him, her glance a shining thread of love that was almost visible across the room. William, apparently giving all his attention to his guests, yet managing to communicate with Fran by a look, a lift of the eyebrows, a smile – and getting an answer by return, as in that moment at dinner when, with a spoon to her mouth, she had inquired of him whether the soup was all it should be, and without pausing in his easy conversation with Anthea he had assured her that it was perfect. How did they do it?

They had reached Anthea's cottage, on the lane that led up to Castle Hill. He drew the car up, and turned towards her. He knew that above everything else tonight, he had been conscious of her presence there, of her beauty that drew his eyes towards her too often, of the scent of her as she had sat beside him at dinner, and the breaking down of her reserve as the warmth of the conversation had softened her eyes; he recalled, too, the sadness he'd surprised in them when Greg had turned from a crisp, brilliant rendering of a Chopin *Polonaise* to stroke from the keys the gentle, soothing Brahms *Lullaby*.

He was about to get out of the car to go round to open the door for her when he noticed that she was attempting to turn up her coat collar, and finding it difficult. He put his left arm round her shoulders to help – and kept it there. She didn't move, or pull away as he had expected, and the next moment his other arm was round her, too, and he was seeking her mouth with his own. He simply could not believe it when she responded. It was what he

321

had been dreaming of – just to hold her for a moment in his arms. Then she spoke – and the bitter tears in her voice showered like ice crystals on the fire inside him.

'No, Terry – no, *please*. Never again. I don't know what happened, but it can't and it mustn't. *No*, Terry! *Never again*.'

She pulled away from him, and sat back in her seat. He could do no other than restrain himself, and do likewise, though he felt crushed, ashamed, debased. He hadn't intended to seduce her there and then, God knew. She was speaking as if he had, and he had to listen, even though his heart was still choking him.

'If we both go on living here, this is bound to happen again, since you have so far refused to take all the hints I've tried to give you. Fran and Beth and Jess have all been trying to engineer what has just happened between us, and will keep on doing so, under the impression that they are being either romantic or kind, or both. They're not – they're being cruel to us both. You must understand that nothing more than a very casual friendship between us is or will ever be possible. I'm sorry, but you may as well know first as last. I don't want to hurt you, but that is the truth.'

In spite of the rage made of all sorts of emotion that was sweeping through him, he didn't believe her. It sounded too much like a speech many times rehearsed, so as to be ready if and when needed. Well, that was hardly surprising. Any man might be tempted to try his luck. He clenched his fists in the dark, and made an icy apology.

'I presume my much-married reputation has gone before me,' he said stiffly. 'I can only assure you that I had no wish to offend you. I never expected you to return the sort of feeling I've had for you since the first time we met, and had no thought of taking any advantage of you. It just happened, and I'm sorry. A doctor has to be extra careful in such matters, but I happen to be a man as well as a doctor. And you did kiss me of your own accord at Beth's so-called "love feast". May I see you safely to your door?'

He got out and went round the car, opening her door as a chauffeur might have done. She made no move to get out, and he was startled to hear what sounded like a muffled sob. 'Terence,' she said, in a much softer voice. 'Please get in again, so that I can say what I must to you. Please.'

He didn't think it wise or dignified, but without being very discourteous, he saw no other way out. He sat in the driver's seat like a ram-rod, as far away from her as he could.

'I'm sorry, too,' she said, 'and I'm not offended, honestly. I was afraid, because no woman is ever blind to such things, or completely indifferent when the man is – what you are. I didn't want to hurt you, or your pride. I like you far too much for that. I just hoped I could trust myself to keep you at a sufficient distance to prevent you from ever getting nearer. You caught me out. If you're a man as well as a doctor, I'm also a woman as well as . . . what I am. I kissed you at the love feast because I wanted to. Forgive me. It's being here among all these others so redolent of love, I think.'

He was more than puzzled. 'I don't want to prolong this,' he said, 'or to offend you again. But when I kissed you just now, you seemed to respond. If everything is so impossible, why did you do that? And why is it so impossible, anyway?'

'I can't tell you. You'll just have to believe me – and you can answer your own other question as well as I could tell you.'

'I suppose what it means is that you're already married?' She shook her head.

'Then is it because I have been married three times, and am obviously no good bet as a husband?'

'I didn't know that,' she said simply. 'I'm sure there must have been good reasons. And you were hurt badly – you're showing it now because I've hurt you again. I didn't mean to.'

'Then if you aren't married now, you must have been hurt too, by some other man. Is that it?'

'Yes. And I have no intention of getting myself hurt in that way again.'

'I swore just the same thing – till I met you,' he said.

She opened the door of the car, and he got out to help her. She stopped him. 'Don't have any hopes, Terry. It is absolutely impossible, quite hopeless. And that's final. Goodnight.'

He stood silent as she passed by him on her way to the cottage door without looking back. Then he turned the car and drove till he came to a spot where he could park, switch off his lights and give way to despair.

He was a different man from what he had been. Women of the Dagmar type would never satisfy him again. He had found out what love was, only to lose the chance of it for ever. He couldn't stay where she was and not be driven crazy by his desire for her. How disappointed Beth and Fran would be – they'd meant so well, and he'd begun to love the place so much. But he would have to pull out and begin all over again. He would be no good to anybody, professionally or otherwise, if he had to endure hurt like this every time they met. Nothing before had hurt half so much as this loss of real love.

It had so nearly been his. And hers? Yes, and hers. He knew it. The memory of that one kiss ran like a flame of pain through him. So she was suffering, too, though that was her own doing. His despair changed to murderous anger. He wanted nothing better than to get his hands on whatever cad had hurt her to the extent that she would never give another man a chance. He knew she meant it. There was no hope.

Fran having declared roundly that she could not and would not tolerate the cold bare church in Lent, their Sunday was their own from every point of view except for Aunt Sar'anne's presence. But she didn't seem half so irritating this morning. William was hugging to himself his secret that he had actually been given the chance to cure the situation and had done it – almost. Perhaps he wouldn't tell Fran after all, till he was quite sure.

Fran felt better, both because of the change in him and because of the warm glow that still lingered from last night. She kept going back to it, wanting to relive it. Then there was the new picture. Not quite like their own, she said, but then what could be?

William admitted to being amazed at the coincidence of Greg's choice of subject at such an appropriate moment, considering he knew nothing whatsoever either of Bob's book or of what William was proposing to do with it. 'And it's a marvellous record for posterity,' he said, 'when the church is no longer there. I'm afraid that may not be long.'

'William, why ever not? What do you mean?'

'Nigel was speaking of it the other day. There's no money about to save churches that are both ruinous and abandoned, and though he still reads the office there once a month, there isn't even a stray cat there now to hear it. Bob's Winnie's become tame, and lives at the farm. It's only a matter of time before it's sold or bulldozed down.'

'But that's unthinkable, especially for Bob. What about his ghosts? And Beth and Elyot's memories of being married there – and all it means to us.'

'It hasn't happened yet, darling. You're doing it again. Running to meet trouble.'

'Well, I like that!' she replied indignantly. 'Who was it that brought the subject up?'

The telephone shrilled, and he picked it up. 'Hello, Beth. I suppose it's Fran you want? Sunday or no Sunday, my study calls. I have work to do. Here she is.'

Beth had heard of Greg's triumph, and was asking for details to make sure she'd got them right before ringing Southside House to congratulate him. 'Did your party last night go well?' she asked.

'Splendidly,' Fran answered. 'We missed you, though. Why do you ask?'

'Terry called in while I was at church this morning. Elyot thinks something's gone wrong for him – that he's had bad news, or something. For one thing, he went to look at their ship model, and warned Elyot he might not be able to go on helping with it.'

'He was as lively as a cricket last night,' Fran said. 'At his very best. He probably had too much champagne.'

'Well, could be, I suppose. I couldn't help wondering if our plan had worked too well, and he's enduring a bout of lovesickness, especially as I'd heard at church that Anthea's had to leave this morning at short notice to go to her sick mother.'

'Drat!' said Fran. 'Fancy fate interfering like that. I was quite encouraged last night. Well, *nil desperandum*. You know the old

325

saying about absence making the heart grow fonder? Fate may be on our side. Keep your fingers crossed, and if you find out anything more, keep me posted.'

Next morning, Sophie was full of the same story. 'It was nice to be having a do 'ere like we used to,' she said. 'Like old times, afore Thirz' was took so bad. But that new doctor seems to hunderstand 'er. 'E's doin' 'er a world of good. We are lucky to ha' got a man like 'im. 'As 'e gone to work?'

'Oh, you mean William. Yes, he's very busy with a bit of special writing.'

'As long as it ain't Aunt driving 'im out of 'is own kitchen,' Sophie said. 'But I didn't think it was. Things 'as been a lot better this last week.'

William was busy. He rang to see if there was any news from Robin Drake. It was only a matter of days now before Roland could submit his plans. The die was cast.

William's spirits rose yet higher. Everything was 'rising' – the word kept cropping up at every verse's end because it was on his mind, pointing to 'Resurgam' being the key to his code. But it didn't work. He sat down patiently to think and try again.

March was living up to its name. Yesterday had been a really springlike day; he had had to take his pullover off while working in his study yesterday morning. Now he was cold without it, but it still hung on the back of his chair where he had thrown it. He reached for it, and pulled it over his head.

'Damnation and the pit!' he said, discovering that he had got it on back to front. He pulled it off again, dazzled in a blaze of possibility. *Back to front?* Why not? Without bothering to change the pullover or put his jacket on again over it, he sat down and began to scribble. MAGRUSERbcdf – to the end of the alphabet.

He barely heard Sophie tell him that his lunch was ready, and that she was going to see how Thirz' was but would be back. He listened though, for the door closing behind her, before leaping to his feet and rushing kitchenwards, yelling at the top of his voice '*Eureka!*'

Fran ran to meet him. 'The code?' she asked, as he swung her off her feet and round and round, as children twizzle each other in the playground.

'Not only the code, my darling. The answer to our other problem, as well!'

Then he sat down, and soberly told her all.

They were looking towards spring and Easter now, with mixed feelings. Pale primroses nestled under seemingly dead hedges against skies of delicately washed cerulean blue, blackening ash-buds and willows reddening against piles of low grey cumulus. Morale was in mid-season, too. There were low days and better days, some bright and cheerful, glad and lit with hope; some dark and long, shadowed by apprehension for which nobody could supply a reason. The strange malady of gay melancholy or melancholy gaiety sometimes alluded to as 'spring fever' was apparently as infectious as the real epidemic of mild influenza that was keeping Terence Hardy busy – so busy that he had time for nobody but his patients, which under the circumstances was a good thing. He needed time to recover before he could face people such as Beth and Elyot or Fran and William again with any kind of equanimity.

Privately, they put his lack of any social lustre down to a mixture of tiredness and lovesickness, believing that it was a mistimed bit of bad luck that Anthea had to be away just then. No one had heard from her, and there seemed little prospect of her return yet.

She was missed at the hotel, and Eric teased William that he was relying on his promise to act as interpreter in an emergency. William sincerely hoped he didn't mean it. He had plenty to do without that, and more once the Easter holiday was over.

Work could begin on the conversion of the old school. The whole village was now agog with the news of what was to happen to it, though few details had been allowed to leak out. William was keeping as low a profile as he could, using 'work' as his excuse for not being around to be trapped into any discussion, argument, conjecture, or speculation with regard to it, when in fact he was in possession of all the facts. He hated having to dissemble, and as usual, wild surmises and exaggerations were afloat on the March breeze like thistledown, sewing seeds of rumour here, there and everywhere. So he stayed at home in safe silence, and worked. It was not a wholly false excuse. Now that he could read the cypher, he was becoming more and more intrigued by what it revealed, and inclined to resent anything that kept him away from it even for an hour.

Fran was trying to knock the many long hours of listening to Aunt Sar'anne's reminiscences into a series good enough to send to her agent under the title of *Call Back Yesterday*. There were times when she could hardly believe her tape-recorder, and had to seek the old lady out and persuade her to tell the tale again, afraid that she must have misinterpreted what she heard. Could conditions have been as Aunt Sar'anne described them so short a time ago? Could anybody have come through them to such a ripe old age so unembittered as Sar'anne was? Fran suspected that some recollections must either have been coloured by exaggeration, or given a patina of nostalgic gloss by the passing of time. She was so sceptical that one lunchtime she confessed to William that she was afraid she would have to tone down the truth or be accused of going over the top into melodrama. He raised his eyebrows at her, and chuckled.

'I was wondering when I was going to have to admit to having the same doubts about the veracity of my seventeenth-century Wagstaffe,' he said. 'If what he recounts is at all true, it will refute most modern historians. But if it isn't, why on earth did he bother to write it? I would have thought it a bit dangerous to write fiction in such a Puritan atmosphere. It reads more like fiction than fact, and yet it has such a ring of authenticity about it that I can't help believing he's recounting fact. Anyway, it doesn't really matter, because I'm proposing to call it fiction, not history. And whatever else I may doubt, his story here and there does coincide with facts which are historically indisputable.

'But that's where we differ from each other. I can't ask my informant how much of it he made up. You've got your information straight from the horse's mouth, and can go back and check. We appear to have exchanged roles. You've become the factual historian, and I the teller of unlikely tales. That's a nice thought.'

However they viewed what they were doing, it kept them busy and, for most of the time, cheerful. Sophie's spirits, by contrast, were sliding downhill again. She grew more morose and gloomy as the days passed, until Fran could bear it no longer, and inveigled her into sitting down for a chat in her study, away from Sar'anne's sharp ears.

'Now, Sophie,' she said. 'Tell me what's the matter. I know a lot of it's to do with Thirzah, but I thought she'd been better lately.'

'So she 'as,' Sophie agreed. 'Only every day as comes is a day nearer to Easter Day and them bells as they mean to ring, do what me and Dan may to persuade 'em not to. We are been taking turn and turn about, like, to stop with 'er while the other goos to church, and there ain't been no bells in Lent. Easter's diff'rent. There ain't never been no Easter Day yet when I ain't been there to sing *Christ the Lord is ris'n today-ay, A-a-a-a-lia-lu-a-yah*' with everybody else. Nor yet Dan'el. And 'e says this year 'e *must* goo – for George's sake. There ain't nothing in the world as 'e wouldn't do for George, do that didn't goo against 'is conscience. And tha's what's worrying 'im this year. 'E don't know wheer 'is duty lays most – with 'Im Above and the church, as well as George as is all'us been 'is friend and so good to 'im – or with Thirz' as is 'is wife.

'I'm told Dan as I'll stop wi' Thurz' do 'e persuade Het to keep me company, but I daresn't be all by myself with 'er when them bells start. Dan mentioned it to the rector, and to George, and asked 'em not to ring 'em this year, just for once, for 'is sake.

'But the rector were real short with 'im, and said if the bells wasn't rung this year come Easter morning, they'd never be rung no more, and there was other folks to be thought about besides us. And George said 'e was surprised at Dan a-asking such a thing 'cos they had plenty to rejoice about as they never expected. Dan reckoned George must ha' meant about the school, 'cos 'e knows very well as George ain't 'isself, and is worrying 'isself to death about something else as 'e ain't even mentioned to Dan.'

'Is he ill?' asked Fran, panicking guiltily at the way she had been neglecting her old friend in the last few weeks.

'We wondered that,' Sophie said. 'But as far as we know 'e ain't 'ad the doctor. Me and Dan thinks as it's something to do with the fam'ly. Y'see, we all'us keep tally o' folks's birthdays and such, and them twins o' Marge's'll be twenty-one come Easter Monday, but not one word hev we 'eard of any do of any sort being made about it.'

'Well, I don't think that's very much to be surprised at,' Fran answered, soothingly. 'Isn't Pansy's baby due just about then? I expect they're going to leave it till the baby's born, and if Pansy can't get home for it, they may have a private family party just for Poppy. George will be disappointed, but won't make himself ill about it.'

'Tha's as maybe,' Sophie replied shortly. 'Us as is knowed the Bridgefoots all our lives can't be expected to know as much about 'em as folks like you. Dan thinks different, and 'e knows more o' George's business than most, only wild 'osses wouldn't drag it out of 'im if 'e'd told Dan to keep it to 'isself. Them as is seen Poppy since she come 'ome say she ain't 'alf the gel she was. Moping and mis'rable, Dan says – but there, we don't know, as I said. Since Marge got so thick with that Choppen, no doubt you know more'n we do.'

Fran was considerably nettled by Sophie's tone. Of course they were in the know about Pansy – or at least about what Eric thought and feared – and certainly Poppy did look wan and listless. But Marjorie had been playing her part, as she had been advised to, like the strong woman she was, and according to Eric had given nothing away. So rumour must be creeping about again, and Fran suspected that this was Sophie's way of probing for the truth. Well, she wasn't going to play. Least said, soonest mended.

'I think it will be easier for George and Molly if none of us ask any questions,' she said, with only the slightest hint of reproof in her voice. 'They'll find their own way of dealing with things. But about Easter Day, and Thirzah – wouldn't Joe come to be with her so that you and Hetty and Dan could all go to church? Joe carries his sort of Christianity about with him, and he'd rather do the rest of you a good turn than make a point of being at church. Thirzah's got nothing against Joe now, has she?'

In spite of herself, Sophie was both relieved and mollified. 'Well!' she exclaimed. 'As I go to school! Fancy us never thinking o' that! No, Joe's the one of us all she ain't got nothing against, which none of us can't understand, considering 'ow she put 'erself out about 'im when 'e took to preaching with that there Welshman as were 'ere. Joe calls to see 'er most days, and she talks to 'im as right as rain, real ordinary, like, as if there ain't nothing wrong with 'er at all. Thenks. I'm sure Dan'll agree with me that that will all be for the best.'

She went off in a much more conciliatory mood, and Fran stopped worrying about the future and went back to Aunt Sar'anne's extraordinary past.


Easter Sunday. Time being as inexorable as always, Easter Day eventually came. It was a glorious morning, and though they would not kneel at the altar rails, Fran and William wanted to be in church that morning with their neighbours, to see it decorated again for the festival, to hear the music, and to listen to the words they knew so well spoken by Nigel's beautiful cultured voice. To both of them, such things approached the spirit of 'and worshipped Him in spirit and in truth' far more effectively than did partaking of the wafer and the wine of communion. Nigel understood, and was glad to see them there at all. They were glad to be there – and to them, that was what mattered.

Sophie's voice, raised in the traditional Easter hymn, drew Fran's attention to the Wainwright pew, and she saw with relief that Daniel was in his accustomed place at her side. That must mean that Joe was keeping watch with Thirzah. It had been a good idea.

Sitting close to the door, they could see out when it was opened to the profusion of daffodils gracing the nearest graves, especially Mary Budd's; and when Nigel came to stand there to greet his congregation as they left, they were among the first to leave, just as the paean of bells began to lace the April sky over their heads with their musical patterns of sound. From the gate they looked back at the church porch, wondering whether or not to wait to speak to George and Molly Bridgefoot, but decided against intruding into what seemed to be a whole family gathering.

'Marjorie's there, and Poppy,' Fran said. 'I expect I was right in supposing that they would celebrate Poppy's birthday tomorrow privately, though perhaps "celebrate" is not quite the right word. We shall hear in the course of time from Eric, and we mustn't congratulate Poppy too soon. It's unlucky. If we find out that all's well during the day tomorrow, we'll walk up to the Old Glebe and leave our present for her on the doorstep.'

They were in consequence the first pedestrians to reach the spot at which a narrow little pathway called Glebe Lane joined Church Road, and down which Daniel and Thirzah had lived in one of the Old Glebe's tied cottages since their wedding day. As they approached the end of Glebe Lane, William broke off in mid sentence, looked around him, and left Fran's side in long loping strides to catch and hold the shorter figure stumbling up the lane with hands clasped to his face. Fran, unable to hear anything because of the noise of the bells, recognized the man as Joe Noble, Sophie's brother-in-law. That he was in pain was evident, and he was stumbling because he was holding across his eyes a large, white handkerchief covered with dark brown stains.

'Thirz',' Joe said in a gasping, choked voice, recognizing William with relief. 'Send Dan'el home quick as you can to her, but keep Soph' and Het out o' the way. It were them bells. She's been took again, and I wasn't ready for 'er, though I'd been listening for 'em as the time come. Quick as lightning, she was.'

'Is she all right?' asked William, in his anxiety almost shaking Joe.

Joe nodded. 'I'm locked 'er in – here's the key.' He took his hands from his face at last, revealing what Fran took to be a severe scald.

'Get home as fast as you can,' William commanded Fran, 'and ring for the doctor to go straight to Thirzah's. Don't worry – I'll see to Joe. Keep the women out of the way.'

332

Fran sped towards home without looking back, and was lucky enough to catch Terry. 'I'm on my way,' he said. 'I've been half-prepared for something of the kind.'

Fran sat down for a moment to get her breath back and think. She'd better take the car back, in case it was needed. Terence would probably have his hands more than full with Thirzah, and Joe's injuries might require hospital treatment.

She left the car at the top of the lane, and began to run down it towards Hiptoft, the cottage where Daniel and Thirzah lived. In the lane outside the cottage was a scene that only a Victorian illustrator could have done full justice to.

The picture-box cottage with its central front door abutted directly on to the lane, and at the door was Daniel, struggling to open it with a key that refused to turn. In his distress, the usually imperturbable Dan was violently alternately pushing and pulling the door until, losing his patience, he began lunging at it with his shoulder. Hetty, small and fluffily helpless in comparison with her tall and upright sister, was clinging to Sophie and screaming – an overture, Fran guessed, to a full fortissimo bout of 'sterrics, justifiably occasioned by the sight of her husband's damaged visage.

Sophie, still and upright as a marble statue and with a face as white and as shadowed with pale green as graveyard stone often is, was thumping Hetty on the back to the accompaniment of her own voice, imitating Thirzah's, saying, 'Now, Het! Now, Het!' with every thump. William, vainly trying to extricate himself from little Steven's hands clinging to his coat-tails, was doing his best to examine Joe's face.

Running towards them, Fran fished in her pocket for a handkerchief – not quite sure whether she would want it to mop up tears or to stifle her own giggles.

Into this animated cartoon came Terence Hardy. He emerged from his car in one movement and took charge, giving orders in a voice raised to an unnatural pitch by the necessity of contending with Dan's battle with the door, Hetty's screams, Sophie's exhortations, and Steven's whining demands to know what was the matter with Grandad, to say nothing of the still-clamouring bells.

'William, stand aside and let me see. I'll attend to Mr Noble as

333

soon as I can. Take him to sit in my car, and keep the injury covered as much as possible from the air. Stop that noise, Mrs Noble. Take the child and go with Mrs Burbage to sit in her car. Mr Bates, let me try that key. Every minute wasted may be crucial.'

The sudden silence as the bells stopped made them all feel dazed and unreal. Daniel handed the key to the doctor with the air of a small child yielding up a concealed sweet to a stern teacher. Terence pulled the door gently towards himself, and the key turned silently in the lock. Daniel stood back to let the doctor in first. Fran, afraid that Sophie would follow and make things worse, ran to stop her; but Sophie knew the danger, and was already pulling Hetty away towards Fran's car. She was trembling, and Fran took her by the arm and escorted her, murmuring words of comfort. All Sophie could do was to say, over and over again, 'I didn't ought to ha' left 'er. They shouldn't ha' made me. They knowed what might 'appen, did them bells maze 'er again. I didn't ought to ha' left 'er.'

'Now stop being silly,' Fran told her sharply. 'We don't know yet what did happen. You stop there in the car while I go and find out.'

William, who had been watching from his post by Joe's side, answered the unspoken appeal of Daniel's eyes to be first over the threshold. As in so many such little homes, the door opened directly into the living-room.

In her place at the corner of the table sat Thirzah, looking quite normal except that her rather small eyes blazed red with anger and in her hand she clutched a long iron poker. At the other corner of the table Dan's chair had been overturned, and broken china lay everywhere – on the floor, on the top of the grate, and all over the table, among pools of strong cold tea. Thirzah ignored Dr Hardy, who might as well have been a transparent, insubstantial ghost. Her anger flowed over her very solid husband.

'Ah! Long looked for come at last,' she spat at him. 'Ain't George Bridgefoot got nothing else for you to do as well as ringing them bells? Didn't I say they was not to be rung? I told you as you'd come home one o' these days and find me done in by some ruffian while you was a-dancing to Bridgefoot's tune. So I was ready for him as come creeping round this morning, knowing as he did I should be here by myself. When he picked the poker up, I hit him with my best teapot, and there it lays, all in bits. Then he come at me with the poker, and smashed all my best china. But he didn't get his own way 'cos I wasn't letting that shrimp of a man as is my very own sister's husband get the better o' me, no more than he could at praying. I shoved him out and locked the door behind him. And if you ever let him set foot across my doorstep again, Dan'el Bates, I'll kill him, that I will! Ringing them bells as I said shouldn't never be rung no more!'

Terence sat down beside her and gently removed the poker from her grasp. Daniel stood mute and helpless, looking from the doctor to William and back for instructions.

'You've had a nasty shock, Mrs Bates,' Hardy said soothingly. 'Sit quiet for a minute or two, and let me see if you're hurt. Is there any brandy in the house, Mr Bates? Good – no, not for your wife. I know she doesn't drink spirits. What she needs is a cup of hot, sweet tea. Ah, Fran! Could you make Mrs Bates a cup of tea?'

He lowered an eyelid at Fran as she filled the electric kettle which, much against her will, Thirzah had agreed to accept as a Christmas present from them last year. He went on talking till it boiled. Fran, looking as helpless as she felt, signalled to him that there was no teapot to make it in.

The doctor rose to speak to Dan, suggesting that he have a good stiff brandy and take one out to Joe, too. He hissed in Fran's ear as he passed her, 'Put the tea in the kettle, and pour yourself a cup out first. Sit down and drink it with her, and if she says it doesn't taste right, tell her it's because it was made in the kettle. I want to get a knock-out sedative down her. I told you I came prepared.'

There were no whole best cups left, either, but Fran found two thick breakfast cups unwashed in the sink, and hastily rinsed them out. The doctor came courteously to carry Thirzah's tea to her.

'Thenks,' she said, suddenly all smiles, and then just as suddenly began to cry over the ruin of all the china 'as had been my Mam's and her Mam's before her'.

'Drink your tea,' said Terence soothingly, 'and then go and lie down in bed. When you're in bed, I'll come up and examine you properly to make sure you are not hurt. Mrs Burbage will come with me.' Much to Fran's surprise, Thirzah made no objection, and ten minutes later was in a deep sleep.

'Now,' said Terence, taking the lead as soon as Fran came down to report that his sedative had worked. 'Sit down, Mr Bates, while I go to see to Mr Noble. Then, if you don't mind, I'd like Dr and Mrs Burbage to hear what I have to say.'

He made a brief examination of Joe in the car, declaring that he had got off lightly. Then he assured Sophie that Thirzah was asleep, and if she would see Hetty and Steven home to the schoolhouse, he would deliver Joe there when he had dressed his wounds. He took Joe with him back to the cottage.

Joe was very shaken, his face white except where the scalding tea had landed on him. His scalp was showing red through his greying hair, and there were cuts and scratches on his forehead from the broken china; but his face had got the worst of it, and one cheek was beginning to blister, while another blister already as big as a large grape bulged from the tip of his nose.

'You've got off very lightly,' Dr Hardy said, seating him on a chair by the table. 'I was afraid for your eyes, but your forehead and your nose saved them. I'll put some dressings on, and give you some painkillers – but if you don't get them infected they'll soon heal. Keep out of the cold, especially the wind, for a few days.'

Fran watched his deft hands at work till Joe resembled a half-wrapped mummy, including blistered hands that he had put up to ward off the boiling liquid. It was quite obvious that Joe trusted him absolutely. 'I shall be right as rain in a couple o' days, Doctor,' he said. 'My skin never has took no harm, all my life.'

Terence didn't argue. He motioned Dan to sit down in his own chair, invited Fran to take over Thirzah's, and pulled one up to the table for himself.

'Now,' he said, 'we must decide what is to be done. That is, I must decide – but I would rather talk it over with you, first. Mr Noble, it would help me if you could tell me exactly what happened.'

'Well,' said Joe, 'as all of you know, somebody had to stop here with Thirzah, and according to Soph' it were Mrs Burbage as

336

suggested it should be me. I was as willing as willing could be, if it was all right with Thirz', and she didn't make no fuss at all. Ain't that so, Dan?'

Daniel agreed that it had been so. She had seemed glad to see Joe at any time lately, and he'd been very good to her.

'So I come straight here when Het went to church. Dan'el was waiting till I got here before he went, and Thirz' seemed to be quite herself, if you know what I mean. We set down and talked for a little while about what was going on, like young Nick Hadley being home up at Castle Hill, and Poppy Gifford with her mother at Monastery Farm, and suchlike. Ordinary things, like. Thirz' was as right as rain. She was keeping her eye on the clock, though, and I thought it might be 'cos she knowed as they intended to ring the bells, it being Easter Day, and wanted to be ready for 'em, as you might say. But she said as how we ought all to be together when the rest come home from church, and they'd want some breakfast, so would I get out all the best china for her to have it ready for 'em. Now I know as well as Dan here does how choice she is o' that china, as was her grandmother's, and never uses it. So I asked her if she was sure she wanted me to get it. That were when I begun to think something might be wrong with her. "It's mine, ain't it?" she said. "And I shall do as I like with it. I shan't let nobody tell me what I can do with what's mine, though I know as both Soph' and Het have got their eyes on it when I'm gone. I shall show 'em today as I shall use it when and how I like. There ain't nobody left in the fam'ly fit to touch it, only me." Well, I didn't answer her, 'cos I know what she thinks about our Wendy, and she's never forgive Het for leaving this church for the one in Hen Street. And she's been so nasty with Soph' since she stood up for Aunt Sar'anne that she can't say bad enough about her. So I thought as if she wanted to aggravate 'em by showing 'em she had the china as was their grandmother's, it would be best to humour her, and I got it all out o' the cupboard for her, and put it on the table. Then she polished it all up with a clean tea-cloth, chatting away to me while I got things out for breakfast till I begun to think she had made up her mind, like, seeing as it was Easter, to let bygones be bygones, and make it up with us all. She kept poking the fire and told me to fill the kettle and get it boiling ready to make the tea. So I did. And when them bells started, I kept my eye on her, but all she said was, "Hark. That's them bells ringing, so they'll be here in a few minutes now. Make the tea, Joe, and stand it on the top o' the grate to draw well afore they come."

'"What?" I says. "In your best teapot?" But I could see as she meant it, so I put the tea in the pot and mashed it from the boiling kettle. Then I turned to put it on the grate, like she'd told me to, and see her lift the poker up to hit me – and I put my hands up to guard my head without thinking as I'd still got the teapot in one of 'em. She didn't hit me – she hit the teapot, and down come the boiling tea all over my face. But she'd still got the poker and was a-coming for me with it. I thought it was 'cos she blamed me for the pot being broke, but I couldn't see out o' my eyes to stop her, so I done the only thing I could – I rushed outside and slammed the door and locked it, and run to find somebody to help.

'Nothing weren't broke then, only the teapot, as I thought she'd hit by mistake. Seems she smashed all the rest soon as I'd gone out, to show Soph' and Het as they'd never get it. I can't think of no other reason.'

'That figures,' the doctor replied. 'She must have been working herself up for another attack of hysteria – centred round not being able to have her own way about the bells, and mixed with her jealousy about her family and Daniel's devotion to George Bridgefoot – which I think is the core of her obsession with the bells. She associates Mr Bridgefoot with bell-ringing. The last time I was sent for to her in the same sort of state, I thought it was only hysteria caused by her anger about the other old lady being here at nights. The obvious thing to do was to remove the old lady.

'This time, it's more difficult to diagnose the situation sensibly. I must put it to you straight, Mr Bates. She has been violent – and though I still think it a case of hysteria, I'm afraid there may be an element of mental unbalance as well. She was too craftily clever, planning to smash the china, though she might not have intended to hit or scald Mr Noble. That may truly have been an accident. That she blamed him for smashing it, and insinuated that he had intended violence to her, is just the sort of cleverness the insane often show. What she didn't think of was that the door was locked from the outside – otherwise we should only have had her word against Mr Noble's.

'If I diagnose it as only hysteria, how long will it be before it happens again? If I refer her to a psychologist, how much will that precipitate a worsening of her condition? You all tell me that she has been much better in every way of late. Dare we risk giving her just one more chance?'

'I'll do my best for her, and to look after her, Doctor,' said Dan humbly. His eyes, like those of a suffering dog, sought Fran's, pleading for help. Only she had any real idea of what it would mean to the entire family if Thirzah had to be referred to a psychologist. Much worse than if she could be sent straight to an asylum, as Ned's wife in the end had had to be.

She explained to Dr Hardy, who listened – and learned. 'Can't you give her at least one more chance?' Fran asked. 'I can see all the difficulties. She may not believe she smashed the china herself. We shall have to think up some tall tale. Do you think she will remember? How much shall we be allowed to tell her?'

'I'll keep her sedated for a few days, and do my best to make her understand what happened without frightening her. I want time to see more of her before committing myself, in any case. But I must warn you, if ever she uses violence on anybody else again, I shall have no option. I will, of course, prescribe tranquillizers, which may be all she needs. But there remains another danger. Her records show that she has been subject to attacks of pain and breathlessness in the past, which Dr Henderson noted that he suspected could be self-induced if she were thwarted; but he also recorded a very high blood-pressure, and it is obvious that she is overweight and gets very little exercise. In the state she was in this morning, her blood-pressure was bound to rise. I shall treat her for that and keep my eye on it in future. But I must warn you that it is often in just such situations as this that strokes occur, and even deaths from heart attacks. She must be kept under medical care, however much she protests, and induced to watch her diet and to take more exercise. I need hardly add she must be kept as calm as is possible.'

'And to begin that treatment,' Fran interposed, 'we must all keep what has happened here this morning absolutely to ourselves. Not a word to anybody – even George, Dan. Joe knows, and can explain to Hetty; I – and William – will make sure that Sophie understands as well.'

'In which case, I'll go up and see her again. As far as anyone else need know, she has had a rather bad attack of her "pain" as in the past, which caused Joe to have an accident and scald himself. Which is why you sent for me. Agreed?'

He came back downstairs, and reported Thirzah still sleeping. Promising Dan he would look in again before bedtime, he left, taking Joe with him, as he had promised, to deliver him home.

'Don't worry, Dan,' William said. 'I'll ring George and tell him you won't be leaving Thirzah for church again today, or be at work for the next few days.'

'And we,' said Fran, 'had better clear this mess up, and then go home.'

They were not surprised when Sophie visited them on her way home from Evensong the same day. She had still been with Hetty when Joe had got home and given them a blow-by-blow account of everything that had been said and done, especially the doctor's warnings about Thirzah in future, and their unanimous resolve not to let anybody know anything except what could not be hidden – that he had been scalded when a teapot broke while he had been visiting Thirzah, and that the shock had brought on her old pain so bad that he'd had to get the doctor, who was keeping her in bed for a few days.

'None o' that is a lie,' Sophie said, 'else I wouldn't have nothing to do with it, be she never so much my sister. I told Joe so. 'E can't speak well enough of that new man. "Tha's a good doctor if ever there was one", 'e said.'

'I think we all agree with him,' Fran answered. 'A lot of it comes from him being such a good man first.'

'Pity as 'e ain't got a wife to match 'im, then,' Sophie retorted shortly. Till that moment, Fran had forgotten Thirzah's moral objections to Terence. There had been no sign of it today – which surely must mean that Thirzah hadn't known at all what she was

340

doing? Dan would have to be on the lookout for trouble when Terence visited her again. But Fran had had enough of the Wainwright family for one day, and was glad when Sophie went home and left them in peace. She said so to William, who agreed.

'By the way,' he said, 'I forgot to mention it before – but when I went to move our car from where you'd left it on the road, Anthea went by in her car. On her way home, I suppose. She didn't notice me.'

Fran didn't reply, and he asked her why. He had hoped he'd just given her something to be pleased about. She shook her head, doubtfully. 'I wish I could hope, but I can't, after this morning. We are all right again, but as Hamlet said, "The time is out of joint".'

Fran and William, caught up by sheer chance in the incident of Thirzah's attack on Joe on Easter Day, had been disturbed, and as Fran said, 'been left with another damned secret to keep'. It was very rarely that she was given to extraneous or vehement qualifying adjectives, and William looked sympathetically at her. She was always carrying other people's secrets; while he, he ruminated somewhat bitterly, often had more to do to keep his own than he could manage. But next morning, they were greeted by such a panorama of dawn glory that Fran thought even the saddest heart must rejoice. She got out of bed to stand by the window to watch it and called William, who also got out of bed to join her. He put his arm round her and said, 'It's coming from the north, though. You can see it moving this way.'

' "Red sky at morning, shepherds' warning" you mean? I suppose it's bound to be so. Yesterday's little how-do-you-do will have a lot of repercussions. I hope not today, though. It's Easter Monday. A public holiday, meant for people to enjoy themselves.'

'What's enjoyment? Ready-made commercial entertainment? There's too much money about, and too little idea of what to do with it. You can't buy happiness. Look who's talking? Yes, that's what I meant. Church End is getting too plush by half.'

The sky had already paled, and the beauty faded. 'Come back to bed and get warm, you dismal Jeremiad,' Fran said. 'Sophie will soon be here.'

Sophie never claimed bank holidays as no-work days. They sometimes wished she would, but in her estimation the only days in the calendar 'hallowed' like the sabbath were holy days, and only these provided exemption from duty to a job for which there was any reward. Bank holidays had no relevance to her.

'She may be a bit late, but she'll come,' Fran continued. 'For one thing, she won't want to spend today alone, after yesterday, and she'll want to talk about it to the only people she can. Us. We shall be expected to hold a long and detailed post mortem on all that happened. I don't know about you, but I had enough of Kezia's family yesterday to last me a lifetime. How we shall manage to keep it all from Aunt Sar'anne's ears I can't conceive. Like all old people, she seems to know by instinct when there's anything secret in the wind. I'd been setting myself up for a more cheerful phase, once Easter was over. Some hope! Everybody else will be looking forward to spring.'

'I doubt that, actually. You said last night that "the time is out of joint" and I'm afraid you may be right. Besides, my sweetheart, we are not "everybody", though to be truthful, I think we act as if we were. We're not satisfied to deal with our own troubles and leave the rest to do the same. We rush in where angels fear to tread, and load ourselves with other people's anxieties as well as our own.'

'I seem to remember you recently expounding a theory that if we all shared each other's troubles, the load on each of us would be less. Are you going back on that? Because if you are, we must cut ourselves deliberately off from our friends. Which is it you want – always supposing we have any choice?'

'Well, what do you propose we do about it?' he asked.

'Compromise,' she said, promptly. 'We were on the spot yesterday, and hadn't any choice. Besides, we inherited Kezia's family with Benedict's. "Heired them", as Bob would say, with the house.'

'A small price to pay for all the rest, isn't it, my darling? We mustn't grumble. Just because things have come right for us just lately, we can't take it for granted that everybody else is as free from worry as we are. What do you mean by "compromise"?'

'Do as we did yesterday. If we're on the spot, wanted or needed, do our best, but not go looking for things to poke our fingers into.' He regarded her with a quizzical look that said plainly that somehow or other she always was on the spot, both wanted and needed, and that it was in her very nature to run to meet trouble, especially other people's.

'I haven't your capacity to hope in the face of experience,' he said. 'Here comes Sophie, and your first chance to try out your compromise theory. I'd like to bet that when the first bit of new trouble comes in at the door, your compromise will fly out of the window. No – I know nothing more than you do. I'm just being more realistic, and not so sanguine as you are. Hello, Sophie. How's Joe this morning?'

As he guessed, she had been to inquire. Joe's face was very sore and blistered, but he was making light of it. 'We should like to know about Thirz',' Sophie said, 'but we daresn't goo near to ask, and there's nobody else as knows.'

'There's Dr Hardy,' Fran said. 'If we see him today, we'll ask. It's bound to get round that something was wrong because of him being there and Dan not going to work today. But we all agreed to try to keep it dark.'

'It's Dan'el who'll suffer most from that,' Sophie said. ''E's never in all 'is life afore kep' anything from George as I know of. I shall be 'appier in my mind when I know 'ow things goo today up at Old Glebe. George'll want Dan, and Dan'll want George, afore this day's out. You mark my words. What am I got to get for dinner?'

'Nothing,' said William, with a swift warning glance at Fran. 'I'm taking Fran out to lunch. It's a general holiday. We decided to go out when we saw what a lovely morning it was.'

'So don't bother about us,' Fran added. 'See that Aunt Sar'anne's got plenty. We plan to leave Poppy's present on our way. If we see anyone, we'll tell you tomorrow.'

'I shall be glad to know myself anyway,' Fran said as soon as

343

Sophie was out of hearing. 'And what's happening at Castle Hill. Nick's home and his "probation" is up.'

'Watch it!' said William, grinning. 'Compromise is trying his wings and only waiting for a window to open.'

Nobody, however, could possibly have foreseen what the red sky at dawn would herald. As Shakespeare said, '*It is the bright day that brings forth the adder.*'

Nick hadn't been home since Christmas. Effendi had seen more of him than any of the others, making a point of meeting Nick whenever he had need to stay in London. The object was not to interfere, but to keep a loving eye on him and to be able to report back, because Nick rarely made contact with them. Jane rang him at intervals to comfort herself. Bob warned her not to overdo it.

'Let him off your apron-strings,' he said. 'Nobody grows up till they've sowed a few wild oats.' Usually she bowed to his practical common sense, but as Easter drew nearer, she took him up on it.

'It's all very well,' she said, 'but he's being very selfish. He isn't the only pebble on the beach. Have you seen Poppy since she's been home? She's pining and I'm more concerned for her – and Marjorie – than I am about him. He's my son and I brought him up, and I think, as you say, that when he gets through this bout of belated adolescence, which I'm pretty sure is all it is, he'll have more sense. He knows that as long as he toes the line of honesty and social respectability, he can be sure of our support. I owe him that. I know you may be right, that he's sowing his wild oats – but he's still a very mixed-up kid, though through no fault of his own. All the same, that doesn't excuse him from considering other people's feelings.

'We can't and I shan't try to interfere with his choice of girlfriends – but I think he owes it to us and to Poppy to come clean with us about her. I know they had some kind of understanding when they were still only kids at school, and she was forbidden to have anything to do with him. But if life's been cruel to Nick since then, he's had compensations. It's been crueller to Poppy. He's gone up in the social scale, and she's gone down. She's doing her best to face up to what's happened, and from the

344

look of her, not doing too well. And as far as I can judge, nobody's taking any notice of her – not realizing the gaps left in her life. You said she was at the bottom of Nick's awful behaviour. I think he's the cause of Poppy wilting before our eyes now. I do wish we knew. Dare we ask him, Bob?'

'No, my pretty,' said Bob, removing his pipe from his mouth to reach across and hold her hand. 'You've just said we mustn't. It would be easier if she wasn't one of the Bridgefoots. They can look after their own.'

'Can, I'm sure. But will they?'

'Wait and see, my beauty. It depends on Nick. Is he staying here, or with Effendi?'

'I don't know,' she answered. 'He just wouldn't say.'

'Don't get it into your head that if he doesn't come here it's because of Jade and Aggie. If he chooses to come here, it may be because Effendi's new home is too close to Monastery Farm. As good a pointer as any – and I keep telling you that in the end it'll turn out right.'

'Then tell me again, Bob. You know how much I believe in you.'

He couldn't and wouldn't give her hope that might prove false. 'I don't *know*,' he said. 'I can only say what I feel. I can't help thinking it'll come right in the end. But I don't feel comfortable about the next little while. It's like old folks saying they know when it's going to rain. They say they feel it in their old bones, and they get rheumatics worst when the bad weather's only brewing up. As soon as it comes, they feel better.

'I feel in my bones that there's some bad weather ahead. Once it's over, we shall all feel better. There, my pretty, that's the best I can do, and I wouldn't say as much as that for anybody but you. I can't tell fortunes, and wouldn't if I could. Besides, I reckon – there's the telephone.'

Jane sprang up to answer it, and came back beaming. 'It was Nick,' she said. 'He's coming tomorrow, and he is staying here.' Bob looked satisfied.

Effendi met Nick at Cambridge and delivered him to Castle Hill in time for their midday meal. The presence of two toddlers robbed it of any constraint. They all made much of Nick, appraising

345

him as they might have done some long-lost treasure. He'd put on weight, Bob said. Jane was glad. 'As long as you can still get your belt round the top of your trousers. I do object to young men with beer-guts, even my own handsome son,' she said. 'What do you do about meals?'

'Cook for myself in my flat, use take-aways, and occasionally go on the splurge. Like all students do. I take jobs when I can where there are canteens, and sometimes as a waiter in hotels and restaurants where meals are laid on. I've done all sorts of jobs, and met all sorts of folk. And I've enjoyed myself in all the usual ways, as well as soaking myself in things I missed when I was a kid – art galleries and museums and concerts. London's a wonderful place to live. But then, so is Old Swithinford. I want the best of both.'

Satisfied, so far, with the Nick who had come back to them, they were careful not to press him for details. When, in the late afternoon, Effendi invited him to go to inspect his new home, Bob and Jane had a chance to talk. They agreed that their 'experiment' seemed to be working.

'At any rate, he chose to come and stay here with us,' Jane gloated.

'He's growed up,' Bob said. 'That's the big difference. I hope he's worked out now where he stands with us. He hasn't mentioned Poppy. I wish he would. I still reckon there's some bad weather to come from that quarter.'

By Sunday evening, any slight restraint among them had completely vanished. There was no sign in Nick of the truculence that had caused him to have to leave them, and later it was Nick himself who asked if it was a good moment for them to talk. He confessed how lonely he'd been at first, and how he'd longed to turn tail and come home; but he'd been almost overwhelmed by having freedom without restraint for the first time – not even shortage of money, as he understood it.

While living with Effendi before, he'd met people of his own age – mostly those connected with the Civil Service; so he'd sought them out, and as Effendi's grandson, had been accepted by them. He admitted how much he'd enjoyed his taste of being

346

a 'man about town', though he'd felt a fish out of water, especially with girls. They were the Sloane Ranger type, mainly. They'd made a dead set at him, and he'd had no idea how to cope. He made a very wry face, and hesitated before going on.

'That all came to a sudden end,' he said, 'and I wasn't sorry. I'd gone to a very up-market cocktail party, and a girl who'd had a lot to drink before I got there came and wrapped herself round me, and kept calling me Justin. She asked me to get her another drink. I was still a raw recruit and asked her what she wanted. She looked offended, and turned on me, saying if I didn't know by now what she drank, there were plenty of others who did. I'd never seen her before – but I didn't know how to escape. So I went to the bar, and found out what she meant. The millionth chance. Another fellow was just turning away from the bar with two drinks, and took them straight to her. She didn't know the difference – he was so much like me that we might have been twins.'

There was a rather uncomfortable pause. 'I take it that one of my half-brothers is called Justin, Effendi? I thought so. I wasn't going to risk it happening again. I went home to my flat, and stayed there. Nobody missed me – I don't suppose they'd ever really known who I was. One never met the same mixture twice. Not what I would call friends.

'So I tried the other end of the scale – popular pubs and night-clubs. They disgusted me. Besides, I was scared at how much my short fling of high-life had cut into my allowance. I looked for jobs, and took my entertainments free where I could. Then one day I found myself in Charing Cross Road, amongst the second-hand bookshops, and really began to enjoy myself. I wanted to rush home to tell you, but . . .' He stopped suddenly, and said no more.

It was Effendi who asked the question he hadn't answered. 'Have you made up your mind what you want to do?'

'Yes – but I'm afraid it won't please you. I'm sorry to disappoint you, but I can't and won't go to a university. I know it was my one and only aim in life once – but the reason for it then no longer exists. I've missed the ordinary point of entry, and though I may not be all that much older in actual years, I haven't had what you'd call an ordinary sort of life or a standard education. I just shouldn't fit, though the thought of living in Cambridge or Oxford tempts me. That must be about the nearest there is to having the best of both worlds. Cambridge for choice, but that's out. I might try Oxford.'

'Doing what?' Effendi asked.

Nick looked all round before he replied, as if he knew he was taking a great risk. 'Running a second-hand bookshop – high-class and antique books,' he said. 'I've been working in one, and I love it. I could make a success of it. But it would need a lot of outlay, and I still have a lot to learn. Owning one is my pipe-dream.'

'Any business venture requires outlay,' Effendi said. 'Good commercial prospects find backers.' Jane said nothing, knowing that her father was offering help. The youngster was still having it all too easy, and it made her feel uncomfortable. She was afraid of Nemesis. It was left to Bob to put the crucial question.

'Why not Cambridge?' he said, very gently. He already knew the answer.

'Because it's too near home. Everything and everybody I love is here, but I'm the odd one out. Honestly! I'm not being cranky or bitter or anything. Being away has made me realize it. A sort of cuckoo in everybody's nest. Take Mum, for example. If ever anybody deserved to be happy now, it's her. She shouldn't have to be bothered by me any longer. We always knew when I was a kid and we only had each other that as soon as I left school we should have to be parted – though we couldn't have believed how things have turned out. But if I'd gone to a university, I'd have had to leave home. Isn't that how it should be? Then think about Effendi. He's got a new life, and needs to look forward, not back. He couldn't, with me always under his feet, reminding him of what's all past and done with now. Nor do I want to be a parasite – on anybody. This is my home, but I want a chance to forget the past, too. I had real friends here, but that's all changed. Robert's dead, and Charles is married. He'll always be a friend, but it's different now he's got a farm and a wife. I know I'd be welcome about there, but it couldn't be like old times. I was born an outsider, and made one again when I lost my memory. So I'll stay away, though of course I'll come and visit often.'

348

Bob spoke again, gently. 'And where does Poppy fit into the picture?' he asked.

Jane gasped, but Nick appeared not to resent the question.

'Nowhere,' he said. 'She's made that clear. That's the real trouble. I don't want to have to meet her, this time or ever again if I can possibly avoid it.' He stood up suddenly, handsome and mature – yet very young and vulnerable. 'That's why I'm going back to London early on Tuesday morning. I'd love to stay longer, but I know she's home, and I don't want to risk meeting her. So if you agree, I'll go back to work in the Charing Cross Road, where I can have a full-time job, and learn everything I can about the antique book trade while I investigate the possibility of finding something in Oxford. I think I could spend my life there, with my work and books. Other girls don't interest me.'

Jane had begun to cry quietly.

'Don't cry, Mum. I'm sorry I was such a pain in the neck to you last year, but something of the kind had to happen. I've learned a lot about myself, as you said I would. I've got a lot more sense than I had then, and less of the swelled head that finding Effendi was my grandfather had given me. What on earth does it matter who or what my father was? I'm me, as I am. You told me, when I was kicking up such a fuss, that my father was a gentleman. He wasn't – he was a rotten bastard who let Mum down. I don't want to know him, or anything about him. I'd rather he'd had a kind heart than any coronet. I want to forget him, however blue his blood was, and be content with just Mum. I had to be when I was little. I've got Effendi and Bob now. Why should I want him? That's what the oldest Petrie said – but I hadn't enough sense to listen to her then. I'll tell her one of these days how right she was.'

Jane and Effendi were both very moved. Again it was Bob who was left to answer. 'Keep that up, my boy, and you'll do,' he said. Then he got up and went out into the darkness, to leave the other three alone together.

It hadn't been a happy Easter for the Bridgefoots, in spite of Marjorie's stoic resolution not to let her family know how totally she had lost touch with Pansy. Such a close family had difficulty in keeping things from each other. They were all anxious for George's sake. They'd tried to keep his mind centred on the church and the way things there had turned out. Nobody was fooled. Easter Monday was the twins' birthday, and they didn't succeed in making him forget it. To please him and Molly, they were all going to have lunch together at the Old Glebe; but Poppy had insisted that any real celebration should be left till Pansy could be there.

Poppy had come home listless and low in spirit. The contrast between her and Charlie, also on vacation, only served to pinpoint Poppy's dejection. Charlie bubbled over with talk about her work, but Poppy said languidly that she'd lost all interest in hers. The thought of going back made her feel ill, because she knew she'd fail her finals next year, and didn't care if she did. She sat around, bored and lifeless, doing what was asked of her without protest but without a spark of observable enthusiasm, until at last Marjorie's patience gave out.

'I suppose you're coming to church with me in the morning?' Marjorie asked.

'I suppose I shall have to,' Poppy replied, pulling a face.

'Yes, you will have to,' her mother snapped sharply. 'For your Grandad's sake if nothing else. I suppose you're going to tell me that you're too tired and want to stay in bed. Well, you won't. And what's more, once Monday's over, you'll go to see the doctor or tell me yourself what's the matter with you. Till then, try to think a bit about others as well as yourself. Are you ill?'

'No. Just fed up with everything and everybody.'

Marjorie set her lips and said no more, but was relieved when Poppy did get up and accompany her to church next morning. The rest of the day dragged by, enlivened by the rumour, grossly exaggerated, of Joe's accident. Molly rang up and suggested they should walk up for tea with her, because Charles and Charlie were there. Poppy didn't want to bother. Marjorie told her that a bit of young company would do her good.

'Not if it's my idiot cousin drooling over the wife who can do no wrong,' Poppy flared back. But she went. George was disappointed because Lucy, his youngest daughter, had rung to say she and Alex couldn't make it after all for Monday lunch – Alex was a doctor and had been summoned to attend a cabinet minister. George said he wasn't surprised. It never rained but it poured. He'd just heard that Dan wouldn't be at work for the rest of the week.

'Just when I needed extra help,' George growled. Molly could hardly believe her ears. It was about the first time she'd ever heard George grumble about work. Charles noticed it, too. 'If you're worried about the cows, I'll come up and see to them,' he said.

'No, you won't,' Charlie chimed in. 'I'm the animal specialist, and I simply adore Daisy and Dora. Even if Dora decided to calve, I could manage – but I daresay Charles would come and help.' Charles looked at her with an expression that said if she asked him to get the cat to play the fiddle to Dora to persuade her to drop her calf on the moon, he'd hey-diddle-diddle it into reality for her somehow.

Poppy turned away. Her expression said just as plainly, 'You two make me sick.' 'Come on, Mum,' she said. 'Let's go home. We shall see everybody again tomorrow, and I'm tired and haven't been warm since I left church this morning. It was like a tomb.'

So they went back to Monastery Farm, where Poppy apologized, looking very pale and wan, and shed a few tears. Marjorie, full of sympathy and contrition, tucked her up on the settee, gave her a drink of hot milk laced with brandy, and was relieved to see that she soon warmed up and fell asleep. Then she went through to the other side of the house to consult Eric, afraid that Poppy might be genuinely ill. She found Nigel with Eric, and poured out her story to them. 'I wonder if I ought to get the doctor. I think she may have glandular fever.'

'We'd rather expected her to be a bit off-colour,' Eric said.

'She's probably dreading the thought of tomorrow without Pansy. After all, they are twins. She may be picking up from out of the ether what Pansy's feeling about not being here.'

'I hope Pansy's all right,' said Marjorie. 'I mean, *she* may be having her baby all alone in a strange place with none of us near her. We're all worried. If only we knew where she was.'

Eric went to sit beside her. 'Just go on being patient with Poppy,' he said. 'Once tomorrow's over, I think a few days' holiday away would do her more good than a doctor. There are too many memories here for her to cope with, poor child.'

'I'll think about it,' Marjorie said, comforted as always by Eric's concern and practical sense.

Poppy had awakened when Marjorie went back, and her mother saw that she had been crying. 'Sorry, Mum,' Poppy said. 'I didn't mean to be bitchy. I just feel so miserable – and Mum, I don't want to try and be happy just because it's my birthday. It's Pansy's as well, and it could have been so different! I know how awful it is for you, and I ought to be helping you, not making it worse. But there's nothing to make any effort for. I can't pretend all the time, like I had to this afternoon. Charles and Charlie so wrapped up in each other, and me the odd one out – when there used to be Robert and Nick and Pansy. I want Pansy! Why doesn't she want me? Why doesn't anybody want me?'

She began to cry in earnest, and couldn't stop. Pent-up misery so long simmering had at last boiled over. She made no noise, no fuss. She sobbed quietly and despairingly, soddened in her own tears. Marjorie had never before dealt with such a prolonged display of hopelessness, and after about an hour could endure it no longer on her own. She rang Eric, and asked him to come through. He arrived within two minutes, went to where Poppy still lay uncontrollably sobbing, and recognized at once the complete breakdown of the defences the girl had been so diligently constructing round herself for far too long.

'Ought I to get the doctor?' Marjorie asked, as if that were the only remedy possible. It wasn't like her. One word too much of sympathy, and Eric would have two to deal with. He went to the door, and shouted for Nigel. The moral medicine man.

Nigel had heard a great deal from Eric, besides what he had

observed for himself. He took in the situation at a glance, and took charge.

'No doctor can cure heartbreak,' Nigel said. 'Only love can ever do that, and even love needs help, sometimes. We can't do anything yet but let her cry herself out, even if it takes all night. She needs to get rid of all the grief she's been storing up. Eric, I think we may need some brandy on hand. Marjorie, what you need is a strong cup of tea. Go and make us all one. We may have a long night ahead of us.'

When the tea came, Nigel sat down by Poppy and lifted her into a sitting position. 'Now, Poppy, drink this. Sit up straight, and give yourself a chance to get some good deep breaths. That's better. Try just a few sips.' She seemed soothed by his presence, and obeyed the tone of command in his voice.

Eric came back with a brandy bottle and some glasses, and set them on an occasional table close at hand. Nigel, sitting on the edge of the settee, kept Poppy's hand in his when he urged her to lie down again, this time facing into the room.

'Good girl,' he said, motioning to Eric and Marjorie to bring their chairs closer. The effect he intended was to give her a sense that they were rebuilding round her her collapsed moral defences. Nobody spoke.

The sobs were beginning to subside a little, and the girl's breathing was gradually becoming deeper and more regular. Nigel squeezed the hand he still held.

'There, that's better, isn't it? You see, you're really quite safe. We've made a wall of love round you, and you feel better already, don't you? Pour us all a brandy, Eric. I think we could all do with it now.'

Poppy made no protest when he pulled her up again to a sitting position and put a very small tot of brandy into her hand. 'Now,' he said, 'we're going to drink to those we love who aren't here with us. Then we'll sit quiet and think about them. They need us as much as we need them.'

They drank and set their glasses down, and absolute silence reigned, except for Poppy's gasping sobs. Marjorie thought time must have stopped. She was beyond coherent thought, but tried to concentrate on Pansy. Eric was looking somewhere into the distance, and Nigel knew with whom his thoughts were – but Nigel himself looked at Poppy, holding her eyes with his own, as if he were compelling her to think as he did. He radiated peace, and even hope. Poppy succumbed to his will. He leaned over her, and took her head on to his shoulder. '*Those* we love,' he whispered into her ear. 'Those we love.' She opened her tear-reddened eyes as wide as she could to make sure she had understood what she thought he was saying. Then she gave a great sigh, and her eyelids fluttered down. She drooped and went limp in his encircling arm.

'Sleep's the best medicine in the world for her now. I suggest that Eric and I carry her to bed just as she is,' Nigel said. 'I wouldn't mind betting she hasn't slept properly for months. She's worn out, physically, mentally, and spiritually.' She didn't rouse at all as they carried her to her bed, covered her, and left her to sleep.

'Now you go to bed as well,' Eric told Marjorie. 'Don't risk waking Poppy, however long she sleeps. Nigel and I will bivouac down here, to be on the spot. Never mind tomorrow – let it look after itself when it comes. We may not be done with this emergency yet, but whatever happens, you'll be better for a good sleep, too. I shall have to be up and away early, but you'll know where I am if you need me, and Nigel will stay within call next door.' Dazed with exhaustion and emotion, Marjorie went and slept.

She was astounded to find that it was past nine 'clock next morning when she woke. Memory flooded back to her, and remembrance of what day it was. What was in store considering Poppy's breakdown last night? She longed to pretend that she was ill, and stay safe in bed, but that was impossible. There was Dad to think about. She washed and dressed with speed, and went softly across the creaky old landing to look in on Poppy.

The bed was empty. Pinned to the pillow was a note.

'*Sorry, Mum. I just can't face today without Pansy. Forgive me, and don't panic. I'll be back.*'

She stood stock still with the note in her hand, read it again, and swore.

'Bloody selfish little bitch,' she said, glaring at the empty bed

354

as if anger could conjure back into it the daughter she longed to spank. 'How could she!'

She got as far as the head of the stairs. Rage made her as rigid as the newel posts, and her legs refused to carry her down. 'Don't panic,' Poppy had written. Marjorie's head came up, and she screwed up the note in her hand. Panic? Not bloody likely! She'd find Poppy and get her to the Old Glebe by one o'clock if she had to drag her there by the hair. Didn't she think of anybody but herself? What about her grandfather, waiting with that huge cheque in his pocket for her – besides all the rest? What about her, who for twenty-one years had suffered so much in silence for the sake of those twins? A fat lot they cared for her!

She wasn't prepared to make any excuses for Poppy. Perhaps it was time to face up to the fact that her children weren't fit to belong to her family. No doubt that's what they said among themselves. It was only to be expected, seeing who their father was, and she should have had more sense than to marry him.

Her fury began to subside. It was as well that she had kept her grip on the newel post, as the starch of rage began to be washed away by fear. She had to get help.

Nigel came in at the front door facing the bottom of the stairs at that moment. He paused, and she tossed him the crumpled note, descended slowly, and sat down on the bottom step. 'What shall I do? What can I do?' she asked, over and over again. 'Where's she gone?'

Nigel answered crisply, 'I have no more idea than you, but it doesn't surprise me. After last night, she'd have had to be superhuman to go through with your plans for today. Come through and we'll talk. But the answer is clear enough. We can do nothing but keep calm and wait for her to come back. When the gathering of the clan is over.'

She was stunned by his apparently deliberate, unfeeling bluntness. She sat up, infuriated by his intimation that but for him she would have acted like Beryl Bean. She retorted angrily, 'It's all very well for you! She isn't your daughter.'

'True. But you involved me, didn't you? Why ask me what to do, if it doesn't concern me? You want my help, but you're afraid my advice won't suit you. Now sit still, calm down, and think. I

355

did warn you. She cried herself out and went to sleep last night from sheer physical exhaustion. The pain was still there when she woke up, and I presume that like any animal in pain, she acted on instinct and ran. We must put ourselves in her place, and think where she'd go. Then if we can do anything, we will.'

'But there's no time! I can't let Dad know. A shock like this will kill him!'

'Not if I know him,' Nigel answered. '*He* knows where to turn for help. All you're doing is panicking. Who is it you're concerned for? Your father? Yourself? The Bridgefoot family pride? Or that poor child? Don't you trust her at all? What do you want?'

'To find her! To get her back. I won't have Dad and Mum upset by her tantrums!'

'Tantrums? She's heart-broken, and not because of Pansy. Surely you know that? Young love's brittle and fragile, but in her case it's genuine. Her pain at being rejected by Nick is mixed up with disillusionment and disappointment and anger, because she doesn't know why it's gone wrong. She's borne it all alone because she loves you and wanted to spare you. A load of misery like that would have floored anybody, let alone a girl of her age and sensibility. It's her capacity for loving that makes her so vulnerable. She must have been dreading today, and when it came to it, she lost her courage. Just lit out for Injun territory, with no thought or plan. Quite likely if she comes back to her senses soon enough, she'll hare back faster than she went, in time for lunch. And you call that a tantrum!'

'She knows it will be Dad who she'll hurt most. After all he's done for her!'

'That's a spurious argument I can't and won't listen to. Whatever he's done for any of you, he's done to please himself, as all parents and grandparents do. Your father's about the last person to give what he couldn't afford. So don't try that argument on me. He wouldn't. If he can't give her what he intended to give her today, he won't have lost the chance. Every day's a birthday if it's a happy day. Now let's be practical. She can't have got far, yet.'

'No,' Marjorie said. 'She must be on foot. She's got no transport.'

'Now you're being sensible. Any guess as to where she may have gone?'

'Not to any of the family – it's them she doesn't want to face. Nor towards Castle Hill, because of Nick being there. To the church, or the graveyard? That's where I went when I ran away.'

'As I heard from Eric, you were not wanting to hide. Quite the reverse. She knows of that episode, would guess we should look there, and would avoid it. She may have made for the Swithinford road to hitch a lift, but to get there she'd have to go through the village. Someone may have seen her. We mustn't hope for too much, but it's a chance. I have some pastoral calls to make there anyway, so I'll get off at once, and ask tactfully of whoever I see or meet. You make sure she's actually gone anywhere. Search every nook and cranny in the house. And all the complex of buildings – as it's a bank holiday, nobody's at work. Don't let on to anybody else that she's missing till you have to – and if you can be strong enough to do that, I'll make a bargain with you. If you have to go up to the Glebe without her at lunchtime, I'll come too, and stand by you. Spare your parents as long as you can, and don't give up hope.'

His didactic voice softened. 'Love can and does work miracles, sometimes.'

'Even for me? I doubt it. But I'll try, and promise not to panic while you've gone. Don't be too long, that's all. I'll be OK.'

This was more like the Marjorie he knew. He had no qualms about leaving her now. She was George's daughter, and a Bridgefoot again.

The spectacle of the dawn sky had got others out of bed early as well as William and Fran. It had roused Charles and Charlie, in their beautiful bedroom in their beautiful home 'down Danesum'. They watched it from their window, and as soon as it began to fade, Charlie asked which of them was going up to the Glebe to do the cows, as promised. Charles was adamant that it should be his job. What would she do?

'What I've been meaning to do for ages. Give Ginger a good grooming, and then take him out. He's getting restive for want of a good gallop – and so am I. He really doesn't get enough exercise. Do you mind?'

'Not as long as you saddle him up properly and stay on his

357

back. I don't want you falling at any other man's feet like you did at mine!' He added seriously, 'You will be careful, won't you? Where are you thinking of going?'

'Up to Castle Hill. He knows every inch of it up there, and it's the only place I can get a really good gallop and be back in time to change for lunch. If I put all my clothes together, will you take them up to the Glebe with you, so that if I should get a bit late, I can change there? I promise not to be late enough to give you any cause to worry. Just you be careful not to let Daisy or Dora gore you.'

He laughed. She meant that she was as safe on a horse as he was in a cowshed.

As a special favour to Eric, Jess had agreed to be on duty in the hotel, because as well as being fully booked, there were always a lot of casual diners on bank holidays. He found her already in her office a few minutes after nine, looking a little anxious.

'Call from London,' she said. 'A party of French and German academics, in London for a conference, but free for today and wanting to see King's College Chapel and Ely Cathedral. We are being honoured by their presence because we happen to sit comfortably in a bit of rural English countryside within reach of both, or so I was informed. I took the call myself, so now I know. We had been graciously chosen because whoever recommended us said we had a linguist on our staff. Who is it, you or me? Lunch for ten of them at 1.30 p.m.'

'They'll all speak English better than I do,' he said. 'Your French will get us through – but it would happen when Anthea's away.'

'The conference secretary who spoke to me made rather a point of it,' she said. 'It sounds as if some of them at least may be a bit long in the tooth, and stuffy. Grown up before English became the lingua franca. Perhaps they may still expect us to converse with them in Latin.' Her expressive eyebrows shot up, and he watched a mischievous suggestion find its way to her tongue. 'What about enlisting the services of my erudite brother?' she asked. 'Didn't he promise to come as an interpreter if ever you were in a tight spot for one?'

'He did, and he shall be held to it,' Eric grinned. 'Especially as even Anthea couldn't have told them where the loos are in Latin.' He picked up the telephone.

'We were coming up to lunch in any case,' William said. 'So I'll be on the spot if you should need my services, but you won't. Academics these days who can't get by in English? I know a lot about vacation conferences. The conference secretary wants them off her hands for the day so that she's free to go on the spree with her boyfriend, or one of the younger and more attractive conferencees, if there is such a word. But if you are genuinely in any doubt, why not give Anthea a ring? I know she came back.'

'Will do,' said Eric with relief, and rang off.

Nick had got up early, rather regretting his decision to leave again so soon. He said he was going for a walk, to fix 'home' in his mind's eye, till he should see it again. 'Besides, it's such a lovely day,' he said.

'Don't forget the wood,' Bob said. 'I think the oxlips may be coming out.'

'I'll go there on my way back,' he said, 'and pick Mum a bunch if they are out. I'm only going down the lane as far as the cottage we lived in. I'll be back well before lunch.'

Under the benign and beaming April sun, the flat fields of East Anglia lay spread out like chessboards ready for an Olympian tournament. The gods had chosen their pieces, and set them out – kings, queens, bishops, knights, and rooks, with a handful of pawns thrown in by chance from an academic-cum-holiday course on 'The Effect of the Reformation on English Rural Life'.

Just before eleven o'clock, Charlie made the first move. Having seen Charles off to attend to the cows, she groomed Ginger to her satisfaction, had a bath and donned her riding habit. Then she saddled up Ginger, and set off to take her place on the chequerboard of the gods.

She was in no hurry, but Ginger was frisky, wanting to kick up his heels and go for it. She held him in and schooled him to a sedate walk all the way up the unfrequented Danesum Lane and as far as the Old Glebe, where she found Grandad Bridgefoot standing by the gate enjoying the spring sunshine.

'You're a sight for sore eyes, you are,' he said. 'Do you want

Charles? He's in the house. You needn't have bothered about the cows you know, either of you. But we're always glad of an excuse to see you. Where are you off to?'

'Only to give Ginger a bit of exercise, really,' she said. 'I'm going up to see Dad and Jane first, and then let him have his head for a good gallop. Don't worry, I'll be back for lunch. Charles has brought my things to change. Have you seen Poppy this morning?'

The old man's face clouded. 'No,' he said. 'Nor spoken to her yet. Gran tried to ring as soon as we thought they would be up, but the phone was engaged.'

'Yes, we tried too, to wish her a happy birthday – but I expect everybody has had the same idea. What's Charles doing?'

'Helping Dobson. Not that I blame him. It's a holiday, and his Mum and Dad are both here, expecting Aunt Marge and Poppy. I was watching for them.'

'We'll all be here at lunchtime,' she said, leaning down to kiss him. 'I'm going their way, so if I meet them I'll hurry them up to help Dobson as well.'

He chuckled, and slapped Ginger on the rump. She delighted him in so many ways. She never let one of his country sayings slip by her without letting him know she had added it to her vocabulary. He hoped he'd live long enough to see their first child. They'd promised him a boy, as soon as it could be managed after Charlie had finished her first degree.

He watched her go, turning and leaning his back against the five-barred gate into the farmyard. He was having to get used to helping Dobson himself, now – watching other people do the work he had previously always done himself. Not that he asked for or needed help yet. He was still a good figure of a man, over six feet tall, and as far as he knew, hale and hearty except for his arthritic hip. He spent a fair amount of time thinking about the future and his great-grandchildren, disappointed that Charles and Charlie's would not be his first. Pansy's would. It would probably take after the Giffords, as Pansy herself did, or the Baileys, neither of which he had much time for. But there – as Mother would say, 'Every baby brings its own love with it.' It didn't matter much which family they favoured in looks, as long as the Bridgefoot character was there somewhere. Charlie looked back before she reached the end of Glebe Lane, and raised her crop to him. He waved back, and went on waiting for Poppy.

Outside Monastery House, Charlie pulled Ginger to a standstill again, called greetings and waited. There was no answer, so she concluded that by going down Glebe Lane she had missed Aunt Marjorie and Poppy going round by car on the main road. She felt uneasy, and made up her mind that as soon as she reached Castle Hill she'd make some excuse to phone Charles to make sure all was well. She was becoming more and more aware that she had inherited a lot of her father's fenland feyness.

Time was passing, so she broke into a trot, and made for the road that led up to her father's farm, along which she had taken the toss from Ginger that had landed her at Charles's feet, then into his car, then into his arms, and finally into his bed. Good old Ginger! She patted his neck, and let him canter. Once she was past the only cottage on that hard road, she could let him have his head. The gate which he had refused that fateful day, and which led across fields to her father's farm, was only a hundred yards or so farther on. A man on foot appeared in sight and made her pull Ginger up short again.

'Nick!' she called. 'Nick! How marvellous to see you! When did you get here?' She slid off Ginger's back, keeping the reins over her arm as Nick went, rather shame-faced, to be hugged and kissed.

'You've been here since Friday and not let us know, or come to see us? Charles will be disappointed. Why not? Is anything wrong?'

She looked puzzled and hurt. After all, Nick was her step-brother now, and Charles his oldest and closest friend. She couldn't believe Nick had grown away from them to such an extent in six months, however posh and successful he'd become. Not that he was looking either self-satisfied or successful at that moment. He was flushed with embarrassment and guilt.

'Don't be cross with me. Or with Mum and Effendi,' he said. 'We've had to talk things out, and make a lot of decisions. I know I ought to have got in touch with you and Charles, but . . . Charlie, I thought you might understand. I didn't really want to see

361

anybody, 'specially any of the Bridgefoots. I stayed up at the farm so that I shouldn't, over the weekend. I'm going back to London early tomorrow.'

'Oh, Nick!' she said. 'If we'd only known, we'd have kept quiet about you being home. What you mean is that you didn't want to meet Poppy, and be hurt again. Perhaps it would have been a bit difficult this particular weekend. It's her twenty-first birthday today.'

'Do you think I've forgotten?' he said. 'I did think of sending her some flowers, anonymously, but she'd have guessed, and I didn't want to spoil things for her. Is she having a party?'

His tone was so wistful that Charlie could hardly bear it. She was almost glad to be able to tell him the truth. 'No. She's refused point-blank to celebrate her birthday in any way without Pansy. All that's happening is that we are having lunch together – and if I don't soon go I shan't have time for a good gallop after all. I'll put things right with Charles, so don't worry about that. He'll understand.' She leaned forward to kiss him again before remounting.

'Watch out,' he said. 'The woman who lives in our old cottage is just backing her car out. Don't go for a minute. She may be coming this way.' He pulled her, and Ginger, nearer to the side of the narrow track, which was enclosed by hedges thick with their first burst of greenery, and the huge horse-chestnut tree in the opposite hedge just beyond the cottage which was sending heavenwards a host of beflowered spikes. They watched as Anthea reversed into the lane, did a three-point turn, and headed towards the village, away from them.

Then it happened, near enough for them to see every detail. From the bottom of the hedge on the cottage side of the track, a large cock-pheasant, screaming his raucous cry, rose and flew straight into the windscreen of the car. The impact killed it, but not before it had screeched again, spread its great wings and fluttered down on to the bonnet in a bloody mass of spattered feathers. Anthea, with no idea what it was she had hit, swung her wheel hard in the opposite direction from which it had come, and stood, as she thought, on her brakes. But in her fright her foot had come down hard on the accelerator instead. The car leapt

362

forward, skidded, and with a crash of crumpling metal and splintering glass, hit the trunk of the tree. Then there were screams such as neither Nick nor Charlie had ever imagined.

Charlie dropped Ginger's reins, and ran. Nick, slower to react, caught her up before they reached the accident. They took in at a glance that it had not been a head-on impact. The car had slewed round in its skid, and only the passenger side had been badly smashed. The windscreen was still whole, and so indeed was the driver's side window. But inside, Anthea, with head thrown back, was uttering such squeals of terror as Charlie would have thought impossible for one human voice to produce. She had been told by her brother and some of her father's fen labourers of the dreadful, hellish, demon-like noise of a back-garden pig-killing in days of yore. They had always made her feel sick, yet she had been forced to go on listening. Now she was hearing the same sort of sounds from a human throat, it seemed to her arising from the same cause. Not the pain, but the terror of the doomed victim. Anthea did not seem to be able to move.

Nick, his face as white as mashed potato, was leaning inside the broken window on one side as Charlie struggled to open the driver's side door. There were words now, among the screams – or else the screams were made up of strangled words. 'Seat-belts' was all the sense she could make. 'Seat-belts. *Seat-belts.*' Then the pig-killing began again.

'Where is the bloody thing?' Nick was yelling to Charlie. 'Your side! Your side!'

'She isn't wearing it.'

'Below the dashboard.' He was only confusing Charlie, who was desperately fumbling for the seat-belt she couldn't locate.

'No, not the belt! The ignition. Switch off. Switch it off! The engine's still running. It may fire!'

The professional calm that Charlie was being taught to cultivate came to her aid. Nick had pinpointed the worst acute danger. She reached for the ignition key and turned it. The car stopped its shuddering, and its driver stopped her indescribable squeals. She did not attempt to move, even when Charlie opened the passenger door.

'Is she trapped?' Nick asked. Charlie shook her head. 'I don't think she's hurt much at all. Come on, Miss Pelham. Can you move? We'll help.'

Anthea seemed to come to her senses, put out her dainty feet and stood up. Then, as Nick and Charlie, one each side of her, tried to urge her away from the wreck, she stiffened in their grasp, stood rigid for a second or two, and fell flat. There was no help at hand but the two of them. They had to act.

'Don't try to move her,' Charlie ordered sharply. 'We might kill her.'

'So will the car if it goes up in flames, which it's very likely to if the tank's punctured. Better to risk moving her than that.'

Charlie agreed. 'We won't try to lift her – but we could drag her away from the car.'

Anthea remained deeply unconscious as they did what they could. Charlie whipped off her hacking jacket and they slipped it under Anthea's waist so that Charlie could support her head as Nick, using the jacket as a hand-hold, dragged her a few inches at a time across to the opposite verge. Then Charlie knelt down beside her.

'We must get the doctor or an ambulance. Dr Hardy's closest, and ambulances are likely to be busy. She may only be in a dead faint, but it could be whiplash injury to her neck. Lend me your jacket to cover her with, and run for the doctor – next door to Effendi. You may be lucky and catch him at home. If he isn't, get Effendi to ring for an ambulance. I'll stay here. Oh, and please ask Effendi to ring Charles at Glebe and tell him to come to help me. Ask Effendi as well to stand by with his car at the ready in case we need another. Come back as quick as you can, because if there's nothing else you can do you can go after Ginger and take him up for Dad to look after till I can fetch him. Go on – don't worry about me. I'll be all right.'

She sat down by Anthea's head, smoothing back the dark hair and watching her breathe. She dared do no more. The sun was quite warm, but once Nick had left her, Charlie began to feel cold and started to shiver. It seemed for ever before Dr Hardy leapt from his car and kneeled down beside her. Following the doctor's car came Charles in his, with Nick at his side.

'Tell me as exactly as you can what happened,' Hardy said,

364

'before I try to examine her. Good girl for having enough sense not to try to move her or revive her.'

Charlie did her best in a few short sentences.

'Was she wearing her seat-belt?'

'No. But she was screaming terribly and I thought I heard her say "seat-belts" two or three times. She didn't try to get out till we made her. Then she collapsed.'

Very cautiously, he began to carry out a preliminary examination where she lay.

'No very obvious injury,' he said. 'Fright and shock could account for the collapse, but I can't be sure, till I can examine her more thoroughly. Perhaps we can get her inside. We could carry her if we could improvise a stretcher.'

Charles went into the adjacent field and ripped a hurdle out of a temporary sheep-fence.

'I know where the key's kept, if it isn't in her handbag. Shall I look?' asked Nick. It was in her handbag. Charlie ran upstairs for a blanket. They pulled a divan away from the wall under the window, and laid her flat upon it.

'Her pulse is weak – but I shouldn't be very popular for sending her to a hospital till I've made sure it's nothing worse than a faint. Thank heaven you're here, Mrs Bridgefoot, to prevent any breach of medical etiquette. I take it you can stay with me?'

Charlie looked at her watch, and then at Charles. To her dismay, he was shaking his head. 'Why not?' she mouthed at him.

'Dr Hardy,' said Charles, 'I'm sorry, but this isn't the only emergency. I was coming from Glebe to find Charlie, and picked the rector up. In fact, he waved me down. My cousin Poppy's gone missing, and can't be found. My aunt's in a dreadful state, and I was on my way to fetch my wife from Castle Hill to be with her, when I passed Nick running this way and picked him up, too. Couldn't he help you?'

'He could if he was here,' said Charlie. 'He's gone.'

It was true. The second shock – of hearing of Poppy's disappearance – had been too much for him. He'd gone to where nobody could see him being violently sick.

'You get back to Aunt Marge and do what you can,' Charlie said. 'I'm needed here.'

Charles didn't stop to argue. He knew Charlie in that mood. They didn't want Grandad to know until all hope of finding Poppy in time had gone. Thinking swiftly, he decided to find a substitute for Charlie at Anthea's side, so as to leave himself and his car free to join the search for Poppy. Mrs Burbage. Hadn't Grandad – and himself – often turned to her before when they were in trouble?

Terence leaned over the patient, his stethoscope in his ears. He slapped her face gently, calling her name. 'Anthea. Anthea! Come on, wake up. You're quite safe now. I'm here with you – Terry. So is young Mrs Bridgefoot.'

He was stroking her forehead, and smoothing back the corona of black curls round the pale, exquisite face with a very tender hand. Charlie was surprised, both at his use of Christian names in a professional situation, and by his tone. But he looked worried.

He began, hesitantly, Charlie thought, to unbutton the high-necked blouse.

'Would you like me to do that?' she asked – and saw his evident relief. He turned to his doctor's bag so as to be looking the other way as Charlie pulled back the blouse from Anthea's throat.

'Dr Hardy!' she exclaimed. He turned and with one stride was back by the divan on the opposite side to Charlie. Both were staring down at a throat and chest terribly scarred, discoloured and puckered. The reason for the high-necked uniform was suddenly clear.

'My God! Burns. Awful burns,' said Terry, pulling the blouse back further. The scars ran right across to her left shoulder. They removed the blouse altogether. The scars went down her arm, into the armpit and along the underside of the left arm as far as the elbow. 'I'm afraid we shall have to get her bra off, too,' he said.

Charlie understood his reluctance, and slid her hand underneath to undo the tiny hooks at the back. Then she gently slipped the strap down the sound right arm, and revealed one beautiful, satin-skinned, pointed little breast that stood proudly forward under their gaze, till Charlie lifted the bra to remove it. The other breast came with it, a foam prosthesis dangling helplessly from

366

Charlie's hand, while under it were scars and evidence of extensive skin grafting running down to waist level, and below.

Charlie noticed the doctor's trembling hands as he returned to his examination. 'I'm afraid we must try to turn her over,' he said. 'I think it may be a bit of luck that she is still out.' Expertly she was turned on to her face, and his sensitive hands soon established no spinal injury. Moreover, she began to stir. He leapt to his feet as the sound of another car stopping outside somehow restored the scene from nightmare to reality.

'Fran!' he said. 'Fran! Thank God you could come.'

Charlie slipped away, to go and cry on Charles's shoulder. The last few minutes had been the worst ordeal she'd ever encountered. No, said Charles, Poppy had not been found.

Charles had arrived at Benedict's just as William and Fran were ready to drive out *en route* for the hotel, and poured out his jumbled rigmarole to them.

'Do come, please Mrs Burbage!' he pleaded. 'Aunt Marge is in a terrible state now, sure that Poppy has committed suicide. Nick was there but he turned green and scarpered, and you were the only person I could think of to help us out. You know Miss Pelham better than we do. I'm sure she'd rather find you there with her when she comes round than Charlie, even if Charlie wasn't wanted somewhere else.'

Fran was scrambling out of their car before he had finished. 'Of course I'll come,' she said. Then, turning to William, 'We know now why Anthea didn't turn up to help Eric when he appealed to her, so it's lucky for him that you'll be there to deal with the polyglot academics who are pretending they don't understand rural English tongues. You'll probably enjoy yourself no end – and you know where I am if you need me, or vice-versa. Come on, Charles, let's go.'

Terence had pulled himself together, and was trying to be the professional doctor, rather than a very shaken man. It was clear to him now that Anthea was going to regain consciousness at any minute, and he knew he ought not to be the person she set eyes on when she realized that her sad secret had been exposed.

He asked Charlie to find another blanket, and they spread it over her, tucking it right up under her chin. His relief on seeing Fran almost undid him; he thanked Charlie and sent her out to Charles rather hastily. He wanted a few words with Fran before Anthea's twitching eyelids lifted and her eyes stayed open.

'It really is the most terrible injury,' he said, 'though they've made as good a job at patching her up as I've ever seen. From the look of the scars, I'd say she came here more or less straight out of hospital – it's as recent as that. I guess a car accident in which the car burst into flames and she was trapped. More than enough to account for this trauma – and a lot of other things.' Fran didn't need to ask what he meant.

'Fran,' he said, rather pleadingly, 'it's been a shock to me, too. Do you mind if I leave her with you, now? I swear to you that I wouldn't if I thought she'd need me still as a doctor – but I'm sure she won't. Treat her for shock when she comes round – and let her cry if she wants to, or talk. I'll arrange for cover from one of my partners, so as to be available if you should need me – or indeed if the Bridgefoots do. Heaven forbid that they should! She'll be coming round any minute now, I think. I'll get away, if you're sure you don't mind.'

Her heart was wrung for him, as well as for the supine woman. She had not seen the scarred body, but she guessed she would have to steel herself to help when Anthea came round.

'I'll manage,' she said. 'Young Charlie's set me an example. She is a brick! And so are you. Off you go – I'll get you back if I have to. And once William's free, he'll come and stand by, too.' She leaned forward and kissed him. 'Go home and look after yourself,' she said.

He pulled a wry face. 'I'm shattered. When I've had time to come to terms with it, I'll be back to see her. As her doctor – as long as you are here to chaperone her.'

When he had gone, she put the kettle on, got everything she could think of ready for any further drama when Anthea regained consciousness, and then sat down on the divan by her side. With infinite care she pulled back the covering blanket from under the chin, far enough to reveal her neck and the misshapen shoulder and upper arm. As Terry had said, it explained so much; so many little things they had not been able to understand before. William's report of her saying she liked handsome men to keep their distance. Christmas morning, when she had slipped on the ice – that injured arm wouldn't have let her get up till she had got over the pain of falling on it, and of course the muscles had probably been affected. And her left hand – did she sometimes have difficulty in raising it? Was that why she hadn't taken Terry's hand in the circle round the table at the pancake love feast? Fran remembered that she had not made any objection when in his indignation he had picked it up in his own and held it. Besides, she had kissed him later on. Fran covered up the shoulder again, and stroked Anthea's face.

The great dark eyes opened, and Fran's heart contracted again as she watched recognition, awful terror, and then memory return. As Anthea closed them again, tears began to run down her face and she clung to Fran's hand, and gasping sobs shook her. Fran cradled her in her arms and crooned over her as she would have done a baby, stroking her hair and face till at last the trembling stopped. Then she lifted Anthea up to lean on her shoulder, and said, 'You're quite safe now, in your own home, and in a minute I'm going to make us some tea. You fainted, that's all. Your car's a write-off, but you weren't hurt, honestly. It was lucky that Charlie Bridgefoot and Nick Hadley were on the spot and saw it happen. They carried you in.'

'Did they see?' Anthea asked, pushing the blanket down and exposing all the rest that Fran had not yet seen and could never have imagined. She shook her head, unable to speak.

'Then who undressed me?'

While Fran hesitated between the truth and a white lie, the pain in Anthea's eyes told her what Anthea's question meant. Before she had time to speak, Anthea answered it herself. 'So he has been here,' she said, her face first suffusing with scarlet before turning again to white crumpled paper. 'They sent for him – and he knows.'

Nothing but the singing of the electric kettle broke the dreadful silence that followed. Then Anthea sat up, cuddling the blanket round her, while Fran made the tea. Anthea took the cup from her, now wearing her usual rather hard, brittle smile.

'In some ways, it's a relief,' she said. 'But it means I can't stay here. I came in the first place to be alone, where nobody knew me, till I could accept how it had to be for the rest of my life. But you were all too kind. You wouldn't let me. So I ran away and stayed away long enough for me to get used to being lonely again. I thought I could bear it, but I can't. So I shall have to leave, as soon as I can – for his sake more than my own. Get out of his sight and spare him embarrassment, now that he knows the truth. His livelihood is here. Mine isn't. Perhaps this was a blessing in disguise.'

Her mouth twisted as she tried to control it. 'You can't beat fate, can you, Fran? Why did this accident have to happen to me? But it's no good crying over spilt milk. I thought I'd got over that childishness before I ever came here. Please help me to dress.' They were adjusting the prosthesis when Anthea said abruptly, 'Why don't you ask?'

'Because if you want to tell me, you will,' Fran answered. So Anthea did. She had been an air hostess. She had read languages at university with that in mind, and had had no difficulty in finding a job with one of the world's biggest airlines.

Fran didn't wonder at that. Ten years younger than she was now, her beauty and charm could have got her anywhere!

'Being an air hostess isn't all it's cracked up to be,' Anthea said. 'A plane in flight is a little world on its own – people behave as if they're cut off from earth. Somehow the belief's got round that air hostesses are fair game for any man out on the loose. And pilots are too attractive by half, in any case. It stands to reason – they have to be almost supermen, and when they are handsome, and free of matrimonial ties, earning huge salaries by standards such as mine, what do you expect? I had a wonderful time, till I fell in love with one of them.

'I know now, in my disillusionment, what my attraction was for him. I had standards of my own that a lot of my colleagues had long ago abandoned – I've heard since that the men used to have bets on which of them could get me into bed first. Harry won his bet. He did it by offering marriage – when it should be convenient. Two years later, we actually set a date for it. I think still that he'd begun to love me enough to want to feel sure of

370

me, or else he was getting more competition from younger men and not finding it quite so easy to play the field. I don't know, and I can't tell, now.

'We had an emergency – and as captain of the aircraft he was all I had ever thought him. He got us down. Have you ever realized what it's like to be trapped in a plane you know is going to crash? Then it looked as if we were going to make it after all, and we did, as far as the airfield. But as we touched down, the crash came, and we burst into flames. My duty was to get the passengers out. Need I tell you any more? Harry? Oh, he just walked out, completely unhurt. He always had the devil's own luck.

'They whipped me into hospital, and as soon as they'd let him, he came to see me – I could have told anybody from that moment what would happen. He was kind – and kept visiting me in hospital, at longer and longer intervals, sending me flowers and presents, till they had done all they could for me. Then he gracefully and courteously withdrew from any commitment to me. He was quite honest about it – men don't like damaged goods, especially when they can take their pick of undamaged ones. My face and my legs – which is what most men look at first – were as good as they'd ever been. That was the irony. I had to learn to keep men at a distance so that they never saw any more of me. Not that I cared much, at first. I thought I'd learned enough about them to last me the rest of my life. I had enough money to do whatever I wanted – so my first thought was to withdraw from my sort of world till I'd come to terms with a world that for me no longer included men.' Her mouth twisted, and she went on in a low voice. 'I landed myself in a tiny village where the first people I met were Greg Taliaferro, Eric Choppen and your William, and then Elyot Franks and the parson and the doctor – all with such different values from the men I'd got used to. I did try hard, Fran, believe me. I shall simply have to find another place to hide to start all over again.'

She turned away and covered her face. Fran left her to cry. What else could she do, other than curse the gods, and tell Anthea that she'd promised to ring William?

She waited a while till silence and deep breathing told her that exhaustion had once again brought the sweet relief of sleep. Then she crept into the tiny hall, shut the door behind her, and dialled Terence Hardy's number.

Nick had run away, not only from the scene of the accident, but from himself. He'd got up conscious that he'd burnt his boats behind him, and though there had been no objections, getting his own way meant that in future he'd be out on his own. A different Nick, who must put the past behind him and go his own way. But what on Saturday had seemed possible and desirable was now shot through with nostalgia. When he left tomorrow, for good, he would be leaving a lot behind. A lot of himself. Little Nick Hadley, who had no father and whose mother worked in the fields; the scared first-day-at-school little Nick, befriended and protected by Charles Bridgefoot and Robert Fairey, who had thereafter shared with him things his mother's poverty couldn't provide. They had become a trio which had remained inseparable until in the course of time adolescence and three girls made it into a sextet. Nobody expected that adolescent phase to last long, and it hadn't. Tragedy had struck. Twice. First when Robert had died, and again when Nick himself had been the victim. A passing van had laid him out, by that time an ambitious schoolboy determined to make his way to a university so as to keep himself in the picture with his girl, to whose father he was socially and financially unacceptable. Yet it had been into her arms, quite literally, that he had fallen from a strawstack and got his memory back, only to find himself rejected again, this time by the girl herself.

Why? Because he was no longer the same Nick? Between being laid out in a coma and falling off the stack, there had been that strange interlude of being someone else who couldn't remember anything before the accident. The poverty-stricken illegitimate son of the village charwoman had come round in hospital with no memory of his past, to find himself the pampered grandson of a distinguished, influential and wealthy diplomat, and the son of a woman he didn't remember who was the wife of a man he didn't know, any more than he recognized his friend Charles, or the girl called Poppy. It was all very peculiar, that strange life within another life that 'they' said he had had ... Who could understand except the one who'd been in it?

Now that time had gone, too, and another phase about to begin. One in which Poppy had no part – except forever in his regained memory as his first and last love, and the only one he wanted. Like Charles with Charlie, except that they had been lucky, while he – but he mustn't grumble. It was only that memories were too strong today. Memories of the time when he and his mother had at last begun to climb out of the worst of their humble poverty, and he had been so contented to work hard at his books in the almost unbelievable luxury (by contrast) of the cottage down the hill on the way to the village. He turned his steps towards it, the place where his adolescent dreams had been born, and ran straight into another accident with a victim laid out in much the same state as he had been. He hadn't wanted to meet Charlie, let alone Charles, or to hear what they said – which was that Poppy, his Poppy, had disappeared. He caught the word 'suicide' and his head reeled while his stomach turned over. Not that she was 'his' Poppy. She belonged to some other fellow at the university to which she, not he, had 'made it'; and there was nothing – *nothing* – that he could do. Filled with despair, he obeyed the most primitive instinct of all, and ran towards home and his mother.

He stopped to vomit under a hedge, and as his head cleared he became aware of Ginger peacefully cropping grass in the gateway where Charles's new car had startled him into refusing the gate, and had thrown Charlie at Charles's feet.

Nick didn't want to have to face anybody, yet. There was no need. Ginger knew where he was. All Nick had to do was to let him through the gate, tie up the reins, and slap his rump. He would take himself home to what had until very recently been his stable. Nick's thoughts went back to what he'd heard.

He began to ask himself questions. Why had Poppy run away? Why on earth should her mother fear *suicide*? He stopped walking, and stood still as his unwilling mind made a connection. *Why had his mother run away from Effendi?* To face a future alone because his blackguard father had abandoned her, and before she could disgrace her own father. Was the Bridgefoot family being protected for the same reason? What could *he* do? Nothing. Wait. Just shut the present out!

He wandered on as far as the gate where he had met Emerald

Petrie. What a pig-headed, arrogant, ungrateful and stupid idiot he'd been then. He'd deserved the dressing-down she had given him; but he didn't deserve this anguish, now. If he went home, he'd break down again and pour it all out – but he mustn't. For Poppy's sake and for his mother's. She still loved him, if Poppy didn't. He'd promised Bob he'd go and pick some oxlips for her. His head still felt queer, but he was able to think again. He could hide in the wood – except that Bob's feyness would tell him not only where, but when to look for him, if, as feared, this morning's shocks should cause amnesia again.

He kept behind the hedge till he came out at the back of the church and went into the wood. He sat down under a tree with his back to the trunk, and waited for the next wave of nausea to pass. The woods were very soothing, so tranquil in their age and beauty, yet noisily stirring with new life as the rooks busied themselves with their nestlings. Yin and Yang he thought, gazing upwards to the rookery above him. There were two sides to everything.

He felt cold, and needed to move, so he got up and stumbled through a miniature jungle of oxlips and bluebells, till the scent came up to him like incense and dulled the awful pain that was inside him. Then he stopped, and began to pick the flowers till his hands would hold no more. He stood at the edge of the wood long enough to take his bearings and square his shoulders to face whatever he had to.

In front of him lay the farmyard, with the long barn and the adjacent strawstack from which he had fallen. At this time of the year the stack was surrounded by loose straw that collected at its base as it was cut away each day to straw the bullock yard. There were so many associations with the past here, particularly of that uncomfortably bewildering period just after his memory had returned, when he recalled both sides of his curiously bifurcated life, but couldn't fit them together. They had never united. The bits from which he had to make yet another life were all there, and ought to fit together; but they didn't hold. Any upset like this morning's scattered them. He was afraid that he might never be quite normal, never again feel wholly secure. He'd said that he would always be the odd man out, but he hadn't wanted anybody to stress the word 'odd'.

Once back in London, he would consult Alex Marland, Charles's psychiatrist uncle, again, but it must wait. He wouldn't leave tomorrow; he had to stop long enough to know what had happened to Poppy. If she had run away, especially for the reason he'd surmised, the time might come when she needed his help. He wouldn't allow the possibility of suicide. His mother had never given in – so why should Poppy?

He moved on, carrying the bunch of oxlips, towards the strawstack. If he climbed to the top of it, he would have a wonderful observation post of all the surrounding countryside. He could be alone, and watch the fields for any sign of Poppy. It was still only a few minutes past twelve. What an interminably long morning it had been.

He stood in the April sunshine at the base of the stack, trying not to remember too vividly the last time he had been there, with Poppy in his arms. She was the missing adhesive that could put his life together again. His eyes filled with tears, and his chest felt tight with anger against the fate that seemed bent on making an Aunt Sally of him. He threw the huge bunch of flowers down at the spot where he had fallen, and then flung himself after it on to the loose straw.

It wriggled, and jiggled, and yelped. From it rose a dark curly head bestrewn with flowers and bedraggled with wisps of straw. He had gone mad! He must have done.

'Poppy?' he said. 'Poppy! What on earth are you doing there?'

'What do you think, you silly idiot? Hiding. What are you playing at?'

'Hide and seek, apparently. I was looking – for you.'

They eyed each other, while she struggled to stand up. He put out a hand and hauled her to her feet. She was rumpled and crumpled, rather pale, and bedizened with straws and an odd oxlip that had got entangled in her hair. He, too, was draped in wispy loose straw and a few stray bluebells. They eyed each other as if neither ever wanted to look away again. The oxlip slipped from her hair and touched her neck as it fell. She screamed. 'Nick, please! There's a spider on my neck.'

He sprang to her side and looked for the offending creature, touching her as if he still didn't believe she was real. 'Not a spider,'

375

he said. 'Only a flower.' Their faces were very close as his fingertips made quite sure.

'It's a beetle – and it's on you now! Stand still,' she said. She tried to knock it off, but succeeded only in giving him a rather ineffectual box on the ear. He looked indignant, and she startled, and both faces suddenly creased into hysterical laughter. His arms closed round her and the beetle was forgotten. Who could bother about a beetle? They had each other . . . They pulled apart, but the sight of each other brought back gurgles of helpless, carefree laughter. It was hardly the romantic reconciliation either had been day-dreaming of, but who cared?

'Oh, Poppy, have you come back to me again?'

'I hope so. Journeys end in lovers' meetings, don't they?'

'Does that mean you love me as much as I love you?'

'Do you mean you didn't know? I called you a blithering idiot. What's the time?'

'Nearly half past twelve. Why?'

'We've got to be down at Grandad's for lunch at one o'clock.'

'Heavens – you'll have to get your skates on! You won't have time to change. Let me get all the straw off and tidy you up.'

'What do you mean, tidy *me* up? It's you that needs tidying up! If you think I'm going to take you with me looking such a guy, you've got another think coming.'

'But I haven't been invited!'

She kissed him to shut him up. 'Don't be a bigger idiot than you can help,' she said. 'I'm not going to let you out of my sight. Come on – let's get going. Just as we are.'

'I must let Mum and Bob know where I am.'

'Ring them from Glebe. *Come on* – we shall have to run all the way as it is.'

Fran let Terence in with her finger to her lips. Anthea was asleep on the divan, just as he had left her, though now dressed. They stood in the hall while she whispered to him most of what Anthea had told her.

'So now it's up to you, I think,' she said. 'If you're here as her doctor, I'll stay. If you're here as her friend, I'll get out of the way. I shall only have to ring the hotel for William to come and get me. Which would you prefer?'

'Both,' he said. 'Ring William, but stay till I'm sure I'm wanted in either role. If I'm not, I shall have to ask you to stay a bit longer with her. But what about your lunch?'

'What about yours, if it's you who stays? Let me tell William to bring you something from the hotel.' He agreed, and Fran got William on the other end of the phone. She didn't tell him much, or hold out much hope that she'd be able to go back with him; Anthea was all right and asleep, but she herself was hungry and thought her patient would be better for some food when she woke. She had to wait till the doctor came back and released her.

William was disappointed, and said so. 'It's been the most enormous fun,' he said. 'Jess is doing a superb job as a hostess, and Eric's dropping in on us every minute he can spare. I'd hoped you might be able to get here to have lunch with us, but I see you can't leave till somebody else takes over. Any news of you-know-who?'

'Not a word,' she answered sadly. 'Poor old George.'

'What sort of food shall I bring?' he asked. 'I'll be there in about ten minutes, because I ought to be back here myself before we begin on lunch.'

She could not resist a hint. 'Something light – like the food of love,' she said.

He sounded quite stumped. 'What on earth for? I can't bring pancakes, can I?'

'No – I was only joking. I meant something light and airy, not too solid for someone who's been knocked out – physically, mentally and emotionally.'

'I'll ask Jess,' he said. 'And I'll bring something more substantial for you. Thank goodness you don't diet. I detest fussy eaters. See you soon.' She didn't really care whether she had anything to eat or not. She was much more concerned about the outcome of the next few minutes. When she judged the time was right, she opened the door and let the doctor through.

He put his stethoscope into his ears and leaned over Anthea. She opened her eyes, and they darkened with pain at the sight of him. Fran held her breath. Terence sat down on the edge of the divan, and waited.

'Fran's still here,' he said. 'May I examine you again?'

She set her chin and her lips firmly, and nodded assent.

Slowly, he began to undo the buttons that closed the high-necked blouse over the scars, and applied his stethoscope to her heart. The foam prosthesis was in the way. He gently pulled the bra-strap over the shoulder, and lifted the bra to one side. Then he removed his stethoscope, got to his knees and raised his patient up on his arm to help her sit up. But he was watching her face, and she his. The arm tightened around her, and she didn't pull away. The discoloured scar and the skin-graft where her left breast should have been were bared. Fran watched, still unsure, as he ran his fingers down the scar on her neck, then over the shoulder and down her arm till he held her hand in his. The slight pressure he applied was returned.

'That's good,' he said. 'Everything seems to be OK.' He turned his head, and Fran took it as a signal that the words meant she could go. William arrived with his package, and again Fran stood in the tiny hall discouraging any speech. She snuggled up to William, and they waited.

The door to the sitting-room still stood a little ajar, and after a minute or two, she peeped. Terry had lowered his head and laid his face against the mangled shoulder. When he turned his head to kiss the worst of the scars, Fran closed the door without making a sound, and beckoned William outside.

'Leave the food by the telephone,' she whispered. 'It won't be wanted just yet.'

They were getting very anxious up at the Old Glebe as the appointed time for lunch neared and only Rosemary and Brian were there. Rosemary was trying to keep the old couple's mind on lunch.

'Are you sure I've set the table properly,' she said. 'There's you two and us two and Charles and Charlie and Marjorie and Poppy. Eight.'

Brian scowled at her – counting those who would be there was the very last thing she should have done. There ought to have been nine, counting Pansy.

'We've cooked enough for a regiment,' she said. 'I think Mother still imagines she's got a troop of hungry men coming in from a harvest field.'

George was not taken in. He was aware that something was wrong. He went to the door, looking towards the road. And here, at last, was a car. He watched the rector hand Marjorie out – a limp, tear-sodden Marjorie, but no Poppy.

He went forward to meet them as Charles and Charlie drove up. A very dishevelled Charlie, without her riding jacket, and with her hair still tied back as it had been all those hours ago for the gallop on Ginger she never got. The old man moved with sagging gait to join them. Taking Marjorie into his arms, he looked over her head at the rector. 'No sign of her yet, then?' he asked.

For once Nigel was tongue-tied. His normal way of coping with tragedy depended on the people involved, but George was no ordinary man – neither as worldly-wise as himself, nor a humble, simple, ignorant countryman to whom one offered superficial, on-the-spot solace of a spiritual kind. He was a man deeply committed to his Christian beliefs.

Charles and Charlie were gawping at the two of them, making the only sense they could of that exchange between the rector and his churchwarden. *Grandad had known all along.* He'd been trusting to prayer all the morning, and his faith had let him down. They knew what that could do to him, and their sympathy switched from Aunt Marge to her father. Grandad. Such a blow must surely be too much for him to withstand. Yet still he held his head high, refusing in the face of all evidence to believe that hope was dead. 'Come in,' he said. 'You as well, Rector. We must still eat.'

Nigel decided he couldn't leave them. They might need him as a priest; and even more as a friend. The door to the house stood open, and at it George stood aside to let the others pass.

'Wait a minute, Grandad,' Charles said urgently, laying his hand on George's arm. 'Who is going to tell Gran?'

Charlie turned away, unable to bear the sadness on the old man's face. Then she turned back and grabbed his arm, her voice raised into a triumphant crow like that of a yard-bird at dawn. She had trouble in shaping the words that let out her paeon of joy.

379

'Nobody,' she cried. 'Nobody has to! Look, she's here! Nick's found her!'

The news was rung through to the hotel, where Fran sat at table with William and the foreign academics, not able to concentrate because her mind was darting to and fro between the Old Glebe and the cottage where she had left Anthea and Terry. They mustn't take the second outcome for granted because the first had, after all, turned out well. But she couldn't help but hope. She said as much to William, who bade her concentrate on the good news and enjoy the rest of her lunch. It was, he said, one of those situations when one just had to wait. Didn't they know enough about waiting to be patient a bit longer?

At home again that evening, they discussed the extraordinary events of the day.

'I think,' said Fran, 'I shall always dread Easter in future. It seems as if fate, or the gods, or whatever you care to call who or whatever it is that pulls the strings, saves things up for Easter time. This is the third year in succession that we have spent Easter on a big dipper of emotion and strain. It must be something to do with the weather.'

He gave it thought before replying. 'More to do with the season, I imagine. It's a time of opposites, isn't it? As you say, like the weather. Dark one day, sunny the next. It wasn't just by chance that the Christian Church set death and resurrection in apposition to each other when all nature was doing the same. They alternate, like all opposites. If you forget the ritual part of it and stop to consider, every day is an Easter day for somebody. Humanity couldn't survive if hope didn't somehow always counter despair. The trouble with a lot of us is that it's so much easier to go downhill than uphill, and when the signposts aren't there, we get lost, as we did in the blackout when there were no signposts anyway. Poppy ran away, and what did we all do? Blundered about in the dark, sure that though we didn't know where "away" was, we did know where it wasn't. "She won't go anywhere near Castle Hill," we said. We should have known better, because Charles and Charlie had spelt out to us what Poppy and Nick had meant to each other once. But we jumped to the same conclusion this morning as everybody else, without thinking properly. We hadn't the sense to realize that *away* from her family might to her unconsciously mean *towards* Nick. We should have remembered Pandora's vase – when you're overwhelmed with trouble, hope is always left at the bottom of the otherwise empty pot. If you ask me, today's been a jolly hopeful day. All the signposts have been put back, even for Terry and Anthea.'

She nodded. 'Like the lark over the battlefield, and the rose in the graveyard, in that poem of your father's called *The Skein of Hope*. Fancy him remembering larks and baby rabbits to write about in the trenches on the Somme! What a lovely man he must have been. I love him. I want him back.'

'No hope of that, my darling. Won't his son do?'

Possibly because they had happened on a public holiday, or perhaps because there were explanations more or less ready to hand, none of the extraordinary cluster of events of Easter Monday became nine-day wonders. Anthea Pelham's accident couldn't be overlooked, but car accidents weren't really news any longer – and it did account for the doctor's car being seen outside her house several times in that week.

The Bridgefoots kept things to themselves, in the belief that all's well that ends well; not even Dan, who wasn't at work and on hand that week, was given any details. He, too, was keeping tight-lipped about the events nearer home last Sunday.

Beth and Fran were quietly triumphant. Their matchmaking plans seemed to be well on course. They kept a low profile, however, even with each other, till Terence had paid a visit to both, and though warning them not to make too much of it, left them even more hopeful.

They agreed with him that to make haste slowly was by far his best policy. Anthea was suffering from the effects not only of a nasty accident, but of a long period of stress. It was legitimate for her to remain his patient, one who had to be visited every day by her doctor for the time being; a situation too ordinary for hawk-eyed scandal-mongers to notice and set rumours afoot.

The Bridgefoots and the Bellamys, both more than delighted at the sudden reversal of the situation with regard to Poppy and Nick, also had enough common sense to play it down and not interfere. It was to Charles and Charlie that the two reunited youngsters looked for support and understanding, because once Easter Monday itself was past, they were having difficulty in coming to terms with the surprise and suddenness of their re-conciliation. It had all been very queer. Both of them had been through a very traumatic period.

Nick tried to explain how he felt. He had, he said, a peculiar illusion that the last three or four years had been clipped out of his life. He *knew* what had happened during those years, in the same way that you know what you've been dreaming, but like a dream when you wake up, it no longer seems as real as it did while you were asleep. He and Poppy had returned to reality at the same point at which, with regard to each other, they had been during the summer before his accident; they were having to pick up their relationship again from there. But the intervening experience had changed both in subtle ways they had to find out, about themselves as well as about each other.

It was easier for other people to understand how his experience had affected Nick than it was to see why Poppy had behaved as she had; even her mother hadn't understood what she had been through, though Nigel had seemed to know by instinct what she had suffered and why she had wanted to keep Nick at arm's length in the time before that awful Monday when she had bolted because she could take no more.

Charlie had done a lot of thinking about it, the feyness she had inherited from her fenland ancestry giving her a bit more insight than a lot of girls her age might have had. She tried to explain to Charles what a dreadful experience the succession of traumatic incidents in Poppy's lifetime had mounted up to, all put together, and which had begun as far back as the time Marjorie's twins had left school. That was the point when they had begun to show differences, for though till that time they had been encouraged to be seen to be the identical twins, they were not. Poppy, as the

382

more amenable of the two, had been persuaded till then to follow the trend for private education and horses to be the symbols of their father's 'success', which suited Pansy. It had been Poppy who had had to keep her sister's guilty secret about going to bed with Robert Fairey – while at the same time being forbidden to speak even to Nick. When he had been knocked out by the van and had disappeared from view, she had not dared to show that she cared.

Her dream had vanished, and then had turned into nightmare. She had actually been with her mother on that terrible New Year's Eve when, through a bedroom door at Bailey's vulgar party, they had both seen her drink-sodden father 'having it off' with his fancy woman . . . and Poppy had had to bear the brunt of the immediate shock to her mother.

They had gone straight from that party, stunned as her mother had been, to keep the promise Marjorie had given to her father to be at the special New Year's Eve service at the church; and there, for the first time since his accident, Poppy had encountered Nick, who did not recognize her and politely ignored her. (Nobody had thought to tell her that he was suffering from complete amnesia!) She, in her own state of shock, had taken his behaviour as proof that, as she had been told, since his grandfather had turned up and claimed him he had withdrawn himself from all his childhood associates. In vain thereafter did Charles try to tell her the sad truth that Nick knew nobody. She was in no state to believe anything but that her mother and father were separating, and even contemplating divorce. Then her father had been killed, and as village gossip soon had it, her mother had consoled herself with Eric Choppen.

Utterly disillusioned, in self-defence, she had invented another sweetheart 'at college' – of whom Nick had heard and put his own interpretation upon when after Charles and Charlie's wedding, Poppy had apparently been doing her best to give him the push. He had believed that to be because he had been, and was still to some extent, damaged physically and mentally. He had been glad to escape any further emotional distress by getting away from it all with his grandfather.

Charlie, discussing them with Charles, had declared that it was

383

no wonder Poppy had acted so strangely – or both of them, if it came to it. That their thoughts for the future were once more centred around each other now was clear – but it was almost as if they had gone back to being the unsophisticated and innocent children they had been at sixteen. There was no more urgency about their relationship now than there had been then. They'd had to school themselves to wait, then, and they seemed to want to live through the missing years now as they would have had to then, if the drama hadn't overtaken them. They wanted to make the most of their adolescent dreams and romance.

'It's just as if we were back in the old days, and might find Robert and Pansy in the next room at any minute,' Nick told Charles. 'As if we have just gone on from where we were then. Now we're sure of each other, it doesn't seem to matter, somehow.'

Charles listened with a sympathy he didn't wholly understand. He certainly hadn't been content to wait when there was no reason to. But people differed. He admitted that.

'Charlie's father knows how you feel,' he said. 'He said yesterday he'd always known it would "come right" for you, and that it's no good anybody thinking they know best what you should do now. And he said more or less what you've just said – that without knowing it you're still half waiting for Robert and Pansy to come back and make the set up before you can start the dance. That we should all keep out of it and let you get used to it as it is now. Robert's gone for ever, but Pansy isn't, and Bob said nobody should forget that Poppy and she are twins who grew up almost like two halves of the same person. He thinks Poppy can't plan properly for anything till she knows what's happening to Pansy. Charlie agrees with her father. So as long as you're not worrying, perhaps it is best to let things just take their time.'

Nick was quite happy to do so. Part of his motivation was to prove to everybody that he could manage without relying too much on Effendi. Loving support he would welcome – but he wanted to show he could stand on his own feet. He went back to London after the next weekend, and Poppy soon afterwards returned to college, with a new incentive to work. Marjorie, considerably cheered by Poppy, became even more worried about Pansy. It was being borne in upon all the family that there was more to Pansy's complete silence than they yet knew. But all was unusually quiet.

Lacking other excitement, the sale of the old school became the talking point, with the undertow of complaint that was to be expected. Because the whole project had been eased through the legal stages, even planning permission, without much fuss, most people had not accepted it as anything more than a rumour till Eric's workmen actually appeared on the scene.

At that point, Nigel took his congregation into his confidence, and explained to them that it was a fact, made possible by an 'anonymous donor' who had bought the property and given it back to the church. There were one or two conditions – that the donor's name should never be disclosed, and that for the next fifty years the donor had the right to choose the tenant of the largest ground-floor flat. The rector hoped that Mary Budd Close might be given the status of a charity, as almshouses had been in the past.

'Just fancy!' said Sophie next morning. 'Wouldn't Miss ha' been pleased! But you can't never please everybody. There's some as are grumbling a'ready and saying whoever it is as is give the money should ha' done it proper, so as there weren't no picking and choosing about who should live there, 'cos that were bound to cause trouble. Them as think they know everything are saying as nothing shouldn't ha' been done till we all knowed the rules as to who can and who can't be let live there. Some say as only church folk should, not chapel folks or them as don't go nowhere. Some think only them born in the parish ought to be considered. And some 'old as nobody as didn't go to Miss's school ought to be allowed to live in a place named after 'er. Thirz' 'as got it all worked out in 'er mind who it was as found the money, and says if she's right 'e's the one to 'ave first say in it, and that being so, it'll most likely be her and Dan gets it first. She reckons as she gets short o' breath gooing up 'er stairs, and a flat is just what she needs.'

Fran was flabbergasted. If Thirzah really had got such a fantastic notion into her head, there were difficulties ahead that none of them had foreseen. It must also indicate that Thirzah's deranged state of mind could no longer be doubted.

'Have you talked to her lately?' she asked Sophie rather anxiously. 'I didn't know you'd even seen her again since Easter Sunday!'

'No – well you ain't 'ad much time to talk to me since then, hev you? You're both been stuck away in them studies as if you'd got something to be ashamed of. I should ha' told you, do I'd 'ad the chance. The new doctor stopped me one day soon after that Sunday, and asked if I'd been to see Thirz'. 'E said 'e'd like us to, and 'ow it was quite likely as she wouldn't remember nothing. So we asked Dan, and 'e asked 'er whether we should be welcome, and she said she was willing to forgive and forget what me and Het 'ad done to 'er, but not Joe as 'ad smashed all 'er best china. So by that we thought we'd better 'umour 'er. She were as right as rain, and went on about the school, and this 'ere monogamous donor, as she said couldn't be nobody but George Bridgefoot. After all, she said, 'e'd made a lot o' money as 'e didn't hev no right to by turning old Esther Palmer out of 'er house and 'ome, and she didn't wonder as 'is conscience wasn't easy. "So tha's why them places is got to be kept for us old folk, 'specially such as me as can't get up and down stairs no more," she said. "George knows he should ha' done more for me and Dan when 'e give up and robbed Dan of 'is job. If 'e don't make it up to us by seeing as we get that place as ain't got no stairs, 'e'll hev thorns in 'is pillow for the rest of 'is life."

'We just set and let 'er talk. Nobody said her nay. We know very well as Dan wouldn't never want it, but we do think Thirz may be right about it being George as is give it.'

Fran felt disturbed by this silly but unexpected development. 'I hope Thirzah hasn't set her heart on it,' she said. 'Goodness knows what it may do to her if she's disappointed. Nobody knows who gave the money!'

'Somebody does,' Sophie answered serenely. ''Im as give it does, and the rector. They say George 'as to be a trustee by law 'cos 'e's the rector's warden, and the doctor, though what a newcomer like 'im 'as got to do with it, I myself can't make out.'

William, inclined to be amused, said that they might have expected it. Fran replied that it was a good thing there would be four flats. Aunt Sar'anne only needed one.

386

'Are you suggesting that the trustees install Thirzah and Sar'anne under one roof?' he asked. 'That would be asking for trouble! I must warn Nigel. We should have known there would be a lot of speculation about the donor. Sophie's got one thing right. If ever a modern man could be said to be monogamous, it's him.'

'Your logic is as faulty as your grammar,' she said, laughing. 'How does anyone know it's a "he"? Are donors always male?'

'In this case, it's Sophie's logic that's at fault,' he said. 'It was a judge in the USA who was the real donor – as likely to be a woman these days as a man, and whether monogamous or not I haven't a clue.' He was so relaxed and casual about it that Fran wondered why she couldn't be. It would sort itself out in time.

Meanwhile, it was a hot topic in the village. Beryl Bean was as sure of the identity of the donor as Thirzah was. 'Who could it be, only that there undertaker from London, Jane Hadley's father?' she said. 'If undertakers ain't got guilty consciences, they ought to have – the money they make out o' folks when they're in trouble. Daylight robbery, funerals is.'

Elyot learned, via Terence and much to his chagrin, that he was the favourite candidate for the honour, and said as much to William in the presence of Eric and Nigel, who both enjoyed the joke enormously. Apart from William and Fran and the solicitor, through whom all communication was to be made, they were the only people who knew the truth. Elyot didn't. At the request of the 'monogamous donor', not even the other two trustees were to be informed. So the rumblings rumbled on, the spring sprang into being, and the restoration went purposefully ahead. The school was being turned into four very desirable little dwellings.

Nigel consulted William about a date for the inevitable opening ceremony, so that he could advertise for applications for the tenancies. He realized that this stage would put a bit of a strain on William and Fran, but he really didn't see how it could be avoided. He felt sure he could rely on the bishop to perform a ceremony such as unlocking the door with a specially gilded key, as usual. Would that do?

William said he supposed so, though they would rather not have been consulted. Nigel laughed. 'You two aren't well enough versed in conspiracy. There has to be an official opening – at which you must be conspicuously present. You couldn't not be there to pay your respects to the memory of Miss Budd without giving the game away, could you? Everybody with a bank account is suspected of being the culprit.'

All very well, and they saw the point; but Fran's mind would rush forward to anticipate trouble, especially for Sophie, because of Thirzah's fantastic theories. 'Have you agreed how you will choose the lucky tenants?' she asked. 'Who will be eligible, and so on? If the very old have to make applications themselves, they won't bother. They'll mistrust forms to fill in, think what a commotion moving would cause them, and stay where they are rather than go to any trouble. On the other hand, if anybody suggested doing it for them, they'd be offended. They'd take that either as interference or too clear a hint that somebody wanted to get rid of them. Couldn't they have to be recommended, and if put on a selected shortlist, only at that point asked whether or not they want to be considered? Aunt Sar'anne wouldn't apply – but Elyot knows our situation regarding her, and would recommend her. She'd be a bit hard put to it to refuse it, then.'

Nigel welcomed the suggestion. 'It's surprising how difficult it is to give anybody anything,' he said. 'They always think there must be a catch in it. I think your idea is brilliant. It would prevent us getting applications from people trying to get something for nothing, and though such a scheme might be open to corruption, I can't think there's much risk of George or Dr Hardy taking bribes. How right Yorkshire people are in saying "There's nowt so queer as folk."'

It pleased Elyot to do anything he could to help ease them of their burden of an uninvited permanent guest, besides being glad of the chance to demonstrate that he was not the 'monogamous donor'. So finally there came an evening when Nigel called at Benedict's and asked to see Mrs Potts – to inform her that Mr Franks had recommended her for consideration as one of the tenants of the new flats, and the trustees had decided, on the grounds that she was by far the oldest applicant and her present accommodation was only temporary, that she should be given the first refusal of the best one.

Mrs Potts was not overjoyed. 'That's only a bit o' eye-wash, that is,' she cackled when she reported to Fran and William after Nigel had left. 'It's just them smarmy church folk making out how fair and above-board it all is. I know 'em. When it comes to it, they'll find some reason why it can't be me. You'll see. I needn't worrit myself, and more needn't you, 'cos I shan't hev to go. I were born chapel, and shall die chapel, like my folks afore me. Besides, they know as I'm all right where I am. But if they was to let me have it, it wouldn't half be a crowner for Thirz'! I'd take it just to do her one in the eye!'

'That's torn it,' said Fran, after Aunt Sar'anne had withdrawn. 'I had a feeling we were in for trouble. She isn't going to leave us without a fuss.'

'She'll have to,' said William shortly. 'Thirzah's intervention may help.' Something was getting on William's nerves again, and Fran was edgy in consequence.

'And what if they get at each other's throats about it? It would send Sophie round the bend, and upset our applecart!' she said.

'It hasn't happened yet. I told you. It's that family vendetta still going on, and will till one of them's dead. But that isn't our fault, and is nothing to do with us.'

Fran felt storms in the air again, though she didn't know why. However hard she tried, it seemed she was like the snail that laboriously climbed four feet up a wall only to slip down three again. For some reason, it was all getting to be too much fuss about nothing, making her depressed. She was irritated with William for not seeing the shadow that the forthcoming opening event was already casting before it.

'How can you say that?' she retorted. 'It's everything to do with us! So are the consequences. What on earth should we do without Sophie – or her without us? It's all very well for you!'

He turned to face her, stung by her critical tone. 'Well, I like that! I give away a fortune to please you, and all the thanks I get is that you blame me for the unlikely possibility that we may lose our daily help!'

Now he really had pulled the wrong string. Her voice went cold. 'Are you by any chance referring to Sophie?' she asked, spilling pump water down his spine. 'Because to me, Sophie is much, much more than a daily help. I consider her a friend. And

389

you didn't give away a fortune to please me. As a matter of fact, I knew nothing about it till you'd got it all cut and dried.'

He could hardly believe his ears. 'But Fran – surely you didn't want the bloody money? You said you didn't! That's why I kept the whole thing secret.'

'No, of course I didn't want the money. But I'd have liked to be told, or even consulted. You might have known that dealing with it in such an underhand way would make me wonder why. You knew I would support you. I suppose because I'm now only your wife, you took my agreement for granted.'

He had gone white, and she knew the signs, but she couldn't stop.

'I don't normally keep secrets from you, do I?'

'No – only those about anything to do with your other wife!' (She saw him flinch, and hated herself, but the words on her tongue would not be stayed.) 'Are we never going to be rid of her? I'm fed up to the back teeth with keeping secrets, but you seem to love it. Especially about her. If the memory of her is so precious to you that you want to keep it to yourself, for God's sake say so. I won't ask any more questions.'

'Don't be such a jealous fool, Fran. You're just being childish. It isn't like you.'

'No, any more than taking such a step without a word to me is like you!' she flared. 'Look what it's done so far! Got us involved in village argument of the sort we both hate. Mixed us up in a feud that doesn't worry you at all because it proves a historical point for you to say it's left over from something going back for generations – and which if you're right will probably end in Aunt Sar'anne either dying here on us or having to go into an old folks' home after all. Then I should feel guilty for the rest of my life. I haven't felt guilty about Janice for a long time, but if I dare let myself dwell on this, I shall. I've been wondering why things haven't been like they used to be with us. Now I know what I do know, I suspect a lot of it is because of her, and this damn money.'

'You always have been suspicious!'

'I shouldn't need to be, if you didn't play everything about her so close to your chest.'

She knew how unfair to him she was being, but resentment

was bubbling up inside her and she couldn't keep it down. 'Why did you do it like that, William? Why?' He saw that she was going to cry, but for once it had no effect on him. What on earth had he done to deserve this? 'I don't know. You're so suspicious I can't keep up with you. You're asking questions you know perfectly well I can't answer. Why do such things happen? I suppose it's fate.'

'Fate? What do you mean by fate? Somebody once said that the consequences of one's own actions are what men call fate.'

He stood up, and looked the way he was feeling. Was she deliberately trying to pick a quarrel with him? If so, she hadn't chosen a good time. He didn't for once feel at all propitiatory. She thought that never before had she ever seen him so fed up with her.

'Another of your bloody quotations? Can't you ever say anything without quoting? Is your mind so second-hand that you always have to rely on somebody else having said anything worth saying first? They irritate me past bearing – especially when you don't know who you're quoting. The next time you quote at me, I shall walk out on you. There's a limit to what any man can stand.'

She looked so offended, so affronted, so hurt, that now he wanted desperately to retreat, but didn't know how to. It was all so unexpected, and so unbelievably puerile. But there was no doubt how truly upset she was. He began to feel it must be his fault.

'Whoever it was that did say it was right for once,' he said. 'I agree that this is the consequence of my own actions – in ever marrying her at all, for ever thinking I could get rid of her, for ever believing you loved me enough to forgive me, and certainly for ever expecting that whatever I did with the money would please anybody. Only a complete idiot would have tried to give it away. Nobody in his right mind these days tries to get rid of *money*. Robin Drake told me I was mad, and I know Eric agrees with him. Maybe Nigel does, as well, but I didn't expect you to! I thought we agreed that the things we think worth having, no amount of money can buy. One reason I was in such a hurry to get rid of it was lest it should prove the precious bane the Bible says it is.'

'Who's doing the quoting now?'

'Well, at least I know where it comes from.'

It was all so childish that she looked, and he felt, that at any moment she might slap him. He tried hard to regain some self-control. 'It's too late for me to change anything,' he said. 'I shall have to go through with it now, but I'll be damned if I'll go to an opening ceremony and play the hypocrite in public! Or anything else they've planned. As to us – if you'll just tell me what it is you want me to do, I'll do it and then clear out and leave you and your precious Sophie together, like you were before I gate-crashed. If you've had enough just lately, so have I. I thought we'd got over it, but it's obvious that we haven't. Our guardian angel's deserted us. The Burbages will not be at home in future.'

Fran looked up towards the picture that wasn't there. She had never felt so utterly desolate before in all her life, and burst into a fit of the most passionate weeping he had ever witnessed. He didn't know how to bear it, but as he had no idea what had caused the idiotic quarrel, he had none as to how to stop it. She could keep it up for hours, and he knew he couldn't take it. He was so nearly out of his mind with despair that if it went on he'd be ill again. *Had* he given her any cause? He must have done, though he certainly hadn't meant to. That damned old woman always there had soured everything for them. And if he could think in those terms of their poor, dependent old lodger, perhaps he was guilty of everything Fran accused him of being.

He had been daft to rush into the business of the old school before telling her anything about it. He'd thought he was doing it to save her any anxiety – but he knew now that his real reason had been that he didn't want to bring up any mention of Janice. He now saw the futility of trying to do the impossible. Janice would always be there in her memory, whatever he said or did. It was probably the knowledge of that which had allowed him to let her goad him into retaliating. But he needn't have been so nasty. She didn't usually react like this, and he began to wonder if she was ill, or had some family worry she hadn't told him about.

There was no way he could un-say things he'd said, which only made him feel angrier than ever. He stood silent, looking down on the crumpled heap of womanhood he wouldn't have recognized as his Fran if she hadn't been sitting in her chair (opposite his) in the sitting-room that had been 'theirs' till a few minutes ago, and in which if he didn't somehow put things right quick there would be no place for him in future. If it was her pride that was telling him to go, his pride wouldn't let him stay. He was too much in her debt already. That was the trouble. They knew each other too well – and he hadn't allowed for that dogged, characteristic East Anglian pride of hers.

Helpless, despairing anger rose up again till it almost choked him. Was she really prepared to give up all they'd had between them on a tiny matter of pride like this? Well, if she was, she wasn't what he had believed her to be, and they'd been living in a fools' paradise. It might as well come to an end here and now as later.

In the ensuing aching silence, Cat, who had been sitting at his feet gazing adoringly up at him, asked in that loving, subdued throaty voice of hers what was the matter, and why he didn't sit down again so that she could sit on his chest. Out of sheer habit, he bent and picked her up to soothe her, and her immediate purring response and the feel of her seemed to become the symbol of everything he was about to lose. She wasn't his cat. She was Fran's – his first gift to her when he had admitted to himself how much he loved her, and that now he had met her again life would never be the same without her. He had to suppose that she no longer felt the same about him – and he couldn't stay where she was if she didn't. He must *not* allow the memory of the time he had given her the kitten to break him down now.

Fran had looked up, and was thinking just the same thing. He was holding Cat, but not in his usual loving, caressing way. Fran had a momentary glimpse of the indignation in Cat's glorious violet eyes at such treatment before he suddenly thrust her away from him, and threw her bodily into Fran's lap. 'Your cat, I believe, Mrs Catherwood,' he said.

Fran grabbed at Cat, but dropped her, and sprang to her feet facing him, spitting anger. 'How dare you  –' she began, but words choked her. She caught her breath on a sob, and couldn't get it back. She sought desperately to find her handkerchief, pressed the little scrap of cambric to her mouth, but still coughed and spluttered till he feared she was in real trouble, perhaps even in danger. He moved to help her, and trod heavily on Cat as he turned Fran round and hit her on the back between the shoulders much harder than he had meant to. She staggered, took the hankie from her mouth and gave way. Cat had let out such a yowl as she had never before uttered, and streaked out of the door with a bottle-brush tail big enough, as Fran said afterwards, to have cleaned a flue with. The sob that had got stuck in her throat had turned itself into the bubble of mirth that always lurked close to the surface, and she began to laugh half hysterically, peal upon peal, till she felt weak at the knees and put out both her hands to seek support from William. As his arms closed round her, he began to laugh as well. They laughed in unison, relief being too much for either to be able to stop. He led her to his chair, sank into it and pulled her down on to his knee, but it was a considerable time before they regained any semblance of middle-aged decorum.

With her face on his chest they gradually resumed some normality. 'Oh, my darling, my darling, are you all right, now?' he asked.

She sat up and nodded, wiping her face with the little wet ball that had once been a crisply laundered and folded handkerchief. 'Of course I am. Don't worry, sweetheart, please! Whatever happened to us? I just don't know what got into me! Unless it was that we had both been bottling things up till something had to give. It was all my fault! I didn't mean a word of it. I'm so sorry.'

'Nor did I,' he said. 'Whatever could have made us behave like that!'

She shook her head, and said again, 'I've no idea. Fate, I suppose.'

'Oh, don't make me laugh again, please!' he said. 'Not if you love me. I can't laugh any more. It hurts too much.' He hid his face against her and she stroked his head and kissed his hair till he raised his mouth to her instead, and tears began to slide down both their faces.

They were both so utterly exhausted by that unexpected journey across such Himalayan peaks of emotion they could do nothing but sit, she in her own chair and he at her feet, till exhaustion turned into lassitude of the languorous kind that a roaring fire induces in a weary traveller on a cold winter night. It was very late before they moved, going to bed without bothering even to make their customary bedtime drink.

'I love you,' he said. 'More than ever before. Quote all you like – I love it. You wouldn't be my Fran if you didn't, and I couldn't bear it. Because you are mine, now and for ever.'

'Go to sleep,' she said, stroking his face. 'We must have caught our guardian angel napping.'

'He doesn't like Aunt Sar'anne being here,' he murmured, 'any more than I do.'

'She won't be, much longer,' Fran replied. 'Not a minute longer than I can help. Go to sleep.' He took a deep, sighing breath of content, and did. Just like that.

Remembrance returned the moment she opened her eyes next morning, bringing a flood of contrition. There had to be reasons why she was acting so much out of character. Perhaps it was that she was, after all, at 'that age'.

She despised women who made a fuss, and once over thirty-five made their age the excuse for every little tantrum or indisposition till they turned sixty. She'd often been very scathing on the subject, blaming the modern mania for giving anything even remotely connected with sex far too much attention. The menopause, like pregnancy, was a perfectly natural process. But trying to account for her irrational outburst yesterday made her wonder if it did have something to do with her recent depression, and what applied to her might equally apply to Sophie. Thirzah's breakdown might have started from it, too, for all she knew. Perhaps she had been a bit too dismissive of it, but to know one's enemy was half the battle. She'd seek medical help if she had to, but she wouldn't indulge in such dramatic contretemps at William's expense again.

She felt guilty and remorseful. She knew from past experience that he wouldn't, because he couldn't, bounce back from the quarrel as fast and as full of new energy as she would. It would take him several days to get over it, and she must do all she could to help. He was still asleep. She crept out of bed and stood looking down at his sleeping face. The pain of loving him so much was almost physical, and she longed to bend and kiss him – but that would rouse him and rob him of the rest and calm that were his best medicine. Let him sleep.

Early as it was, she got up and crept downstairs. She made herself her morning tea, and sat down to apply a clearer mind to the problem of inducing Sar'anne to accept the flat without causing Thirzah an apoplectic fit. She was thinking clearly now, with reason rather than emotion. This business of Janice's death and the disposal of the unexpected assets had thrown them into confusion because they were not yet adjusted to the modern world. In the matter of relationships and so-called 'morality' they were in as much confusion as Sophie was when confronted with metric instead of imperial measures.

Times changed, but people didn't do it at the drop of a hat. She suddenly saw, quite clearly, that she and William had from the very beginning been both as unable and as unwilling to change their outlook on the matter of their relationship, particularly with regard to guilt feelings towards or concerning Janice, as Sophie was to deal with grammes instead of the ounces she had always been used to. She herself had been as unwilling to let go of the old, especially as far as living in an old community went, as William had. They'd converted because they had to – but they still thought in the old ways first. Time had changed the nature of the old community, but it hadn't changed the individuals who, put together, made up the new. William had acted by the rules of the past, when for all sorts of reasons he'd had to keep Janice and all that pertained to her under wraps. By 'modern' standards, they had no obligation to old Sar'anne, yet they'd let her get under their skins to the point at which she'd nearly broken them apart. She herself had been too soft-hearted, and William too secretive, because they weren't willing to throw away the old and embrace the new without protest. But desperate maladies required desperate remedies, and yesterday's malady had indeed been desperate.

They had to get it straight now, before it had time to infect any but themselves. William had acted in a typically male way –

yesterday's way. He had not expected his magnanimous plan to rid himself of the last remnants of Janice to be derailed by the personal antipathy of two silly old women – a statement that itself needed examination. One of them was thirty years older than the other, but both belonged to an age when change had been a slow process. That's what led William to say their antipathy went back to a generation-old family quarrel. But while she was glad that the community still retained a lot of old and trusted values, it now had to exist in the modern, postwar world. As the personnel within it changed, so did the values. She and William couldn't cling entirely to the old, as they had been unconsciously trying to do.

William's customary secrecy about Janice, a bit of old-fashioned morality left over from the past, no longer applied to a modern ruthless society of brittle relationships wherein it was everyone for himself and the State take the hindermost. There was a large sum of money involved, and nowadays money was god. Neither she nor William wanted to abandon the old and give in wholly to the new, so compromise was the only way out. If this particular matter were not to get worse, it had to be stopped now, this very day, before any details of it leaked out – especially of any dissension between Thirzah (ill) and Sar'anne (old) as to which of them should get the best flat. The situation needed a touch of old-fashioned feminine guile rather than male common sense.

It wasn't evenly balanced. Sar'anne was old only in years. Thirzah was old in mind. Fran was struck by that thought. Was what was the matter with Thirzah possibly the onset of premature senile dementia?

Old people did become stubborn. They resented giving up the reins of their lives to anybody – family, friends, or 'the Welfare'. Fran was sympathetic towards Aunt Sar'anne, but there was no sense in giving in to her. Her presence in their house had not been meant to be permanent. William had provided splendid alternative accommodation, and she must be made to take it.

Thirzah was a different case. She'd always been masterful, used to getting her own way because those closest to her had taken the course of least resistance. As a result, she had become a complete tyrant, a dictator, a female Caligula. Now that her mind was failing, she was a positive danger. If William's plan of action was not to be completely nullified by her unreasonable antipathy to her aged aunt, something had to be done quickly. Aunt Sar'anne must be prevented at once from springing out of her lair like a spider, as soon as she heard Sophie's voice, to break the news of Nigel's visit and thereby 'get her blow in fust'.

William appeared, looking, as she had expected, washed out. She had no time to begin a long discussion with him, but she had to ask one or two questions.

'Darling – I don't want to open yesterday up again, but the matter's urgent if we aren't going to let this silly business between Sar'anne and Thirzah wreck everything. You've done your best. Will you let me try to nip this in the bud?'

He was only too glad to. He wasn't prone to headaches, but he had got up with a bad one this morning. To be alone in his study would be the quickest way to get rid of it. He told her so, adding that he trusted her absolutely.

'Then may I change your instructions a bit, and let George and Terence know the truth? It isn't fair on them to have to work in the dark, and I may need help from both of them. They're called trustees; we ought to be able to trust them.'

'We can,' he said. 'It was only for your sake I kept everything so dark.'

'Right,' she said. 'Leave it to me. Have your breakfast, go into your study and stay there. I'm about to play the conspirator, with a lot of white lies thrown in. As far as Sophie and Sar'anne will know, you have a bilious attack. You are, and always will be Galahad – well, up to a certain point – but for today I'm going to be Morgan la Faye, and full of wicked woman's wiles.'

He kissed her, blessed her common sense, and went.

She needed an ally, and it had to be Sophie the all-too-truthful. She would have to lay her cards on the table and pray that Sophie would see reason; but before she came, Fran had to deal with Sar'anne. She went to the door of Eeyore's Tail, and told Sar'anne that William was ill and it would be wise for her to stay where she was today. When the old woman began to argue, Fran informed her bluntly that she had no option. She must not expose herself to infection.

Now for Sophie. 'Hello, Sophie,' she said when she arrived shortly after. 'Don't stop to change into your apron. I need to talk to you straight away – in my study. The kitchen's too close to the keyhole, and I think your aunt will get earache before the day's out. There's nothing wrong, honestly. Bring your things in with you while I make us a cup of tea.'

If there was one thing that Sophie loved, it was to be taken secretly into Fran and William's confidence. She made no demur, and once she was settled, Fran began to talk. Without letting on that they knew more than anybody else about the donor, she told Sophie about the rector's visit last evening. In view of what Sophie had told her of Thirzah's expectations, it looked as if there might be trouble. Aunt Sar'anne had made it plain that the only reason she'd leave Benedict's willingly would be to do Thirzah's hopes down. It was Thirzah who had turned her out into the street. She wanted to have a bit of her own back.

'Now,' Fran said, 'Dr Hardy has made it plain that if Thirzah has another turn like the last, he can't answer for the consequences. I'm afraid the news of this genuine offer to Aunt Sar'anne, when she's set her heart on having the new flat, will cause her to flip again. It's up to me and you to prevent that if we possibly can.'

'I never took much 'eed o' what Thirz' said,' said Sophie, looking helpless. 'I knowed as Dan wouldn't move. 'E were born there! 'E won't want no flat nor yet no charity. So I never thought no more would come of it, 'cos I never expected Thirz' to be put in for it. Seems she 'as been. She told me so last night. She reckons it's the doctor as done it 'cos 'e knows 'ow bad she is. But I never expected Aunt to be give it, either, and what that'll do to Thirz' when she 'ears of it don't bear thinking about.'

To Fran's surprise, she went on, wisely and sensibly and without getting upset. 'It don't take no doctor to see as she can't go on as she is. Since that last do, we're all knowed as it's only a matter o' time afore it 'appens again, and she may hev to be took away. If that's the will of 'Im Above we must abide by it.

'And sorry to say it as I am, she can't be let to go on getting worse. She's been making our lives a misery for too long as it is. It were 'er as persuaded Mam not to let Jelly come courting

399

me – 'cos she were married, and Het were courting, and if I'd been married an' all, she'd ha' 'ad to 'elp look after Mam. When Jelly was killed, 'er conscience pricked 'er so she 'ad to make 'erself believe as she 'ad done right. She's like that. She believes what it suits 'er to. Like she did about Wendy – never give the poor gel a chance, and it's a wonder it didn't kill Joe, what with one thing and another. And as for Dan, 'e ain't 'alf 'ad a packet with 'er! I'm sure I don't know 'ow 'e's stood it. 'E couldn't ha' done if it 'adn't been for George.

'You see, Dan 'ad all'us been sweet on Joe's sister Em'ly, but she died o' diptheria just afore they was going to get married. Then Thirz' set 'er cap at 'im, and 'e didn't care much what 'appened, so 'e married 'er. Poor ol' Dan! 'E did 'ope 'e'd 'ave some child'en, but Thirz never fell. P'raps it's all to the good, as things 'ave turned out. But I don't see what we can do.'

'Aunt Sar'anne doesn't want to go anywhere,' said Fran, 'but she'll soon have to, and this flat is a godsend. We've got to make her take it, and persuade Thirzah to change her mind. I have an idea, but it depends on you being willing to help me.' The look of indignation at being doubted that Sophie turned on her would have made a rogue elephant wince. Fran understood it. 'Even if it means pretending things that aren't true?'

Sophie hadn't expected that, and didn't reply immediately. Instead, she sat silently contemplating the hands lying folded in her lap. Whether she was consulting the Almighty or Jelly, Fran couldn't decide. There didn't seem to her to be a lot of difference, as far as Sophie was concerned. She waited.

'Fran,' Sophie said, looking up with her eyes so clear and deep that Fran felt she could almost see through them into eternity, 'I wouldn't goo against 'ow I was brought up or do nothing as I thought was wrong for nobody, only you. But I remember when Miss asked me to – to 'elp 'er to settle things between 'im and you that day 'e come back 'ome, as went against everything as I'd all'us believed in. Miss made me see as it were right, and I'm never doubted as I done right. What do you want me to do now?'

'Tell lies – you to Thirzah and me to Aunt Sar'anne. I'll tell her that I've heard if she doesn't take first offer, Thirzah will get the

400

flat. You tell Thirzah you know that if she goes to live in the flat, George has promised Aunt Sar'anne she can have their cottage. I think that should settle it both ways.'

Sophie's eyes were shining when she looked up. 'I reckon you know 'em both as well as I do,' she said. 'Do you want me to go back to Thirz's now, straight off?'

'Might as well,' Fran said. 'You've still got your coat on.'

Fran watched her go, and then went in to put William wise. She was, as he said, a constant delight to him, even if she did occasionally cast him into her own fiery furnace.

'There's just one snag,' he said. 'You've involved George, without his consent.'

'Not without thinking,' she said. 'That's why I wanted to be able to tell him the truth, and why we are interfering. My guess is that he'll be tickled by my stratagem. He'll sympathize with us about Sar'anne, because of the trouble Esther Palmer caused Brian and Rosemary, and he'll do it for Dan. Besides, he'll play if only to please me. I'm going to catch him straight away, before any of it leaks out to Beryl Bean. Oh – and I've thought of something else. I think we ought to ask Nigel to hold up the opening ceremony till we know about the Summer Exhibition. Greg's bound to want us to go with him to the private view, and ten to one they'll coincide. Don't let's risk it.'

He'd forgotten his headache. 'Whatever you say, my Oracle,' he agreed.

Fran went first to the old surgery, asked to see Terence on a non-medical matter, and was asked to wait. He finished his surgery, and invited her into his consulting-room. She began by asking him how Anthea was, and had the pleasure of seeing him flush. Everything was going as well as could be hoped or expected, he said. He was taking nothing for granted, but – well, life was worth living again. He had hopes. They were being very discreet, which was frustrating but, they thought, wise. Anthea didn't want her story to be common knowledge, and in that he was prepared to back her. It was enough for him to know that behind the scars was a woman with a spirit as unscarred and appealing as her beautiful face. What held him back, if anything, was that she had been so badly hurt by the man she thought had loved her, and that he had failed other women three times. Dare he trust himself not to do it again? So far, they hadn't spent enough time together for either to be sure of the next step.

'You need a little assistance from your friends, I think,' Fran said. 'It's time Greg and Jess got us all together. They'll have good reason to throw a party soon, when the Summer Exhibition opens, if not before. Or perhaps Beth could find some reason for celebration. Just at present, William and I have reasons for keeping ourselves out of the limelight a bit. That's what I came to see you about.'

She proceeded to put him in possession of all the facts, including her bit of subterfuge with Thirzah and Sar'anne. He showed a professional ability not to let his feelings show at the disclosure of William as 'the man', and with regard to Thirzah told her that he was afraid that her surmise on premature dementia might be correct, though of course he couldn't discuss another patient with her.

'However, as a Mary Budd trustee, and especially now I am in possession of the facts, I see no reason for not telling you that as far as I know her name hasn't been put forward at all. It must be another of her deranged fantasies, if she truly thinks she stands any chance of being the specially selected tenant. She, of course, believes in her fantasies. That's the danger. When her fancied hopes are frustrated, she has a tendency towards violence, as we know. At present, there's little I can do but keep an eye on her and give her mild sedatives. Is there any reason for the antagonism towards Mrs Potts?'

Fran explained William's theory, which he could hardly credit, but was interested to hear all the same. 'You learn a lot in a place like this, where you really get to know your patients,' he said. 'Especially about yourself. Luckily, Mrs Bates seems to have forgotten that at first I was anathema to her as one of the original sons of Belial! I let it upset me, and failed to connect it with any mental confusion on her part. I ought to have been a better doctor. Her obsession with my failed marriages should have given me a clue. It isn't uncommon for women whose sexual feelings have been repressed over a long period to dwell on sex almost exclusively in senility. I am afraid that it may be a sad case of dementia praecox.'

'Poor old Thirzah,' Fran said. 'We mustn't be too hard on her. She played her part in keeping you with us, and bringing you and Anthea together. Keep it up. I must be off now to see if I can catch George.'

She came upon him leaning over a five-barred gate, pulling the cows' ears and feeding them tit-bits. Fran joined in. After cats, she considered cows, especially these soft-eyed, velvet-muzzled Jerseys, the most beautiful of all animals, partly because their breath always smelled so sweet, as if they had been eating the very essence of spring. Daisy licked her as she leaned on the gate and told George what she had gone to tell him. He made no comment, but his placid manner indicated that the identity of the donor was no great surprise to him, and his reaction to the Thirzah–Sar'anne situation showed only a regretful acceptance of what might have been expected.

'I knowed a bit about that,' he said. 'Dan's been up to tell me. When Sophie told Thirz' this morning what you sent her to say about what you were supposed to have heard from me, Dan come rushing down here to ask me if it was the truth.

'"You know me better than that, Dan, surely," I said. "You know as I ain't one to go bladging about things as are secret, nor Fran Burbage neither. And as a trustee o' the school business, I have to be trusted to keep my mouth shut, if nothing else."

'"Ah!" says Dan. "And I reckon you know me well enough b'now to know as I shan't agree to go and live nowhere else. I were born in that cottage and I shall die there. So I knowed it couldn't be you as 'ad recommended us to be moved into one o' them fancy places with no upstairs nor no garden nor nothing as I'm been used to all my life. If Thirzah had set her heart on going, do she'd had the chance, she'd ha' had to goo by herself. I were just a-gooing to tell her so when Soph' went on to say how well everything had turned out like, and what a nice change it would be for us at our time o' life, besides Aunt Sar'anne being able to settle into my place, after all these year of not heving no place of her own. I couldn't believe my own ears – but I were nearly frit

403

by seeing what it done to Thirz'. She 'eld 'er breath till she were scarlet in the face and looked as if she'd bust before she could get the words out.

'"Then she started – just like she all'us does when she gets in one o' her tempers. 'Her come to live 'ere?' she bust out. 'That she shall not. Ain't I said as that woman shall never come over this doorstep again? I hev swore before the Lord of 'Osts as she shall never set foot in this 'ouse, and may 'E strike me dead if she ever do. But I knowed as George Bridgefoot never meant us no good,' she said – and a lot more as I shan't repeat. Well you know how she goes on once she's started. 'Put me out o' my 'ome as I come to when I was fust married 'e shall not, nor no rector nor doctor neither. I will not be moved out to let her come here,' she said – and she meant it, as I could see. Soph' done 'er best to calm her down, and tipped me the wink to come up and ask you to tell me the truth of it while she were still there to stop wi' Thirz'."

'"Well Dan," I said. "I don't know as I can. As far as I know, there ain't no truth to tell. It's just another of Thirz's fancies. So if I was you I should go home afore she hits Soph' over the head with the frying-pan, and tell her as it's nothing but a tale as is got about."'

'I am sorry I had to involve you,' Fran said. 'But I wanted you to know the truth, anyway. It was William who didn't want anybody to know – not even me in the first place. He was only trying to save me embarrassment, because it was his first wife's money. We had an awful row about it in the end. I hate having secrets to keep. At least I can share that one with you.'

They were both leaning with their arms on the gate. He put his right arm round her shoulders and drew her towards him. 'We've shared a lot of secrets before now, my gel,' he said. 'And there's nobody else I'd rather share mine with than you. So let me give you a bit of advice. I shall never tell nobody what I know no more than Daisy or Dora will – but if you ain't careful, you'll go on telling yourself lies about William. You must have showed him you were jealous of that woman you just called "his first wife" to make him do such a thing. She wasn't ever his wife, not like you are. She was only a woman as he went to bed with – and

404

because he's the man he is, he was daft enough to think he had to marry her to get her there. That don't make her into anything but a bought woman. About as much of a wife to him as any of King Solomon's three hundred concubines. It's always the same in wartime. Folks tie themselves to the wrong folk for the wrong reasons, like my poor Marjorie did, and thousands of others. Come and see Dora's calf, and then get back to your man. He'll be waiting for you. All's well that ends well.'

She found Sophie back at Benedict's, and they compared stories. 'I ain't seen Aunt Sar'anne, yet,' Sophie said. 'I reckon she's a-sulking. But I looked in on 'im when I got back. 'E were a'snoring, so I didn't wake 'im. We are only got cold meat and taters done in their jackets for dinner, so I made 'im 'is favourite apple-pie, and a Queen o' Puddings for Aunt. Will that do?'

Fran put out her hand to squeeze Sophie's across the table. 'Jelly's a very wise man,' she said. 'I'll bet he went with you every step between here and Thirzah's house, didn't he? And told you exactly what to say?'

There was no need for Sophie to answer. Fran appreciated the Almighty's ability to choose his deputies. They'd certainly served Him well this morning.

After the storm, the calm. A purposeful calm, everywhere. The rector, with George, had collected Aunt Sar'anne and taken her for a tour of inspection of her prospective home, and she had returned to Benedict's overwhelmed. After which, there was no more demur about her acceptance of the tenancy.

'Only I shall be lonely there,' she said. 'I'm been so happy here, with Soph' about and you to talk to about old times, and such.' Fran felt a twinge of guilt, and did her best to make the old lady believe that none of them had any intention of abandoning her just because she no longer lived in their house.

'I know as Soph'll do her best for me, so long as Thirz'll let

405

her. Takes after the other side o' her fam'ly, Soph' does. If it weren't for Thirz' we should be right enough.'

'Thirzah won't stop us from coming to see you, and taking you out now and again,' Fran promised. 'And in any case, it isn't quite ready for you to go into yet. The rector's having to wait to fix a date for the opening that will suit the bishop.'

That was a fib, but it served. The date was being held up so as not to clash with the opening of the Summer Exhibition. William and Fran had accepted Greg's invitation to be his special guests at the private view, and they were looking forward to it as they rarely looked forward to leaving home for any reason at this pleasant time of the year. They had reached a new plateau of mutual contentment.

'Darling,' said Fran to William when he put up his plate for a second helping of cabinet pudding made almost entirely of cream and brandy, 'ought you to? I don't know if I ought to let you! Sophie said only yesterday that you were putting on weight.'

'If she's right, it's only because I'd been losing it first, worrying myself to death about you. When you get down, my barometer falls to dangerous levels and betokens gales. It's set fair again now – for a long time to come, I think.'

She hoped he was right, and saw no reason to doubt him. The heavy clouds that had lain over all the village were lifting. It was only when Fran gave the matter some serious thought that she comprehended how stormy had been the time since 'Tilda's curse' had descended on them.

She said so to William. 'It's another new phase,' he said. 'We've had to deal with a whole batch of things one after another, and it's only the last few straws that begin to make the load too heavy. Looking back, I agree it has been a bit of a bumpy ride. Not just for us, but all round. Things have settled down.'

'Especially for Jess and Greg!' she said. 'Can you believe that Greg is the man you described to me before I'd ever met him as "that hopeless husband of Jess's"? A charming but feckless ne'er-do-well who couldn't keep your sister from starving without your help?'

'One learns,' he said. 'I was fed up by myself, and I didn't want him on my plate. What I didn't understand was that he'd given up trying, not for lack of ability, but for lack of encouragement after failure. Jess had killed his ambition by showing him she regarded him as a failure in every way, though she knew quite well who it was that had failed. She played the martyr so often that she'd very nearly become one. Only she was rapidly becoming a bitchy, jealous old cat as well. But to see her now —' He spread out his hands as if to demonstrate the impossibility of believing her to be the same woman.

'We didn't know the cause,' Fran said. 'We had no right to judge her, really. Our trouble was that we felt guilty about our association, and thought she was judging us. We can give ourselves a bit of credit for holding out and helping when we could – and the two of them a lot for forgiving and forgetting and grabbing a new start with both hands when the chance came.'

'Jonce has been the real saviour,' he said. 'I try not to think about that, because while Crystal lives there will always be a question mark over his future. The longer he's with them, the less chance she has of reclaiming him, but I wish it were legally settled. As I promised, I'll fight her through the courts if I have to, though Greg could afford to do it himself, now. Well, if he can't, it's only a question of time after this exhibition. I wonder what Jonce will turn out to be when he's a man? Who he'll take after?'

'That's been one of the bumps, hasn't it? One identity crisis after another. Why was that, do you think? Just chance, or fate, or whatever?'

'Something to do with modern society, perhaps. The young follow fashion in behaviour as they do in clothes. Whether or not they like tight jeans and long hair they'd rather be like everybody else than be seen to be different. So while they sow their wild oats all over the place, their parents, who were responsible for the hippies of the babyboom years, wonder where it will end. It'll be a wise child who'll know its own father in future. That may be why so many want to establish who they are before it's too late. I suppose if it comes to it we'd all rather be oak trees than tumble-weeds. Not that not knowing your own bloodline is any-thing new – especially among royalty and the aristocracy in general. It mattered then, because it was a question of passing on privilege. Does it now? It's only when it becomes a purely personal matter

407

that not knowing begins to chafe. I got myself in a sweat about it last year. I wanted to know who it was that I took after. I was lucky – chance let me find out. It made a difference to me if to nobody else.

'Nick made his mother and his grandfather miserable, to say nothing of Bob – and what happened? They let him loose, and within six weeks he'd found out for himself, and turned his back on a so-called aristocratic bloodline in favour of being himself as he was brought up. A wise choice. Our genes do count, but then, so does security. I'm silly to worry about the Petries. Nothing can now happen to the four oldest unless they want it to – and God knows what will happen to Basher! But then comes Jonce – the one who matters most to me because he is John's son. The most vulnerable because he remembers – Jade and Aggie don't. I can't help thinking about it, because of Thirzah. It's her genes at fault in the first place and the way she was brought up in the second. What chance of being a nice woman did she ever have?'

Fran had been listening and following her own trend of thought at the same time. 'I was thinking along those lines myself as I came home after seeing George the other day – about Thirzah especially. We know well enough that she takes after Kezia, and Sophie after her father. Genes must have counted most in Sophie's case, because her father didn't live long enough to bring her up. But that applied to a lot of our generation, didn't it? Your own father had no hand in bringing you up, and if I tell the truth neither did mine. We both owe our nurture to Grandfather. Perhaps that's why we get along so well together.'

'It's a fascinating subject,' he said, 'but we ought to get an early night – it'll be a long day for us tomorrow. Good old Greg! Whoever would have thought it!'

'That's what I said an hour and a half ago,' she answered. 'And they say women talk!'

He stopped and faced her at the bottom of the stairs. 'So which would you rather have now? A talkative historian or a silent old curmudgeon who thinks but never speaks?'

'I want you forever just as you are.'

'Good,' he said. 'That was exactly the answer I'd got ready if you had asked the question.'

They drove to London in the early evening of a beautiful day, two middle-aged, middle-class couples dressed for an occasion. William looked his distinguished best; Jess, whose fine bone-structure was so often disguised by casual wear, had taken the trouble to be smartly feminine. Fran noted that the family resemblance between them was strong tonight. Perhaps it had been the air of sadness on Jess's face until this year that had masked the likeness. She herself and Greg were built from a different mould. She had long ago come to terms with being a size or two larger than the fashionable figure, and made no concessions to it. She dressed to suit her personality, and got away with comfortable panache. Greg, not so tall as William and more sturdily built, was by nature flamboyant, and looked so whatever he wore. Jess remarked on it as she inspected him outside Southside House when they were ready to set off in William's car.

'It's Greg's day,' William reminded her. 'We're only the entourage.' It was indicative of the happy relationship between the four of them now that the two men sat together in the front, and the women left them to deal with the journey while they enjoyed being together.

They parked and walked to the Academy. None of them was a stranger there, but never before had they been guests at a private view. Greg went very quiet, and Jess moved to his side. Fran dropped back beside William, alert to the possibility of Greg's emotional nature getting the better of him. That was where the reserve that William and his sister shared might prove inadequate. It all depended now on what they found, once up the steps and into the gallery.

They moved, wine-filled glasses in hand, among the milling crowd, trying not to show too much interest – but there was no need to look carefully to find what they had come to see. Even from the length of the whole gallery they could see that Aunt Sar'anne had been given a place of honour right in the centre of the end wall – and that there was always a group of spectators standing before it. More than satisfied, Greg turned away and went to look for his other two paintings, Jess at his side. William and Fran let them go. As an artist, Greg had arrived.

Fran and William could relax, because it was clear that everything was better than any of them could have hoped. They waited till they could get near enough to see the picture properly. It was staggering what the frame and the lighting did to enhance it in that setting.

'Ta-li-a-ferro,' said a youngish man with a notebook in his hand. 'Where have I seen that name before? You can't forget a name like that.'

'You won't be allowed to,' said another voice. 'He's no amateur trying his luck. The man's an artist. There are two others by him listed. Let's go and look for them.'

William consulted their catalogue. The crowd had grown thicker, and wine was still flowing, and progress from side to side was slow. 'The other two pictures are both in here as well,' he said, using his height to see better. 'One on each side, I think.'

They worked their way across to *Girls with Babies*. It was bearing the 'sold' label, in spite of the very large price Greg had put on it because, like most artists when it came to it, he didn't want to part with it. He said it felt like selling your own children. They wondered if he knew it had been sold, but Fran said they mustn't look for him. She guessed he had been overcome and that Jess had wisely led him to somewhere a bit less public. They thoroughly enjoyed looking at the rest of the show, and by the time they got round to *The Burbages at Home* the crush had begun to thin.

'I think one of us had better go and try to find them,' Fran said, 'and if you don't mind, I think it should be me. You'd be dreadfully embarrassed if you found him sitting in a corner weeping, with Jess standing in front of him like the mother of a child who has wet his pants. Besides, he would rather it be me than you to see him like that.'

William knew she spoke only the truth, and was glad to be excused. She left him still looking up their own picture in the catalogue. That, at least, was not for sale, and the catalogue said so. N F S. 'Lent by Dr and Mrs William Burbage.'

410

William found himself by the side of another man of his own type, though perhaps a few years younger, whose face was vaguely familiar to him. He noticed that he was getting rather searching glances in return. Anxious now about Fran, he came to the conclusion that they must have met in the past at some academic conference, and decided he would not enter into a conversation. Next minute, Fran was back. Everything was all right, she said, but Greg was a bit excited and was suggesting dinner before starting the journey back – so perhaps they should go now.

As they left, William noticed the stranger's gaze intent upon Fran, too. If only he could remember where they had met before – but he couldn't. Possibly at the hotel? Just in case, he gave the stranger a slight bow of acknowledgement, and they left.

'Sorry about that, old chap,' said Greg as soon as they were alone. 'But it was a bit too much to take all at once, and I was afraid somebody might find out who I was. I couldn't have carried on a civilized conversation. So let's go and celebrate – at my expense, for once. Fancy the two girls being snapped up like that.'

'Not fancy at all,' said Jess. 'Fact. And I'm so proud of you!' Which she proved by bursting into tears in the street. It didn't matter. This was London, after all, not Old Swithinford. Nobody noticed a woman they didn't know in tears, or cared what she was crying about.

Bob Bellamy, getting out of bed as usual at 5 a.m. the next morning, looked out of the window and saw that it was going to be a lovely day. There was a summer mist lying low on the fields, but the sun would soon be shining through it.

He turned to look back at Jane, still asleep with her two cats, Ali and Baba, stretched out on the foot of the bed. He crept about noiselessly so as not to rouse her. It wouldn't be long before Jade and Aggie did, either in bed with her or jumping about all over her; and she wouldn't care in the least. In fact, she loved it – as he did. He felt unusually happy this morning, and didn't know

411

why; though experience had taught him that when he felt like this, things were likely to go well. It was the other side of the sixth sense that warned him of trouble to come.

He thought about it as he went about his routine yard-work. Things were already going so well that he didn't see how they could be much better, though he did know that Jane still harboured a couple of doubts she thought she was hiding from him. One was that Nick might go off the rails again, and lose the confidence and the purpose he had regained. The other was a bit of apprehension that until things were finally settled once and for all, they couldn't be sure of keeping Jade and Aggie, their 'two stray kittens'. The alternative didn't bear thinking about, and this morning Bob saw no need to.

When he looked across the stackyard towards the little church so close by on the hill, the picture enchanted him. The top of the church tower stood out of the mist, with here and there a glimpse of the red roof of the nave lower down, as swirling, thin grey mist shot with all the colours of the rainbow like sequins on a diaphanous scarf drifted round it at the sun's warm bidding. He stood and watched. To him, such time was never thought of as 'wasted'.

It was an hour and a half later that, having fed all his pets as well as his yard animals, he met the postman's van and took the letters from the postman through the window to save him the trouble of getting out. There was a letter addressed to Jane in Nick's hand. Well, she'd be pleased with that. Nick didn't often bother to set pen to paper while there was a telephone to hand. This must be something personal, meant for his mother's eyes. Bob had no fear, this glorious morning, that it could spell trouble.

Eric Choppen had exactly the same thoughts as he picked up the letters from the mat at Monastery Farm, and sorted his own from those addressed to Marjorie. He always carried a feeble hope that one morning he might pick up one with a foreign stamp and know it was from Pansy, but that scent was growing cold. Marjorie no longer expected such a letter. This morning, there was one for her from Poppy, which helped. He placed it with one or two others on the hall table for her to find when she came downstairs, glanced at his own uninteresting lot, and went into the kitchen to make his breakfast and take a look at *The Times*. Next moment, he was reaching for the telephone. 'Greg? Good, you are up! Have you seen this morning's *Times*?'

'No – I take the *Telegraph* and the *Guardian*. Why?'

'Have you looked at them yet?'

'They haven't come. Why? What are you so excited about?'

'Get your kettle on and a bit of toast ready for me. I'm on my way.'

It took him less than five minutes to reach Southside House. He met the paperboy at Greg's gate, and carried the papers still folded into the house. He had brought his own copy of *The Times*, which he spread out before his puzzled friend, his normally staid businessman's morning face wreathed in smiles. He seized Greg's hand and shook it vigorously, saying, 'Congratulations, my dear fellow. Take a look at this.'

So Greg looked down, and there it was. On the front page, a sub-headline:

## Picture of the Year: *Aunt Sar'anne*

and under it a large photograph of the painting, with columns of print round it eulogizing it and its creator, simply given as Taliaferro.

Greg was speechless, and opened up his own papers. They had it, too, with additional information about the other two paintings both having drawn a lot of attention, one having been sold early to an anonymous buyer, and the picture of the year to a provincial gallery of note in East Anglia.

Eric ate his toast and drank his coffee standing. There was no sign of Jess. 'I'll have more if I want it at the hotel,' he said to the still-bemused artist. 'Tell Jess I don't expect her this morning till she's ready to come. Go on, man, go up and show her!'

As soon as he reached the hotel, Eric rang William to tell him to look out for the announcement. He said they mustn't expect much sense out of Greg for a while yet, but they left their copy of *The Times* open on the kitchen table for Aunt Sar'anne to see, and sped to Southside House as fast as they could.

'It's incredible,' Greg kept saying. 'I don't believe it. Dreams like this don't come true.'

'Oh, yes they do,' countered Jess, swooping on little Jonce, still in his pyjamas, and swinging him up to put his legs round her waist while she hugged him in ecstatic joy.

Greg looked at his wife and the child with eyes blurred by such an intensity of love that Fran could hardly bear it. He turned to her and William. 'If I could be as sure of that as I am of this,' he said huskily, putting a finger on *The Times*, 'I think I could have nothing else in the world to wish for.'

Thirzah had been too quiet lately. It worried Dan more than her tirades did. He felt his responsibility for her condition, and found talking to George about it a great consolation. George listened, because he knew talking would ease Dan's mind, but he was too honest to be anything but a Job's comforter.

'She blames me, you see,' Dan said. 'She won't go out, and nobody comes to ours as she wants. Soph' and Het both come reg'lar, but she don't want 'em. If they as much as pick up a tea-cloth she watches like a hawk to see as they don't put it in their bag. If they try to do anything to help her, she says, "I can look after myself. I ain't like some as I could mention," meaning old Sar'anne. I hadn't ought to a-stood out against her about Sar'anne in the first place. I'm sure I didn't mean nobody no harm.'

George listened, sympathized, and prayed. He also did his best to convince Dan that it would have happened in the course of time, Aunt or no Aunt. People's minds were like clocks, he thought. Some went on ticking and telling the right time till they stopped because they were worn out. Others got a little bit of their machinery wrong, and couldn't tell the right time. Sometimes they could be put right, but mostly once they started going wrong, they only got worse.

'It's in her blood, Dan,' he said. 'We should ha' thought about it a long while ago, when she begun to get so masterful as nobody could do nothing right for her. She'd find fault with God Hisself if things didn't go as she wanted 'em. All anybody can do now is to be as kind to her as she'll let 'em and be prepared for anything to happen at any minute.'

Since Easter Sunday, even her tongue had quietened down and they had all begun to believe that Dr Hardy's medicine was doing her good. There had been a bit of improvement, in that she seemed to have forgotten her dislike of the bells. The only time she showed signs of getting herself worked up was at any mention of Sar'anne. As neither of the women concerned wanted to see or hear anything about the other, it wasn't very difficult to avoid the subject. At any rate, Dan went off to his beloved cows in less apprehension as time passed and Daisy got closer and closer to calving. He had made sure today that Thirz' had everything she wanted before he left, and set off to Glebe in a mood to match the morning. George met him, and said he thought Daisy had started to calve. Dan forgot everything else.

They had delivered a lovely heifer calf, and were cleaning themselves up when Molly came rushing out of the house, shouting excitedly for George and waving a newspaper in her hand. 'George! Come and look at this!'

He took the flimsy sheets from her. It wasn't the paper they had taken every day for donkey's years – even without his specs he could see that. It was something called the *Swithinford Clarion*.

'What have we got this for?' he asked, puzzled at her obvious excitement.

'It's one o' them new papers they put through everybody's door, free,' she said. 'I didn't come out here just to tell you that! Here's your glasses. Look at the front page!'

### Local Artist Makes Good

Local artist Gregory Taliaferro's portrait of an old lady also born and bred in our district is this morning causing a sensation as the 'picture of the year' at the Summer Exhibition at the Royal Academy in London –

And below it, of course, was a photograph of the portrait of Sar'anne.

'Do you mean as they might ha' put one like that through our door?' Dan asked. ''Cos if so, I'd better be getting off home as fast as I can.'

They never did know what had happened. When Dan opened the door, he found Thirzah stretched out on the floor by the side of the table, on which lay a copy of the newspaper, still folded as it had been pushed through the letterbox. Thirzah was breathing stertorously, and one look at her sent Dan running back to the Glebe for help.

'Cerebral haemorrhage,' said Dr Hardy. 'Don't move her till the ambulance arrives. Get her things ready for hospital. It may be only for a few days either way, but she may go on a long time, and even recover. Don't despair.'

It was Fran, herself feeling quite shaken, who had to deliver the news to Sophie. She stood still for half a minute, then began to take off her apron with such calm that Fran wondered if she understood; but folding her apron, she fetched her coat and put it on, saying she'd best get off straight away to tell Het and Joe, before they all went down to 'see to things' together.

'Let William take you in the car,' Fran suggested.

'No thenks. I shall be better a-walking, taking it in, like. You goo and tell Aunt, and expect me again when you see me.'

Fran did as she was bidden, and went, rather apprehensively, to spoil Sar'anne's euphoric morning. She went back afterwards to William, in a meditative mood that she needed to share with somebody. 'It's incredible,' she said. 'I couldn't believe Sophie could take it with such calm – but we still seem to have a lot to learn. It was Aunt Sar'anne who was upset, though all she said was, "Dear Oh dear! That ain't fair. It ought to ha' been me. I'm had my day, but Thirz' ain't no age at all. But there, we're all got to go sometime." And she went on looking through the *Clarion* "for sale" column as if I'd told her the cat had been sick, not bothering at all about her own portrait being on the front page of the first issue. It seems to me that all the learned philosophers and psychologists could have saved a lot of time and ink. A. A. Milne said it all for them in one sentence. "*You never can tell with heffalumps*" – or bees, or people.'

416

'I expect,' said William, 'you learn to take all sorts of things in your stride by the time you're ninety-odd.' The front doorbell prevented the conversation being taken any further. As there was no Sophie to answer it, William went himself, and found he was face to face with the man who only last evening, while looking at their own picture in its new setting, had been standing at his side.

'Dr Burbage? Professor William Burbage?'

'Yes?' Both were hesitant.

'Dr Burbage – I must apologize for this intrusion, but I believe we almost met last evening at the private view. My name is Cochrane, Theodore Cochrane, art critic for the BBC. Could you possibly spare me a few minutes of your time?'

William was surprised. Of course he should have recognized the man. He'd seen him often on the screen. But what could he possibly want?

'Sir Theodore Cochrane! How silly of me not to recognize you last night. Do come in. How can I help you?'

'I need information, and I think it just possible you may be able to help me. I couldn't help but identify you in the flesh from Taliaferro's likeness of you, especially when your wife appeared as well. I checked the catalogue, remembered who you were, and looked you up. The picture itself was so obviously a Gainsborough-inspired chimney-piece that I deduced it must have been a commission. I only began to think I'd made a mistake when I got here – the foreground is different.'

'It's as it was when the original Gainsborough it replaced was painted,' William said. 'That had to be sold after the First War. Please come in, and if you will allow me, I'll just tell my wife. Ah – here she is.'

Fran was introduced, raised her eyebrows at William in interrogation, and led the visitor into the sitting-room.

'You have another Taliaferro!' he said, standing before it. 'Very fine, but not up to the standard we saw last night. You're very lucky, though.'

Fran laughed. 'Give the poor man a chance,' she said. 'It isn't actually finished properly yet. He had to find us something to fill the gap.'

Cochrane looked startled. 'I must be on the right track! I guessed

417

that as you had commissioned him, you might be able to tell me something about him. But you speak as if you know him personally?'

'We ought to,' William said. 'He's my brother-in-law.'

There was a momentary pause in which Cochrane looked unbelieving and William lifted his eyebrows at Fran. What could a man of this visitor's eminence in the art world possibly want to know about Greg more than he could have learned in five minutes through normal channels? Ought they not to find out, before they gave out any further information? Greg the artist was one thing; Greg the private man was another. Cochrane saw, and interpreted their silent communication with each other correctly.

'I can see I must lay my cards on the table,' he said. 'I have a very personal, and rather delicate problem which he might be able to help me solve. I haven't had time since last night to do my homework properly, and in any case I'm hesitant either to encroach or to confide in him till I know something of him. Why wasn't he in evidence last night? Is he a recluse?'

Fran burst out laughing. 'Far from it! He's an absolute darling. And he was there last night – so overcome that he went and hid! But I'm not at all sure you would get much sense out of him today. We've been round to visit him this morning, and he's in a state of euphoria – a bit like a hot air balloon, not really with us. "*Up above the world so high, like a diamond in the sky*".'

Cochrane's face lit up. What a pleasant couple he had hit on, even if he hadn't actually gained his objective. They gave him confidence, and he took the plunge.

'You are obviously being circumspect in guarding the new star twinkling in the art world's sky,' he said. 'But my problem is very personal, very confidential, and urgent. It's possible you could help me as well as he if he lives locally. May I ask you a few questions?'

William gave Fran a loving, amused smile. It was no good – she simply could not escape other people's personal problems. 'If we can be of any help to you, I can assure you of complete confidentiality,' he said. 'May I get you a drink, first? Alcoholic, or coffee?'

'Both, I imagine,' Fran said, and went off to make the coffee while William suggested a brandy to go with it. Cochrane appeared to be labouring under a lot of stress.

'We are a little out of routine this morning,' William said, trying to break the tension. 'We've been robbed of our factotum for the time being. There's nobody else here. So please feel free to be as frank as you wish.'

Fran brought the coffee, and William set a brandy by their visitor's side.

'It must be my lucky star that brought me here,' he said.

They waited till he had restored himself a little. He began by asking if they had noticed that Greg's other picture, *Girls Carrying Babies*, had been sold. They had.

'I bought it,' Cochrane said. 'Not only because it's a masterpiece. I wanted to ask him about those two exquisite models.'

'Well, that's no problem for us to answer,' Fran said. 'They're not artists' models in the sense you mean. Just a couple of sisters from the village – both used to being draped with babies from the time they could first toddle. I think that's probably the hidden strength of Greg's picture. It's so natural – and somehow, so symbolic. But there's no mystery about it. He happened to be at a party when they came through a door just like that, and he photographed the scene in his mind. He's been making sketches of them ever since. We've seen one of them this morning.'

William, with his eye on Cochrane as Fran chatted, wondered if the man was going to pass out. But he pulled himself together, and asked, 'Then will you tell me who they are and what you know of them?' Fran tacitly passed the reply to William.

'They're part of rather a long story, I'm afraid. They arrived here as members of a hippy family who settled in a derelict house down a lane right out of the village. By chance we made their acquaintance – the family's, I mean. Their father (William had a little difficulty with his own voice) became a very dear friend. He died of lung cancer. Their mother, who'd never been much in evidence, cleared off, taking only one boy with her, and leaving seven other children abandoned. People in the village came to the rescue – Greg Taliaferro and my sister among them. That's the best of living in a place that is still a real community. It only happened last year, and so far, they're all still here. As Fran said, we've seen one of the girls this morning. Greg and Jess took one of the smaller children, a boy still only four, and got his sister in last night to baby-sit while they were out. The older of the two girls in the painting, Emerald.'

Cochrane set his glass down with a shaking hand. '*Emerald?* Her name is Emerald?'

'The four girls all have names of precious stones, the four boys of semi-precious. Their mother's name was Crystal and her surname Garnett. I expect that's the origin of such names.'

'And their father?'

'Oh, the man looking after them wasn't the actual father of any but the one Greg and Jess have – he's named Jasper, but we've re-named him for his father, so he's Jonce now. He – the father and my friend – was a drop-out from the medical profession, and – well, we loved him. He saved the lives of the five of them once, and thereafter couldn't desert them, till he had to.'

'So one of the two girls in my picture is named Emerald – and the other?'

'Amethyst.' It was Fran who answered this time, and looking closely at her questioner, she added, 'Why do you ask? Does it matter?'

'To me, it does. Very much.'

He put his hand in his pocket, found his handkerchief, and held it to his mouth for a moment. Then he said, rather brokenly, 'They are my daughters. Emerald, certainly – and Amethyst almost certainly. They're so much like their mother was once – though I couldn't believe last night but that it might be a nasty trick fate was playing on me. It was too much of a coincidence to be true. Now, of course, your story has proved it. I should like to hear it all, one day.'

'You shall,' promised William. 'But not now.'

'I want to see them.'

Fran sprang to her feet, horrified, and as William could see, putting on her armour. 'To claim them?' she asked. 'Oh no! No! You can't! You mustn't! They absolutely revere and adore the memory of the man who brought them up, and they have a very happy home now with another couple of our friends who are able to give them everything they need, including love. What possible

420

right have you to push your nose in and spoil things for any of them? *You* ran away and left them to be brought up in a hippy camp by a woman you had by then discovered to be a drug addict, I suppose. You have no right to them at all! Keep out of it. If you're suffering pangs of conscience now, in my opinion you've got what you asked for. You deserve it – but they don't! Did you ever wonder what had happened to them between leaving them in Wales and seeing that picture of them last night? I doubt it! *They must never know you exist.*'

She sat down, and began to cry. William went to her, held her and said, 'Ssh, darling, ssh! Of course you are quite right – but remember that Sir Theodore is our guest, and we haven't heard his side of the story at all. Why don't you go and make some soup and sandwiches for us all, while I sort out the rest?'

She went, all fiery indignation, not knowing what she might do or say if she stayed.

When she had gone, William said, 'I apologize for my wife's outburst – she's emotional about something else this morning anyway. But she's right, you know. We can't stop you, of course, doing whatever you want to. But Emerald's over eighteen, and can choose for herself. Ammy's seventeen, and not to be pushed about, either. Their present protector is a magistrate with an aristocratic background, but also an ex-naval officer to whom I would trust my own life, or Fran's, without question. I know your part in it as far as the birth of Emerald, because my friend told me before he died. He guessed, and we agreed because they are in age so close together and so much alike, that whoever fathered Emerald had probably also fathered Amethyst. We gave him the benefit of the doubt that he might not have known he had left Crystal pregnant again.

'By the time the man they called their father began to be really ill, their mother had saddled him with eight children to care for, only one of them his own. She already had five when he found them and saved them. I'm sorry, but I think Fran's right. We all have to pay for past mistakes, especially if we have feelings and want to put things right. But in this case, it might actually do harm. You would do yourself no good, defeat all that John did for them, and spoil the new security they've found. There is, I take it, no proof of your paternity? In which case, I do beg of you to think again, and never disclose to them or anybody else what you have just told us.'

Cochrane smiled, rather wanly and sardonically. 'My dear man,' he said, 'that's my problem. Whatever I, personally, may feel, I must prevent it from ever coming to light, somehow. I didn't mean to blurt it out like that. I was going to beg for your discretion, but I can see I need have no worry on that score. For one thing, I have a reputation and a public image to keep up. For another, I have a wife and three sons who have no idea at all of that part of my life, and if I can help it, will never know. When we were at university together, Crystal was as beautiful as those girls are now – and we were both caught up in the rebellious student phase, experimenting with drugs and sex like all the rest. We bolted when she told me she was pregnant, to do our own thing, and "be free". She liked the life, and got hooked on the drugs. I didn't. So, as you say, I quit. I didn't know about Amethyst, honestly, until yesterday, but my conscience has never been clear about Emerald. The whole thing wasn't all that uncommon just then, though I thought I was the only villain. My family accepted me back into the fold, and I simply let sleeping dogs lie. Of course I knew Crystal's family quite well, and knew that they had cast her off with an adequate allowance to live on, though not one to cover the hard drugs she'd graduated to. I guessed she'd found some other man to batten on. What had she got to live on when the man died?'

'Her children's allowances, mainly. It was a very difficult situation for me – my friend left them morally in my care. "Morally" is hardly the right word. Fran and I were both over fifty, too old to be considered as foster parents, even if we could have managed so large a family; but we were not acceptable to the powers-that-be anyway, not at that time being respectably married. The police had been involved from the time of the man's death, so of course they informed the welfare people about the abandoned children. We hoped the police wouldn't be able to trace the mother if we kept our heads down. She was welcome to the allowances, illegal though it may have been on her part to go on drawing them – but she wasn't welcome to those lovely children. Our hope was that she wouldn't want them, as long as she went on getting the allowances, though those for the two eldest have now stopped.'

'Yes. That's when she began to blackmail me. That's what comes of having a public image – she got at me through the BBC, and – well, to keep her quiet, I paid up. She was always infernally clever, you know – there was nothing wrong with her but her idiotic ideas about personal freedom and a completely amoral attitude towards anybody else. Financially, it wasn't a problem, though one always puts oneself in hock to a blackmailer once you part with any money at all. The trouble was that she could always keep tabs on me, but she never let me know how to get back to her. She employed a sort of agent – a Welshman named Pugh.'

'Good God!' exclaimed William. '*Dafydd Pugh?*'

'You obviously know the man. He was just as cagey. He used a poste-restante address in Macynlleth, to which I had to send what she demanded. My only alternative was to go to the police and have them trace her – but with what possible effects on me, my career, and my wife and children? It seemed to me that I had no option left but to let her win. Then, only a few days ago, I had a personal letter from Pugh. An extraordinary sort of epistle. He sounded like a red-hot gospeller!'

'He is,' said William grimly. 'He helped her to vamoose, with all that John had provided for the family's welfare and to which she hadn't an atom of right – but in his queer, muddled Puritanical mind, he genuinely believed what he was doing to be God's will. Calvanist at heart in the first place, no doubt, but adulterated in the years between by contact with all sorts of other strange but independent sectarians and free-thinkers, right down to the latest sort of modern evangelism. A gifted orator, I believe, once in the pulpit with an audience in front of him. Youngish, good-looking, well-spoken. A crank with a religious bee in his bonnet. He did genuinely try to help the entire family in his way by "bringing them to God". He set himself to save Crystal's soul from the devil by prayer. He was naïve, with a mission, and no match for her. She wound him round her little finger, and he was able to persuade himself that she had been the victim of wicked sinners who had led her astray and then let her down.

'Of course, the truth must have been that she used all her charm on him and he was crazy about her. But he denied himself any satisfaction – other than the suffering it caused him and the belief that he was serving God by doing what she asked of him in a final attempt to save her soul from hell.'

'That all fits,' Cochrane said. 'There was no address on his letter, which in spite of its biblical style and content did eventually make sense. He was still doing what he considered his God required of him by writing it. Though he had striven with Satan until the last, he had lost the battle, which meant that the two girls she had had by me were out in the wicked world somewhere unprotected. She had died of a drug overdose, and he had done what she had requested him to do in the event of her "being at rest in the bosom of Christ" – sent me a copy of her death certificate, and the birth certificates of her two oldest children, for whom he now expects me to take entire responsibility.'

William sat as if turned to stone, unable to believe it. Such incredibly *good* news. Cochrane didn't notice. He had got up, and was striding about the room.

'Can you understand?' he said. 'It meant that somewhere there were two orphaned girls for whose existence I was responsible. I may have been a rebellious prat in my student days, and I have enough sense to know that there must be thousands upon thousands of other men who suspect they may have grown-up offspring they don't know of, or vice versa. But it was like some form of madness we went through at that time. I think I proved, when I left Crystal in Wales, that I'd got over it, and wanted out. I couldn't take a year-old baby with me – I couldn't even prove she was mine. I did know that Crystal's family could well afford to keep her and her child if she, too, gave up and went home. But since that letter arrived, I have been almost out of my mind with anxiety. I couldn't get out of all the commitments I had concerning the exhibition – that's my job. But once it was over, and I could find a good enough excuse, I intended going to Wales to find Pugh, and perhaps through him trace my daughters and do what I could for them anonymously. Then I went to the private view last night and – well, you know the rest.'

He sat down again, pale, tense and visibly trembling. William put out a hand, and the other man took it. Somewhere in the distance they both heard Fran's voice calling them to come and eat her improvised lunch.

'Can you bear to come and eat something?' William asked. 'It would truly be best for you if you can. And – if you think you can manage it, say nothing of what you have just told me to Fran? As you saw, she's already on a knife-edge of emotion this morning. I give you my word of honour that both the girls are well and happy, and likely to remain so. I'll keep in touch with you to let you know of any further developments – but there won't be any. You can please yourself about keeping in touch with me, but since you are what you are, and admire Greg and his work, I see no reason why you shouldn't visit us again in your private or professional capacity or both, and we'll find some way of making sure you meet the girls, as the lucky owner of Greg's famous picture of them who would like to see them in the flesh. There's nothing in the world but my knowledge of all that you have told me to connect you in any way with Crystal. You need not fear Pugh. Believe me, he won't put his head above the parapet. He was an accessory before the fact of her stealing about twenty thousand pounds' worth of goods!'

'Are you coming?' said Fran from the door. 'The soup will be cold already.'

William had learned his lesson about keeping things from Fran. As soon as they were alone, he told her. The entire pattern with regard to the Petrie children's security in future must be altered by the death of Crystal; but, he said, he thought he must make quite sure where they all stood before giving any false hopes to anybody.

Overwhelmed as she was, Fran's ability to use her head rather than her heart had returned to her. 'I don't think Greg could take much more good news just at present,' she said. 'It would make him afraid of his own good luck. And if it all turns out well in the end, it will be cause for a great celebration, which just at the moment we couldn't consider. Sophie, Hetty and particularly Joe have all been very much part of the story that this may very well be a satisfactory ending to. One can't say "happy", considering it

425

has taken the death of that idiotic woman to bring it about. And with Thirzah still dithering on the verge of life and death, the most we can do is to keep what we know up our sleeves for the present, and hope.' She paused, then added, 'Another thread of the identity tangle. Does any of it really matter?'

'I don't know,' said William. 'It's an unanswered question that has always been asked. Nobody has ever been able to settle it, and I don't suppose they ever will. I think it's a bit like believing in God. Your reason may not want to accept any of the images the different religions have made of God, but when it comes to the crunch most people like the feeling that there's something somewhere greater than themselves. Without a god of some kind, they feel unattached, like astronauts feel weightless in space. It gives us some hold on our own reality to know what and where our roots are. If pressed to give an answer one way or the other, I think I'd have to say it's much more important what you are than who you are – but it's nice to know, all the same. I find it everlastingly interesting – but then, so did Francis Bacon, and other thinkers millennia before him and his inquiring bunch of seventeenth-century friends. Is anything new?'

'If you mean that philosophically, I don't know. If you mean have I heard any news, yes. Jane rang up to say she's had a long letter from Nick – telling her that he and Poppy want to get engaged on his birthday in September. Only engaged, because Poppy has still another year to go at university, and he wants to find a niche in the antique book market, in Cambridge if possible. They are prepared to be old-fashioned, and have a long engagement. A consummation devoutly to be wished, and to be thankful for, I think.'

'The Bridgefoots think so, too, according to Eric, whom I saw for a few minutes this morning. Marjorie has had the same sort of letter from Poppy. Of course, just at the moment, George is very concerned about Thirzah, as it affects Dan. But I'll bet Molly and the rest of the women are already planning for a huge harvest supper cum engagement party.'

'We shan't wait for that,' Fran said. 'Once we can let our news about the children out, we'll throw a party here for everybody.'

*

Thirzah lay comatose in hospital. To their surprise, Sophie turned up to work the next Monday morning very much her ordinary self, and with little outward show of feeling about the situation. Fran asked at once about Thirzah, and Sophie showed no compunction in saying just what she thought and felt.

'It's in God's hands,' she said, 'and we must abide by 'Is will. But if she was to go peaceful, now, I should give thanks. It would be a 'appy release, and not only for 'er. None of us, 'specially poor old Dan'el, would never rest easy no more about 'er if she got better and come 'ome again. And she wouldn't be 'appy, because she's forgot 'ow to be. Everything and everybody's been wrong for 'er for a goodish while, but it got worse so gradual, like, we didn't notice it. Joe and me said so last night when he drove me to see 'er. He reckoned she could ha' been responsible for a lot o' Het's sterricks. Het says it were to get away from 'er as she j'ined that church at Hen Street and got in with that man as led to all their trouble. I know as Thirz' never forgive me for getting that money Jelly left me – but there, she's turned against us all for reasons we shall never know, do she get better or not.'

Fran tried to be sympathetic, but in her heart she knew Sophie was right. 'We mustn't blame her,' she said gently. 'None of us can help being ill – and this is all part of her illness. If it is the sort of illness that gets worse as you grow older, perhaps it would be better if she didn't live to be very old.'

'Ah. We can't do no more but wait. 'Ow's Aunt taking it?'

'I can't tell you because I don't know,' Fran said truthfully. 'We haven't seen much of her since she heard about it. If I hadn't known how they felt about each other, I should have said she was grieving in solitude and silence.'

'That don't surprise me,' Sophie said. 'It's very often like that. They are kin to each other, and blood's thicker than water. They didn't never get on with each other 'cos they was brought up not to. There's all'us some in every fam'ly as don't or won't get on with the others. But though I say it, Aunt's all'us been a nicer woman than Thirz', be she never so much my sister. If Aunt's a-grieving, it's 'cos that's one more in the fam'ly likely to go, so there'll soon won't be none of us left.'

'Go in and see her and talk to her,' said Fran. 'I think that would please her.'

Nigel arrived while Sophie was gone. He felt a bit guilty, he said – he had agreed to put the opening of Mary Budd Close off till after the exhibition on their behalf, but he knew how much they wanted their house to themselves again, and now he was having to prevaricate because of Thirzah. He felt that at least they must wait to arrange it till they knew which way it was likely to go with her. He had seen Dr Hardy, who had not given him much hope that she would ever recover entirely, but on the other hand, she might last for years. Too long to wait, now that the flats were ready.

They assured him that he need not worry on their account. They were afraid Sar'anne was a bit down just at present about Thirzah; but once she was over the shock, whatever the outcome, her new home would give her something to look forward to.

As it happened, they didn't have to wait long. Thirzah had another stroke and died three days later.

It took the best part of a month after the funeral for them all to adjust to the change. William was glad of the respite. He had a problem he didn't know how to solve.

Fran thought that a month was quite long enough for Benedict's to be in mourning for Thirzah, and began to plan her celebration party, to take place immediately after the opening of Mary Budd Close and the installation of Aunt Sar'anne into her new home.

The guests would be only those couples who had so generously and altruistically stepped forward to take in and care for the seven abandoned Petrie children when their 'father' had died and their mother had abandoned them. In the order in which they had come forward to do so, they were Greg and Jess, Bob and Jane, Elyot and Beth, and Roland and Monica. Perhaps the last couple, with two businesses to run and twins of their own, might not have been quite so willing in the first instance but for Eric's help – but they would now be no more willing than any of the others to part with their 'adopted' children. Monica had far-reaching plans for her two to be trained as models for the cat-walk. So Eric ought also to be included in their gathering. And what large roles in the drama while it was all actually happening had Sophie, Joe, and even Hetty played. They, too, must be part of the celebration somehow. Well, Sophie would be there in any case, and lacking Thirzah, might perhaps accept Hetty as her substitute – in which case Joe, dear Joe, could be invited to help Ned. Then they would all be on the spot to hear what good news William had to tell them.

She outlined all this to William, who said it was fine but for one thing. He had given his word to Cochrane that he would never disclose his part in any of it. So how in the Lord's blessing, as Ned would say, was he supposed to have heard anything about Crystal's death? Sooner or later, of course, it would be found out that she was no longer drawing her children's allowances, perhaps eventually being reported to the police, who would then be obliged to find the children – and everything would be made public knowledge, with heaven knows what consequences.

No, he was *not* being a Jeremiah and looking on the dark side – only realistic. He thought that what was already a heaven-sent solution to the local welfare officer would simply be made firm and finalized; but that meant questions being asked of him that he wasn't prepared to answer. One complication was that Basher, who would by now be about ten, was still alive somewhere, whereabouts unknown. John Petrie had been careful to word his will not to exclude Basher from his 'family', so his trustees had a duty to him to find, and if possible to arrange for the care of the black sheep, Basher, as well as all the others. Not a particularly pleasant prospect.

She mustn't forget that he, William, who had so far taken it upon himself to see to most of the official business, was not the sole executor. The other was Joe, who must be put into the picture as soon as possible – but that raised another difficulty. Joe had almost idolized Dafydd Pugh – until he had become Crystal's cat's-paw, helped her to abandon four helpless girls, and involved him in that terrible trek to Wales to find the three little boys. It had ended in John's death and Joe playing the Good Samaritan.

Good, simple-hearted Joe had not been able to believe the wicked-
ness of what his 'friend' Pugh had done. He would be extremely
distressed, if nothing more, ever to have to have any dealings with
Pugh again – even if they could find him. It was quite possible
that once Crystal was dead, it had come home to Pugh that he
had in fact committed a felony in helping her to steal the vehicle
and camping equipment she'd had no right to, and thereafter in
helping her to go on stealing from the DHSS, to say nothing of
blackmailing Cochrane. He could very well have skipped out of
the country. So, said an anxious William to a happy-hearted Fran,
what did she advise?

'Stop worrying,' she said. '"*Take the cash, and let the credit go.*" As
Thirzah would have said, doubtless the Lord will provide. Or as
dear old Mary Budd did say, "Leave it to the gods." They often
have a trick in their hands if only we let them play the cards they
hold their way.'

He rejoiced at her optimism. Once they had their home to
themselves again, she had bounced back to being herself, and that
cheered him. He'd take her advice and let a week or two pass
before stirring anything up, and see what happened.

When it did, it came from an unexpected quarter. He was down
in the garden one morning, enjoying the sunshine and the view
of the church across the trees, when Joe came into view down
the tradesmen's path on his old bike. He was the only person
who ever used that path, and William waited for him under a big
hornbeam that was almost his favourite tree in their garden.

Joe looked distressed, and William went to meet him.

'Morning, Joe. What's the matter? Van packed up on you?'

'No, Sir. It's this here, as come this morning afore Het were
up. I wanted to ask you what to do afore she see it.' 'It' was a
letter, a single sheet only. There was no address.

Dear Brother-in-Christ,

    I write to you from the depths of despair that I have failed
the dear Lord by following the devices and desires of my own
heart instead of heeding His warning to beware the snares of

430

the Evil One. As with Adam in the Garden of Eden, the woman tempted me, and though I did not eat, I allowed her to lead me into other ways of sin.

I assisted her in breaking some of God's Holy Commandments, in especial the eighth, and the seventh also, for did not Christ say that he who looks at a woman with lust in his heart, the same has committed adultery? Christ knoweth all hearts, and because of my sins He has denied me that which I had set my heart upon, which was to bring the woman Crystal to the Lord with all her sins forgiven.

Instead, He has taken her unto Himself, with all her sins still upon her head. She is dead. It grieves me to say that she died of an overdose of the drugs she swore to me she had renounced for ever because of my help and my prayers for her.

The angel with the flaming sword is at the gates and I cannot get back into His garden to go on with His work in this country. I leave tonight for another land where infidels abound, and you will hear no more of me.

However, my conscience is not at rest because of the child Carnelian or Basher, who has now been deserted by me as well as by the mother who bore him. He has left the camp in Wales where he was in company with the man she said was his father, though he denies it. But he finds the child useful in working his evil tricks on other innocent people. I wish I could tell you where to find the boy and so at least rescue him from a sinful life in this world and the fires of hell in the next. It would ease the heavy burden on my conscience that I must carry with me for ever.

I beseech you to pray for him as well as for your sinful but repentant brother-in-the-sight-of-God,

D.P.


William read to the end, his stomach turning against the unbelievable ranting hypocrisy, while at the same time being filled with pity at the waste of such a good mind and a spirit so well meaning on such false and feeble, handed-down pseudo-religious trash. Pugh's mind was like a lump of good putty, liable to take an impression from whatever it came into contact with, but resting on a set base of biblical text learned, no doubt, in his childhood. The result was a mish-mash of beliefs bearing little resemblance to anything but the worst of the modern cults, which like the free-thinkers of the seventeenth century, created their God to suit themselves. Had Pugh lived then, he was just the sort of fanatic who would have joined the sect that called themselves Adamites, worshipping God 'free of original sin' as Adam and Eve did – stark naked.

Yet even so, Pugh was a man with a conscience, and at the last he had obeyed it and drawn their attention to the moral danger young Basher had been left in. Well, he and Joe would have to face that, sometime or other; but at this moment, all William could really think of was that Pugh's letter had solved his knotty problem. He told Joe as much as he dare, withholding Cochrane's name only.

Joe was no putty-minded man. He understood what William told him, grasping all the significance of his own sense in bringing the letter direct to his friend. That William Burbage the erstwhile Cambridge professor was his friend, he never doubted.

'Do you think we ought to do anything to try to find that little hell-hound?' Joe asked. William shook his head. 'It would only be a waste of time and money, and do him no good. He's as fly as they come. He's his mother's son. As soon as he's in any kind of want or need, he'll find us. She will have briefed him well, and the greatest influence on him has been the community of free-thinkers into which he was born. His mother was too clever even for John. She made sure that he had no influence on Basher, so that she always had one on her side and to do her illegal errands. Such a lost lamb already, Joe, that I fear even your shepherding could never bring home rejoicing. Let us be glad about the seven who are safe in the fold. May I keep this?'

Joe nodded, adding, 'We done our best, Sir. We couldn't do no more.'

Armed with the letter and the copy of Crystal's death certificate, William set to work, and had very little difficulty in getting temporary arrangements made permanent.

He and Fran agreed that when they had released the news to the respective adoptive or foster parents, their part in it was done. It was up to each couple, then, to tell the children as much or as little as they thought fit.

'That's all very well,' Fran said, 'but the four girls will tell each other, anyway. The little ones are different. I imagine Bob and Jane will want to change Jade and Aggie's name by deed-poll to Bellamy, but what about Jonce?'

'I shouldn't want to agree to him becoming Taliaferro, however well known it becomes,' William said. 'I am so glad Grandfather left me my own father's name. I should feel guilty towards John if I let Jonce grow up anything but Voss-Dering. All four girls, I'm sure, will insist on remaining Petries. That gives them the identifiable roots we were discussing the other day.'

Fran, a little bit apprehensive about the first party after Thirzah's death, found that her worries were needless. She was more than surprised by Hetty's attitude towards Sophie, accepting her as first-horse but still being willing to pull her weight. Fran was also more than surprised at Hetty's behaviour and capabilities. It began to dawn on all of them that Sophie and Joe had been right, and that Thirzah had had more to answer for than had been realized in her lifetime. Nobody could put the clock back, or undo what had been done; but if ever there was a man willing to forgive and forget, it was Joe. It seemed, from all they saw of Hetty that night, that she had enough sense to recognize the fresh start her home-life had been given, and to make the most of it. She and Joe, too, had a child to bring up as well as they knew how. William said that if anybody did know how to bring a child up, it was Joe.

Eric had felt rather an odd man out at Fran's get-together of the Church Enders who had met together at Benedict's to celebrate the resolution of the problem of the future of the Petrie children. He had had no direct participation in giving homes to any of the seven children who were now literally orphaned, though he was

433

glad to have had a secondary role in standing behind Monica and Roland regarding the two they had sheltered.

As he drove home, he took stock of his own position there among the rest. He had arrived in the village a complete stranger, almost an alien, with plans to turn the village and its community upside down and inside out, to suck out of it all those characteristics that he could turn to his own and his partners' commercial advantage. Instead of which it had sucked him into itself and had taken him to its heart. It had, in fact, saved him as a man, converted him into a support for its crumbling community values, and given him no small part to play in its future. He was now almost as much a part of it as the Wagstaffes or the Wainwrights or the Bridgefoots, especially since the tendrils of his own family had become entwined round their ancient roots. His own grand-children were also the grandchildren of Fran and William.

The Bridgefoot family had not been represented at tonight's gathering, and in a curious way he had missed them, because they were at the very heart of the community he now cared so much about; besides, he had become personally involved with them, too, because of his deep friendship and affection for his tenant Marjorie, who occupied half of his overlarge house and supplied that female element in his life that was necessary for both companionship and social balance.

His relationship with her had been settled once and for all when she had first moved in. Gossip that had linked them together in any other sort of relationship had forced them into complete honesty with each other; they both knew exactly where they stood. The agony of his grief at losing his adored wife had now worn down to an ache, which for much of the time was dulled by work and companionship. But the pain of that grief still stabbed him like a stiletto in his ribs when her name was mentioned. He would never recover enough to want Marjorie or any other woman to take Annette's place. And that was what was so good about his friendship with Marjorie. She wanted nothing else any more than he did. However, living in such close propinquity and finding each other so completely compatible, they were the warmest of friends.

He had missed her tonight as his social counterpart more than usual, because just at present she was rather on his mind. She wasn't happy, and he knew why. All the rest of her close family were bubbling over with joy and anticipation at the thought of her daughter Poppy's engagement to Nick. She couldn't share it because of her worry about Poppy's twin, Pansy.

Plans for a triple celebration party for Nick's coming-of-age, the engagement, and George's seventieth 'milestone' birthday were already well afoot. Marjorie hadn't said much about it, but her brother Brian had been to consult him about the venue.

In the past, all such Bridgefoot celebrations had been held in the large and beautiful old tithe barn at the Glebe, especially since its restoration; but this time it had, apparently, been George himself who had vetoed the barn. Brian was fairly certain that the reason was that this time it was as much a Bellamy/Hadley-Gordon function as a Bridgefoot one, and it would have gone absolutely against the grain for George to allow the expense to fall anywhere but on himself if it had been held on Bridgefoot premises. Brian had added a rider that Eric had been able to understand.

'Besides, he wants Charles's wedding to be the last true family occasion till he can be sure there'll be other Bridgefoots to keep the tradition up. I'm pretty sure that in the course of time Dad'll get his wish for a Bridgefoot grandson, but Marjorie's family's different. I know she would much rather it was held on neutral ground, and we couldn't have a much better "do" than the Burbages' wedding party. The hotel, thanks to you, looks and feels so much a part of the old village that we forget it hasn't always been.'

That made sense to Eric. Glad as Marjorie was for Poppy, it only emphasized that her other daughter was missing. That would always be so either till Pansy turned up again, or Marjorie grew to accept that she never would. His heart ached for her.

Before he reached home, he had come to a conclusion. Neither outcome was likely without some action on somebody's part, and if there had to be a *deus ex machina* it was he who would have to set it up. For one thing, only he had enough inside knowledge to try, and for another, no one would suspect him of interfering. There was no time to be lost if, as he feared, it might be necessary to track Pansy as far as the continent. He went to bed in deep thought, and got up next morning cheered by having to plan a manoeuvre in the same sort of detail as he had in the past planned commando raids.

He packed a bag, saw to his passport, and had his car serviced. While that was being done, he took a walk as far as the do-it-yourself shop, and told Mrs Bean crisply and coldly that he had something to say to her husband in private.

She blustered that 'Kenneth' was not at home – but like a snake whose venom had been removed, she was afraid and showed it.

'So where is he? His car's in the garage, I see. I suggest we go back to the hotel for a chat.' His voice was cold, with an air of command that scared Beryl even more. She called her husband, who came, shuffling and truculent, from behind the shop to enquire what Eric wanted with him.

'Only a private word or two,' said Eric. 'In my office – for your sake.' Red in the face and nervous, Kenneth agreed.

Beryl lost her cool. 'Don't you tell him nothink,' she screamed at her unhappy husband. 'He ain't got no right to ask you. He ain't the police – and they never found out nothing from you. You just remember that.'

Kenneth turned on her with undisguised fury. 'You shut your gob, and keep it shut,' he said. 'Else I'll shut it for you, d'yer hear?'

'Not while I'm here you won't,' said Eric calmly. 'She's right, anyway. I'm neither a policeman nor a spy for them. As far as the police are concerned, they can do their own questioning. But nobody hits a woman while I'm about. So pull yourself together, man, and act like one. Shall we go?'

Eric was beginning to enjoy himself. If there was anything he knew, it was how to handle men. He didn't know Kid Bean well, but he had summed him up before they reached the hotel. He was typical of the sort of countryman whose native intelligence and ability were above average and would have served him well all his life if he'd been content to rely on them. But he'd been spurred on to 'vaulting ambition' by jealousy of his brother's good fortune in winning a premium bond jackpot, and thereafter by cupidity, flattery, and a nagging wife with too wide a mouth. Nevertheless, Eric judged him to be a man whose business sense was still keen.

He took Bean up in the lift to his own sanctum, and sat him down with a stiff drink. Then he told him that he already knew of Bailey's involvement in the fraud that was still national news, and that he guessed Kid had been bribed by promises to become Bailey's local sub-contractor. He was careful not to level a single specific charge against the wilting man before him, but hinted that there were worse revelations still to come. With so many much bigger fish for the police to catch in those muddy waters, they wouldn't bother about small fry like him. As a rival developer, all he desired was to keep his own name and reputation well out of it – which involved keeping tabs on all the Baileys. Ken must remember that until the day when they had skipped out without warning, Eric had had in his employ the wife of Arnold Bailey's clerk of the works. He had good reasons for wanting to know where that couple were now, as well as others of the Bailey faction.

Eric was well aware of what he was doing; he had thought he might have had to unleash on Ken all the invective he had spared William, but he had seen the advantage of changing his tactics and puncturing the soft underbelly of Ken's inflated ego. The man was not a fool. Besides his native wit, he was possessed of the countryman's crafty nous for self-preservation. The longer Eric talked in this strain, the more confidence Kenneth managed to retrieve.

'So, all I want to ask you is if you know now where the Chessmans are?'

'Abroad,' Ken answered. 'Somewhere in France. Using her name.'

'And young Darren Bailey? I know he has been living in Deal, because I went to see him there, but he was away and his wife told me he'd had to break his appointment with me because they were about to move overseas. Have they gone to France, too?'

Eric's keen eye noted that Ken's wilting belligerence was leaving in its wake an air of embarrassment more difficult to understand. He sat stubbornly silent.

'Look, man,' said Eric. 'I was going to make you an offer. It's quite obvious to me that you're a good businessman who was doing well till Bailey put his oar in. I guess your friend Arnold has skedaddled not only owing you money, but leaving you carrying the can for him. So why are you trying to protect him? He's let you down, and your business is suffering. I suppose he's promised to reward you in the course of time for keeping your head down till the danger's over. You're backing the wrong horse, you know. By the time he keeps his promise, you'll be bankrupt. You've had a good little business here, but people are moving away from it – towards Hen Street and Lane's End. What you need to do is to follow the trade. Bailey showed you a quicker, less honest way of making money – but that bubble's burst.

'I'm offering you a deal. Your shop's an eyesore in this end of the village, but it is built on to the front of a three-hundred-year-old cottage of considerable size and charm. I'll give you enough for the premises to let you begin again on your own account in Lane's End, if you'll put me on the track of young Darren as well as the Chessmans. It's nothing at all to do with me in any other way what happens to them as long as they don't try to hide behind me. Arnold himself has more sense. It's his son I don't trust. Why are you trying to hide his get-rich-quick antics that even his father doesn't know?'

This was a complete shot in the dark, but the colour that flooded up over Kid's face told Eric he had bagged something with it. 'It ain't nothing like that, as far as I know,' Ken said. 'But he owes me money as I lent him, and I did promise him as I wouldn't let his father know. I daren't let Beryl know, neither. You know what she is. She wouldn't be proud to boast about being so friendly with them if she knowed all I do. It would be a blessing for us to get out and start somewhere else, 'specially if it were to be up Lane's End way. Beryl would agree to that.'

'OK. So where are Darren Bailey and his wife?'

When the truth burst from Ken, it was not what Eric had expected. Ken was glad to talk, and Eric let him, and sat back and listened.

Darren had been trying to break away from his father and set up a similar business on his own in the south, in partnership with a young architect he had met at a race-meeting. Pansy was in the family way, so they let on they were married – but they weren't, and never had been. Darren had told him that because he had been buying and selling 'government surplus' supplied through them without making sure it had ever been paid for in the first place, he was in trouble as deep as any of them. He'd believed it, after the police had questioned him.

When it had begun to get too hot for Darren and his new partner, they'd tried to get Pansy to raise some money from her grandfather; but she'd found out the truth and refused to raise a penny. That was when Darren had put pressure on Ken to lend them what he could raise, and as soon as he'd let them have as much as he could, they'd cleared off. He'd been trying to find Darren, but the flat was empty. That's all he knew.

Eric felt he had kicked over an ants' nest. But as with a raid on enemy territory, once you'd landed with your face blackened, there was nothing for it but to go on, attack, and pray that you'd be able to carry out what you'd set out to do. He'd get no more out of the snuffling, limp man in front of him. 'Have another drink,' he said, pouring it out. 'Then pull yourself together and go home and put my offer to your wife. If she agrees, I'll still play – on condition that you never breathe a word of what you've just told me to anybody. I've got to go away, but I'll see you as soon as I get back about the details of a deal with you, if you want to go ahead with it. And if I ever hear any more of young Bailey, I'll let you know. There may be a chance you'll get your money back some day, though I wouldn't bet on it.'

When Kid had gone, Eric sat in as helpless a state of indecision about what to do next as he had ever been in his life. Perhaps he should have known better than to poke a stick into a wasps' nest! But he had done, and now he had to deal with the wasps. Unless there were some way out that at present he couldn't see, he'd only made things worse, not only for Marjorie, but for them all. He needed advice – and there was only one person he could consult. He went straight to Nigel, and told him all.

'Pansy must be found,' was Nigel's first comment.

'Of course. Just tell me how and where to begin.'

'Oh, I don't suppose there is the least likelihood that *you* could find her. You've got no authority even to be looking for her – it

439

will be a case of hospitals, hostels for the homeless, homes for unmarried mothers – even perhaps prison. Why do you suppose she's chosen to disappear? Because she won't bring shame on her family, poor child. She doesn't want to be found. If you succeeded, she wouldn't consider coming home with you. She'd swear she didn't know you. Accuse you of molesting her. A middle-aged widower, too well off for his needs, with no woman in tow? You'd get nowhere without involving the police or her family. I don't see that *you* can help. But I can. A dog-collar gets you a long way. I could pull strings. And I have useful connections from my days in the Guards. So I propose you let me take on the search. No – I won't agree that it's too bloody silly for anything! On the contrary, it's eminently sensible. Yours will be the harder part, my boy – to stay put and let me go. Act normally, support Marjorie with regard to the party, and wait. If what I find is bad, we may have to lie quiet about it till the party's over. If, on the other hand –'

'Keep in touch every day, won't you?' said Eric, tacitly if reluctantly submitting.

'I know you don't put much trust in anything or anybody other than yourself, Eric, but there are times when you need to. This is one of them. If you don't put any trust in God, put some in me and let me stand in for Him. You know I won't let you down if it's humanly possible not to, but that's where He has the advantage.'

Eric humbly acquiesced. Nigel made a few *ad hoc* arrangements, and left next day to visit 'a dear friend, a clergyman, who lives in Canterbury'. It occurred to nobody to ask questions.

Nigel rang to say he had arrived, was being made much of, and had already gained some information as to how to set about his task. Eric told him it had been one of the longest days he ever remembered, because he'd had to dissemble every time he'd met Marjorie. But he had had other things to occupy both his mind and his time. He'd thought he had exhausted the supply of old cottages in Church End, not expecting there was any possibility that the Beans would be moved from their glaringly modern business premises, though he had known there was a traditional cottage behind it. Even old inhabitants had forgotten about it, because long before the advent of the DIY shop it had been obscured by the ramshackle buildings and sheds from which Kid and Jelly had conducted their equally ramshackle but thoroughly efficient odd-jobbers' business.

He had rung Kenneth Bean and told him that his other plans having been cancelled, the next move was up to them. Getting some encouragement, he suggested a visit for him to inspect the cottage and see what possibilities it offered.

They were good. It would mean completely demolishing both the new shop and the old sheds, but what would be left then was, as in so many other cases, 'twin houses' which had been hastily turned into one. Though it would never be large, it would be adequately roomy and, restored as he would do it, beautiful into the bargain. He had not known that behind it lay a neglected large and pleasant old orchard and garden. All in all, it was a very desirable property for him to acquire. If he decided not to keep it as a holiday home, it would be easily saleable – and if the rest of the Church End lot didn't give him a medal as a public benefactor for removing the eyesore of the garish new shop, they ought. He had come home considerably cheered.

Three days later Nigel reported success in tracking Pansy down. It was not only a sad story but a difficult situation, he said, to which there was no instant solution. Could he deal with it now in his own way, before coming home to explain the details in private? (Meaning, as Eric knew, with Marjorie nowhere in the offing.)

'I think all will be well,' Nigel said, 'but it may take some time. I'll be back tomorrow evening, and I'll meet you at the hotel. But we'll eat before I begin. We've been through worse times than this together. You'll feel better when you know the worst – and the best that may follow, if you agree to my plans.'

What Eric was told was that with the help of Nigel's friend, and the friend's somewhat younger and very practically minded wife, it had not taken them long to locate Pansy – in a Church of England hostel for the homeless. Their only real difficulty had been caused by the fact that they hadn't known whether to look for a Bailey or a Gifford, and eventually found she had used neither name. She had registered herself in hospital as Patricia Fairey.

'Hospital?' asked Eric, sharply.

Nigel assented. 'Only to be expected,' he said gently. 'Poor child!' The shock of finding herself so callously deserted by her pseudo-husband had brought on labour two months too soon. She had been all alone, in a flat from which the telephone had been cut off. A neighbour had finally heard her and she had been rushed to hospital, too late to save the baby.

'That may be a mercy, in the long run,' Nigel said. 'It's not for us to judge. She'd haemorrhaged badly, and was in no state to be questioned till she'd had time to concoct a new identity and a tale to mislead enquiries about herself. She told them that she was over twenty-one, and had run away from home to live with her boyfriend, who had welshed on her. They'd been living in a furnished flat, but he hadn't rented it in his proper name – he'd called himself Fred Darren, and she had no idea where he'd gone. She'd packed her few belongings in the suitcase they had found with her, and was preparing to leave the flat to go for help when she'd passed out. The rest they knew. The last thing she could or would do was to go home.

She hadn't been fit to leave hospital for nearly a month. Nigel had been to the hospital and heard the doctors' side of it. She'd been very ill, but the main difficulty had been that she'd had no will to live. Nigel had paused at that point, and both were silent.

'Of course,' Nigel said, 'her main trouble now is guilt. She told me, when at last I got through to her, that she had broken every single one of the ten commandments – including the sixth. She was responsible for the child's life, and its death. She didn't care what happened to her now, except to make sure she never disgraces her family, or hurts them again more than she did by throwing

442

her lot in with the Baileys. By God, Eric, that girl's got guts! There was no question of her creeping back home with a sorry tale. She'd made her bed, and if she had to go on living, she was prepared to lie on it.'

Once out of hospital, she'd been cared for by the social services, who'd found her a place in a hostel. It was there that Nigel had found her. She'd recognized him on sight, and the surprise had broken her down to telling him all the story. He'd been afraid that if he took his eyes off her, she'd disappear again. Besides, if he persuaded her to return home with him, all that she had put herself through to avoid being an embarrassment to her family would have been wasted. She was nearly unrecognizable as the girl she had been – and she still needed more time before coming home, though he thought he had persuaded her that to do so would be best. She'd cried herself into a state of exhaustion by that time, so he'd felt he was safe in leaving her till the morning, and had gone back to Canterbury – where he had told his hosts all there was to tell.

'My old friend's wife was once the matron of a hospital. He's a clergyman. Both are the sort that are the salt of the earth,' Nigel said. 'They went with me next morning, and the upshot of it is that they'll take her, keep her and look after her till she's ready to come back. If love and care and good company can restore her, she'll soon be herself again physically, and will be able to face all that coming back means. When that time comes, our task will be to prepare her family to receive her.'

'Leave Marjorie to me,' Eric said. 'I don't know how to thank you!'

'Me? My dear fellow, give thanks where they are due.' That was the nearest Nigel ever got to preaching, but Eric knew what he meant. He put out one of his big, strong, hairy-backed hands, and Nigel took it in a grip that said more than thousands of words.

Life went on. Sophie arrived bursting one morning about a month later, just as harvest was beginning.

She had barely got inside the kitchen before exclaiming, 'Have you heard the news? Kid Bean's a-selling up! I know it's the truth, 'cos Beryl told me so not more'n ten minutes ago with 'er own lips! She say there ain't enough trade 'ere now so many people are gone to live at Lane's End and Hen Street, so they are bought the little general shop at Hen Street where Het used to do 'er shopping. It were a good little business as is gone downhill since the shopkeeper died and his wife had to have paid 'elp to keep it going. Beryl thinks Olive 'Opkins'll go on working for 'er, so as Kid can build 'is old business up again from there.'

Fran was used to playing Sophie's game. She was now expected to ask leading questions, to give Sophie the chance to tell all the rest without laying herself open to the charge of 'gossiping' by repeating rumours that 'she couldn't vouch for the truth of'.

'I wonder who's bought Kid's shop?' she said. 'Did Beryl tell you?'

'Tha's going to be pulled down! And all Kid and my Jelly's old buildings as were good enough for 'em till Kid got too big for 'is boots.'

'Well!' said Fran unguardedly. 'That's something to be thankful for, at any rate.'

Sophie looked slightly offended – anything that had once belonged to her Jelly was sanctified. But she went on, 'It's that Mr Choppen as is bought the place, to do the same as 'e does with any old place as 'e can get 'is 'ands on to do up. Fancy! That little 'ouse where my Jelly were born, and 'is father afore 'im, and 'is father afore that. I daresay Mr Choppen'll make it look as good as 'e 'as done all the others. It used to be two cottages once, afore Jelly's father and mother took it over. Their grandfather used to live in one, and Jelly's mother and father in the other till they 'ad so many child'en that they needed both. But it'll make somebody a good 'ome, that I will say.'

Harvest was over before they heard the next instalment. Dr Hardy was finding his pad at the old surgery barely big enough for his needs, and Effendi had no objection to taking it back from him.

'Though what that doctor needs such a big place for, I can't think,' Sophie remarked. 'From what I 'ear, 'e's 'ardly ever at 'ome, only when 'e's on call, like. 'E spends a most of 'is time up at the Old Rectory, it seems, 'elping the Commander with making a ship or something. And that Miss Pelham very near lives there an' all, since she's got over 'er haccident. She and Mis' Franks get on as well together, seems, like the doctor and the Commander do.'

'Tell me something I don't know,' Fran thought, but was careful not to say. She and Beth were still keeping their fingers crossed as the romance silently ripened. Terence's move was more than a straw in the wind.

Next, Sophie also broke the news that Pansy had been heard of, and would soon be coming home. Fran couldn't wait to get William away from his study to tell him how hopeful things look on all fronts.

Eric and Nigel kept silent about Pansy as long as they dared. George was greatly looking forward to his birthday, averring that when you got to his age, birthdays meant more.

'Not for the reasons you think, neither,' he said. 'I shall be here for many another birthday yet. But you're never too old to learn. I've enjoyed this year as I never expected to, except for one or two things as can't be helped. We can't expect life to be all sunshine. We've got plenty to be pleased about, what with one thing and another.'

Just before George's birthday, Eric told Marjorie about Pansy, while Nigel broke the news to all the rest. When she was ready to come, there would be no difficulty. The sturdy old family would have no qualms about opening their arms and taking her into them again.

'Would anybody who knows them expect anything else?' Fran asked William. 'It's only the practical application of the parable of the lost sheep. They'll all enjoy the party more for knowing, whatever anybody else cares to say or think. That it's being held in the hotel is in itself another landmark. The George Bridgefoot we first got to know would have been dead set against having any family gathering anywhere but under his own roof. It's a sign of the times.'

William took her more seriously than she had expected. 'Yes,' he agreed. 'There have been so many changes since we came back here that it's difficult to remember them except in aggregate. Little ripples bring the tide in as far and as often as big waves. Historians make it sound as if you could draw a hard and fast line precisely between one tide-mark and the next – which may be convenient for them, but it isn't really possible. History's the record of passing time, and time is seamless. It just goes on and on.'

Fran took that up. Time was a mystery that never failed to fascinate her.

> ' "Tomorrow, and tomorrow, and tomorrow
> Creeps in this petty pace from day to day
> Till the last syllable of recorded time"

'Which means, of course, while I have been quoting those words. Or, as T. S. Eliot wrote, "*History is now.*" Poets do make you think.'

William nodded. 'But historians have something to be said for them. If I were forced to give a statement as to the moment when it was necessary for us to change tense and could say, "It has changed," instead of "It is changing," I think I should have to declare it to have been the day we buried Thirzah.'

Fran gave it some thought before deciding that she agreed with him. Things had been different since then. Take Sophie. Freed from Thirzah's domination, she had become a different person in many ways. The mantle of Elijah-cum-Thirzah had not fallen, as Fran had feared it would, upon Elisha-cum-Sophie. Far from it. Instead, Sophie had shaken off the yoke that for so long had

446

obliged her to go in whatever direction Thirzah's reins had directed. An indication of this had been her willingness to help Aunt Sar'anne to settle into her new home, visit her there, and take Hetty with her. Joe and Dan got on well together again, as they hadn't been allowed to since before Wendy had had little Steven. The church congregation no longer feared Thirzah's loud, didactic tongue.

Though she and William had never before formulated such a thought, Fran now saw Thirzah as a symbol of the past. They had seen it being buried with Thirzah, and a new epoch born, as they had watched her coffin being lowered into the grave.

*'Wheat and tares together sown, Unto joy or sorrow grown.'* They had sung that, Thirzah's favourite hymn, before committing her and the past for ever to the earth. What the future would bring, only time itself would tell.

Considering the hope that the future held for them all, Fran remarked, 'I think Sophie must have been right about Tilda's Curse. For a little while, everything seemed to go wrong – but since the night of Greg's private view, the tide has turned.'

'That's life,' William said. 'Whatever the poets say, roads don't wind uphill all the way.'

She laughed and said, 'They don't all take that miserable Victorian outlook. Don Marquis didn't, for one. You know, the American poet who looked at life through the eyes of Archie and Mehitabel – a cockroach and an alley-cat. Mehitabel says

> "Life's too damn funny
> For me to explain.
> It's kicks or money,
> Life's too damn funny.
> It's one day sunny
> The next day rain.
> Life's too damn funny
> For me to explain."

'I think he got it right. I like my philosophy spiced with wit and short enough to quote – even if it does prove that I have only a second-hand mind.'

'Whatever idiot dared say that about you?'

'An academic historian called William Burbage.'

He looked so rueful that she had to lean forward and drop a kiss on him.

'Please, my precious one, never remind me of that again – if you really love me!'

'Funny,' she said, 'but I do.'

# READ MORE IN PENGUIN

In every corner of the world, on every subject under the sun, Penguin represents quality and variety – the very best in publishing today.

For complete information about books available from Penguin – including Puffins, Penguin Classics and Arkana – and how to order them, write to us at the appropriate address below. Please note that for copyright reasons the selection of books varies from country to country.

**In the United Kingdom**: Please write to *Dept. EP, Penguin Books Ltd, Bath Road, Harmondsworth, West Drayton, Middlesex UB7 0DA*

**In the United States**: Please write to *Consumer Sales, Penguin Putnam Inc., P.O. Box 999, Dept. 17109, Bergenfield, New Jersey 07621-0120.* VISA and MasterCard holders call 1-800-253-6476 to order Penguin titles

**In Canada**: Please write to *Penguin Books Canada Ltd, 10 Alcorn Avenue, Suite 300, Toronto, Ontario M4V 3B2*

**In Australia**: Please write to *Penguin Books Australia Ltd, P.O. Box 257, Ringwood, Victoria 3134*

**In New Zealand**: Please write to *Penguin Books (NZ) Ltd, Private Bag 102902, North Shore Mail Centre, Auckland 10*

**In India**: Please write to *Penguin Books India Pvt Ltd, 210 Chiranjiv Tower, 43 Nehru Place, New Delhi 110 019*

**In the Netherlands**: Please write to *Penguin Books Netherlands bv, Postbus 3507, NL-1001 AH Amsterdam*

**In Germany**: Please write to *Penguin Books Deutschland GmbH, Metzlerstrasse 26, 60594 Frankfurt am Main*

**In Spain**: Please write to *Penguin Books S. A., Bravo Murillo 19, 1° B, 28015 Madrid*

**In Italy**: Please write to *Penguin Italia s.r.l., Via Benedetto Croce 2, 20094 Corsico, Milano*

**In France**: Please write to *Penguin France, Le Carré Wilson, 62 rue Benjamin Baillaud, 31500 Toulouse*

**In Japan**: Please write to *Penguin Books Japan Ltd, Kaneko Building, 2-3-25 Koraku, Bunkyo-Ku, Tokyo 112*

**In South Africa**: Please write to *Penguin Books South Africa (Pty) Ltd, Private Bag X14, Parkview, 2122 Johannesburg*

# BY THE SAME AUTHOR

*Her collection of short stories:*

**The Chequer-Board**

A disturbed and unhappy schoolgirl; an unsuspected suicide; 'fen-tiger' survivors of two world wars – these are just a few of the vibrant and vulnerable characters elegized in Sybil Marshall's remarkable short stories.

In 'Felo de Se' a sudden death evokes memories of a proud man and his humble subordinate, whose destinies were decided by an exquisite piece of silverware. Fred Wood and Beresford Blake are 'Twin Halves', two men bizarrely battling out their frustrations over a yew hedge and thirty-seven cats. The strict upbringing of Lavinia, devoted to her brothers and to 'Mother dear' is brought humorously up to date in 'A Question of Sex', and in 'The Nightingale Ode' Alys ponders the loveless childhood she has overcome, and the inscrutable ways of fate.

'Sybil Marshall's world is one of mystery and miracle, but it is inhabited by ordinary people leading everyday lives ... In this collection of tales from the Fens, it is once again her deep, unrivalled knowledge of country life, and her sharp eye for character and situation, that give her work its charm' – Robert McCrum in the *Mail on Sunday*

# BY THE SAME AUTHOR

*Her autobiographical memoirs:*

### A Pride of Tigers

Sybil Marshall can claim to be a true 'fen-tiger' – one of the last survivors of a proud and resistant species.

She was born just before the First World War into the seventh generation of a vast tribal family all of whom had been born and raised below sea-level, within a few flat miles of Ramsey in one of the most isolated of the black fens of Huntingdonshire.

Redolent with the wit and *joie de vivre* of a wonderful raconteur, *A Pride of Tigers* concentrates on a 'tiny area approximately one mile square' but evokes a whole world. Work, dress, food, fashions, customs – everything from a mouth-watering recipe for onion dumplings to the advent of the wireless is recorded in a book vividly populated with 'fen-tigers'.

### The Silver New Nothing

Here Sybil Marshall recounts the childhood adventures she shared with her family. One of three children, she had many aunts and uncles – the source of old tales and new gossip – constant mischief to get into and a range of fascinating characters who taught her about life.

With the freshness of a child's perception she recounts the most vivid memories of her early days, from the mysterious 'scientist' who lodged with her aunt, to the time the parsley bed was dug up to find out where babies came from. She tells of the tramp who visited them and regaled them with stories, of skating on the frozen fen, of the first bomb of the war and of a riotous fracas between the women at the local fair.

Rich in warmth, humour and affection, these evocative memories hauntingly recapture a time long gone by.

# BY THE SAME AUTHOR

### A Nest of Magpies

Fran and her stepcousin William spent an idyllic childhood at Benedict's, Fran's grandfather's house, in Old Swithinford. Now widowed, Fran learns that Benedict's is up for sale. While overseeing its restoration, Fran renews old friendships and forms new ones. But it is her relationship with William that takes on a new dimension, and William's unhappy marriage forces them to face a profound moral dilemma . . .

'Sybil Marshall has a good ear for local dialects and a good eye for observing individuals, but it is the intensity she brings to the plight of her narrator, which makes this fictional début so impressive' – *The Times Literary Supplement*

### Sharp through the Hawthorn

Scandalizing certain established villagers of Old Swithinford, Fran and William are now living together as man and wife in their childhood home of Benedict's. But change comes in the shape of the beautiful but embittered daughter of the local Rector, and it falls to Fran and William to hold together the village community.

'A sprawling, passionately sincere saga of a village in East Anglia on the cusp of social and sexual change' – *Mail on Sunday*

### Strip the Willow

At Benedict's Fran and William's love remains unchanging, but with the advent of wealthy developers, the ancient place seems set to face its greatest threat yet. When the church fails to hold the community together, Fran and William must inevitably be drawn into the fight to protect the land that has been their home for half a century.

'The rendering of local speech and character is often little short of brilliant' – *Guardian*